From the Pages of
The Pilgrim's Progress

As I walked through the wilderness of this world, I lighted on a certain place, where was a Den, and I laid me down in *that* place to sleep: And as I slept, I dreamed a Dream.   (page 13)

What are the things you seek, since you leave all the World to find them?   (page 17)

It is a hard matter for a man to go down into the Valley of *Humiliation*, as thou art now, and to catch no slip by the way.   (page 66)

I will talk of things Heavenly, or things Earthly; things Moral, or things Evangelical; things Sacred, or things Prophane; things past, or things to come; things foreign, or things at home; things more essential, or things circumstantial; provided that all be done to our Profit.   (page 90)

Almost five thousand years agone, there were Pilgrims walking to the Cœlestial City, as these two honest persons are; and *Beelzebub*, *Apollyon*, and *Legion*, with their companions, perceiving by the path that the Pilgrims made, that their Way to the City lay through this town of *Vanity*, they contrived here to set up a Fair; a Fair, wherein should be sold *all Sorts of Vanity*, and that it should last all the year long; therefore, at this Fair, are all such merchandizes sold, as houses, lands, trades, places, honours, preferments, titles, countries, kingdoms, lusts, pleasures; and delights of all sorts, as whores, bawds, wives, husbands, children, masters, servants, lives, blood, bodies, souls, silver, gold, pearls, precious stones, and what not?
                                                             (page 102)

Hanging is too good for him, said Mr. *Cruelty*.   (page 112)

JOHN BUNYAN.

AFTER A DRAWING FROM THE LIFE BY R. WHITE.

PRESERVED IN THE BRITISH MUSEUM

THE
PILGRIM'S PROGRESS

John Bunyan

*With an Introduction and Notes
by David Hawkes*

George Stade
Consulting Editorial Director

JB

BARNES & NOBLE CLASSICS

NEW YORK

𝒥ℬ

BARNES & NOBLE CLASSICS

NEW YORK

Published by Barnes & Noble Books
122 Fifth Avenue
New York, NY 10011

www.barnesandnoble.com/classics

The first part of *The Pilgrim's Progress From This World, to That Which is to Come:
Delivered Under the Similitude of a Dream Wherein is Discovered, the Manner of His
Setting Out, His Dangerous Journey; and Safe Arrival at the Desired Countrey* was
published in 1678, and the second part followed in 1684. The present text converts
the long "S" of Bunyan's English to a modern, short "S" throughout but retains most
other antiquated conventions. The illustrations in this edition appeared in various
editions of *The Pilgrim's Progress* published during John Bunyan's lifetime.

Published in 2005 by Barnes & Noble Classics with new Introduction, Notes,
Biography, Chronology, Inspired By, Comments & Questions, and For Further Reading.

Introduction, Notes, and For Further Reading
Copyright © 2005 by David Hawkes.

Note on John Bunyan, The World of John Bunyan and
The Pilgrim's Progress, Inspired by *The Pilgrim's Progress*, and Comments & Questions
Copyright © 2005 by Barnes & Noble, Inc.

The Pilgrim's Progress
ISBN 1-59308-254-1
LC Control Number 2004115315

Produced and published in conjunction with:
Fine Creative Media, Inc.
322 Eighth Avenue
New York, NY 10001

Michael J. Fine, President and Publisher

Printed in the United States of America

QM

1 3 5 7 9 10 8 6 4 2

FIRST PRINTING

John Bunyan

John Bunyan, who described himself as "a tinker, and a poor man," lived in England during a period of great upheaval that included civil war, an epidemic of the plague, the Great Fire of London, and intense religious persecution of dissenters who did not conform with the teachings and liturgy of the Church of England. Bunyan was born near Bedford, in the village of Elstow, in 1628. His father was a tinker who repaired metal household objects such as pans and kettles. Tinkers were generally itinerants, or even gypsies, but the Bunyan family owned a cottage. John was sent to the village school to learn to read and write, although beyond that he was largely self-taught. In his spiritual memoir, *Grace Abounding to the Chief of Sinners* (1666), he claims to have had a happy childhood, but one that was intermittently tormented by dreams of "devils and hellish fiends." These powerful nightmares were precursors to the visions that motivated his religious conversion years later. Until that time, Bunyan claimed to have been involved in "all manner of vice and ungodliness."

When Bunyan was sixteen, his mother and his sister died a month apart, and the young man was conscripted to serve in the Civil War on the side of the Parliamentary Army. Although he did not see combat, he was exposed during that time to the radical Puritan preaching of the period, which encouraged him to break from the Church of England. When his garrison was dissolved, Bunyan moved back to Elstow, married, and took up work as a tinker.

When his eldest daughter, Mary, was born blind, Bunyan experienced a spiritual crisis. He became an active member of the nonconformist church St. John's of Bedford, where he began preaching. His simple, straightforward manner of spreading the gospel earned him a devoted following among his peers. His first printed work, *Some Gospel Truths Opened*, appeared in 1656.

When the Protectorate of Oliver Cromwell ended and the monarchy was restored in 1660, nonconformist religious sects were persecuted, and in 1661 Bunyan was arrested for leading a secret religious meeting. He was jailed on a three-month sentence that turned into one that lasted twelve years because he refused to say he would give up preaching. During his imprisonment Bunyan wrote prolifically, producing among other works *Grace Abounding to the Chief of Sinners*, *The Holy City* (1665), and his allegorical masterpiece, *The Pilgrim's Progress*. Published in 1678, shortly after he was released from a second prison term, this time of six months, *The Pilgrim's Progress* was an instant success; it remains one of the most translated and reprinted works of all time.

Bunyan preached widely in the years that followed. He published more than forty works in his lifetime, including a novel-like story, *The Life and Death of Mr. Badman* (1680); another allegory, *The Holy War* (1682); and *The Second Part of the Pilgrim's Progress* (1684). In 1688 John Bunyan contracted pneumonia and died. He was buried alongside other religious dissenters in Bunhill Fields, London.

Table of Contents

List of Illustrations

The World of John Bunyan and
The Pilgrim's Progress

1628 John Bunyan is born in November in the village of Elstow, England, near the town of Bedford. He is the oldest of the four children of Thomas and Margaret Bunyan, who are tinkers, mending metal ware such as kettles and pans. Although tinkers are generally transients who travel the countryside in search of work, the Bunyans own a cottage and send their son to the village schools. Bunyan has a happy childhood, including games with friends on the town green, yet is plagued by dreams of "devils and hellish fiends."

1629– Charles I dissolves the Parliament of 1628 and will rule with-
1640 out a parliament for the next eleven years.

1640 Charles I convenes what will be known as the Short Parliament but dissolves it in less than a month. Late in the year he convenes the Long Parliament, which will last until 1653.

1642 Civil war breaks out in England; the conflict between Charles I and Parliament will continue until 1645.

1644 Bunyan's mother dies. A month later his sister also dies, and his father remarries a month after that. In November Bunyan joins the Army of the Parliament in the war against Charles I and is stationed in the garrison at Newport Pagnell. John Milton's *Aeropagitica* is published.

1645 Bunyan does not see combat, but he is exposed to many new ideas, including Puritan tracts.

1646 Parliamentary forces are victorious over those of Charles I.

1647 Bunyan returns to Elstow and works as a tinker. Parliamentary forces kidnap the King.

1648 Bunyan marries his first wife, whose name is unknown; they will have four children.

1649 Charles I is tried and executed. Parliament abolishes the monarchy, and the Commonwealth is declared.

1650   After Bunyan's first child, Mary, is born blind, he reevaluates his life, which he comes to consider sinful and ungodly.

1651   Thomas Hobbes publishes *Leviathan*, a work of political philosophy that examines the role of sovereign power.

1653   Joining those who desire a more direct and pared-down form of worship than the Church of England offers, Bunyan affiliates with the Baptist St. John's Church of Bedford and befriends the pastor, John Gifford. After a near-fatal fall from a boat into the Bedford River, Bunyan feels he was saved by God's mercy. Religious suppression of nonconformist groups, such as the Ranters and Levellers, is rampant. The Protectorate is established, with Oliver Cromwell as protector.

1655   Bunyan moves to St. Cuthbert's Street in Bedford and takes a position as deacon of St. John's, where he begins preaching. John Gifford dies.

1656   Bunyan begins to preach beyond St. John's. His first printed work, an attack on Quakers called *Some Gospel Truths Opened*, appears.

1657   In response to Quaker outrage, he writes a defense entitled *A Vindication of Some Gospel Truths Opened*.

1658   Bunyan's first wife dies. *A Few Sighs from Hell* is published. In February Cromwell dissolves Parliament; in August he dies and is succeeded by his son Richard.

1659   Bunyan marries a woman named Elizabeth. His reputation as a powerful preacher grows. *The Doctrine of the Law and Grace Unfolded* is published.

1660   This momentous year witnesses the end of the Cromwell Protectorate and the restoration of the monarchy of Charles II; the latter is accompanied by a move to unify the country under the Church of England. Independent congregations, such as the ones Bunyan leads, are shut down. When authorities catch him holding a nonconformist meeting in Samsell, he is arrested.

1661   A three-month sentence in the county jail will extend to twelve years, since Bunyan will not agree to abandon nonconformist preaching. Elizabeth pleads with England's Chief Justice to release her husband, but her petition is denied. While in jail, Bunyan makes bootlaces to sell to support his family; he receives visitors and is allowed the occasional day of leave to return to his nearby home. He will write constantly during this time; early in his imprisonment he authors *The Holy City* and his spiritual memoir, *Grace Abounding to the Chief of Sinners.* John Whiteman and Samuel Fenn are appointed pastors of the Bedford Church.

1665   *The Holy City* is published. The citizens of London battle an epidemic of plague, which had broken out in late 1664 and will ravage the city until early 1666.

1666   *Grace Abounding to the Chief of Sinners* is published. The Great Fire devastates London.

1667   John Milton's *Paradise Lost* is published.

1668   Bunyan works during the second half of his imprisonment on his best-known book, the allegorical *The Pilgrim's Progress.*

1672   John Whiteman dies, and Bunyan is appointed pastor while still in prison. King Charles II issues the Declaration of Indulgence to the Nonconformists, and Bunyan is released from prison. Gaining a wider following and the appellation "Bishop Bunyan," he preaches throughout the countryside.

1673   Charles II withdraws the Declaration of Indulgence.

1676   *The Strait Gate* is published.

1677   Bunyan is returned to prison for six months.

1678   Bunyan's masterpiece, *The Pilgrim's Progress from This World to That Which Is to Come,* is published to instant success; ten editions appear in as many years. Translated into more than 200 languages, it remains one of history's most widely read texts. Bunyan will publish close to forty additional works during his lifetime.

1680   *The Life and Death of Mr. Badman,* considered a sequel to *The Pilgrim's Progress,* is published.

1682   Another allegorical work, *The Holy War,* is published.

1684   In an attempt to refute a proliferation of imitations and counterfeit sequels to *The Pilgrim's Progress,* Bunyan publishes *The Pilgrim's Progress: The Second Part,* the tale of Christian's wife, Christiana.

1685   Worried about religious persecution, Bunyan deeds all he owns to his wife to avoid confiscation of his property. Charles II dies and is succeeded by James II.

1686   *A Book for Boys and Girls,* in which poems comment on emblematic pictures, is published.

1687 Isaac Newton's *Principia Mathematica* is published.

1688 After riding from London to Reading in the rain after reconciling a quarreling father and son, Bunyan contracts pneumonia; he dies on August 31. He is buried in Bunhill Fields, London, alongside other Dissenters of the era. William of Orange lands in England.

1689 James II is deposed, and William and Mary are crowned. Bunyan's unpublished works will continue to be printed in the years that follow.

Introduction

To understand fully *The Pilgrim's Progress*, we must remember that it was written in prison. Imprisonment is its major theme, and escape from prison is its primary purpose. Although Bunyan was without a doubt incarcerated in the literal, physical sense while he composed his work, he did not believe that he was truly in jail. He was convinced that, as Richard Lovelace had written in "To Althea, from Prison" (1642), "Stone walls do not a prison make, / Nor iron bars a cage," and Bunyan echoed the sentiment in his own "Prison Meditations" (1665; quoted from *The Works of John Bunyan*, edited by George Offor, vol. 1, p. 64; see "For Further Reading"):

> I am, indeed, in prison now
> In body, but my mind
> Is free to study Christ, and how
> Unto me he is kind.
>
> For though men keep my outward man
> Within their locks and bars,
> Yet by the faith of Christ I can
> Mount higher than the stars.

As far as Bunyan was concerned, the real prisoners were outside the walls, in the world. *The Pilgrim's Progress* aims to establish two deeply counterintuitive propositions: that its author is not in jail, and that its readers are. But while Bunyan argues that the world is the prison of the soul, he also offers us a way to escape from the world. The book's subtitle, *From This World to That Which Is to Come*, indicates our ultimate destination, but the world "to come" is to be reached by a way not measurable in space or time. The pilgrim's progress is not a literal journey along a physical road, but an exercise in semiotics: a reinterpretation of the world. As Stanley Fish puts it, Bunyan's work teaches us that "the truth about the world is not to be found within its own confines or configurations, but from the vantage point of a perspective that transforms it" (*Self-consuming Artifacts*, p. 237).

In the course of his journey the hero, named Christian, learns to understand the world as an allegory. He comes to perceive his experience as a series of signs that point toward nonmaterial, spiritual referents, and this constitutes his liberation. But before he can escape from prison, he must become aware that he is in one. The progress toward an allegorical interpretation of reality is simultaneously a process of alienation from the mundane world of experience. *The Pilgrim's Progress* shows us a man who becomes a stranger to the world, to the extent of rejecting empirical sense perception, as well as the laws, morality, and behavioral standards of society. The first lesson Christian learns after his conversion is that "Mr. Worldly Wiseman is an alien."

Allegory has often been described as a suitable mode to represent the alienated, objectified character of worldly experience. This line of reasoning originates with Walter Benjamin's seminal analysis of the genre in *The Origin of German Tragic Drama* (1928). Benjamin argues that allegory's purpose is to teach us that the experiential world—the "carnal" or "fleshly" dimension, in Bunyan's terms—is fallen into a disharmonious relation with its Creator: "Allegory itself was sown by Christianity. For it was absolutely decisive for this mode of thought that not only transitoriness, but also guilt should seem evidently to have its home in the province of idols and of the flesh" (p. 224). Plato had argued that, because the material world is transitory, it is also illusory, and to take empirical appearances for reality thus constitutes a philosophical error. But Christianity introduced an ethical dimension to this argument. From the Christian perspective, taking appearances for reality is not only erroneous, but also sinful, and in *The Pilgrim's Progress*, understanding this fact is the first step on the way to redemption. This is a paradoxical operation, however, for the process of understanding that creation is alienated from the Creator simultaneously involves the recognition of another, spiritual, realm to which the carnal world points the way. As Benjamin puts it:

> It will be immediately apparent, especially to anyone who is familiar with allegorical textual exegesis, that all of the things which are used to signify derive, from the very fact of their pointing to something

else, a power which makes them appear no longer commensurable with profane things, which raises them onto a higher plane, and which can, indeed, sanctify them. Considered in allegorical terms, then, the profane world is both elevated and devalued (p. 175).

The idea that human beings are strangers in a fallen world is a fundamental tenet of Christianity. But there were also local, historical reasons why Bunyan should have been attracted to the theme of alienation. His contemporary John Milton also found the alienation of the world from its Creator a timely topic for literature, and many critics have remarked upon the thematic and chronological proximity of what Christopher Hill calls "the two great epics of Biblical Puritanism in defeat" (*The English Bible and the Seventeenth-century Revolution*, p. 372): *The Pilgrim's Progress* (1678) and *Paradise Lost* (1667). Milton and Bunyan had both fought for the English revolution, the former with the pen, the latter with the sword. Both were imprisoned after the restoration of the monarchy in 1660, although Milton's incarceration was brief. Both devoted the succeeding years to the composition of complex theological allegories that explained the defeat of their cause by suggesting that God had temporarily abandoned the world to the machinations of Satan, and both of the resulting narratives claimed to show how it was nevertheless possible to break free of Satanic, alienated perception and achieve what Milton calls "a Paradise within thee, happier far" (book 12). *Paradise Lost* and *The Pilgrim's Progress* are both works of liberation theology.

The similarities between them do not extend to form, however. Milton's learned, allusive poetry occupies a quite different aesthetic, and social, stratum from Bunyan's earthy, vernacular prose. Bunyan was not the first poor man to write English literature, but he was the first to write in the language of the poor. If *Paradise Lost* anatomizes the grandiose despair of the intellectual, *The Pilgrim's Progress* studies the psychological effects of alienation as they were experienced by ordinary English people. It has often been described as the first English novel, on the grounds that it is an extended, fictional prose narrative featuring a narrator and characters who speak and act independently, but the description is also apt on thematic grounds. The Hungarian philosopher Georg Lukács's famous definition of the novel genre, in *The Theory of the Novel*, as "the epic of a world that has been abandoned by God" fits *The Pilgrim's Progress* precisely. Unlike the epics of Homer, Virgil, and Milton, Bunyan's story does not concern itself with the actions of divine beings. It is firmly, resolutely earth-bound, and the fantastic, supernatural figures and events it describes are understood to be re-readings of literal, earthly experience. The walking allegorical abstractions who people *The Pilgrim's Progress* are not visitors from another dimension, such as Homer's Olympus or Milton's heaven. Rather, they reflect Christian's interpretation of reality as a set of signs pointing to referents in the "world that is to come," and the epic "progress" he undergoes consists in the recognition of spiritual significance in the alienated, objectified, "carnal" world of experience.

II

For two hundred years, *The Pilgrim's Progress* was, after the Bible, the most widely read book in the English-speaking world. Its phenomenal popularity indicates that it speaks to the experience of the common people, and historians such as E. P. Thompson have acknowledged it as one of the "foundation texts of the English working-class movement" (*The Making of the English Working-class*, p. 34). This rare ability to speak to the masses is doubtless the product of the author's background. Bunyan has often been charged with exaggerating both the poverty of his childhood and the depravity of his youth in his spiritual autobiography, *Grace Abounding to the Chief of Sinners* (1666), but there is little evidence to support these accusations. He was born in 1628, in the village of Elstow near the town of Bedford, and his father was a tinker. According to Bunyan, this constituted "a low and inconsiderable generation; my father's house being of that rank that is meanest, and most despised of all the families of the land" (*Grace Abounding to the Chief of Sinners and A Relation of the Imprisonment of Mr. John Bunyan*, 1987, p. 7). Critics have disputed this characterization, noting that the Bunyan family had been resident in Bedfordshire for generations, and thus do not seem to have belonged to the quasi-pariah, hereditary caste of itinerant tinkers who were often equated with gypsies in early modern England. John Bunyan did follow his father into the trade, however, and it would be surprising if some of the opprobrium attached to traveling tinkers did not rub off on the sedentary practitioners of the craft. The word "tinker" remains an epithet in parts of Britain to this day, often used interchangeably with "pikey," a derogatory term for gypsies. When Bunyan's wife appealed on his behalf to the Lord Chief Justice of England, she claimed that "because he is a tinker, and a poor man; therefore he is despised, and cannot have justice" (*Grace Abounding to the Chief of Sinners and A Relation of the Imprisonment of Mr. John Bunyan*, p. 107).

Although Bunyan's parents were illiterate, he attended school and learned to read and write, as he puts it, "according to the rate of other poor men's children" (*Grace Abounding*, p. 7). This little learning he "soon forgot" on leaving school; literacy was neither required nor expected of a tinker, and the young Bunyan preferred to spend his leisure hours in pursuit of more physical pleasures. *Grace Abounding* tells us that he spent his days "in sin," risking "disgrace and open shame," and dedicating himself to "all unrighteousness" (p. 8). Exactly which vices Bunyan refers to here has been the matter of some dispute. He mentions "cursing, swearing, lying, and blaspheming," but he also castigates himself for such innocuous pleasures as bell ringing and playing the ball game tip-cat on the village green. Such wholesome diversions are at odds with his insistence that "I did still let loose the reins to my lusts, and delighted in all transgressions against the law of God: so that until I came to the state of marriage I was the very ring-leader of all the youth that kept me company, into all manner of vice and ungodliness" (p. 8).

This inconsistency has led some to conclude that Bunyan is sparing his readers' blushes, refusing to titillate, and resting content with hints as to the nature of his more lurid transgressions. He certainly had reason to guard his reputation jealously; *Grace Abounding* mentions that even after his conversion he was accused of keeping "my misses, my whores, my bastards, yea, two wives at once" (p. 76) and that it was "rumored up and down among the people that I was a witch, a Jesuit, a highwayman, and the like" (p. 75). Critics generally accept Bunyan's denial of these charges with regard to his life after conversion, but they are divided as to whether there was anything in his youthful experience that might have given them plausibility. Christopher Hill claims that Bunyan led "a group of wide boys in his village . . . there is no escaping the libertine ideas which he records in *Grace Abounding*, and with which he continued to struggle for the rest of his life" (*The English Bible and the Seventeenth-century Revolution*, p. 386). But most earlier commentators, especially the committed Christians who form the majority, wish to limit the young

Bunyan's vices to those he explicitly mentions. The problem with this argument is that he can then come to appear as a paranoid spiritual masochist, obsessively fearful of damnation for absurdly trivial sins. This is, in fact, how he has often been portrayed by enlightened liberals in the tradition of Thomas Babington Macaulay.

It seems most likely that, after his conversion, Bunyan simply did not differentiate between degrees of sinfulness. His entire unregenerate life would have appeared, from his redeemed perspective, utterly depraved, and this would apply to games of tip-cat just as much as to the explicitly sexual "uncleanness" that he mentions observing in his companions. The entire phenomenal world was alien to the converted Bunyan, not just those elements within it that moralists identify as sinful. As he puts it in *The Strait Gate* (1676; quoted from *The Works of John Bunyan*, edited by Offor, vol. 1, p. 370):

> The world hateth thee if thou be a Christian; the men of the world hate thee; the things of the world are snares for thee, even thy bed and table, thy wife and husband, yea, thy most lawful enjoyments have in them that will certainly sink thy soul to hell, if thou dost not strive against the snares that are in them.

The point Bunyan wants to establish in his autobiography is that he remained "shy of women from my first conversion" (*Grace Abounding*, p. 77). He is content to allow the individual reader to speculate on what may have happened prior to that event. His formal conversion did not take place until 1653, but he would have been exposed to radical religious ideas long before that. In 1642, when Bunyan was fourteen, civil war broke out between King Charles I and forces under the banner of the Parliament. The reasons for the conflict were complex, and different social groups fought for different causes. Much of the aristocracy and landed gentry resented Charles's refusal to call Parliament for eleven years, his imposition of arbitrary taxes, and his attempt to set up a system of absolute monarchy. Merchants objected to his bestowal of trading monopolies on favorites, and to the costly extravagance of court life. Among the common people there were demands for an extension of the franchise and a redistribution of land. And "Puritans" of all classes took issue with the official state Church of England, which they considered repressively hierarchical and overly enamored of quasi-

Papist ritual and ornamentation. Such political, economic, and religious ferment must have made some impression on even the heedlessly hedonistic young Bunyan. Bedfordshire was a center of Puritan influence, which may have contributed to the guilt-induced "fearful dreams," "fearful visions," and "apprehensions of devils and wicked spirits" (p. 8) that, in *Grace Abounding*, Bunyan reports experiencing in the midst of his sinful pleasures.

Bunyan's mother died in 1644; she was followed a month later by his sister, and his father remarried a month after that. The disruption this presumably caused in his family may have contributed to Bunyan's decision to join the Parliamentary Army in arms against the King. He enlisted in 1644 and remained on active service for three years. It is uncertain whether he fought in any battles—although much of his work, especially *The Holy War* (1682), shows a keen interest in and knowledge of military operations—but we know that he was stationed in the garrison at Newport Pagnell, which was a hotbed of radical opinion throughout the war. During Bunyan's time as a soldier the Parliamentary Army became the primary venue in which the ideas of groups like the Levellers and the Ranters took hold. His teenage years would have been filled with the clamor of voices advocating such startling notions as democracy, free love, and communism, and the impression they made on the sensitive boy was deep and lasting, though by no means unequivocally benign.

The Civil War ended in 1647 with the defeat of the Royalists and the capture of the King. Bunyan was demobbed the same year and returned to Bedford to follow his former trade and patterns of behavior. The late 1640s and early 1650s were years of convulsive upheaval in the state, and also within the minds of individuals. The execution of King Charles in 1649 permanently divided the main body of revolutionaries into moderate Presbyterians, who advocated retaining a state church and a monarchy, and radical Independents, who favored greater religious toleration and a republic. Power soon passed from the former to the latter, creating a climate favorable to root-and-branch reformation of church, state, and individual morality. The repercussions of these developments reverberated loudly in Bunyan's soul, and between 1647 and 1653 he vacillated wildly in his religious opinions and personal behavior.

The life of a soldier doubtless provided ample opportunity for vice, and by the time he left the army Bunyan regarded himself as a thoroughly hardened man. His regeneration was inaugurated by his marriage in 1648 to "a wife whose father was counted godly" (*Grace Abounding*, p. 9). The couple quickly had four children, including a girl who was born blind. Like Bunyan himself, his wife was "as poor as poor might be," and her dowry consisted of two religious books, Arthur Dent's *The Plain Man's Pathway to Heaven* (1601) and Lewis Bayly's *The Practice of Piety* (1612). The first of these, with its pilgrimage motif, clearly influenced *The Pilgrim's Progress*, but Bunyan tells us only that he "sometimes" read the books, finding in them "some things that were somewhat pleasing to me" but taking "no conviction" from their arguments (p. 9).

This germinal spiritual education brought Bunyan no relief from the torturing remorse for sin that continued to afflict him, and he began to seek succor in public religious observance. He went through a stage of scrupulous attendance at church and underwent an "outward reformation" that astonished his neighbors, "for this my conversion was as great, as for Tom of Bethlehem to become a sober man" (*Grace Abounding*, p. 13). This external change found no correspondence in his soul, however, and Bunyan tells us that he remained "a poor painted hypocrite" in spite of his ostensible holiness. In theological terms, he was passing through a phase of "works righteousness," in which he believed that salvation was attainable by obedience to the moral law and participation in religious ceremony. In this condition he fetishized the visible trappings of religion:

> I was so overrun with the spirit of superstition, that I adored, and that with great devotion, even all things (both the high place, priest, clerk, vestments, service and what else) belonging to the church; counting all things holy that were therein contained (p. 10).

Lacking any subjective correlative, such idolatrous observance inevitably lapsed, and Bunyan periodically returned to his "wicked life." At such times he was tempted by the doctrines of the Ranters, a sect who seemed to occupy the opposite end of the religious spectrum from the respectable churchgoers of his previous acquaintance. The Ranters were antinomian—that is to say, they extrapolated the Calvinist doctrine that God's "elect" were predestined for salvation into a belief that such "saints" were entirely free of any earthly law, and thus at liberty to practice any vice or hold any opinion that they deemed fit:

> I happened to light into several people's company; who though strict in religion formerly, yet were also swept away by these Ranters. These would also talk with me of their ways, and condemn me as legal and dark, pretending that they only had attained to perfection that could do what they would and not sin. O these temptations were suitable to my flesh, I being but a young man and my nature in its prime (*Grace Abounding*, p. 16).

So Bunyan's initial interest in religion provoked him to ricochet between a strict adherence to the external ceremonies and morality of the church, and an antinomian disavowal of any ethical constraint whatsoever. He was torn, in the language of the day, between "legalism" and "licence." His final conversion followed an epiphany by which he came to understand that the terms of this opposition were mutually definitive, so that the apparent contradiction between legalism and licence masked their interdependence, and the two tendencies were revealed as different sides of the same coin. License, in fact, takes for granted the power of the law, and merely claims an exemption from it. The point, however, was to disregard the law entirely in matters of faith. Bunyan achieved this revelation after careful study of Martin Luther's *Commentary on the Epistle to the Galatians* (1535), and it is no exaggeration to say that his entire subsequent life, and especially the doctrines and aesthetic mode of *The Pilgrim's Progress*, were determined by his interpretation of this book.

III

Grace Abounding depicts Bunyan's discovery of Luther's work as an act of divine Providence. In the midst of his tribulation, "the God in whose hands are all our days and ways, did cast into my hand, one day, a book of Martin Luther, his comment on the Galatians" (pp. 34–35). Despite the text's antiquity, Bunyan was amazed to find "my condition in his experience, so largely and profoundly handled, as if his book had been written out of my heart" (p. 35). What delighted him was Luther's assertion that it was impossible for human beings to obey the moral law. In fact, Luther argued that the law's purpose was to bring us to a conviction of our own irremediably sinful nature and our inability to please God through our own works. If we can resist the consequent temptation to despair, we are then driven to seek salvation through faith in the efficacy of Christ's sacrifice. This doctrine of "justification by faith alone" stimulated in Bunyan a psychological revolution against the vicious circle of sin and remorse that had almost ruined his life:

> Besides, [Luther] doth most gravely also in that book debate of the rise of these temptations, namely, blasphemy, desperation, and the like, showing that the law of Moses, as well as the devil, death, and hell, hath a very great hand therein; the which at first was very strange to me, but considering and watching, I found it so indeed. But of all particulars here I intend nothing, only this methinks I must let fall before all men, I do prefer this book of Martin Luther upon the Galatians, (excepting the Holy Bible) before all the books that ever I had seen, as most fit for a wounded conscience (p. 35).

Paul's epistle to the Galatians takes issue with the apostle Peter's opinion that Christians ought to follow the Mosaic law. As Paul points out, this would obviate the need for a new religion, relegating Christianity to the status of a sect within Judaism: "If righteousness come by the law, then Christ is dead in vain" (2:21; King James Version). In chapter four, he illustrates the proper relationship between the law of Moses and faith in Christ by means of an "allegory":

22: For it is written, that Abraham had two sons, the one by a bondmaid, the other by a freewoman.

23: But he who was of the bondwoman was born after the flesh; but he of the freewoman was by promise.

24: Which things are an allegory: for these are the two covenants; the one from the mount Sinai, which gendereth to bondage, which is Agar.

25: For this Agar is mount Sinai in Arabia, and answereth to Jerusalem which now is, and is in bondage with her children.

26: But Jerusalem which is above is free, which is the mother of us all.

The law is necessary insofar as we are not free, it is the "schoolmaster" that brings us to faith by instructing us as to the nature of our sinful condition. But the law is incapable of effecting our salvation; hence the necessity of Christ's sacrifice. This act redeems all humanity from sin, and all that is necessary to be saved is to have faith in this fact. In order to understand Bunyan's allegorical mode in *The Pilgrim's Progress* we must note here that Paul illustrates this argument by reference to the method of biblical interpretation known as "typology." He reads the Old Testament story of Abraham's two wives, the bondwoman Hagar and the free woman Sarah, as an allegory depicting the New Testament doctrine of justification by faith. To insist on a literalistic reading of the story would be, in Paul's view, to remain ignorant of the difference between the law and the gospel. Paul's epistle thus establishes the connection between literalism and legalism that dominates Bunyan's aesthetic practice. *The Pilgrim's Progress* insists that we must view the world of the flesh as an extended allegory, and this constant referral of material signs to spiritual meanings is the journey that its hero undertakes.

Like Paul and Bunyan, Luther spent many years in the vain attempt to achieve righteousness through obedience to the law in its civil, moral, and ceremonial guises. The Reformation began with his realization that this was impossible, and that justification before God could be attained only through faith in Christ. This entailed a radical, absolute separation between the fleshly righteousness of the law and the spiritual righteousness of grace: "But we imagine as it were two worlds, the one heavenly and the other earthly. In these we place these two kinds of righteousness, being separate the one far from the other" (*Commentary on the Epistle to the Galatians*, reprinted in *Selections from His Writings*, p. 104). Luther's dichotomy involves the division of every aspect of experience along these lines, and the *Commentary* constructs a lengthy series of binary oppositions on this basis. These oppositions are so prominent throughout *The Pilgrim's Progress* that a visual aid may be useful as a mnemonic:

Justice / Mercy
Law / Grace
Works / Faith
Flesh / Spirit

Type / Antitype
Literal / Allegorical
Old Man / New Man
Moses / Christ
First Adam / Second Adam
Old Testament / New Testament
Body / Soul
Active Righteousness / Passive Righteousness
Earth / Heaven
Alienation / Reconciliation
Death / Life
Damnation / Salvation
Imprisonment / Liberty

For Luther, as for Bunyan, the first terms of these oppositions are all connected to each other, as are the second terms. He emphasizes this unity throughout the *Commentary*: "For the flesh or the old man must be coupled with the law and works: the spirit or new man must be joined with the promise of God and his mercy" (p. 103), and "such a respect there is between the justified conscience and the law, as is between Christ raised up from the grave, and the grave; and as is between Peter delivered from the prison, and the prison" (p. 120). Such connections inform the logic of Bunyan's practice in *The Pilgrim's Progress*, and the subtitle he gave to his *A Book for Boys and Girls; or, Temporal Things Spriritualized* (1686; later titled *Divine Emblems; or, Temporal Things Spiritualized*) applies equally to his allegorical epic. The figural is coupled with the spiritual and the literal with the fleshly, and the act of interpretation is a journey from one to the other. As well as remembering these analogies, however, we must simultaneously bear in mind the irreducible nature of the contradiction between the first and second terms of these oppositions. Luther insists that a Christian must always be "putting a difference" (p. 144) between them. As a result, he or she will perceive a set of meanings in experience that are "hidden in a mystery, which the world does not know" (p. 101). It is easy to see why Bunyan would have found ease for his troubled conscience in Luther's words:

Wherefore, when you see a man terrified and cast down with the sense and feeling of his sin, say unto him: Brother, thou dost not rightly distinguish; thou placest the law in thy conscience, which should be placed in the flesh. Awake, arise up, and remember that thou must believe in Christ the conqueror of the law and sin. With this faith thou shalt mount up above and beyond the law, into that heaven of grace where is no law or sin (p. 119).

This is the journey traveled by Christian in *The Pilgrim's Progress*. He leaves behind the first terms of Luther's oppositions, and "mounts" (or walks, in Bunyan's metaphor) to the second. But Luther's uncompromising differentiation between the law and grace was potentially a dangerous doctrine. Such declarations as "a Christian man, if ye define him rightly, is free from all laws" (*Commentary*, p. 112) were seized on by antinomian sects like the Anabaptists and used to justify social revolution and the abandonment of ethical constraints on behavior. Luther regarded this as an egregious misreading of his doctrine, as the *Commentary* makes clear:

> This we see at this day in the fantastical spirits and authors of sects, which teach nothing, neither can teach anything aright, concerning this righteousness of grace. The words indeed they have taken out of our mouth and writings, and these only do they speak and write. But the thing itself they are not able to deliver and straitly to urge, because they neither do nor can understand it, since they cleave only to the righteousness of the law. Therefore they are and remain exactors of the law, having no power to ascend higher than that active righteousness (p. 106).

Luther argues that the antinomians are just as subject to the law as overt legalists. Their puerile rebellion against the law is its mirror-image; their behavior is determined by the law just as surely as that of the advocates of works righteousness. Both groups believe that their salvation consists in their actions. For Luther, in contrast, the law occupied a different dimension from salvation, and neither obedience nor disobedience was relevant to justification before God. Bunyan found in Luther's argument the solution to his twin temptations toward legalism and license. Much of his work, especially *The Pilgrim's Progress*, features fierce attacks on both legalists and antinomians, and Bunyan always contends that the opposition between them is false. Both groups, he tirelessly reminds us, remain under the law, but for Bunyan the only way to salvation is to transcend the sphere of the law altogether.

IV

Bunyan's study of *Commentary on the Epistle to the Galatians* was well-timed. Shortly before he encountered Luther, Bunyan had become acquainted with the man who became the single greatest influence on his life, pastor John Gifford, the leader of the Baptist congregation at Bedford. Before his conversion Gifford had lived a notoriously disreputable life, famed for wild drinking and gambling. He had served as a soldier in the Royalist army, and been captured and sentenced to death, but he had escaped from prison. This detail of his mentor's biography evidently impressed itself deeply on Bunyan's mind, as did Gifford's miraculous transformation from despised degenerate to respected congregational elder. Bunyan soon attached himself to Gifford's congregation, and in 1653 he was formally baptized in the River Ouse.

Male members of the congregation who felt moved by the Spirit were encouraged to preach, and Bunyan soon discovered his vocation. He first addressed private assemblies "though with much weakness and infirmity," as he modestly claims in *Grace Abounding* (p. 68). He learned quickly however, and in 1656 he was appointed to an official and regular preaching post. By all accounts he was an astonishing preacher, even by the standards of an age full of astonishing preachers. His written works, with their pungent emphases, energetic imagery, and rapid-fire repetition give some idea of the impression he must have made, and his fame soon spread throughout southeastern England.

He therefore inevitably became embroiled in the fierce sectarian disputes that roiled the land during the last years of the interregnum, and the first opponents he encountered were the Quakers. The Quakers Bunyan knew were very different from those of today. George Offor, the great Victorian editor of his *Collected Works*, goes so far as to note that "The word 'quakers' must not be misunderstood as referring to the society of friends, but to some deluded individuals calling themselves quakers; the friends were not formed into a society for some years after this was written" (vol. 2, p. 133). In fact, however, Bunyan fashions the "Quakers" into precisely the kind of enemy he required to inaugurate his polemical career. Bunyan viewed, and evidently needed to view, the Quakers as legalistic antinomians. They function in his work as allegorical personifications of the complicity between the law and license, the discovery of which had precipitated Bunyan's conversion.

His charges were not altogether groundless: Like the Ranters, who were in decline by the mid-1650s, the Quakers believed in the essential goodness of the human soul; they rejected the Calvinist idea of "total depravity" that was so important to Bunyan; they believed that their own soul, or "inner light," was a higher authority than the Bible; and they treated the term "Christ" as referring to interior qualities within the believer rather than to the historical Jesus of Nazareth. But Bunyan thought that the Quakers were even worse than the Ranters. At least the latter group had openly revealed their depravity by public indulgence in vice; the Quakers had the fiendish cunning to conceal their wickedness behind a screen of outwardly holy, unimpeachably sinless conduct. As Bunyan explains in *A Vindication of Gospel Truths* (1656):

And really I tell thee (reader) plainly, that for the generality, the very opinions that are held at this day by the Quakers, are the same that long ago were held by the Ranters. Only the Ranters had made them threadbare at an alehouse, and the Quakers have set a new gloss upon them again, by an outward legal holiness (*Works*, vol. 2, p. 183).

Bunyan saw the Quakers as combining two kinds of self-righteousness: the happy antinomian faith in their own intrinsic goodness, and the Pharisaical smugness of external legalism. In *Some Gospel Truths Opened* (1656) he accounts for the attraction they evidently held for many of his neighbors by noting their ability to attract both libertines and legalists. He scorns those "who at this day are so carried away with the quakers delusions: namely, a company of loose ranters, and light notionists, with here and there a legalist" (*Works*, vol. 1, p. 133). Surprising as it may seem to us, this controversy was of enormous public interest and popular influence in revolutionary Bedfordshire. Bunyan entered into a "pamphlet war" with a Quaker firebrand named Edward Burroughs, and the passionate debate between these two young men (Bunyan was twenty-eight, Burroughs twenty-three) won widespread attention. The struggle against

Quakerism made Bunyan's reputation, and he would return to the terms of this argument throughout his career.

He was still not free of the terrifying guilt that had tortured him all his life; he would be liberated from that only when physically imprisoned. But the nature of his remorse now changed. He no longer blasphemed or swore, nor did he even indulge in bell-ringing or tip-cat, but he did experience, and submit to, what he calls "a more grievous and dreadful temptation than before." He describes it in *Grace Abounding*:

> And that was to sell and part with this most blessed Christ, to exchange him for the things of this life; for any thing: the temptation lay upon me for the space of a year, and did follow me so continually, that I was not rid of it one day in a month, no, not sometimes one hour in many days together, unless I was asleep. . . . It did always in almost whatever I thought, intermix itself therewith, in such sort that I could neither eat my food, stoop for a pin, chop a stick, or cast mine eye to look on this or that, but still the temptation would come, *Sell Christ for this, or sell Christ for that; sell him, sell him.* Sometimes it would run in my thoughts not so little as a hundred times together, sell him, sell him, sell him (pp. 35–36).

It sounds as though every aspect of Bunyan's experience of the world was clouded by an insistent temptation to commodify Christ. He eventually succumbed to this pressure, allowing the thought "Let him go if he will" pass through his mind. Meditation on the precedents of Esau, who exchanged his "birthright" (a typological figure for redemption) for a "mess of pottage," and Judas, who betrayed Jesus for thirty pieces of silver, firmly convinced him that "I had sold my Saviour." Worse still, he was sure that this "selling" of Christ constituted the "sin against the Holy Ghost" that Jesus describes as unforgivable, and so he plunged into the deepest depression of his life.

What did Bunyan mean by "selling" Christ, and why did he fear it more than any other sin? Throughout his life, he was interested in affairs that we would call "economic," although the modern idea that there exists some identifiable object or realm called "the economy" that can be segregated from other fields of experience was unknown to him. One of his earliest works, *A Few Sighs from Hell* (1658), is a lengthy commentary on the parable of the rich man and Lazarus the beggar, in which money becomes a trope for legalism and worldliness in general. One of his latest, *The Life and Death of Mr. Badman* (1680), depicts a trader in unspecified "commodities," whose reprobation is signaled by his blithe ignorance of his own allegorical status. Mr. Badman does not understand that he is predestined to badness, that it is his essence and nature, but rather regards himself as a free subjective agent. As he boasts: "Now I enjoy my self, and am master of my own ways, and not they of me" (*The Life and Death of Mr. Badman*, p. 84). *The Pilgrim's Progress* features many worldly characters who express a similarly misplaced confidence in their liberty from allegorical constraints. For example, "By-Ends" (that is, "Self-interest") proclaims, "This is not my name, but indeed it is a nickname that is given me by some that cannot abide me." Christian soon corrects him on this point, observing that "this name belongs to you more properly than you are willing we should think it doth," and he is proved right when By-Ends falls to his death into the silver mine at Lucre Hill.

Like most of his contemporaries, Bunyan connected market behavior with "covetousness." In *Christian Behaviour* he claims:

> It is covetousness in the seller, that puts him to say of his traffic, it is better than it is, that he may heighten the price of it; and covetousness in the buyer, that prompts him to say worse of a thing than he thinks in his conscience it is (*Works*, vol. 2, p. 566).

What Bunyan considers sinful "covetousness" is, today, the very foundation of theoretical and practical economics. We have largely forgotten the ethical objections to the market that were so familiar to Bunyan. He often points, for example, to the biblical texts in which Paul identifies "covetousness" with "idolatry" (Colossians 3:5, Ephesians 5:5), thus linking market exchange with the adoration of images. Bunyan believed that financial value constituted an artificial, man-made, and thus illusory set of meanings imposed upon the natural, Godly, and thus true significance of the world. As Luther had put it: "Money is the word of the devil, through which he creates everything in the world, just as God creates through the true word" (quoted in Shell, *Money, Language and Thought*, p. 84, note 1).

To "sell" Christ, then, would be to replace this true significance with the false, and it appeared to Bunyan that many of his contemporaries were doing just that. Over the preceding two centuries, the massive influx of American gold into Europe had helped give rise to a money-based, market economy. Any act of market exchange assumes an illusory equivalence between the objects being exchanged, and in a developed market economy this equivalence is expressed through the medium of money. The burgeoning of the market, which rapidly gathered pace after the Restoration, seems to have produced in many people a deeply rooted, almost ineradicable temptation to "sell" Christ: "to exchange him for the things of this life, for any thing." This was certainly Bunyan's most terrible and tenacious temptation, and he had to be physically separated from the world before he could be free of it. *The Pilgrim's Progress* presents Vanity Fair, where Christian is imprisoned and his companion Faithful executed, as the most dangerous territory of all. As Thomas Luxon explains:

> Christian basically defines the things of the world and those who credit them as real, as things for sale, indeed things always already sold. . . . This includes even the very selves who value such things; such people, asserts Christian, sell "themselves out right" without even knowing it. The once-born are doomed to the status of commodities—things of this world (*Literal Figures*, p. 197).

This connection, lost to us but vital for Bunyan, between financial value and idolatry, explains why the temptation to "sell" Christ was so horrifyingly persistent in his mind. His world was visibly being taken over by the false image of money, and its people were turning into living commodities, who sold their labor—that is, themselves— for money on a daily basis. The animate abstractions who populate *The Pilgrim's Progress* illustrate Bunyan's reflections on the spiritual consequences of these developments.

V

Bunyan's first wife, whose name we do not know, died in 1658, and he remarried a woman named Elizabeth the following year. Elizabeth Bunyan was evidently much younger than her husband; one of the judges to whom she appealed in 1661 remarked that she seemed too young to have four children, and she had to explain that she was their stepmother (*Grace Abounding to the Chief of Sinners and A Re-*

lation of the Imprisonment of Mr. John Bunyan, p. 107). This second marriage eventually produced two children, but not before it was interrupted by Bunyan's arrest and imprisonment. His preaching and pamphleteering had brought him fame throughout southeastern England, but it also attracted the wrong kind of attention. After King Charles II took the throne in 1660, Anglicanism was reestablished as the sole legal religion, dissenters were persecuted under the repressive laws known as the Clarendon Code, and popular, unofficial preachers like Bunyan became obvious targets for the authorities. He was warned of his impending arrest, but he hungered for the martyr's crown. He refused to escape or hide, and when brought to trial he boasted of his intention to repeat his offense at the earliest opportunity. He had been psychologically prepared for this moment by years of meditation on the superiority of faith to the moral law, and he did not shrink from extending this to the civil law of the land. His refusal to cease preaching left the judges no choice. Bunyan was sent to jail where, with brief, irregular intervals of liberty, he remained for the next twelve years.

This external oppression seems actually to have come as a relief from the more ferocious interior persecution to which Bunyan had previously subjected himself. As he admits in "Prison Meditations": "Here, though in bonds, I have release / From guilt, which else would bite" (quoted in *Works*, vol. 1, p. 64). The conditions under which he was held varied with the temper of the local authorities and the fluctuations in state policy. Seventeenth-century jails were never pleasant—dirt, disease, and overcrowding caused the death of thousands of incarcerated nonconformists, including Bunyan's Quaker antagonist Edward Burroughs. But Bunyan was generally allowed to have food brought to him from home, to preach to his fellow prisoners, to support his family by making bootlaces, and even to leave the jail periodically, in order to attend church or visit his family. Most important, he was allowed to write. Bunyan consolidated his reputation in jail, partly because his heroic defiance of the law inspired admiration and emulation throughout the nonconformist congregations, but also because of the steady stream of poems, pamphlets, and memoirs that issued from his pen. The most famous of his works to be published while he was in jail was his spiritual autobiography, *Grace Abounding to the Chief of Sinners* (1666), which became a model for the religious experience of dissenters throughout England. By the time of his release in 1672, Bunyan was a famous man.

Considerable public attention therefore focused on the controversy that occupied him during the final months of his incarceration, in which Bunyan came into conflict with another branch of the legalist/libertine alliance. Edward Fowler, later bishop of Gloucester, was then rector of the parish of Norhill, near Bedford. He had been a Puritan during the interregnum but had turned his coat at the Restoration, conforming to the Anglican Church, and his current position was the reward for his treachery. Such men often rationalized their behavior through the doctrine of Latitudinarianism, which suggested that believers should be allowed "latitude" in their faith, and that many doctrinal points were "things indifferent," over which it was permissible to differ. Bunyan, who had spent more than a decade in prison for his refusal to compromise on doctrinal points, was understandably unsympathetic to this position. He was driven into a fury when Fowler published *The Design of Christianity* in 1671. This book's emphasis on the inherent goodness of man, and its stress on the importance of civility and personal morality in religious practice, seemed to Bunyan to represent the same unholy alliance of legalism and antinomianism he had encountered in the Quakers. Fowler presented Christ as a clubbable English gentleman:

> He was a Person of the Greatest Freedom, Affability, and Courtesie, there was nothing in his Conversation that was at all Austere, Crabbed or Unpleasant. Though he was always serious, yet he was never sour, sullenly Grave, Morose or Cynical; but of a marvelously conversable, sociable and benign temper (quoted in Roger Pooley, "Plain and Simple: Bunyan's Style," in *John Bunyan: Conventicle and Parnassus*, edited by N. H. Keeble).

Such sentiments have led many critics to find a personification of Fowler in Mr. Worldly Wiseman, who directs Christian out of the way, to the house of Mr. Legality and his "simpering" son Civility. In *A Defence of the Doctrine of Justification by Faith* (1672), Bunyan wonders what madness can have provoked "you, Sir, a pretended minister of the word, so vilely to expose to public view the rottenness of your heart" (*Works*, vol. 2, p. 281). He deftly identifies Fowler's assertion of the basic morality of human nature as "the self-same which our late ungodly heretics the Quakers have made such a stir to promote and exalt" (*Works*, vol. 2, p. 286), and he includes an appendix juxtaposing quotations from Fowler with corresponding passages from the work of the Quaker William Penn. Fowler gave as good as he got in his reply, *Dirt Wip'd Off* (1672). Uncharitable as it may have been, the vehement tone of the debate attracted public attention, and must have increased the anticipation with which Bunyan's followers anticipated his release.

King Charles II was no friend to the dissenters, but he saw that he could use them to further his ultimate design of reintroducing Roman Catholicism into England. His Declaration of Indulgence (1672) made it possible to follow religions other than Anglicanism, and thus served the interests of Catholics and dissenters alike. Bunyan was released under its terms and immediately became pastor of his congregation. He resumed preaching with a vigor accumulated during his years in jail, and his sermons rapidly became phenomenally popular. Although he traveled widely, often visited London, and was offered many more prominent positions, he refused to move away from his flock in Bedford, and remained resident there, apparently even continuing to work as a tinker. Royal policy toward dissenters was erratic in the 1670s and '80s; Bunyan continued to be subjected to periodic persecution, and he was imprisoned for a further six months in 1677. It was during this period in jail that, most critics agree, he finished writing the first part of *The Pilgrim's Progress*, which he had probably begun in 1668. Bunyan eventually decided to publish it, following lengthy consultation with religious friends and elders, in 1678.

Although the naturalism of *The Pilgrim's Progress* is unprecedented, in many ways it represents the culmination of a lengthy, though largely subterranean, tradition of popular English literature. The anonymous *The Pylgremage of the Sowle* (1483) describes "a full marueylous dreme" (*Works*, vol. 3, p. 33) and features a pilgrim who carries a "scrip" and a "burden," and who is put on trial and examined by the figures of "Justice" and "Mercy." William Langland's *The Vision of Piers Plowman* (c.1370) uses the dream motif and allegorical style, and also employs the voice of the dispossessed to protest against economic oppression. One of the few books we know Bunyan read, Arthur Dent's *The Plaine Man's Pathway to Heaven* (1601), uses the pilgrimage metaphor and contains strident attacks on the market economy. Works like Robert Bruen's *The Pilgrim's Practice* (1621) and Thomas Taylor's *The Pilgrim's Profession* (1624) show how deeply engrained in the English consciousness were the basic techniques and assumptions of Bunyan's masterpiece. Richard Barnard's *The Isle of Man* (1627) depicts a lengthy trial featuring a judge called "Sir Worldly Wise," and such figures as "Mistress Heart," "Sir Luke Warm," and "Sir Silly." The real achievement of *The Pilgrim's Progress* is not originality but comprehensiveness; it is the summation and apex of a centuries-old set of ideas and beliefs.

As such, it could not help but strike a chord in the popular mind. A second edition was published in the same year as the first, and a third, with considerable additions, the following year. The book went through eleven editions in Bunyan's lifetime and was translated into every major language of western Europe. It was especially popular in New England, where the inhabitants already thought of themselves as "pilgrims," and after Bunyan's death it was carried to the ends of the earth by the missionaries who followed in the wake of the British empire. It has never been out of print, and in all probability it is the most widely influential book ever written in English.

For the last decade of his life, Bunyan was in great demand as both preacher and author. He composed a companion volume to *The Pilgrim's Progress*, which traces the path of the reprobate to hell, entitled *The Life and Death of Mr. Badman* (1680). The title character is a personification of Vanity Fair; he represents the market economy, as well as the general nature of sin, and in fact Bunyan comes close to equating the two. A more closely focused *psychomachia*, *The Holy War* (1682), recasts the English Civil War as a battle for the town of Mansoul, fought between the forces of Emmanuel and the Diabolonians. By this time, numerous imitations and even counterfeit sequels to *The Pilgrim's Progress* were circulating, and Bunyan responded by publishing his own *Second Part* in 1684. This work deals with the adventures of the original pilgrim's wife, Christiana, and her retinue of children, friends, and guides. It is sometimes considered as a feminization of the masculine first part. Bunyan had opposed a suggestion that women should be allowed to preach in his church, and the second part includes regular reference to the weakness of women. It would be a mistake, however, to read Christiana too literally, as simply designating the female gender. For Bunyan, a wife symbolized the church, and whereas part one examines the development of the individual soul, part two deals with the salvation of the collective believer, or congregation. The Song of Solomon was believed to depict the church through the metaphor of a "bride," and the vision of a woman fleeing in the wilderness in Revelation 12:14 was also taken as a type of the congregation. Bunyan's own *Christian Behaviour* (1663) describes a wife as "the figure of a church" (*Works*, vol. 2, p. 560), and it is as such that Christiana is best regarded. The characters in part two do not generally personify abstract qualities, as they do in part one, but seem rather to represent character types drawn from Bunyan's pastoral experience. Furthermore, Bunyan skillfully manipulates the allegory, so that his figures become progressively more free from their allegorical confines as they approach the celestial city. Feeble-mind, for example, asks for his feeble mind to be buried in a dunghill.

This shift of emphasis from internal, personal struggle to the practical issues faced by a spiritual guide reflects the fact that part two was written while Bunyan was at liberty to practice his pastoral duties. He continued to do so until the end of his life, and they included interventions in disputes among the faithful as well as regular preaching. In 1688, one such mission took him on a journey from London to Reading, where he successfully reconciled a disinherited son with his estranged father. During the ride back to the capital he was caught in a heavy storm, as a result of which he contracted pneumonia, and he died three weeks later at a friend's house in Holborn. A statue marks the spot today. It is invisible to pedestrians, being set into an alcove two stories above street level, but Bunyan stares directly into the eyes of the passengers on the top deck of the number sixty-eight bus, as they make their painful, halting progress down Kingsway toward the Strand.

David Hawkes is Associate Professor of English at Lehigh University. He is the author of *Idols of the Marketplace* (Palgrave, 2001) and *Ideology* (Routledge, second edition, 2003). His work has appeared in *Milton Studies*, *The Nation*, *Times Literary Supplement*, *Journal of the History of Ideas*, *Huntingdon Library Quarterly*, and *Studies in English Literature*. Professor Hawkes recently received a long-term fellowship from the National Endowment for the Humanities to work on a book-length history and analysis of the Faust myth.

THE
PILGRIM'S PROGRESS

R.W.f.

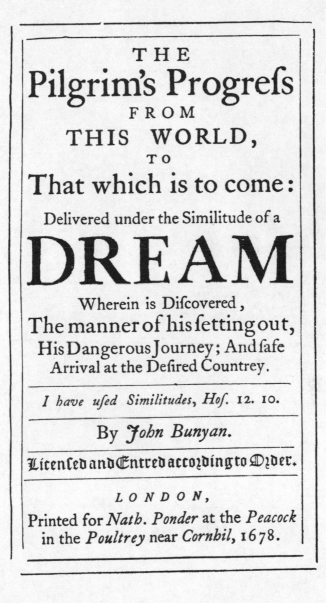

THE
Pilgrim's Progreſs
FROM
THIS WORLD,
TO
That which is to come:

Delivered under the Similitude of a

DREAM

Wherein is Diſcovered,
The manner of his ſetting out,
His Dangerous Journey; And ſafe
Arrival at the Deſired Countrey.

I have uſed Similitudes, Hoſ. 12. 10.

By *John Bunyan.*

Licenſed and Entred according to Order.

LONDON,
Printed for *Nath. Ponder* at the *Peacock*
in the *Poultrey* near *Cornhil,* 1678.

The Author's Apology for his Book.

W hen at the first I took my Pen in hand,
    Thus for to write; I did not understand
    That I at all should make a little Book
In such a mode: Nay, I had undertook
To make another; which, when almost done,
Before I was aware, I this begun.
    And thus it was: I writing of the Way[1]
And Race of Saints[2] in this our Gospel-day,
Fell suddenly into an Allegory[3]
About their Journey, and the Way to Glory,
In more than twenty things, which I set down;
This done, I twenty more had in my crown,
And they again began to multiply,
Like sparks that from the coals of fire do fly.
Nay then, thought I, if that you breed so fast,
I'll put you by yourselves, lest you at last
Should prove ad infinitum, and eat out
The Book that I already am about.
    Well, so I did; but yet I did not think
To show to all the World my Pen and Ink
In such a mode; I only thought to make
I knew not what: nor did I undertake
Thereby to please my Neighbour; no not I,
I did it mine ownself to gratifie.
    Neither did I but vacant seasons spend
In this my scribble; nor did I intend
But to divert my self in doing this,
From worser thoughts,[4] which make me do amiss.
    Thus I set Pen to Paper with delight,
And quickly had my thoughts in black and white.
For having now my Method by the end,

5

Still as I pull'd, it came;° and so I penn'd
It down; until it came at last to be
For length and breadth, the bigness which you see.
      Well, when I had thus put mine ends° together,
I shew'd them others, that I might see whether
They would condemn them, or them justify:
And some said, let them live; some, let them die;
Some said, John, print it; others said, Not so.
Some said, It might do good, others said, No.
      Now was I in a straight, and did not see
Which was the best thing to be done by me:
At last I thought, Since ye are thus divided,
I print it will; and so the case decided.
      For, thought I, Some, I see, would have it done,
Though others in that Channel do not run:
To prove then who advised for the best,
Thus I thought fit to put it to the test.
      I further thought, if now I did deny
Those that would have it thus, to gratifie;
I did not know but hinder them I might
Of that which would to them be great delight.
For those that were not for its coming forth,
I said to them, Offend you, I am loth;
Yet since your Brethren pleased with it be,
Forbear to judge, till you do further see.
      If that thou wilt not read, let it alone;
Some love the meat, some love to pick the bone:
Yea, that I might them better palliate,°
I did too with them thus *Expostulate:*
      May I not write in such a stile as this?
In such a method too, and yet not miss
Mine end, thy good? why may it not be done?

Still as I pull'd, it came Keeble notes that "the image is of a spinner pulling thread from the distaff" (Keeble, ed., *The Pilgrim's Progress*, p. 264; see "For Further Reading"). Bunyan is "spinning a yarn"; **mine ends** The "ends" of the yarn or thread produced by the spinner, as well as "purposes" and "products of my labor"; **palliate** The ninth (1684) and subsequent editions have "moderate."

Dark Clouds bring Waters,[5] when the bright bring none.
Yea, dark or bright, if they their Silver drops
Cause to descend; the Earth, by yielding Crops,
Gives praise to both, and carpeth° not at either,
But treasures up the Fruit they yield together;
Yea, so commixes both, that in her Fruit
None can distinuish this from that; they suit
Her well, when hungry: but if she be full,
She spues° out both, and makes their blessings null.

    You see the ways the Fisher-man doth take
To catch the Fish; what Engines doth he make?
Behold how he engageth all his Wits;
Also his Snares, Lines, Angles, Hooks, and Nets:
Yet Fish there be, that neither Hook, nor Line,
Nor Snare, nor Net, nor Engine can make thine;
They must be grop't for, and be tickled too,
Or they will not be catch't, what e're you do.

    How doth the Fowler seek to catch his Game
By divers means, all which one cannot name?
His Gun, his Nets, his Lime-twigs,° light and bell:
He creeps, he goes, he stands; yea, who can tell
Of all his postures, Yet there's none of these
Will make him master of what Fowls he please.
Yea, he must Pipe and Whistle, to catch this,
Yet if he does so, that *Bird* he will miss.

If that a Pearl may in a Toad's head dwell,[6]
And may be found too in an Oyster-shell;
If things that promise nothing, do contain
What better is than Gold; who will disdain,
(That have an Inkling of it,) there to look,
That they may find it? Now my little Book,
(Though void of all those paintings that may make
It with this or the other Man to take)
Is not without those things that do excel
What° do in brave,° but empty, notions dwell.

---

carpeth Complains; **spues** Spews; **Lime-twigs** Traps to catch birds; **What** Which; **brave** Ostentatious.

Well, yet I am not fully satisfied,
That this your Book will stand when soundly try'd.[7]
   Why, what's the matter! it is dark, what tho'?°
But it is feigned:° *What of that I tro?*°
Some men by feigning words, as dark as mine,
Make truth to spangle, and its rayes to shine.
But they want solidness: Speak man thy mind:
They drown the weak; Metaphors make us blind.[8]
   Solidity, indeed, becomes the Pen
Of him that writeth things Divine to men:
But must I needs want solidness, because
By Metaphors I speak; Was not God's Laws,
His Gospel-Laws, in older time held forth
By Types, Shadows and Metaphors?[9] *Yet loth*
Will any sober man be to find fault
With them, lest he be found for to assault
The highest Wisdom: No, he rather stoops,
And seeks to find out what by pins and loops,
By Calves; and Sheep; by Heifers, and by Rams,
By Birds, and Herbs, and by the blood of Lambs,°
God speaketh to him: And happy is he
That finds the light, and grace that in them be.
   Be not too forward therefore to conclude
That I want solidness; that I am rude:
All things solid in shew, not solid be;°
All things in parables despise not we,
Lest things most hurtful lightly we receive;
And things that good are, of our souls bereave.
   My dark and cloudy words they do but hold
The Truth, as Cabinets inclose the Gold.
   The Prophets used much by Metaphors
To set forth Truth; Yea, whoso considers
Christ, his Apostles too, shall plainly see,

---

what tho'? So what?; **feigned** Fictional; **What of that I tro?** What do I care about that?; **pins and loops . . . Lambs** The first in a series of Old Testament types (see endnote 9 to part one); **All things . . . not solid be** Not everything that appears substantial is truly so.

That Truths to this day in such Mantles° be.
    Am I afraid to say that holy Writ
Which for its Style and Phrase puts down° all Wit,
Is every where so full of all these things,
(Dark Figures, Allegories) yet there springs
From that same Book, that lustre, and those rays
Of light, that turn our darkest nights to days.
    Come, let my Carper° to his Life now look,
And find There darker lines than in my Book
He findeth any; Yea, and let him know,
That in his best things there are worse lines too.[10]
    May we but stand before impartial men,°
To his poor One, I durst° adventure Ten,
That they will take my meaning in these lines
Far better than his Lies in Silver Shrines.°
Come, Truth, altho' in Swaddling-clouts, I find
Informs the Judgment, rectifies the mind;
Pleases the Understanding, makes the Will
Submit; the Memory too it doth fill
With what doth our Imagination° please;
Likewise it tends our troubles to appease.
    Sound words I know, Timothy is to use,[11]
And old Wives Fables he is to refuse;
But yet grave Paul, him no where doth forbid
The use of Parables; in which lay hid
That Gold, those Pearls, and precious stones that were
Worth digging for; and that with greatest care.
    Let me add one word more. O man of God!°
Art thou offended? dost thou wish I had
Put forth my matter in another dress,
Or that I had in things been more express?
Three things let me propound, then I submit
To those that are my betters, as is fit.

Mantles Cloaks; **puts down** Surpasses; **Carper** Complainer; **impartial men** An ironic reference to legal trial by jury; **durst** Dare; **Silver Shrines** Reference to the altars to Diana of Ephesus, mentioned in the Bible, Acts 19:24; **Imagination** The mental faculty of creating images; **man of God!** A religious person, not necessarily an ordained minister.

1. *I find not that I am denied the use*
Of this my method, so I no abuse[12]
Put on the Words, Things, Readers, or be rude°
In handling Figure, or Similitude,
In application; but, all that I may,
Seek the advance of Truth, this or that way:
Deny'd, did I say? Nay, I have leave,
Example too, and that from them that have
God better pleased by their words or ways,
Than any man that breatheth now a-days
Thus to express my mind, thus to declare
Things unto thee, that excellentest are.

2. *I find that men (as high° as Trees) will write*
Dialogue-wise;[13] *yet no man doth them slight,*
For writing so: Indeed if they abuse
Truth, cursed be they, and the craft they use
To that intent; But yet let Truth be free
To make her salleys upon Thee, and Me.[14]
Which way it pleases God: For who knows how,
Better than he that taught us first to Plough,°
To guide our Mind and Pens for his Design?
And he makes base things usher in Divine.

3. *I find that holy Writ in many places*
Hath semblance with this method, where the cases
Do call for one thing, to set forth another;°
Use it I may then, and yet nothing smother
Truth's golden Beams; Nay, by this method may
Make it cast forth its rays as light as day.

And now, before I do put up° my Pen,
I'll shew the profit of my Book, and then
Commit both thee and it unto that hand
That pulls the strong down, and makes weak ones stand.°

---

rude Crude; **high** Eminent; **Plough** That is, to prepare the figurative soil of the mind to receive the seed of the gospel; **the cases . . . set forth another** In other words, the Bible also uses imagery; **put up** Put away; **that hand . . . weak ones stand** The hand of God reverses earthly hierarchies; Bunyan was always interested in the idea of *mundus inversus*, the "world turned upside down."

This Book it chalketh out before thine eyes
The man that seeks the everlasting Prize;
It shews you whence he comes, whither he goes,
What he leaves undone; also what he does:
It also shews you how he runs, and runs
Till he unto the Gate of Glory comes.

It shows too, who set out for life amain,°
As if the lasting Crown they would attain:
Here also you may see the reason why
They lose their labour,° and like Fools do die.

This book will make a Traveller of thee,°
If by its Counsel thou wilt ruled be;
It will direct thee to the Holy Land,°
If thou wilt its Directions understand:
Yea, it will make the slothful, active be;
The Blind also delightful things to see.

Art thou for something rare, and profitable?
Wouldest thou see a Truth within a Fable?
Art thou forgetful? wouldest thou remember
From New-year's-day to the last of December?
Then read my fancies, they will stick like Burs,
And may be to the Helpless, Comforters.

This Book is writ in such a Dialect,[15]
As may the minds of listless men affect:
It seems a Novelty, and yet contains
Nothing but sound and honest Gospel-strains.

Would'st thou divert thyself from Melancholy?
Would'st thou be pleasant, yet be far from folly?
Would'st thou read Riddles, and their Explanation?
Or else be drownded in thy Contemplation?
Dost thou love picking meat?° Or wouldst thou see
A man i' th' Clouds, and hear him speak to thee?

---

amain Strongly; **lose their labour** Waste their effort; **This book . . . of thee** As Stanley Fish, in *Self-consuming Artifacts*, and others have noted, the real action of *The Pilgrim's Progress* takes place within the mind of the reader; **the Holy Land** A good example of a biblical "type": The land of Canaan, promised to the Israelites in the Old Testament, is a prefiguration of the kingdom of Heaven; **picking meat** Dainty food.

Would'st thou be in a Dream, and yet not sleep?
Or, wouldest thou in a moment laugh, and weep?
Wouldest thou lose thyself, and catch no harm?
And find thyself° again without a charm?°
Would'st read thyself,° and read thou know'st not what,
And yet know, whether thou art blest or not,°
By reading the same lines? O then come hither,
And lay my Book, thy Head, and Heart together.

JOHN BUNYAN.

---

lose thyself . . . find thyself The reader will lose his "old man" and find his "new man"; **charm** Magic spell; **read thyself** Bunyan stresses again that the landscape of the book is internal; **blest or not?** Readers' responses to the work will determine whether they are members of the elect or reprobate.

The Pilgrims Progress

In the Similitude of a Dream.

As I walked through the wilderness of this world,° I
lighted on a certain place, where was a Den,° and I
laid me down in *that* place to sleep: And as I slept, *The Jail.*
I dreamed a Dream.° I dreamed, and behold *I saw a Man°*
cloathed with rags, standing in a certain place, with his face Isa. 64. 6.
from° his own house, a Book[16] *in his hand, and a great Burden°* Luke 14. 33.
upon his back. I looked, and saw him open the Book, and read Psalm 38. 4.
therein; and as he read, he wept and trembled; and not being Hab. 2. 2.
Acts 16. 29,
able longer to contain, he brake out with a lamentable cry, 30.
saying, *What shall I do?* *His Outcry.*

In this plight therefore he went home, and refrained him- Acts 2. 37.
self as long as he could, that his wife and children should not
perceive his distress; but he could not be silent long, because
that his trouble increased: Wherefore at length he brake° his
mind to his wife and children; and thus he began to talk to
them: *O my dear Wife*, said he, *and you the Children of my*
bowels, I your dear friend am in myself undone,° by reason of a
Burden that lieth hard upon me: moreover, I am for certain in-
formed, that this our City will be burned with fire from Heaven; *This World.*
in which fearful overthrow, both myself, with thee my wife, and
you my sweet babes, shall miserably come to ruin, except (the

---

the wilderness of this world The alien nature of the earthly environment is
established at the outset; **Den** Cave, but representing the prison in which
Bunyan had his "dream"; **Dream** Bunyan will emulate such biblical inter-
preters of dreams as Joseph (Genesis 41) and Daniel (Daniel 2); **a Man** At
this stage he has given no name; after his conversion we learn that his previous name had been "Graceless"; **from** Turned away from; **Burden** According to Keeble (Keeble, ed., *The Pilgrim's Progress*, p. 265), "The rags signify
the inadequacy of man's own moral effort . . . and the burden the guilt of
sin which that effort cannot remove"; **brake** Opened; **in myself undone** The
man's "self" has undergone a split; he has become alien to his "self."

which yet I see not) some Way of escape may be found, whereby we may be delivered. At this his relations were sore amazed; not for that they believed that what he had said to them was true, but because they thought that some frenzy distemper° had got into his head; therefore it drawing towards night, and they hoping that sleep might settle his brains, with all haste they got him to bed: But the night was as troublesome to him as the day; wherefore, instead of sleeping, he spent it in sighs and tears. So when the morning was come, they would know how he did; he told them *worse* and *worse;* he also set to talk-

Carnal Physick for a sick Soul.

ing to them again, but they began to be hardened;[17] they also thought to drive away his distemper by harsh and surly carriages to him: Sometimes they would deride, sometimes they would chide, and sometimes they would quite neglect him: Wherefore he began to retire himself to his Chamber, to pray for and pity them; and also to condole his own misery: He would also walk solitarily in the fields, sometimes reading and sometimes praying; and thus for some days he spent his time.

Now I saw, upon a time, when he was walking in the fields, that he was (as he was wont) reading in his Book, and greatly distressed in his mind: and as he read, he burst out, as he had

Acts 16. 30, 31.

done before, crying, *What shall I do to be saved?*

I saw also that he looked this way, and that way, as if he would run; yet he stood still, because (as I perceived) he could not tell which way to go. I looked then, and saw a Man named *Evangelist*[18] coming to him, and asked, *Wherefore dost thou cry?*

Heb. 9. 27. Job 16. 21, 22. Ezek. 22. 14.

He answered, Sir, I perceive by the Book in my hand, that I am condemned to die, and after that to come to Judgment; and I find that I am not willing to do the first, nor able to do the second.

Then said *Evangelist*, Why not willing to die, since this life is attended with so many evils? The man answered, Because I fear that this Burden that is upon my back, will sink me lower

---

frenzy distemper Feverish illness.

than the grave; and I shall fall into *Tophet*.° And, Sir, if I be not fit to go to Prison, I am not fit to go to Judgment, and from thence to Execution; and the thoughts of these things make me cry.

Isa. 30. 33.

Then said *Evangelist*, If this be thy condition, Why standest thou still? He answered, Because I know not whither to go. Then he gave him a *Parchment Roll*,° and there was written within, *Fly from the Wrath to come*.

Conviction of the Necessity of flying.
Mat. 3. 7.

The Man therefore read it, and looking upon *Evangelist* very carefully, said, Whither must I fly? Then said *Evangelist*, pointing with his finger over a very wide field, Do you see yonder *Wicket Gate*?[19] The man said, No: Then said the other, Do you see yonder Shining Light?° He said, I think I do. Then said *Evangelist*, Keep that Light in your eye, and go up directly thereto, so shalt thou see the Gate; at which, when thou knockest, it shall be told thee what thou shalt do. So I saw in my dream that the Man began to run: Now he had not run far from his own door, but his Wife and Children[20] perceiving it, began to cry after him to return; but the Man put his fingers in his ears, and ran on crying, *Life! Life! Eternal Life!* So he looked not behind him, but fled towards the middle of the Plain.

Mat. 7. 13, 14.
Psal. 119. 105.
2 Pet. 1. 19.
Christ and the Way to him, cannot be found without the Word.

Luke 14. 26.

Gen. 19. 17.

The Neighbours also came out to see him run, and as he ran some mocked, others threatened, and some cried after him to return; Now among those that did so, there were two that were resolv'd to fetch him back by force. The name of the one was *Obstinate*, and the name of the other *Pliable*.° Now by this time the Man was got a good distance from them; but however, they were resolved to pursue him, which they did, and in a little time they overtook him. Then said the Man, Neighbours, *Wherefore are you come?* They said, To persuade

Jer. 20. 10.
They that fly from the Wrath to come are a gazing stock to the world.
Obstinate and Pliable follow him.

Tophet Hell. Compare Milton's *Paradise Lost* (book 1, line 404); **Parchment Roll** This convinces the man that he needs to escape from the world; it thus represents his assurance of elect status; **Shining Light** The Word, which will show the way to Christ. Compare, on page 345, the endnote to "very well"; **Obstinate . . . Pliable** The first appearance of allegorical figures; Christian perceives the world as an allegory only after he has been convinced of the need to escape from it.

CHRISTIAN NO SOONER LEAVES THE WORLD BUT MEETS
EVANGELIST, WHO LOVINGLY HIM GREETS
WITH TIDINGS OF ANOTHER: AND DOTH SHEW
HIM HOW TO MOUNT TO THAT FROM THIS BELOW.

you to go back with us; but he said, That can by no means be: You dwell (said he) in the City of *Destruction*, (the place also where I was born) I see it to be so:° And dying there, sooner or later, you will sink lower than the grave, into a place that burns with Fire and Brimstone: Be content, good neighbours, and go along with me.

What, said *Obstinate*, and leave our Friends and our Comforts behind us!

Yes, said *Christian*, (for that was his name)° because that all *which you shall forsake*, is not worthy to be compared with a little of that, that I am seeking to enjoy; and if you will go along with me, and hold it, you shall fare as I myself; for there where I go, is enough and to spare; come away and prove° my words. 2 Cor. 4. 18.
Rom. 8. 18.

Luke 15. 17.

Obst. What are the things you seek, since you leave all the World to find them?

Chr. I seek an *Inheritance incorruptible, undefiled, and that fadeth not away:* And it is laid up in Heaven, and safe there, to be bestowed, at the time appointed, on them that diligently seek it. Read it so, if you will, in my Book. 1 Pet. 1. 4.
Heb. 11. 16.

Obst. Tush, said *Obstinate*, away with your Book; will you go back with us, or no?

Chr. No, not I, said the other; because I have laid my hand to the Plough. Luke 9. 62.

Obst. Come then, neighbour *Pliable*, let us turn again, and go home without him; There is a Company of these craz'd-headed coxcombs,° that when they take a fancy by the end, are wiser in their own eyes than seven men that can render a Reason.[21]

Pli. Then said *Pliable*, Don't revile; if what the good *Christian* says, is true, the things he looks after° are better than ours; my heart inclines to go with my Neighbour.

Obst. What! more Fools still? Be ruled by me, and go back;

I see it to be so He now regards his home town as an image; **for that was his name** Christian is so called only after he has recognized the allegorical nature of his surroundings; **prove** Test; **coxcombs** Fools; **looks after** Looks for, searches after.

who knows whither such a brain-sick fellow will lead you? Go back, go back and be wise.

Christian *and* Obstinate *pull for* Pliable's *Soul.*

Chr. Nay, but do thou come with me, neighbour *Pliable;* there are such things to be had which I spoke of, and many more Glories besides; if you believe not me, read here in this Book, and for the truth of what is express'd therein, behold all is confirmed by the Blood of him that made it.

Heb. 9. 17, 18, 19, 20, 21. Pliable *contented to go with* Christian.

Pli. Well, neighbour *Obstinate*, (said *Pliable*) I begin to come to a point, I intend to go along with this good man, and to cast in my Lot with him; but, my good companion, do you know the way to this desired place?

Chr. I am directed by a man whose name is *Evangelist*, to speed me to a little Gate that is before us, where we shall receive instructions about the Way.

Pli. Come then, good neighbour, let us be going. Then they went both together.

Obstinate *goes railing back.*

Obst. And I will go back to my place, said *Obstinate:* I will be no companion of such misled fantastical fellows.

Talk between Christian *and* Pliable.

Now I saw in my dream, that when *Obstinate* was gone back, *Christian* and *Pliable* went talking over the plain; and thus they began their discourse.

Chr. Come, neighbour *Pliable*, how do you do? I am glad you are persuaded to go along with me; and had even *Obstinate* himself but felt what I have felt of the Powers and Terrors of what is yet unseen,° he would not thus lightly have given us the back.

Pli. Come, neighbour *Christian*, since there are none but us two here, tell me now further, what the things are? and how to be enjoyed, whither we are going?

God's things unspeakable.

Chr. I can better conceive of them with my Mind, than speak of them with my Tongue:[22] But yet since you are desirous to know, I will read of them in my Book.

Pli. And do you think that the words of your Book are certainly true?

Tit. 1. 2.

Chr. Yes verily, for it was made by him that cannot lye.

---

the Powers . . . unseen As the subtitle puts it, Christian has already begun his journey "from this world to that which is to come."

Pli. Well said, what things are they?

Chr. There is an endless Kingdom to be inhabited, and everlasting Life to be given us, that we may inhabit that Kingdom for ever. Isa. 45. 17.
John 10. 27,
28, 29.

Pli. Well said; and what else?

Chr. There are Crowns of Glory to be given us; and Garments that will make us shine like the Sun in the firmament of Heaven. 2 Tim. 4. 8.
Rev. 22. 5.
Mat. 13. 43.

Pli. This is very pleasant; and what else?

Chr. There shall be no more crying, nor sorrow; for he that is Owner of the place will wipe all tears from our eyes. Isa. 15. 8.
Rev. 7. 16, 17.
ch. 21. 4.

Pli. And what company shall we have there?

Chr. There we shall be with Seraphims, and Cherubims,° Creatures that will dazzle your eyes to look on them: There also you shall meet with thousands, and ten thousands that have gone before us to that place; none of them are hurtful, but loving and holy, every one walking in the sight of God, and standing in his presence with acceptance for ever: In a word, there we shall see the Elders with their golden Crowns: There we shall see the Holy Virgins with their golden Harps: There we shall see men,° that by the World were cut in pieces, burnt in flames, eaten of beasts, drowned in the Seas, for the Love that they bare to the Lord of the place; all well, and cloathed with Immortality, as with a garment. Isa. 6. 2.
1 Thes. 4. 16,
17. Rev. 5. 11.

Rev. 4. 4.
Rev. 14. 1, 2, 3,
4, 5
John 12. 25.

2 Cor. 5. 2, 3, 5.

Pli. The Hearing of this is enough to ravish one's heart; but are these things to be enjoyed? How shall we get to be Sharers thereof?

Chr. The Lord the Governor of the country, hath recorded *that* in this Book, the substance of which is, if we be truly willing to have it, he will bestow it upon us freely. Isa. 55. 12.
John 7. 37.
John 6. 37.
Rev. 21. 6.
Rev. 22. 17.

Pli. Well, my good companion, glad am I to hear of these things; come on, let us mend° our pace.

Seraphims, and Cherubims Orders of angels; **we shall see men** The martyrs. Like most religious English people, Bunyan knew John Foxe's *Actes and Monuments* (1563), with its vivid depictions of martyrdoms, extremely well; **mend** Improve.

Chr. I cannot go so fast as I would, by reason of this Burden that is on my back.°

The Slough of
Despond.

Now I saw in my dream, that just as they had ended this talk, they drew nigh to a very *miry Slough*° that was in the midst of the plain, and they being heedless, did both fall suddenly into the bog. The name of the Slough was *Despond.*[23] Here therefore they wallowed for a time, being grievously bedaubed with the dirt; and *Christian*, because of the Burden that was on his back, began to sink in the mire.

Pli. Then said *Pliable*, Ah! neighbour *Christian*, where are you now?

Chr. Truly, said *Christian*, I do not know.

Pli. At that *Pliable* began to be offended, and angrily said to his fellow, Is this the happiness you have told me all this

It is not enough to be Pliable.

while of? If we have such ill speed° at our first setting out, what may we expect 'twixt this and our Journey's end? May I get out again with my Life, you shall possess the brave Country alone for me.° And with that he gave a desperate Struggle or two, and got out of the mire on that side of the Slough which was next to his own house; so away he went, and *Christian* saw him no more.

Christian in Trouble seeks still to get further from his own house.

Wherefore *Christian* was left to tumble in the Slough of *Despond* alone; but still he endeavoured to struggle to that side of the Slough that was still further from his own house, and next to the Wicket Gate; the which he did, but could not get out because of the Burden that was upon his back: But I beheld in my dream, that a man came to him, whose name was *Help*,[24] and asked him, *What he did there?*

Chr. Sir, said *Christian*, I was directed this way, by a man called *Evangelist*, who directed me also to yonder Gate, that I might escape the Wrath to come. And as I was going thither, I fell in here.

The Promises.

Help. But why did you not look for the Steps?

Burden that is on my back Note that Pliable is not conscious of any such burden; he lacks Christian's awareness of his own sin; **Slough** Swamp; **speed** Success; **for me** Both "instead of me" and "for all that I care."

Chr. Fear° followed me so hard, that I fled the next way, and fell in.

Help. Then, said he, *Give me thy hand;* so he gave him his hand, and he drew him out, and set him upon sound Ground, and bid him go on his way.

Help *lifts him out.* Psa. 40. 2.

Then I stepped to him° that plucked him out, and said, Sir, wherefore, (since over this place is the way from the City of *Destruction* to yonder Gate,) is it, that this plat° is not mended, that poor Travellers might go thither with more security? And he said unto me, This *miry Slough* is such a place as cannot be mended: It is the descent whither the scum and filth that attends Conviction for° Sin doth continually run, and therefore it is called the Slough of *Despond;* for still as the Sinner is awakened about his lost condition, there ariseth in his Soul many fears and doubts, and discouraging apprehensions, which all of them get together, and settle in this place: And this is the reason of the badness of this ground.

What makes the Slough of Despond.

It is not the pleasure of the King that this place should remain so bad; his labourers° also have, by the directions of his Majesties Surveyors, been for above this sixteen hundred years° employ'd about this patch of ground, if perhaps it might have been mended: Yea, and to my knowledge, said he, *here* hath been swallowed up at least twenty thousand cart loads; yea, Millions of wholsome Instructions,° that have at all seasons been brought from all places of the King's dominions (and they that can tell, say, They are the best materials to make good ground of the place) if so be it might have been mended; but it is the Slough of *Despond* still; and so will be when they have done what they can.

Isa. 35. 3, 4.

True, there are, by the direction of the Lawgiver,° certain

Fear No such character has appeared; rather, Christian has learned to externalize his own fear; **I stepped to him** The narrator makes a rare appearance in the narrative; **plat** Patch of ground; **for** Both "for" and "of"; the pilgrim must convict himself of sin, since this is the first stage on the path to salvation; **his labourers** Anyone doing God's work, not necessarily ordained clergymen; **sixteen hundred years** That is, since the birth of Christ; **wholsome Instructions** The law, which is incapable of saving man from despair; **the Lawgiver** Not Moses, but God, since the "Steps" are glossed in the margin as the biblical promises of salvation.

The Promises
of Forgiveness
and
Acceptance to
Life by Faith
in Christ.

1 Sam. 12. 23.

good and substantial Steps, placed even through the very Midst of this Slough; but at such time as this place doth much spue out its filth, as it doth against change of weather, these steps are hardly seen, or if they be, men, through the dizziness of their heads, step besides; and *then* they are bemired to purpose,° notwithstanding the steps be there; but the ground is good when they are once got in at the Gate.

Pliable is got
home, and is
visited by his
Neighbours.
His
Entertainment
by them at his
return.

Now I saw in my dream, that by this time *Pliable* was got home to his house again. So his Neighbours came to visit him; and some of them called him wise man for coming back; and some called him Fool for hazarding himself with *Christian*; others again did mock at his *Cowardliness*; saying, 'Surely since you began to venture, I would not have been so base to have given out for a few Difficulties.' So *Pliable* sat sneaking° among them. But at last he got more Confidence, and then they all turned their tales,° and began to deride poor *Christian* behind his back. And thus much concerning *Pliable*.

Now as *Christian* was walking solitary by himself, he espied one afar off, come crossing over the field to meet him, and their hap° was to meet *just as they were crossing the way of each other.*

Mr. Worldly
Wiseman
meets with
Christian.

The gentleman's name that met him, was Mr. *Worldly Wiseman*,[25] he dwelt in the town of *Carnal Policy*,° a very great town, and also hard by° from whence *Christian* came. This Man then, meeting with *Christian*, and having some inckling of him (for *Christian's* setting forth from the City of *Destruction*, was much noised abroad, not only in the town where he dwelt, but also it began to be the *Town-talk* in some other places) Master *Worldly Wiseman* therefore having some guess of him,° by beholding his laborious going, by observing his sighs and groans, and the like;

Talk between
Mr. Worldly
Wiseman *and*
Christian.

began thus to enter into some Talk with *Christian*.

World. How now, good fellow,° whither away after this burdened manner?

---

bemired to purpose Really stuck in the mire; **sneaking** Ashamed; **turned their tales** Both "told their stories" and "turned their backs"; **hap** Chance; **Carnal Policy** Worldly calculation; **hard by** Close by; **having some guess of him** Having some idea of who he was; **good fellow** A patronizing mode of address; Wiseman signals that he regards Christian as a social inferior.

Chr. A burdened manner indeed, as ever, I think, poor creature had! And whereas you ask me, *Whither away?* I tell you, Sir,° I am going to yonder Wicket Gate before me; for there, as I am informed, I shall be put into a Way° to be rid of my heavy Burden.

World. Hast thou a Wife and Children?

Chr. Yes; but I am so laden with this Burden, that I cannot take that Pleasure in them as formerly: methinks, I am as if I had none.

1 Cor. 7. 29.

World. Wilt thou hearken to me if I give thee counsel?

Chr. If it be good, I will; for I stand in need of good counsel.

World. I would advise thee then, that thou with all speed get thyself rid of thy Burden; for thou wilt never be settled in thy mind till then: Nor canst thou enjoy the Benefits of the Blessings which God hath bestowed upon thee, till then.

Mr. Worldly Wiseman's *Counsel to* Christian.

Chr. That is that which I seek for, even to be rid of this heavy Burden; but get it off myself, I cannot: Nor is there a Man in our country, that can take it off my shoulders; therefore am I going this Way, as I told you, that I may be rid of my Burden.

World. Who bid thee go this Way to be rid of the Burden?

Chr. A Man that appeared to me to be a very great and honourable person; his name, as I remember, is *Evangelist.*

World. Beshrew him for his counsel,° there is not a more dangerous and troublesome way in the world, than is that unto which he hath directed thee; and that thou shalt find, if thou wilt be ruled by his counsel. Thou hast met with something (as I perceive) already; for I see the dirt of the Slough of *Despond* is upon thee; but that Slough is the Beginning of the sorrows that do attend those that go on in that Way: Hear me, I am older than thou;° thou art like to meet with, in the way which thou goest, Wearisomeness, Painfulness, Hunger, Per-

Mr. Worldly Wiseman *condemns* Evangelist's *Counsel.*

Sir Christian acknowledges Wiseman's superior social status; **Way** Both "path" and "condition"; **Beshrew him for his counsel** Curse him for his advice; **I am older than thou** Worldliness predates Christianity, both in world history and in individual development.

ils, Nakedness, Sword, Lions, Dragons, Darkness, and in a word, Death, and what not?° These things are certainly true, having been confirmed by many Testimonies. And why should a man so carelessly cast away himself, by giving heed to a Stranger?°

The Frame of the Heart of a young Christian.

Chr. Why, Sir, this Burden upon my back is more terrible to me, than are all these things which you have mentioned: Nay, methinks I care not what I meet with in the way, if so be I can also meet with Deliverance from my Burden.

World. How camest thou by thy burden at first?

Chr. By reading this Book in my hand.

Mr. Worldly Wiseman *does not like that Men should be serious in reading the Bible.*

World. I thought so; and it is happened unto thee as to other weak men, who, meddling with things too high for them,° do suddenly fall into thy distractions; which distractions do not only unman men (as thine I perceive have done thee) but they run them upon desperate° ventures, to obtain they know not what.

Chr. I know what I would obtain; it is Ease for my heavy Burden.

World. But why wilt thou seek for ease this way, seeing so many Dangers attend it? especially, since (hadst thou but patience to hear me) I could direct thee to the obtaining of what thou desirest, without the dangers that thou in this way wilt run thyself into: Yea, and the Remedy is at hand. Besides, I will add, that instead of these dangers, thou shalt meet with much Safety, Friendship, and Content.

Chr. Pray, Sir, open this secret to me.

Mr. Worldly *prefers* Morality *before the Strait Gate.*

World. Why in yonder Village (the village is named *Morality*) there dwells a gentleman, whose name is *Legality*,° a very judicious° man (and a man of a very good name) that has

---

Wearisomeness ... what not Note Wiseman's conflation of abstract concepts and physical creatures; **a Stranger** Evangelist is a stranger to the world; **things too high for them** Wiseman is uncomfortable about the lower orders reading the Bible; **desperate** "Hopeless"; perhaps also "criminal"; **Legality** Offor cites the gloss from W. Mason's edition (1778): "Legality is as great an enemy to the cross of Christ as licentiousness" (*Works*, vol. 3, p. 96); **judicious** "Wise," but also implying "legalistic" and "judgmental."

skill to help men off with such Burdens as thine is, from their
shoulders; yea, to my knowledge, he hath done a great deal of
good this way: Ay, and besides, he hath skill to cure those that
are somewhat crazed in their wits with their Burdens. To him,
as I said, thou may'st go, and be help'd presently. His house is
not quite a mile from this place; and if he should not be at
home himself, he hath a pretty young man to his Son, whose
name is *Civility*,° that can do it (to speak on) as well as the old
Gentleman himself: There, I say, thou may'st be eased of thy
Burden, and if thou art not minded to go back to thy former
habitation, as indeed I would not wish thee; thou may'st send
for thy Wife and Children to thee to this Village, where there
are houses now stand empty, one of which thou mayest have
at reasonable rates: Provision is there also cheap and good,
and that which will make thy Life the more happy is, to be
sure there thou shalt live by honest neighbours, in Credit°
and good Fashion.

Now was *Christian* somewhat at a stand;° but presently he
concluded, If this be true which this gentleman hath said, my
wisest course is to take his advice; and with that he thus further spoke.

Chr. Sir, which is my way to this honest man's house?

World. Do you see yonder high Hill?°

Chr. Yes, very well.[26]

World. By that Hill you must go, and the first house you
come at is his.

So *Christian* turned out of his way, to go to Mr. *Legality's*
house for help: But behold, when he was got now hard by the
Hill, it seemed so high, and also that side of it that was next
the Wayside, did hang so much over, that *Christian* was afraid
to venture further, lest the Hill should fall on his head;[27]
wherefore there he stood still, and he wot° not what to do.
Also his Burden now seemed heavier° to him than while he

Margin notes:

Christian *snared by Mr. Worldly Wiseman's Words.*

Mount Sinai.

Christian *afraid that Mount Sinai would fall on his Head.*

Civility Courtesy; **Credit** Credibility, reputation. The word was not yet confined to its financial sense; **at a stand** At a loss; **yonder high hill** Mount Sinai
(Exodus 19:1–3), where Moses received the Ten Commandments (Exodus
20), here representing the law; **wot** Knew; **heavier** The purpose of the law is
to increase our sense of sin.

Exod. 19. 18.
Ver. 16.
Heb. 12. 21.

was in his Way. There came also flashes of fire out of the Hill, that made *Christian* afraid that he should be burned:° Here therefore he sweat and did quake for Fear. And now he began to be sorry that he had taken Mr. *Worldly Wiseman's* counsel; and with that he saw *Evangelist* coming to meet him; at the sight also of whom he began to blush for Shame. So *Evangelist* drew nearer and nearer; and coming up to him, he looked upon him with a severe and dreadful countenance, and thus began to reason with *Christian.*

Evangelist
findeth
Christian
under Mount
Sinai, *and
looketh
severely upon
him.*

Evangelist
*reasons afresh
with*
Christian.

Evan. What doest thou here, *Christian?* said he: At which words, *Christian* knew not what to answer; wherefore at present he stood speechless before him. Then said *Evangelist* farther, Art not thou the Man that I found crying without° the walls of the City of *Destruction?*

Chr. Yes, dear Sir, I am the Man.

Evan. Did not I direct thee the Way to the little Wicket Gate?

Chr. Yes, dear Sir, said *Christian.*

Evan. How is it then that thou art so quickly turned aside? for thou art now out of the way.

Chr. I met with a gentleman so soon as I had got over the Slough of *Despond*, who persuaded me, that I might, in the village before me, find a man that could take off my Burden.

Evan. What was he?

Ch. He looked like a gentleman,° and talked much to me, and got me at last to yield; so I came hither: But when I beheld this Hill, and how it hangs over the way, I suddenly made a stand, lest it should fall on my head.

Evan. What said that gentleman to you?

Ch. Why, he asked me whither I was going? And I told him.

Evan. And what said he then?

Ch. He asked me if I had a family? And I told him: But, said I, I am so loaden with the Burden that is on my back, that I cannot take pleasure in them as formerly.

---

burned That is, in Hell; **without** Outside; **He looked like a gentleman** Note that Evangelist's question about Wiseman's essence—"What was he?"—is answered by reference to his appearance.

Evan. And what said he then?

Ch. He bid me with speed get rid of my burden; and I told him 't was Ease that I sought: And, said I, I am therefore going to yonder Gate, to receive farther direction how I may get to the place of deliverance. So he said that he would shew me a better way, and short, not so attended with Difficulties, as the Way, Sir, that you set me in; which way, said he, will direct you to a gentleman's house that hath skill to take off these Burdens: So I believed him, and turned out of *that* Way into *this*, if haply° I might be soon eased of my Burden. But when I came to this place, and beheld things as they are, I stopped for fear (as I said) of danger: But I now know not what to do.

Evan. Then (said *Evangelist*) stand still a little, that I may shew thee the words of God. So he stood trembling. Then said *Evangelist*, See that ye refuse not him that speaketh; for if they escaped not, who refused him that spake on Earth, much more shall not we escape, if we turn away from him that speaketh from Heaven. He said, moreover, Now the just shall live by faith; but if any man draws back, my soul shall have no pleasure in him. He also did thus apply them,° *Thou art the man* that art running into this misery: Thou hast begun to reject the counsel of the Most High, and to draw back thy foot from the Way of Peace, even almost to the hazarding of thy Perdition.° Heb. 12. 25.
Evangelist
convinces
Christian *of*
his Error.
Heb. 10. 38.

Then *Christian* fell down at his foot as dead, crying, *Wo is me, for I am undone!* At the sight of which, *Evangelist* caught him by the right hand, saying, *All manner of Sin and Blasphemies shall be forgiven unto men; be not faithless, but believing:* Then did *Christian* again a little revive, and stood up trembling, as at first, before *Evangelist*. Mat. 12.
Mark 3.

Then *Evangelist* proceeded, saying, Give more earnest Heed to the things that I shall tell thee of. I will now shew thee who it was that deluded thee, and who it was also to whom he sent thee. The man that met thee, is one *Worldly Wiseman*, Mr. Worldly
Wiseman
described by
Evangelist.
1 John 4. 5.

---

haply By any chance; **apply them** That is, apply the texts to Christian's case; **hazarding of thy Perdition** Risk of your damnation.

WHEN CHRISTIANS UNTO CARNAL MEN GIVE EAR,
OUT OF THEIR WAY THEY GO, AND PAY FOR'T DEAR.
FOR MASTER *WORLDLY WISEMAN* CAN BUT SHEW
A SAINT THE WAY TO BONDAGE AND TO WO.

and rightly is he so called;° partly, because he savoureth only the doctrine of this world; (therefore he always goes to the town of *Morality* to church) and partly, because he loveth that doctrine best; for it saveth him from the Cross;° and because he is of this carnal temper,° therefore he seeketh to pervert my ways, though right. Now there are three things in this man's counsel that thou must utterly abhor.

Gal. 6. 12.

Evangelist *discovers the deceit of Mr. Worldly Wiseman.*

1. His turning thee out of the Way.

2. His labouring to render the Cross odious to thee.

3. And his setting thy feet in that way that leadeth unto the administration of Death.

First, Thou must abhor his turning thee out of the Way; yea, and thine own Consenting thereto; because this is to reject the counsel of God for the sake of the counsel of a *Worldly Wiseman*. The Lord says, *Strive to enter in at the Strait²⁸ Gate*, the gate to which I sent thee; *for strait is the Gate that leadeth unto Life, and few there be that find it.* From this little *Wicket Gate*, and from the Way thereto, hath this wicked man turned thee, to the bringing of thee almost to destruction: hate, therefore, his turning thee out of the Way, and abhor thyself for hearkening to him.

Luke 13. 24.
Mat. 7. 13, 14.

Secondly, Thou must abhor his labouring to render the Cross odious unto thee; for thou art to *prefer it before the treasures in Egypt:* Besides, the King of Glory hath told thee, *That he that will save his life shall lose it:* And, *he that comes after him, and hates not his Father, and Mother, and Wife, and Children, and Brethren, and Sisters, yea and his own Life also, he cannot be my Disciple.* I say therefore, for a man to labour to persuade thee that That shall be thy Death, without which, the Truth hath said, thou canst not have Eternal Life: This doctrine thou must abhor.

Heb. 11. 25, 26.

Mark 8. 35.
John 12. 25.
Mat. 10. 39.
Luke 14. 26.

---

rightly is he so called The various interpretative guides usually emphasize the correspondence between characters' names and their essences; **the Cross** Both "salvation by means of the cross" and "persecution in this world"; **carnal temper** Fleshly character.

Thirdly, Thou must hate his setting of thy feet in the way that leadeth to the ministration of Death. And for this thou must consider to whom he sent thee, and also how unable that Person was to deliver thee from thy Burden.

He to whom thou wast sent for Ease, being by name *Legality*, is the son of the Bondwoman° which now is, and is in bondage with her children, and is in a mystery° this Mount *Sinai*, which thou hast feared will fall on thy head. Now if she with her children are in Bondage, how canst thou expect by them to be made free? This *Legality*, therefore, is not able to set thee free from thy Burden. No man was as yet ever rid of his Burden by him; no, nor ever is like to be: Ye cannot be justified by the Works of the Law; for by the deeds of the law no man living can be rid of his burden: Therefore Mr. *Worldly Wiseman* is an alien,° and Mr. *Legality* a cheat: And for his son *Civility*, notwithstanding his simpering looks, he is but a hypocrite,° and cannot help thee. Believe me, there is nothing in all this noise that thou hast heard of this sottish° man, but a design to beguile thee of thy Salvation, by turning thee from the Way in which I had set thee. After this, *Evangelist* called aloud to the Heavens for confirmation of what he had said; and with that there came Words and Fire° out of the Mountain under which poor *Christian* stood, that made the hair of his flesh stand up: The words were thus pronounced, *As many as are of the Works of the Law, are under the Curse; for it is written, Cursed is every one that continueth not in all things which are written in the Book of the Law, to do them.*°

Now *Christian* looked for° nothing but Death, and began to cry out lamentably; even cursing the time in which he met

Margin notes:
Gal. 4. 21, 22, 23, 24, 25, 26, 27.
The Bondwoman.

Gal. 3. 10.

---

the Bondwoman Hagar, wife of Abraham and mother of Ishmael. In Galatians 4, Paul uses her to represent the condition of mankind under the law; **mystery** Allegory; **an alien** That is, an alien to Christian; Wiseman is of course very much at home in the world, to which Christian is an alien; **hypocrite** Greek for "actor"; used in the New Testament to denote those who formally observe religion but lack inner faith; **sottish** Foolish; **Words and Fire** Bunyan describes biblical texts as physical forces; **As many . . . to do them** It is impossible for fallen man to obey the law, therefore salvation by works is impossible; **looked for** Expected.

with Mr. *Worldly Wiseman;* still calling himself a thousand
fools for hearkening to his counsel: He also was greatly
ashamed to think that this gentleman's arguments, flowing
only from the Flesh, should have that prevalency with him
as to cause him to forsake the right Way. This done, he
applied himself again to *Evangelist* in words and sense as
follows:

Chr. Sir, what think you? Is there Hopes? may I now go
back, and go up to the *Wicket Gate?* Shall I not be abandoned
for this, and sent back from thence ashamed? I am sorry I
have hearkened to this man's counsel; but may my Sin be forgiven?

Evan. Then said *Evangelist* to him, Thy Sin is very great, for
by it thou hast committed two evils; thou hast forsaken the
Way that is good, to tread in forbidden paths; yet will the man
at the Gate receive thee, for he has *good will°* for men; only,
said he, take heed that thou turn not aside again, lest thou
perish from the Way, when his wrath is kindled but a little.
Then did *Christian* address himself to go back; and *Evangelist*, after he had kissed him, gave him one smile, and bid him
God speed; So he went on with haste, neither spake he to any
man by the way; nor if any asked him, would he vouchsafe
them an answer. He went like one that was all the while treading on forbidden ground, and could by no means think himself safe, till again he was got into the Way which he left to
follow Mr. *Worldly Wiseman's* counsel: So in process of time
Christian got up to the Gate. Now over the Gate there was
written, *Knock, and it shall be opened unto you.* He knocked
therefore more than once or twice, saying,

> *May I now enter here? Will he within*
> *Open to sorry Me, though I have bin*
> *An undeserving Rebel? Then shall I*
> *Not fail to sing his lasting Praise on high.*

At last there came a grave person to the Gate, named *Good-
will*, who asked, Who was there? and whence he came, and
what he would have?

Christian
*enquires if he
may yet be
happy.*

Evangelist
comforts him.

Psalm 2. *last
Verse.*

Mat. 7. 8.

Chr. Here is a poor burdened Sinner. I come from the City of *Destruction*,° but am going to Mount *Zion*,° that I may be delivered from the Wrath to come; I would therefore, Sir, since I am informed that by this Gate is the Way thither, know if you are willing to let me in?

The Gate will be opened to broken-hearted sinners.

Goodwill. I am willing with all my heart, said he; and with that he opened the Gate.

Satan envies those that enter the Strait Gate.

So when *Christian* was stepping in, the other gave him a pull: Then said *Christian*, what means that? The other told him, A little distance from this Gate, there is erected a strong castle, of which *Beelzebub*° is the captain; from thence both he, and them that are with him, shoot arrows at those that come up to this Gate, if haply they may die before they can enter in.

Christian *entered the Gate with joy and trembling. Talk between* Goodwill *and* Christian.

Then said *Christian*, I rejoice and tremble. So when he was got in, the man of the Gate asked him who directed him thither.

Chr. Evangelist bid me come hither and knock, (as I did) and he said, that you, Sir, would tell me what I must do.

Goodw. An open Door is set before thee, and no man can shut it.

Chr. Now I begin to reap the Benefits of my hazards.

Goodw. But how is it that you came alone?

Chr. Because none of my neighbours saw their danger, as I saw mine.

Goodw. Did any of them know of your coming?

Chr. Yes, my Wife and Children saw me at the first, and called after me to turn again: Also some of my neighbours stood crying and calling after me to return; but I put my fingers in my ears, and so came on my way.

Goodw. But did none of them follow you to persuade you to go back?

Chr. Yes, both *Obstinate* and *Pliable*: But when they saw that they could not prevail, *Obstinate* went railing° back; but *Pliable* came with me a little way.

City of Destruction The material world; **Mount Zion** In Jerusalem; a biblical trope for the kingdom of heaven; **Beelzebub** Hebrew for "Lord of the Flies"; he is identified with Satan in the marginal note. Other writers, like Milton in *Paradise Lost*, differentiate between Beelzebub and Satan; **railing** Raging.

HE THAT WILL ENTER IN MUST FIRST WITHOUT
STAND KNOCKING AT THE GATE, NOR NEED HE DOUBT,
THAT IS A KNOCKER, BUT TO ENTER IN,
FOR GOD CAN LOVE HIM, AND FORGIVE HIS SIN.

Goodw. But why did he not come through?

Chr. We indeed came both together, until we came at the Slough of *Despond*, into the which we also suddenly fell, and then was my neighbour *Pliable* discouraged, and would not adventure further. Wherefore, getting out again on that side next to his own house, he told me, I should possess the brave country alone for him: So he went *his* way, and I came *mine*. He after *Obstinate*, and I to this Gate.

Goodw. Then said *Goodwill*, Alas, poor man, is the Cœlestial Glory of so small esteem with him, that he counteth it not worth running the hazard of a few difficulties to obtain it?

Chr. Truly, said *Christian*, I have said the truth of *Pliable*, and if I should also say all the truth of myself, it will appear there is no betterment 'twixt him and myself.° 'Tis true, he went back to his own house, but I also turned aside to go in the way of Death, being persuaded thereto by the carnal arguments of one Mr. *Worldly Wiseman*.

Goodw. Oh! did he light upon you? What, he would have had you have sought for ease at the hands of Mr. *Legality;* they are both of them a very cheat; but did you take his counsel?

Chr. Yes, as far as I durst; I went to find out Mr. *Legality*, until I thought that the Mountain that stands by his house would have fallen upon my head; wherefore there I was forced to stop.

Goodw. That mountain has been the death of many, and will be the death of many more: 'Tis well you escaped being by it dashed in pieces.

Chr. Why truly I do not know what had become of me there, had not *Evangelist* happily met me again as I was musing in the midst of my *dumps:*° But it was God's Mercy, that he came to me again, for else I had never come hither. But now I am come, such a one as I am, more fit indeed for death by that mountain, than thus to stand talking with my Lord:

A man may have company when he sets out for Heaven, and yet go thither alone.

Christian accuseth himself before the Man at the Gate.

---

no betterment 'twixt him and myself Self-condemnation was an essential prerequisite of conversion; **dumps** Depression.

But O! what a Favour is this to me, that yet I am admitted entrance here?

Goodw. We make no objections against any, notwithstanding all that they have done before they come hither. They in no wise are cast out; and therefore, good *Christian*, come a little way with me, and I will teach thee about the way thou must go. Look before thee; dost thou see this narrow way? THAT is the way thou must go. It was cast up by the Patriarchs, Prophets, Christ and his Apostles, and it is as strait as a *Rule* can make it: This is the Way thou must go.

Christian comforted again.

John 6. 37.

Christian directed yet on his Way.

Chr. But, said *Christian*, are there no turnings nor windings, by which a Stranger may lose his way?

Christian afraid of losing his Way.

Goodw. Yes, there are many ways *butt*° down upon this; and they are crooked and wide: But *thus* thou mayst distinguish the right from the wrong, the Right only being strait and narrow.

Mat. 7. 14.

Then I saw in my dream, That *Christian* asked him further, If he could not help him off with his Burden that was upon his back? For as yet he had not got rid thereof, nor could he by any means get it off without help.

Christian weary of his Burden.

He told him, As to thy Burden, be content to bear it, until thou comest to the place of *Deliverance;* for there it will fall from thy back of itself.

There is no deliverance from the guilt and burden of Sin, but by the death and blood of Christ.

Then *Christian* began to gird up his loins, and to address himself to his Journey. So the other told him, That by that he was gone some distance from the Gate, he would come at the house of the *Interpreter,*[29] at whose door he should knock, and he would shew him excellent things. Then *Christian* took his leave of his Friend, and he again bid him God speed.

Then he went on till he came at the house of the *Interpreter,* where he *knocked* over and over; at last one came to the door, and asked, Who was there?

Christian comes to the House of the Interpreter.

Chr. Sir, here is a Traveller, who was bid by an acquaintance of the Good Man of this house, to call here for my profit; I would therefore speak with the Master of the house:

---

butt That abut.

So he called for the Master of the house; who after a little time came to *Christian*, and asked him what he would have?

Chr. Sir, said *Christian*, I am a man that am come from the City of *Destruction*, and am going to the Mount *Zion;* and I was told by the Man that stands at the Gate, at the head of this way, that if I called here, you would shew me excellent things, such as would be a help to me in my Journey.

He is entertain'd.

Illumination.

Inter. Then said the *Interpreter*, Come in; I will shew thee that which will be profitable to thee. So he commanded his man to light the Candle, and bid *Christian* follow him: So he had him into a private room, and bid his man open a door;

Christian sees a brave picture.
The fashion of the picture.

the which when he had done, *Christian* saw the picture of a very grave Person° hang up against the wall; and this was the fashion of it, It had eyes lifted up to Heaven, the best of Books° in his hand, the Law of Truth was written upon his lips, the World was behind his back; it° stood as if it pleaded with men, and a Crown of Gold did hang over its head.

Chr. Then said *Christian*, What means this?

1 Cor. 4. 15.

Gal. 4. 19.

Inter. The man whose picture this is, is one of a thousand; he can beget children,° travel in birth with children,° and nurse them himself when they are born. And whereas thou seest him with eyes lift up to Heaven, the best of Books in his hand, and the Law of Truth writ on his lips; it is to shew thee, that his work is to know and unfold dark things to Sinners;

The meaning of the picture.

even as also thou seest him stand as if he pleaded with men; and whereas thou seest the World as cast behind him, and that a Crown hangs over his head; that is to shew thee, that slighting and despising the things that are present,° for the love that he hath to his Master's service, he is sure in the

---

a very grave Person Possibly a generic minister of the gospel, but also perhaps Saint Paul, in particular; **the best of Books** That is, the Bible; **the things that are present** The world of external experience, the appearance of things as they are presented to us; **it** Bunyan refers to the picture, not to the man depicted therein; thus he directs our attention to the medium of signification; **he can beget children** In 1 Corinthians 4:15, Paul writes: "In Christ Jesus I have begotten you through the gospel" (King James Version; henceforth KJV); **travel in birth with children** In Galatians 4:19, Paul refers to "my little children, of whom I travail in birth again until Christ be formed in you" (KJV).

World that comes next, to have Glory for his reward. Now, said the *Interpreter*, I have shewed thee this picture first, because the man whose picture this is, is the only man whom the Lord of the place whither thou art going, hath authorized to be thy Guide in all difficult places thou may'st meet with in the Way: Wherefore take good heed to what I have shewed thee, and bear well in thy mind what thou hast seen; lest in thy Journey thou meet with some that pretend to lead thee right, but their way goes down to death.

Why he shewed him the picture first.

Then he took him by the hand, and led him into a very large parlour that was full of dust, because never swept; the which after he had reviewed a little while, the *Interpreter* called for a man to sweep. Now when he began to sweep, the dust began so abundantly to fly about, that *Christian* had almost therewith been choaked. Then said the *Interpreter* to a *Damsel* that stood by, bring hither Water,° and sprinkle the room; the which when she had done, it was swept and cleansed with pleasure.

Chr. Then said *Christian*, What means this?

Inter. The *Interpreter* answered, This *parlour* is the heart of a man that was never sanctified by the sweet Grace of the Gospel: The *dust* is his Original Sin, and inward Corruptions that have defiled the whole man. He that began to sweep at first, is the *Law;* but she that brought Water, and did sprinkle it, is the *Gospel*. Now, whereas thou sawest that so soon as the first began to sweep, the dust did so fly about, that the room by him could not be cleansed, but that thou wast almost choaked therewith; this is to shew thee, that the Law, instead of cleansing the heart (by its working) from Sin, doth revive, put strength into, and increase it in the soul, even as it doth discover° and forbid it, for it doth not give Power to subdue.°

Rom. 7. 6.
1 Cor. 15. 56.
Rom. 5. 20.

Again, as thou sawest the *Damsel* sprinkle the room with Water, upon which it was cleansed with pleasure; this is to shew thee, that when the Gospel comes in, the sweet and pre-

---

Water Of baptism. However, Bunyan did not require water baptism for the members of his congregation; **discover** Reveal; **it doth not give Power to subdue** A concise statement of Bunyan's Lutheran theology.

cious influences thereof to the heart, then, I say, even as thou sawest the *Damsel* lay the dust by sprinkling the floor with Water, so is Sin vanquished and subdued, and the soul made clean, through the Faith of it, and consequently fit for the King of Glory to inhabit.

John 15. 3.
Ephes. 5. 26.
Acts 15. 9.
Rom. 16. 25,
26.
1 John 5. 13.

I saw, moreover, in my dream, That the *Interpreter* took him by the hand, and had him into a little room, where sat two little children, each one in his chair. The name of the eldest was *Passion*, of the other *Patience*.[30] *Passion* seemed to be much discontent, but *Patience* was very quiet. Then *Christian* asked, What is the reason of the discontent of *Passion?* The *Interpreter* answered, the Governor of them would have him stay for his best things, 'till the beginning of the next year; but he will have all now: But *Patience* is willing to wait.

He shewed him Passion *and* Patience. Passion *will have it now.*

Patience *is for waiting.*

Passion *hath his desire.*

Then I saw that one came to *Passion*, and brought him a bag of Treasure,° and poured it down at his feet; the which he took up and rejoiced therein, and withall laughed *Patience* to scorn: But I beheld but a while, and he had lavished all away, and had nothing left him but rags.

And quickly lavishes all away.
The matter expounded.

Chr. Then said *Christian* to the *Interpreter*, Expound this matter more fully to me.

Inter. So he said, These two lads are Figures;° *Passion* of the men of *this* World, and *Patience* of the men of That which is to come: For as here thou seest, *Passion* will have all now, this year; that is to say, in this world; so are the men of this world: They must have all their good things now, they cannot stay till next year, that is, until the next World, for their portion of good. That proverb, *A Bird in the Hand is worth two in the Bush*, is of more authority with them, than are all the Divine testimonies of the Good of the World to come. But as thou sawest, that he had quickly lavished all away, and had presently left him nothing but rags; so will it be with all such men at the End of this world.

The Worldly man for a bird in the hand.

Chr. Then said *Christian*, Now I see that *Patience* has the best Wisdom, and that upon many accounts. 1. Because he

---

Treasure The things of this world represented in financial form; **Figures** Emblems.

stays° for the *best* things. 2. And also because he will have the
Glory of his, when the other has nothing but rags.

Patience *had the best Wisdom.*

Inter. Nay, you may add another, to wit,° the Glory of the
next World will never wear out; but these are suddenly gone.
Therefore *Passion* had not so much reason to laugh at *Patience*, because he had his good things first, as *Patience* will
have to laugh at *Passion*, because he had his best things last;
for *first* must give place to *last*,° because *last* must have its
time to come; but last gives place to nothing; for there is not
another to succeed: He therefore that hath his portion *first*,
must needs have a Time to spend it; but he that has his portion *last*, must have it lastingly: Therefore it is said of Dives,°
In thy Lifetime thou receivedst thy good things, and likewise
Lazarus° *evil things; but now he is comforted, and thou art tormented.*

Things that are First must give place, but things that are Last are lasting.

Luke 16.

Dives *had his good things first.*

Chr. Then I perceive it is not best to covet[31] things that *are*
now, but to wait for things to come.

Inter. You say truth: *For the things that are seen are* Temporal; *but the things that are not seen are* Eternal:° But though
this be so, yet since things present, and our fleshly appetite
are such near neighbours one to another; and again, because
things to come, and carnal Sense, are such Strangers one to
another: Therefore it is, that the first of these so suddenly fall
into *Amity*,° and that *Distance* is so continued between the
second.

2 Cor. 4. 18. *The first things are but Temporal.*

Then I saw in my dream, that the *Interpreter* took *Christian* by the hand, and led him into a place where was a Fire
burning against a wall, and one standing by it, always casting
much water upon it, to quench it; yet did the Fire burn higher
and hotter.

Then said *Christian*, What means this?

---

stays Waits; to wit That is; first must give place to last Earthly hierarchies
are reversed in heaven; Dives The name associated with the rich man in the
parable of Lazarus in Luke 16; Lazarus In Luke 16:19–31, Lazarus the beggar goes to Abraham's bosom after death, while the rich man goes to Hades.
Bunyan's *A Few Sighs from Hell* (1658) is a commentary on this parable; For
the things . . . Eternal The essential tenet of Platonism; Amity Friendship.

The *Interpreter* answered; This Fire is the Work of Grace°
that is wrought in the heart; he that casts water upon it, to ex-
tinguish and put it out, is the *Devil:* But in that thou seest the
Fire notwithstanding burn higher and hotter, thou shalt also
see the reason of that. So he had him about to the back side
of the wall, where he saw a Man with a Vessel of Oil in his
hand, of which he did also continually cast (but secretly) into
the Fire.

Then said *Christian*, What means this?

The *Interpreter* answered, This is *Christ*, who continually
with the Oil of his Grace maintains the work already begun
in the heart: By the means of which, notwithstanding what
the Devil can do, the souls of his people prove gracious still.
And in that thou sawest, that the Man stood behind the wall
to maintain the Fire; this is to teach thee, That it is hard for
the Tempted to see how this Work of Grace is maintained in
the soul.

I saw also, that the *Interpreter* took him again by the hand,
and led him into a pleasant place, where was builded a stately
Palace, beautiful to behold; at the sight of which, *Christian*
was greatly delighted; he saw also upon the top thereof certain persons walking, who were cloathed all in Gold.

Then said *Christian*, May we go in thither?

Then the *Interpreter* took him and led him up toward the
Door of the Palace; and behold, at the Door stood a great
Company of men, as desirous to go in, but durst not. There
also sat a man at a little distance from the door, at a table side,
with a book, and his inkhorn before him, to take the name of
him that should enter therein: He saw also, that in the door-
way stood many men in armour to keep it, being resolved to
do to the men that would enter, what hurt and mischief they
could. Now was *Christian* somewhat in a maze:° At last, when
every man started back for fear of the armed men, *Christian*
saw a man of a very stout countenance, come up to the man

2 Cor. 12. 9.

---

the Work of Grace This "work" is, of course, performed by Christ, not man;
in a maze The figural and literal senses of the word blur; it is not immediately clear whether the maze is physical or metaphorical.

that sat there to write, saying, *Set down my name, Sir;* the
which when he had done, he saw the man draw his Sword,
and put an Helmet upon his head, and rush toward the Door
upon the armed men, who laid upon him with deadly force:
But the man, not at all discouraged, fell to cutting and hack-
ing most fiercely. So after he had received and given many
wounds to those that attempted to keep him out, he cut his
way through them all, and pressed forward into the Palace; at
which there was a pleasant voice heard from those that were
within, even of those that walked upon the top of the Palace,
saying,

> *Come in, Come in;*
> *Eternal Glory thou shalt win.*

So he went in, and was cloathed with such garments as
they. Then *Christian* smiled, and said, I think verily I know
the meaning of this.°

Now, said *Christian*, let me go hence. Nay, stay (said the *Interpreter*) till I have shewed thee a little more, and after that
thou shalt go on thy way. So he took him by the hand again,
and led him into a very dark room, where there sate° a man
in an Iron Cage.[32]

Now the man, to look on, seemed very sad: he sat with his
eyes looking down to the ground, his hands folded together,
and he sighed as if he would break his heart. Then said *Christian*, What means this? At which the *Interpreter* bid him talk
with the man.

Then said *Christian* to the man, What are thou? The man
answered, I am what I was not once.

Chr. What wast thou once?

Man. The man said, I was once a fair and flourishing Professor,° both in mine own eyes, and also in the eyes of others:

The Valiant Man.

Despair like an Iron Cage.

Luke 8. 13.

I know the meaning of this Christian's interpretive skills are improving: He
has recognized this vision as an allegory of entrance into heaven; **sate** Sat;
Professor Religious man.

I once was, as I thought, fair for the Cœlestial City, and had then even Joy at the thoughts that I should get thither.

Chr. Well, but what art thou now?

Man. I am now a man of *Despair*, and am shut up in it, as in this Iron Cage.[33] I cannot get out; O, *Now* I cannot.

Chr. But how camest thou in this condition?

Man. I left off to watch, and be sober; I laid the reins upon the neck of my lusts;° I sinned against the Light of the Word, and the Goodness of God: I have grieved the Spirit, and he is gone; I tempted the Devil, and he is come to me; I have provoked God to Anger, and he has left me; I have so hardened my heart that I *cannot* repent.

Then said *Christian* to the *Interpreter*, But is there no Hopes for such a man as this? Ask him, said the *Interpreter*.

Chr. Then said *Christian*, Is there no Hope, but you must be kept in the Iron Cage of Despair?

Man. No, none at all.

Chr. Why? The Son of the Blessed is very pitiful.

Heb. 6. 6.
Luke 19. 14.
Heb. 10. 28,
29.

Man. I have crucified him to myself afresh; I have despised his Person, I have despised his Righteousness, I have counted his Blood an unholy thing, I have done despite to° the Spirit of Grace: Therefore I have shut myself out of all the Promises, and there now remains to me nothing but Threatnings, dreadful Threatnings, fearful Threatnings of certain Judgment and fiery Indignation, which shall devour me as an Adversary.

Chr. For what did you bring yourself into this condition?

Man. For the Lusts, Pleasures, and Profits of this World; in the enjoyment of which, I did then promise myself much delight: But now every one of those things also bite me, and gnaw me, like a burning Worm.[34]

Chr. But canst thou not now repent and turn?

Man. God hath denied me Repentance. His Word gives me no encouragement to believe; yea, himself hath shut me up° in this Iron Cage: Nor can all the men in the world let me out.

I laid . . . lusts As if to make them gallop, like a horse; done despite to Despised; himself hath shut me up This is blasphemy, closely linked to despair in Bunyan's mind.

O Eternity! Eternity! How shall I grapple with the Misery that I must meet with in Eternity!

Inter. Then said the *Interpreter* to *Christian*, Let this man's Misery be remembered by thee, and be an everlasting Caution to thee.

Chr. Well, said *Christian*, this is Fearful; God help me to watch and be sober, and to pray that I may shun the Cause of this man's misery. Sir, is it not time for me to go on my way now?

Inter. Tarry° till I shall show thee one thing more, and thou shalt go on thy way.

So he took *Christian* by the hand again, and led him into a chamber, where there was one rising out of bed; and as he put on his raiment,° he shook and trembled. Then said *Christian*, Why doth this man thus tremble? The *Interpreter* then bid him tell to *Christian* the reason of his so doing: So he began and said, This night as I was in my sleep, I dreamed,° and behold the Heavens grew exceeding black; Also it thundred and lightned in most fearful wise, that it put me into an agony. So I looked up in my dream, and saw the clouds rack° at an unusual rate; upon which I heard a great sound of a Trumpet, and saw also a Man sit upon a Cloud, attended with the Thousands of Heaven: They were all in flaming fire, also the Heavens were in a burning flame, I heard then a Voice, saying, Arise ye Dead, and come to Judgment;° and with that the Rocks rent, the Graves opened, and the Dead, that were therein, came forth; some of them were exceeding glad, and looked upward; and some sought to hide themselves under the mountains:[35] Then I saw the Man that sat upon the Cloud, open the Book, and bid the World draw near. Yet there was, by reason of a fierce Flame which issued out and came before him a convenient° distance betwixt him and them, as

1 Cor. 15. 52.
1 Thess. 4.
Jude 15.
John 5. 28.
2 Thess. 1. 8.
Rev. 20. 11, 12, 13, 14.
Isa. 26. 21.
Mich. 7. 16, 17.
Psalm 5. 1, 2, 3.
Dan. 10. 7.

Tarry Wait; **raiment** Clothes; **I dreamed** We are now to be shown a dream within a vision within a dream; **rack** Drive along; **Judgment** The following lines paraphrase various biblical accounts of the Day of Judgment; **convenient** Appropriate;

Mal. 3. 2, 3.
Dan. 7. 9, 10.

Mat. 3. 12.
Chap. 13. 30.
Mal. 4. 1.

Luke 3. 17.

1 Thess. 4. 16,
17.

Rom. 2. 14, 15.

betwixt the Judge and the Prisoners at the bar. I heard it also proclaimed to them that attended on the Man that sat on the Cloud, *Gather together the Tares, the Chaff and Stubble,*° and *cast them into the burning Lake;* and with that the bottomless Pit opened, just whereabout I stood; out of the mouth of which there came, in an abundant manner, smoak, and coals of fire, with hideous noises. It was also said to the same Persons, *Gather my Wheat into the Garner.*° And with that I saw many catch'd up and carried away into the clouds, but I was left behind. I also sought to hide myself, but I could not, for the Man that sat upon the Cloud still kept his Eye upon me: My Sins also came into my mind; and my Conscience did accuse me on every side. Upon this I awakened from my sleep.

Chr. But what was it that made you so afraid of this sight?

Man. Why, I thought that the Day of Judgment was come, and that I was not ready for it: But this frighted me most, that the Angels gathered up several, and left me behind; also the Pit of Hell opened her mouth just where I stood. My Conscience too afflicted me; and, as I thought, the Judge had always his Eye upon me, shewing Indignation in his countenance.

Then said the *Interpreter* to *Christian,* Hast thou considered all these things?

Chr. Yes, and they put me in *Hope* and *Fear.*°

Int. Well, keep all things so in thy mind, that they may be as a *goad* in thy sides, to prick thee forward in the Way thou must go. Then *Christian* began to gird up his loins,[36] and to address himself to his Journey. Then said the *Interpreter,* The *Comforter* be always with thee, good *Christian;* to guide thee in the Way that leads to the City. So *Christian* went on his Way, saying,

> *Here I have seen Things rare and profitable,*
> *Things pleasant, dreadful, Things to make me stable*

---

the Tares, the Chaff and Stubble The reprobate; Garner Granary; Hope and Fear The two states are not contradictory, since both involve anticipation of the world to come, not contentment in the present world.

In what I have begun to take in hand;
Then let me think on them, and understand
Wherefore they shewed me were, and let me be
Thankful, O good Interpreter, *to thee.*

Now I saw in my dream, That the highway up which *Chris-*
tian was to go, was fenced on either side with a wall, and that
wall was called *Salvation.* Up this way therefore did burdened   Isa. 26. 1.
Christian run, but not without great difficulty, because of the
Load on his back.

He ran thus till he came at a place somewhat ascending,
and upon that place stood a *Cross,* and a little below, in the
bottom, a Sepulchre. So I saw in my dream, That just as
Christian came up with the *Cross,* his Burden loosed from off
his shoulders, and fell from off his back, and began to tumble, and so continued to do, till it came to the mouth of the
Sepulchre, where it fell in, and I saw it no more.°

Then was *Christian* glad and lightsome, and said with a   *When God*
merry heart, *He hath given me Rest by his Sorrow, and Life by*   *releases us of*
his Death. Then he stood still a while to look and wonder; for   *our Guilt and*
Burden, we
it was very surprizing to him, that the sight of the Cross   *are as those*
should thus ease him of his Burden. He looked therefore,   *that leap for*
and looked again, even till the springs that were in his head   *Joy.*
sent the waters down his cheeks. Now, as he stood looking   Zech. 12. 10.
and weeping, behold three Shining Ones° came to him and   Mar. 2. 5.
saluted him, with *Peace be to thee;* so the first said to him,
Thy Sins be forgiven; the second stript him of his rags, and
cloathed him with Change of Raiment; the third also set a   Zech. 3. 4.
Mark on his forehead, and gave him a Roll,[37] with a Seal   Eph. 1. 13.
upon it, which he bid him look on as he ran, and that he
should give it in at the Cœlestial Gate; so they went their
way. Then *Christian* gave three leaps for Joy, and went on
singing:

I saw it no more Christian is fully relieved from the guilt of sin by the cross
near the beginning of his journey; **three Shining Ones** According to Sharrock, "Since the first, not the second, says 'Thy sins are forgiven,' three angels rather than the Trinity" (Sharrock, ed., *The Pilgrim's Progress,* p. 390).

A Christian can sing, tho' alone, when God doth give him the Joy of his Heart.

Thus far did I come laden with my Sin;
Nor could ought ease the grief that I was in,
Till I came hither: What a place is this!
Must here be the beginning of my bliss?
Must here the Burden fall from off my back?
Must here the strings that bound it to me crack?
Blest Cross! blest Sepulchre! blest rather be
The Man *that there was put to Shame for me!*

I saw then in my dream, that he went on thus, even until he came at the bottom, where he saw, a little out of the way, three men fast asleep, with Fetters upon their heels. The name of the one was *Simple*, another *Sloth*, and the third *Presumption*.

Simple, Sloth and Presumption.

Christian then seeing them lie in this case, went to them, if peradventure° he might awake them; and cried, You are like them that sleep on the top of a mast, for the Dead Sea° is under you, a Gulph° that hath no bottom: Awake, therefore, and come away; be willing also, and I will help you off with your Irons. He also told them, If he that goeth about like *a roaring Lion*,° comes by, you will certainly become a Prey to his teeth. With that they looked upon him, and began to reply in this sort: *Simple* said, *I see no Danger:* *Sloth* said, *Yet a little more Sleep:* And *Presumption* said, *Every Tub must stand upon his own bottom.*° And so they lay down to sleep again, and *Christian* went on his Way.

Prov. 23. 34.

1 Pet. 5. 8.

There is no Persuasion will do if GOD *openeth not the eyes.*

Yet was he troubled to think, that men in that danger should so little esteem the kindness of him that so freely offered to help them, both by the awakening of them, counselling of them, and proffering to help them off with their Irons. And as he was troubled thereabout, he espied two men come tumbling over the wall, on the Left Hand° of the narrow Way; and they made up apace to him. The name of the one was *Formalist*, and the name of the other *Hypocrisy*.[38] So, as I said, they drew up unto him, who thus entered with them into discourse.

---

peradventure By chance; the Dead Sea The sea of death; Gulph Abyss; he that goeth about like a roaring Lion Satan; Every Tub . . . bottom Every man must rely upon himself; the Left Hand The sinister side.

Chr. Gentlemen, Whence came you, and whither do you go?

Christian talked with them.

Formalist and *Hypocrisy*. We were born in the land of *Vain-Glory*,° and are going for Praise° to Mount *Sion*.

Chr. Why came you not in at the Gate which standeth at the beginning of the Way? Know you not that it is written, That *he that cometh not in by the Door, but climbeth up some other way, the same is a Thief and a Robber?*

John 10. 1.

Form. and *Hyp.* They said, That to go to the Gate for entrance, was by all their countrymen counted too far about; and that therefore their usual way was to make a short cut of it, and to climb over the wall, as they had done.

They that come into the Way, but not by the Door, think that they can say something in Vindication of their own Practice.

Chr. But will it not be counted a trespass against the Lord of the City, whither we are bound, thus to violate his revealed Will?

Form. and *Hyp.* They told him, That as for that, he needed not to trouble his head thereabout; for what they did, they had *Custom* for, and could produce, if need were, Testimony that would witness it, for more than a thousand years.[39]

Chr. But, said *Christian*, will your Practice stand a Trial at Law?

Form. and *Hyp.* They told him that *Custom*, it being of so long standing as above a thousand years, would doubtless now be admitted as a thing legal° by an impartial Judge: And besides, said they, if we get into the Way, what's matter which way we get in? If we are in, we are in: Thou art but in the Way, who, as we perceive, came in at the Gate; and we are also in the Way,[40] that came tumbling over the wall: Wherein now is thy condition better than ours?

Chr. I walk by the Rule of my Master, you walk by the rude working of your fancies.[41] You are counted Thieves already by the Lord of the Way, therefore I doubt you will not be found true men at the End of the Way. You come in by yourselves without his Direction; and shall go out by yourselves, without his Mercy.

Vain-Glory Futile worldly pride; **for Praise** Ambiguous; both "in order to give praise" and "in order to win praise"; **a thing legal** Formalist and Hypocrisy assume they can be justified by the law.

Who's this? The *Pilgrim*. How! 'Tis very true.
Old things are pass'd away; all's become New.
Strange! He's another Man, upon my word;
They be fine Feathers, that make a fine Bird.

To this they made him but little answer; only they bid him look to himself. Then I saw that they went on every man in his way, without much Conference one with another; save that these two men told *Christian*, That as to *Laws* and *Ordinances*, they doubted not but they should as conscientiously do them as he.° Therefore, said they, we see not wherein thou differest from us, but by the *Coat*° that is on thy back, which was, as we trow,° given thee by some of thy neighbours to hide the shame of thy nakedness.

Chr. By Laws and Ordinances you will not be saved, since you came not in by the Door. And as for this *Coat* that is on my back, it was given me by the Lord of the Place whither I go; and that, as you say, to cover my nakedness with. And I take it as a token of his kindness to me; for I had nothing but Rags before; and besides, thus I comfort myself as I go: Surely, think I, when I come to the Gate of the City, the Lord thereof will know me for good, since I have his *Coat* on my back! a *Coat* that he gave me freely in the day that he stript me of my Rags. I have moreover a Mark in my forehead, of which perhaps you have taken no notice, which one of my Lord's most intimate Associates fixed there in the day that my Burden fell off my shoulders. I will tell you, moreover, that I had then given me a Roll sealed, to comfort me by reading, as I go on the Way; I was also bid to give it in at the Cœlestial Gate, in token of my certain going in after it; all which things I doubt you want,° and want them, because you came not in at the Gate.

To these things they gave him no answer, only they looked upon each other, and *laughed*. Then I saw that they went on all, save that *Christian* kept before, who had no more talk but with himself, and that sometimes sighingly, and sometimes comfortably: Also he would be often reading in the Roll, that one of the Shining Ones gave him, by which he was refreshed.

Gal. 2. 16.

Christian has got his Lord's Coat on his back, and is comforted therewith: He is comforted also with his Mark and his Roll.

Christian has talk with himself.

---

as to Laws . . . do them as he This is true, but irrelevant to their salvation; **Coat** The freely granted, or "imputed," righteousness that has replaced the "rags" of Christian's own sinful works; **trow** Believe; **I doubt you want** Both "I think you lack" and "I doubt you desire."

He comes to
the hill
Difficulty.

Isa. 49. 10.

The danger of
turning out of
the Way.

A Word of
Grace.

I beheld then, that they all went on till they came to the foot of the hill *Difficulty*, at the bottom of which was a Spring. There were also in the same place two other ways besides that which came strait from the Gate; one turned to the left hand, and the other to the right, at the bottom of the hill: but the narrow Way lay right up the hill, and the name of the going up the side of the hill is called *Difficulty*.° *Christian* now went to the Spring, and drank thereof to refresh himself, and then began to go up the Hill, saying:

> This Hill, though high, I covet to ascend,
> The Difficulty will not me offend.
> For I perceive the Way to Life lies here:
> Come pluck up Heart, let's neither faint nor fear;
> Better, though difficult, the Right Way to go,
> Than Wrong, though easy, where the End is Wo.

The other two also came to the foot of the hill; but when they saw that the hill was steep and high; and that there were two other ways to go; and supposing also that these two ways might meet again with that up which *Christian* went, on the other side of the hill: Therefore they were resolved to go in those ways. Now the name of one of those ways was *Danger*, and the name of the other *Destruction*. So the one took the way which is called *Danger*, which led him into a great Wood, and the other took directly up the way to *Destruction*, which led him into a wide field, full of dark Mountains, where he stumbled and fell, and rose no more.

I looked then after *Christian*, to see him go up the hill, where I perceived he fell from running to going,° and from going to clambering upon his hands and his knees, because of the steepness of the place. Now about the midway to the top of the hill, was a pleasant *Arbour*, made by the Lord of the Hill, for the refreshment of weary Travellers; thither therefore *Christian* got, where also he sat down to rest him: Then he

---

and the name . . . Difficulty Note that it is no longer the hill itself that is named "Difficulty," but the act of climbing it; going Walking.

pulled his Roll out of his bosom, and read therein to his Comfort; he also now began afresh to take a review of the Coat or Garment that was given him as he stood by the Cross. Thus pleasing himself a while, he at last fell into a Slumber, and thence into a fast Sleep,° which detained him in that place until it was almost night: and in his Sleep his Roll fell out of his hand. Now as he was sleeping, there came one to him,° and awaked him, saying, *Go to the ant, thou Sluggard; consider her ways, and be wise:* And with that *Christian* suddenly started up, and sped him on his Way, and went apace till he came to the top of the hill.

He that sleeps is a Loser.
Prov. 6. 6.

Now when he was got to the top of the hill, there came two men running against him amain; the name of the one was *Timorous*, and of the other *Mistrust*: To whom *Christian* said, Sirs, What's the matter you run the wrong way? *Timorous* answered, That they were going to the City of *Zion*,° and had got up that difficult place: But, said he, the farther we go, the more Danger we meet with; wherefore we turned, and are going back again.

Christian *meets with* Mistrust *and* Timorous.

Yes, said *Mistrust*, for just before us lies a couple of Lions[42] in the Way; (whether sleeping or waking we know not)° and we could not think, if we came within reach, but they would presently pull us in pieces.

Chr. Then said *Christian*, You make me afraid: But whither shall I fly to be safe? If I go back to mine own country, that is prepared for Fire and Brimstone, and I shall certainly perish there: If I can get to the Cœlestial City, I am sure to be in safety there: I must venture; to go back, is nothing but death; to go forward, is Fear of death, and Life everlasting beyond it: I will yet go forward. So *Mistrust* and *Timorous* ran down the hill, and *Christian* went on his Way. But thinking again of what he had heard from the men, he

Christian *shakes off* Fear.

---

fast Sleep Representing the complacency that comes from contemplating one's elect status (Christian's "roll"); there came one to him The biblical text seems to become an active entity here; the City of Zion Mount Zion, in Jerusalem, is a biblical type of heaven; whether sleeping or waking we know not State policy toward dissenters varied widely between 1660 and 1688.

Shall they who Wrong *begin* yet Rightly *end*?
Shall they at all have Safety for their friend?
No, no, in head-strong manner they set out,
And head-long will they fall at last no doubt.

felt in his bosom for his Roll, that he might read therein, and
be comforted; but he felt, and found it not. Then was *Christian* in great distress, and knew not what to do; for he wanted
that which used to relieve him; and that which should have
been his Pass into the Cœlestial City. Here therefore he
began to be much perplexed, and knew not what to do; at
last he bethought himself ° that he had slept in the Arbour
that is on the side of the hill; and falling down upon his
knees, he asked God Forgiveness for that his foolish act, and
then went back to look for his Roll. But all the Way he went
back, who can sufficiently set forth the sorrow of *Christian's*
heart? Sometimes he sighed, sometimes he wept, and oftentimes he chid° himself for being so foolish to fall asleep in
that place which was erected only for a little refreshment
from his weariness. Thus therefore he went back, carefully
looking on this side and on that, all the way as he went, if
happily he might find the Roll that had been his comfort so
many times in his Journey. He went thus till he came again
in sight of the Arbour where he sat and slept; but that sight
renewed his sorrow the more, by bringing again even afresh,
his evil of sleeping into his mind. Thus therefore he now
went on bewailing his sinful sleep, saying, O *wretched Man
that I am!* that I should sleep in the Day-time! that I should
sleep in the midst of Difficulty! that I should so indulge the
Flesh, as to use that rest, for ease to my flesh,° which the
LORD of the Hill hath erected only for the relief of the Spirits of Pilgrims! How many steps have I took in vain! (Thus it
happen'd to *Israel*,° for their Sin they were sent back again by
the way of the Red Sea) and I am made to tread those steps
with Sorrow, which I might have trod with Delight, had it
not been for this sinful Sleep. How far might I have been on
my Way by this time! I am made to tread those steps thrice

*Christian
missed his
Roll wherein
he used to
take Comfort.*

*He is
perplexed for
his Roll.*

*Christian
bewails his
foolish
Sleeping.*

Rev. 2.
1 Thess. 5. 7, 8.

---

bethought himself "Remembered," but the phrase suggests a differentiation
between Christian's consciousness and his essence, or self; **chid** Criticized;
Flesh . . . flesh The "flesh" refers to both the body and to a carnal orienta-
tion of the mind; **Israel** The wandering of the Israelites in the desert was a
biblical type for the inner pilgrimage of the individual soul.

over, which I needed not to have trod but once: Yea, now also I am like to be benighted,° for the Day is almost spent: O that I had not slept! Now by this time he was come to the *Arbour* again, where for a while he sat down and wept; but at last (as *Christian* would have it) looking sorrowfully down under the settle,° there he espied his Roll; the which he with trembling and haste catched up and put into his bosom. But who can tell how joyful this man was, when he had gotten his Roll again? For this Roll was the Assurance of his Life, and Acceptance at the desired Haven. Therefore he laid it up in his bosom, gave Thanks to GOD for directing his eye to the place where it lay, and with Joy and Tears betook himself again to his Journey. But, O how nimbly now did he go up the rest of the Hill! Yet, before he got up, the Sun went down upon *Christian;* and this made him again recall the vanity of his sleeping to his remembrance; and thus he again began to condole with himself: O thou sinful Sleep! how for thy sake am I like to be benighted in my Journey: I must walk without the Sun, darkness must cover the path of my feet, and I must hear the noise of doleful creatures, because of my sinful Sleep! Now also he remembered the story that *Mistrust* and *Timorous* told him of, how they were frighted with the sight of the Lions. Then said *Christian* to himself again, These Beasts range in the Night for their prey, and if they should meet with me in the dark, how should I shift them?° How should I escape being by them torn in pieces? Thus he went on his Way; but while he was thus bewailing his unhappy miscarriage, he lift up his eyes, and behold there was a very stately palace before him, the name of which was *Beautiful*,[43] and it stood just by the Highway side.

So I saw in my dream, that he made haste and went forward, that if possible he might get Lodging there. Now before he had gone far, he entered into a very narrow Passage, which was about a furlong off the Porter's lodge, and looking very

Christian
*findeth his
Roll where he
lost it.*

---

benighted Both literally and figuratively; the term refers to external and internal conditions simultaneously; **settle** Bench; **shift them** Both "deal with them" and "get them out of the way."

narrowly before him as he went, he espied two Lions in the way.° Now, thought he, I see the dangers that *Mistrust* and *Timorous* were driven back by. (The Lions were chained, but he saw not the chains.)° Then he was afraid, and thought also himself to go back after them, for he thought nothing but death was before him: But the Porter° at the Lodge, whose name is *Watchful*, perceiving that *Christian* made a Halt, as if he would go back, cried unto him, saying, Is thy Strength so small? Fear not the Lions, for they are chain'd, and are placed there for Trial of Faith, where it is, and for Discovery° of those that have none: Keep in the *midst* of the Path, and no hurt shall come unto thee.

Mark 13. 14.

Then I saw that he went on trembling for fear of the Lions; but taking good heed to the directions of the Porter, he heard them roar, but they did him no harm. Then he clapt his hands, and went on till he came and stood before the Gate where the Porter was. Then said *Christian* to the Porter, Sir, What house is this? and, May I lodge here to-night? The Porter answered, This house was built by the Lord of the Hill, and he built it for the relief and security of Pilgrims. The Porter also asked whence he was, and whither he was going?

Chr. I am come from the City of *Destruction*, and am going to Mount *Zion;* but because the Sun is now set, I desire, if I may, to lodge here to-night.

Porter. What is your Name?

Chr. My name is now *Christian*, but my name at the first was *Graceless:*° I came of the race of *Japheth*, whom God will persuade to dwell in the Tents of *Shem*.°

Gen. 9.27.

Port. But how doth it happen that you come so late? The Sun is set.

---

two Lions in the way The civil and ecclesiastical authorities forbade membership in dissenting churches; **The Lions . . . saw not the chains** Penal laws against dissenters were often not enforced, but the arbitrary nature of their application was small comfort to their victims; **the Porter** The pastor; **Discovery** Exposure; **Graceless** Christian gives himself this name retroactively; after his conversion he understands that he was previously "Graceless," but before it he is referred to simply as a "man"; **Japheth . . . Shem** Sons of Noah. See the Bible, Genesis 9:27: "God shall enlarge Japheth, and he shall dwell in the tents of Shem; and Canaan shall be his servant" (KJV).

DIFFICULTY IS BEHIND, FEAR IS BEFORE,
THOUGH HE'S GOT ON THE HILL, THE LIONS ROAR.
A CHRISTIAN MAN IS NEVER LONG AT EASE:
WHEN ONE FRIGHT'S GONE, ANOTHER DOTH HIM SEIZE.

Chr. I had been here sooner, but that, wretched man that I am, I slept in the *Arbour* that stands on the Hill-side! Nay, I had, notwithstanding that, been here much sooner, but that in my Sleep I lost my Evidence,° and came without it to the brow of the Hill, and then feeling for it, and finding it not, I was forced, with Sorrow of Heart, to go back to the place where I slept my Sleep,° where I found it, and now I am come.

Port. Well, I will call out one of the Virgins of this place, who will, (if she likes your Talk) bring you in to the rest of the Family, according to the rules of the house. So *Watchful* the Porter rang a bell, at the sound of which came out of the door of the house a grave and beautiful damsel, named *Discretion*, and asked why she was called?

The Porter answered, This man is in a Journey from the City of *Destruction* to Mount *Zion*, but being weary and be-nighted, he asked me if he might lodge here to-night: So I told him I would call for thee, who, after Discourse had with him, mayest do as seemeth thee good, even according to the Law of the house.

Then she asked him, whence he was, and whither he was going? And he told her.° She asked him also, how he got into the Way? and he told her. Then she asked him, what he had seen and met with in the Way? and he told her. And at last she asked his Name? So he said, It is *Christian;* and I have so much the more a desire to lodge here to-night, because by what I perceive, this Place was built by the Lord of the Hill, for the relief and security of Pilgrims: So she smiled, but the water stood in her eyes:° And after a little pause, she said, I will call forth two or three more of the Family. So she ran to the door and called out *Prudence, Piety*, and *Charity;*[44] who after a little more discourse with him, had him into the Family; and many of them meeting him at the Threshold of the House, said, Come in, thou blessed of the Lord; this House

---

my Evidence His roll; **I slept my sleep** Note that "sleep" becomes a transitive verb; Christian's sleep is an object to him; **and he told her** New members of the congregation were expected to give personal accounts of their conversion experiences; **the water stood in her eyes** A rare naturalistic touch.

was built by the Lord of the Hill, on purpose to entertain such Pilgrims in. Then he bowed his head, and followed them into the House: So when he was come in, and set down, they gave him something to drink, and consented together that until Supper was ready, some of them should have some particular discourse with *Christian*, for the best Improvement° of Time, and they appointed *Piety*, and *Prudence*, and *Charity*, to discourse with him; and thus they began:

Piety discourses him.

Piety. Come, good *Christian*, since we have been so loving to you, to receive you into our House this night, let us, if perhaps we may better ourselves thereby, talk with you of all things that have happened to you in your Pilgrimage.

Chr. With a very good will, and I am glad that you are so well disposed.

Piety. What moved you at first to betake yourself to a Pilgrim's Life?

How Christian was driven out of his own Country.

Chr. I was driven out of my Native Country by a dreadful sound that was in mine ears; to wit, That unavoidable destruction did attend me, if I abode in that place where I was.

Piety. But how did it happen that you came out of your Country this Way?

How he got into the Way to Zion.

Chr. It was as God would have it; for when I was under the fears of destruction, I did not know whither to go; but by chance there came a Man, even to me, (as I was trembling and weeping,) whose name is *Evangelist*, and he directed me to the Wicket Gate, which else I should never have found, and so set me into the Way that hath led me directly to this House.

Piety. But did you not come by the House of the *Interpreter*?

A Rehearsal of what he saw in the Way.

Chr. Yes, and did see such things there, the remembrance of which will stick by me as long as I live: Especially three things, to wit, How Christ, in despite of *Satan*, maintains his Work of Grace in the heart; how the Man had sinned himself quite out of hopes of God's Mercy; and also the dream of him that thought in his sleep the Day of Judgment was come.

Improvement Improving use.

Piety. Why, Did you hear him tell his dream?

Chr. Yes, and a dreadful one it was, I thought; it made my heart ache as he was telling of it; but yet I am glad I heard it.

Piety. Was that all that you saw at the House of the *Interpreter?*

Chr. No, he took me and had me where he showed me a stately Palace, and how the people were clad in Gold that were in it; and how there came a venturous° man, and cut his Way through the armed men that stood in the Door to keep him out; and how he was bid to come in, and win Eternal Glory: Methought those things did ravish my heart! I could have staid at that good man's house a twelve-month, but that I knew I had further to go.

Piety. And what saw you else in the Way?

Chr. Saw! Why, I went but a little further, and I saw one, as I thought in my mind, hang bleeding upon a Tree; and the very Sight of him made my Burden fall off my back, (for I groaned under a weary Burden) but then it fell down from off me. 'Twas a strange thing to me, for I never saw such a thing before: Yea, and while I stood looking up, (for then I could not forbear looking) Three Shining Ones came to me: One of them testified that my Sins were forgiven me; another stript me of my Rags, and gave me this 'broidered Coat which you see; and the third set the Mark which you see in my forehead, and gave me this sealed Roll; (and with that he plucked it out of his Bosom.)

Piety. But you saw more than this, did you not?

Chr. The things that I have told you, were the best; yet some other small matters I saw, as namely I saw three men, *Simple, Sloth,* and *Presumption,* lie asleep a little out of the Way as I came, with Irons° upon their heels; but do you think I could awake them! I also saw *Formality* and *Hypocrisy* come tumbling over the wall, to go (as they pretended) to *Zion,* but they were quickly lost; even as I myself did tell them, but they would not believe: But, above all, I found it *hard work* to get

---

venturous Daring; **Irons** Fetters.

up this Hill, and as hard to come by the Lions mouths: and truly if it had not been for the good man, the Porter that stands at the Gate, I do not know, but that, after all, I might have gone back again; but now I thank God I am here, and I thank you for receiving of me.

Then *Prudence* thought good to ask him a few questions, and desired his answer to them.

Prudence
discourses
him.

Prudence. Do you not think sometimes of the Country from whence you came?

Christian's
thoughts of
his Native
Country.

Chr. Yea, but with much *Shame* and *Detestation:* Truly, if I had been mindful of that Country from whence I came out, I might have had opportunity to have returned; but now I desire a better Country; this is, a Heavenly.

Heb. 11. 15, 16.

Prud. Do you not yet bear away with you some of the things that then you were conversant withal?

Christian
distasted with
Carnal
Cogitations.

Chr. Yes, but greatly against my will; especially my inward and carnal Cogitations,° with which all my countrymen, as well as myself, were delighted; but now all those things are my Grief; and might I but choose mine own things, I would choose never to think of those things more; but when I would be doing of that which is best, that which is worst is with me.

Christian's
Choice.
Rom. 7.

Prud. Do you not find sometimes, as if those things were vanquished, which at other times are your Perplexity?

Christian's
Golden
Hours.

Chr. Yes, but that is but seldom; but they are to me Golden Hours, in which such things happen to me.°

Prud. Can you remember by what Means you find your annoyances at times, as if they were vanquished?

How
Christian
gets Power
against his
Corruptions.

Chr. Yes, when I think what I saw at the Cross, that will do it; and when I look upon my 'broidered Coat, that will do it; also when I look into the Roll that I carry in my bosom, that will do it; and when my thoughts wax° warm about whither I am going, that will do it.

Prud. And what is it that makes you so desirous to go to Mount *Zion?*

---

inward and carnal Cogitations Although they were "inward," his thoughts were also fleshly; happen to me Christian experiences his thoughts as external things that "happen to" him; wax Become.

Chr. Why, there I hope to see him *alive* that did hang *dead* on the Cross; and there I hope to be rid of all those things, that to this day are in me an Annoyance to me: There they say there is no Death, and there I shall dwell with such Company as I like best. For, to tell you truth, I love him, because I was by him eased of my Burden; and I am weary of my inward Sickness: I would fain° be where I shall die no more, and with the Company that shall continually cry, *Holy, Holy, Holy.*

Why Christian would be at Mount Zion.
Isa. 25. 8.
Rev. 21. 4.

Then said *Charity* to *Christian*, Have you a Family? Are you a married man?

Charity discourses him.

Chr. I have a Wife and four small Children.[45]

Charity. And why did you not bring them along with you?

Chr. Then *Christian* wept[46] and said, Oh! how willingly would I have done it! but they were all of them utterly averse to my going on Pilgrimage.

Christian's Love to his Wife and Children.

Cha. But you should have talked to them, and have endeavoured to have shown them the Danger of being behind.

Chr. So I did; and told them also what God had shewed to me of the destruction of our City; but I seemed to them as one that mocked, and they believed me not.

Cha. And did you pray to God that he would bless your Counsel to them?

Chr. Yes, and that with much Affection;° for you must think that my Wife and poor Children were very dear unto me.

Cha. But did you tell them of your own Sorrow, and Fear of Destruction? For I suppose that destruction was visible enough to you?

Chr. Yes, over, and over, and over. They might also see my Fears in my Countenance, in my Tears, and also in my trembling under the apprehension of the Judgment that did hang over our heads; but all was not sufficient to prevail with them to come with me.

Christian's *Fears of perishing might be read in his very Countenance.*

Cha. But what could they say for themselves why they came not?

I would fain I want to; **Affection** Feeling.

The Cause why his Wife and Children did not go with him.

Chr. Why, my Wife was afraid of losing this World; and my Children were given to the foolish Delights of Youth: So what by one thing and what by another, they left me to wander in this manner alone.

Cha. But did you not with your vain Life damp° all that you by Words used by way of persuasion to bring them away with you?

Chr. Indeed I cannot commend my Life, for I am conscious to myself° of many failings therein: I know also, that a man by his Conversation° may soon overthrow what by Argument or Persuasion he doth labour to fasten upon others for their good. Yet, this I can say, I was very wary of giving them occasion, by any unseemly action, to make them averse to going on Pilgrimage. Yea, for this very thing, they would tell me I was too precise,° and that I denied myself of things (for their sakes) in which they saw no evil. Nay, I think I may say, that, if what they saw in me did hinder them, it was my great Tenderness in° sinning against God, or of doing any Wrong to my Neighbour.

Cha. Indeed *Cain* hated his brother, because his own works were Evil, and his brother's Righteous; and if thy Wife and Children have been offended with thee for this, they thereby shew themselves to be implacable° to good; and thou hast delivered° thy soul from their Blood.

Now I saw in my dream, That thus they sat talking together until Supper was ready. So when they had made ready, they sat down to meat: Now the Table was furnished with fat° Things, and with Wine that was well refined; and all their talk at the Table was about the LORD of the Hill; as, namely, about what HE had done, and wherefore HE did what HE did, and why HE had built that House; and by what they said, I perceived° that HE had been a *great Warrior*, and had fought

Christian's good Conversation before his Wife and Children.

1 John 3. 12. *Christian clear of their Blood if they perish.*

Ezek. 3. 19.

What Christian *had to his Supper. Their Talk at Supper-Time.*

---

damp Render ineffective; **conscious to myself** Christian's consciousness is distinct from his self; **Conversation** Behavior; **precise** Puritanical: a "precision" was a puritan; **Tenderness in** Sensitivity to; **implacable** Impervious; **delivered** Exonerated; **fat** Attractive or desirable; **I perceived** The narrator is learning from Christian's discourse.

with, and slain him that had the Power of Death, but not Heb. 2. 14, 15. without great Danger to himself, which made me love him the more.

For, as they said, and as I believe, (said *Christian*)° he did it with the Loss of much Blood; but that which put Glory of Grace into all he did, was, that he did it of pure Love to his Country. And besides, there were some of them of the Houshold that said, they had seen and spoke with him since he did die on the Cross; and they have attested, that they had it from his own lips, that he is such a Lover of poor Pilgrims, that the like is not to be found from the East to the West.

They moreover gave an Instance of what they affirmed, and that was, He had stript himself of his Glory, that he might do this for the Poor;° and that they heard him say and affirm, *That he would not dwell in the Mountain of* Zion *alone.* They said moreover, That he had made many Pilgrims princes, though by nature° they were beggars born, and their original had been the dunghill.°

Christ makes
Princes of
Beggars.
1 Sam. 2. 8,
Ps. 113. 7.

Thus they discoursed together till late at night; and after they had committed themselves to their Lord for Protection, they betook themselves to rest: The Pilgrim they laid in a large upper chamber, whose window opened towards the Sun-rising: The name of the chamber was *Peace*, where he slept till break of Day, and then he awoke and sang,

Christian's
Bed-chamber.

> *Where am I now! Is this the Love and Care*
> *Of* Jesus; *for the men that Pilgrims are,*
> *Thus to provide! That I should be forgiven,*
> *And dwell already the next door to Heaven!*

So, in the morning, they all got up; and, after some more discourse, they told him that he should not depart till they had shewed him the *Rarities*° of that place. And first they had him

---

said Christian The narrator blends into the fictional representation of himself; **for the Poor** Bunyan always considered the poor to be God's chosen people; **by nature** According to the flesh; **dunghill** Garbage dump, where the poorest scavenged for food; **Rarities** Wonders, signs.

into the Study, where they shewed him Records° of the greatest antiquity; in which, as I remember my dream, they shewed him first the *Pedigree* of the Lord of the Hill, that he was the Son of the Ancient of Days,° and came by an Eternal Generation:° Here also was more fully recorded the Acts that he had done, and the Names of many hundreds that he had taken into his service; and how he had placed them in such Habitations, that he could neither by Length of Days, nor Decays of Nature, be dissolved.

Then they read to him some of the worthy Acts that some of his Servants had done: As how they had subdued Kingdoms, wrought Righteousness, obtained Promises, stopped the Mouths of Lions, quenched the Violence of Fire, escaped the Edge of the Sword, out of Weakness were made strong, waxed valiant in Fight, and turned to Flight the Armies of the *Aliens.*°

Then they read again in another part of the Records of the House, where it was shewed how willing their Lord was to receive into his Favour, any, even any, though they in time past had offered great Affronts to his Person and Proceedings. Here also were several other histories of many other famous things, of all which *Christian* had a view: As of things both Ancient and Modern; together with Prophecies and Predictions of things that have their certain accomplishment, both to the dread and amazement of Enemies, and the comfort and solace of Pilgrims.

The next day they took him, and had him into the Armory, where they shewed him all manner of Furniture,° which their Lord had provided for Pilgrims, as Sword, Shield, Helmet, Breast-plate, *All-Prayer*, and Shoes that would not wear out. And there was here enough of this to harness° out as many

Christian had into the Study and what he saw there.

Heb. 11. 33, 34.

Christian had into the Armory.

Records The Bible, now read in a more historical way than the purely iconic images at the Interpreter's House; **Ancient of Days** A term for God used in Daniel 7:9; **Eternal Generation** His generation took place in eternity, and He is eternally being generated; **the Aliens** In the Bible, the foreign nations surrounding Israel; but in Bunyan's typology, the worldly, from whom Christian has become alienated; **Furniture** Equipment; **harness** To arm.

men, for the service of their Lord, as there be Stars in the Heaven for multitude.

They also shewed him some of the Engines° with which some of his Servants had done wonderful things. They shewed him *Moses'* Rod, the Hammer and Nail with which *Jael* slew *Sisera*, the Pitchers, Trumpets, and Lamps too, with which *Gideon* put to Flight the Armies of *Midian*. Then they shewed him the Ox's Goad, wherewith *Shamgar* slew Six Hundred men. They shewed him also the Jaw-Bone with which *Samson* did such mighty Feats: They shewed him moreover the Sling and Stone with which *David* slew *Goliah* of *Gath;* and the Sword also with which their Lord will kill the Man of Sin,[47] in the Day that he shall rise up to the Prey. They shewed him besides many excellent things, with which *Christian* was much delighted. This done, they went to their Rest again.

Christian made to see Ancient things.

Then I saw in my dream, That on the morrow he got up to go forwards, but they desired him to stay till the next day also; and then said they, we will (if the day be clear) show you the Delectable Mountains;[48] which, they said, would yet farther add to his Comfort, because they were nearer the desired Haven than the place where at present he was; so he consented and staid. When the morning was up, they had him to the top of the House, and bid him look South: So he did; and behold, at a great Distance, he saw a most pleasant mountainous Country, beautified with Woods, Vineyards, Fruits of all sorts, Flowers also, with Springs and Fountains, very delectable to behold. Then he asked the name of the Country. They said, It was *Emanuel's Land;*[49] and it is as common,° said they, as this *Hill* is to and for all the Pilgrims. And when thou comest there, from thence thou mayest see to the Gate of the Cœlestial City, as the Shepherds that live there will make appear.

Christian shewed the Delectable Mountains.

Isa. 33. 16, 17.

Now he bethought himself of setting forward, and they were willing he should. But first, said they, let us go again into

Christian sets forward.

Engines Weapons. See the footnote to "two-edged sword" on page 71; **common** Communal. The privatizing of "common" land was a pressing issue in seventeenth-century England.

the Armory: So they did; and when he came there, they harnessed him from head to foot, with what was of Proof,° lest perhaps he should meet with Assaults in the Way. He being therefore thus accoutred,° walketh out with his Friends to the Gate, and there he asked the Porter, If he saw any Pilgrim pass by? Then the Porter answered, Yes.

Chr. Pray, did you know him? said he.

Port. I asked his name, and he told me it was *Faithful.*

Chr. O, said *Christian*, I know him; he is my Townsman, my near neighbour, he comes from the place where I was born: How far do you think he may be before?°

Port. He is got by this time below the Hill.

Chr. Well, said *Christian*, good *Porter*, the Lord be with thee, and add to all thy blessings much increase for the kindness that thou hast shewed to me.

Then he began to go forward; but *Discretion, Piety, Charity*, and *Prudence*, would accompany him down to the foot of the Hill. So they went on together, reiterating their former discourses,[50] till they came to go down the Hill. Then said *Christian*, As it was *difficult* coming up, so, (so far as I can see,) it is *dangerous* going down. Yes, said *Prudence*, so it is; for

it is a hard matter for a man to go down into the Valley of *Humiliation*, as thou art now, and to catch no slip by the Way; therefore, said they, are we come out to accompany thee down the Hill. So he began to go down, but very warily; yet he caught a slip or two.

Then I saw in my dream, That these good Companions (when *Christian* was got down to the bottom of the Hill) gave him a loaf of bread, a bottle of wine, and a cluster of raisins; and then he went his Way.

But now in this Valley of *Humiliation*, poor *Christian* was hard put to it; for he had gone but a little Way, before he espied a foul *Fiend*° coming over the field to meet him: His name is *Apollyon*.[51] Then did *Christian* begin to be afraid, and

---

of Proof Impenetrable; **accoutred** Equipped; **before** Ahead; **a foul Fiend** A dirty devil. "Fiend" is the Old English word for "enemy," as "Satan" is the Hebrew.

WHILST *CHRISTIAN* IS AMONG HIS GODLY FRIENDS,
THEIR GOLDEN MOUTHS MAKE HIM SUFFICIENT 'MENDS
FOR ALL HIS GRIEFS; AND WHEN THEY LET HIM GO,
HE'S CLAD WITH NORTHERN STEEL FROM TOP TO TOE.

to cast in his mind whether to go back or to stand his ground.

Christian *has no Armour for his back.*

But he considered again, that he had no Armour for his back, and therefore thought that to turn the back to him might give him greater advantage, with ease to pierce him with his Darts;

Christian's *Resolution on the approach of* Apollyon.

therefore he resolved to venture,° and stand his ground: For, thought he, had I no more in mine Eye° than the saving of my life, 'twould be the best way to stand.

So he went on, and *Apollyon* met him: Now the Monster was hideous to behold: He was cloathed with scales like a fish; (and they are his Pride)° he had wings like a dragon, feet like a bear, and out of his belly came fire and smoke, and his mouth was as the mouth of a lion. When he was come up to *Christian*, he beheld him with a disdainful countenance, and thus began to question with him.

Discourse betwixt Christian *and* Apollyon.

Apollyon. Whence come you? and whither are you bound?

Chr. I am come from the City of *Destruction*, which is the Place of all Evil, and am going to the City of *Zion*.

Apol. By this I perceive thou art one of my subjects; for all that country is mine, and I am the Prince and God of it. How is it then that thou hast run away from thy King? Were it not that I hope thou mayest do me more service, I would strike thee now at one blow to the ground.

Rom. 6. 23.

Chr. I was born indeed in your Dominions, but your Service was hard, and your wages such as a man could not live on; *for the Wages of Sin is Death;* therefore, when I was come to years,° I did as other considerate° persons do, look out, if perhaps I might mend° myself.

Apol. There is no prince that will thus lightly lose his subjects, neither will I as yet lose thee; but since thou complainest of thy service and wages, be content to go back; what our Country will afford, I do here promise to give thee.

Apollyon's *Flattery.*

Chr. But I have let myself to° another, even to the King of princes, and how can I, with fairness, go back with thee?

---

venture Dare; **in mine Eye** As my aim; **they are his Pride** Meaning both that the scales are the allegorical figure for Apollyon's pride and that he is proud of his scales; **to years** To maturity; **considerate** Prudent; **mend** Improve; **let myself to** Engaged myself in service to.

Apol. Thou hast done in this according to the Proverb, changed *a Bad for a Worse:* But it is ordinary for those that have professed themselves his Servants, after a while to give him the slip, and return again to me: Do thou so too, and all shall be well.

Chr. I have given him my Faith, and sworn my Allegiance to him, How then can I go back from this, and not be hanged as a Traitor?

Apol. Thou didst the same to me, and yet I am willing to pass by all, if now thou wilt turn again and go back.

Chr. What I promised thee was in my non-age;° and besides, I count° that the Prince under whose Banner now I stand, is able to absolve me; yea, and to pardon also what I did as to my Compliance with thee: And besides, (O thou destroying *Apollyon*) to speak Truth, I like his Service, his Wages, his Servants, his Government, his Company, and Country, better than thine; and therefore leave off to persuade me further, I am his servant, and I will follow him.

Apol. Consider again, when thou art in cool blood, what thou art like to meet with in the Way that thou goest. Thou knowest, that for the most part, his Servants come to an ill End, because they are transgressors against me and my Ways. How many of them have been put to shameful deaths! And besides, thou countest his service better than mine, whereas he never came yet from the Place where he is, to deliver any that served him out of our hands: But as for me, how many times, as all the World very well knows, have I delivered, either by Power or Fraud, those that have faithfully served me, from him and his, though taken by them? And so I will deliver thee.

Chr. His forbearing at present to deliver them, is on purpose to try their Love, whether they will cleave to him to the End: And as for the ill end thou sayest they come to, that is most glorious in their account:° But, for present Deliverance,

Apollyon
undervalues
Christ's
Service.

[Apollyon
pretends to be
merciful. 1st
Edit. 1678
only.]

Apollyon
pleads the
grievous Ends
of Christians,
to dissuade
Christian
from
persisting in
his Way.

---

non-age Before the legal age of maturity, hence in the pre-conversion condition of being under the law; **count** Reckon; **account** Reckoning.

they do not much expect it; for they stay° for their Glory, and then they shall have it, when their Prince comes in his, and the Glory of the Angels.

Apol. Thou hast already been unfaithful in thy service to him; and how dost thou think to receive Wages of him?

Chr. Wherein, O *Apollyon!* have I been unfaithful to him?

Apollyon
pleads
Christian's
Infirmities
against him.

Apol. Thou didst faint at first setting out, when thou wast almost choaked in the Gulph of *Despond;* thou didst attempt wrong ways to be rid of thy Burden, whereas thou shouldest have stayed till thy Prince had taken it off. Thou didst sinfully sleep, and lose thy choice Things. Thou wast also almost persuaded to go back at the sight of the Lions: And when thou talkest of thy Journey, and of what thou hast heard and seen, thou art inwardly desirous of Vain-glory in all that thou sayest or dost.

Chr. All this is true, and much more, which thou hast left out; but the Prince whom I serve and honour, is merciful and ready to forgive: But besides, these Infirmities possessed me in thy Country; for there I sucked them in, and I have groaned under them, been sorry for them, and have obtained Pardon of my Prince.

Apollyon *in a*
Rage falls
upon
Christian.

Apol. Then *Apollyon* broke out into a grievous Rage, saying, I am an Enemy to this Prince; I hate his Person, his Laws, and People: I am come out on purpose to withstand thee.

Chr. Apollyon, beware what you do; for I am in the King's highway, the Way of Holiness; therefore take heed to yourself.

Apol. Then *Apollyon* straddled quite over the whole breadth of the Way, and said, I am void of Fear in this matter; prepare thyself to die; for I swear by my infernal Den,° That thou shalt go no further: Here will I spill thy Soul!°

And with that he threw a flaming Dart at his breast; but *Christian* had a Shield in his hand, with which he caught it, and so prevented the danger of that.

Then did *Christian* draw;° for he saw it was time to bestir

---

stay Wait; **Den** Hell, but Bunyan uses the word to signify his prison on page 13 and elsewhere; **Here will I spill thy Soul!** Apollyon imagines that the soul is part of the physical body; **draw** That is, draw his sword.

him;° and *Apollyon* as fast made at him, throwing Darts as thick as hail; by the which, notwithstanding all that *Christian* could do to avoid it, *Apollyon* wounded him in his *head*, his *hand*, and *foot*. This made *Christian* give a little back: *Apollyon*, therefore, followed his Work amain, and *Christian* again took Courage, and resisted as manfully as he could. This sore Combat lasted for above half a day, even till *Christian* was almost quite spent. For you must know that *Christian*, by reason of his Wounds, must needs grow weaker and weaker.

Christian wounded in his Understanding, Faith, and Conversation.

Then *Apollyon* espying his opportunity, began to gather up close to *Christian*, and wrestling with him, gave him a dreadful Fall; and with that *Christian's* Sword flew out of his hand. Then said *Apollyon*, *I am sure of thee now*: And with that he had almost pressed him to Death; so that *Christian* began to despair of Life. But, as God would have it, while *Apollyon* was fetching of ° his last blow, thereby to make a full end of this good man, *Christian* nimbly reached out his hand for his Sword, and caught it, saying, *Rejoyce not against me, O mine Enemy! when I fall I shall arise*; and with that gave him a deadly thrust, which made him give back, as one that had received his mortal wound. *Christian* perceiving that, made at him again; saying, *Nay, in all these things we are more than Conquerors, through him that loved us*. And with that *Apollyon* spread forth his Dragon's wings, and sped him away, that *Christian* saw him no more.

Apollyon casteth Christian down to the Ground.

Christian's Victory over Apollyon.

Mic. 7. 8.

Rom. 8. 37. Jam. 4. 7.

In this Combat no man can imagine, unless he had seen and heard as I did, what yelling and hideous roaring *Apollyon* made all the time of the fight: He spake like a Dragon: And on the other side, what sighs and groans burst from *Christian's* heart. I never saw him all the while give so much as one pleasant look, till he perceived he had wounded *Apollyon* with his two-edged Sword;° then, indeed, he did smile, and look upward: But it was the dreadfullest Fight that ever I saw.

A brief Relation of the Combat, by the spectator.

---

bestir him Take action; **fetching of** Preparing for; **two-edged sword** Compare Milton's "Lycidas" (1638): "But that two-handed engine at the door / Stands ready to smite once, and smite no more" (lines 130–131).

A MORE UNEQUAL MATCH CAN HARDLY BE:
CHRISTIAN MUST FIGHT AN ANGEL; BUT YOU SEE
THE VALIANT MAN, BY HANDLING SWORD AND SHIELD
DOTH MAKE HIM, THO' A DRAGON, QUIT THE FIELD.

So when the Battle was over, *Christian* said, I will here give Thanks to him that hath delivered me out of the mouth of the *Lion*, to him that did help me against *Apollyon*. And so he did; saying,

> Great Beelzebub, *the Captain of this Fiend,*
> *Design'd my Ruin; therefore to this end*
> *He sent him harness'd out; and he with rage,*
> *That hellish was, did fiercely me engage:*
> *But blessed* Michael° *helped me, and I,*
> *By dint of Sword, did quickly make him fly:*
> *Therefore to him let me give lasting Praise,*
> *And Thank, and bless his holy Name always.*

Then there came to him a Hand with some of the leaves of the Tree of Life, the which *Christian* took and applied to the wounds that he had received in the battle, and was healed immediately. He also sat down in that place to eat bread, and to drink of the bottle that was given him a little before; so being refreshed, he addressed himself to his Journey, with his Sword drawn in his hand; for he said, I know not but some other Enemy may be at hand. But he met with no other affront from *Apollyon* quite through this Valley.

Now at the end of this Valley was another, called, *The Valley of the Shadow of Death*, and *Christian* must needs go through it, because the Way to the Cœlestial City lay through the midst of it: Now this Valley is a very solitary place. The prophet *Jeremiah* thus describes it: A wilderness, a land of desarts, and of pits; a land of drought, and of the shadow of death, a land that no man (but a Christian)° passeth through, and where no man dwelt.

Now here *Christian* was worse put to it than in his fight with *Apollyon;* as by the sequel° you shall see.

I saw then in my dream, That when *Christian* was got to

Margin notes:
Christian *gives God* thanks for Deliverance.

Christian *goes on his Journey with his Sword drawn in his hand.*

The Valley of the Shadow of Death.

Jer. 2. 6.

Michael The warrior angel in the Bible, Revelation 12:7. Note that the character has not appeared; Christian refers to his own courage as "Michael"; **but a Christian** This is Bunyan's interjection; **sequel** That is, what follows.

The Children of the Spies go back.

Numb. 13.
the borders of the *Shadow of Death*, there met him two men, children of them that brought up an evil report of the good land, making haste to go back; to whom *Christian* spake as follows:

Chr. Whither are you going?

Men. They said, Back! Back! And we would have you to do so too, if either Life or Peace is prized by you.

Chr. Why! What's the matter? said *Christian*.

Men. Matter! said they, we were going that Way as you are going, and went as far as we durst; and indeed we were almost past coming back; for had we gone a little farther, we had not been here to bring the news to thee.

Chr. But what have you met with? said *Christian*.

Psal. 44. 19.
Psal. 107. 10.
Men. Why we were almost in the Valley of the Shadow of Death, but that by good hap° we looked before us, and saw the danger before we came to it.

Chr. But what have you seen? said *Christian*.

Men. Seen! Why the Valley itself, which is as dark as pitch: We also saw there the Hobgoblins, Satyrs,° and Dragons of the Pit: We heard also in that Valley a continual howling and yelling, as of a people under unutterable misery, who there sat
Job. 3. 5.
ch. 10. 22.
bound in affliction and irons;° and over that Valley hangs the discouraging clouds of Confusion: Death also doth always spread his wings over it. In a word, it is every whit° dreadful, being utterly without Order.

Jer. 2. 5.
Chr. Then said *Christian*, I perceive not yet, by what you have said, but that this is my Way to the desired Haven.

Men. Be it thy Way, we will not choose it for ours.

So they parted, and *Christian* went on his Way, but still with his Sword drawn in his hand, for fear lest he should be assaulted.

Psal. 69. 14.
I saw then in my dream, so far as this Valley reached, there was on the right hand a very deep Ditch: That Ditch is it, into

---

hap Luck; **Satyrs** According to Sharrock, "not classical, but Biblical satyrs" (Sharrock, ed., *The Pilgrim's Progress*, p. 393); **affliction and irons** Note the elision between physical and mental fetters; **every whit** Every bit.

which the blind have led the blind in all ages, and have both
there miserably perished. Again, behold, on the left hand, there
was a very dangerous Quag,[52] into which, if even a good man
falls, he finds no bottom for his foot to stand on: Into that
Quag King *David*° once did fall, and had, no doubt, therein
been smothered, had not he that is able plucked him out.

The pathway was here also exceeding narrow, and therefore good *Christian* was the more put to it; for when he
sought, in the Dark, to shun the Ditch on the one hand, he
was ready to tip over into the Mire on the other: Also when
he sought to escape the Mire, without great carefulness he
would be ready to fall into the Ditch. Thus he went on, and I
heard him here sigh bitterly: For besides the dangers mentioned above, the pathway was here so dark, that oftimes,
when he lift up his foot to set forward, he knew not where, or
upon what, he should set it next.

About the midst of this Valley, I perceived the mouth of
Hell° to be, and it stood also hard by° the Wayside: Now,
thought *Christian*, what shall I do? And ever and anon the
flame and smoke would come out in such abundance, with
sparks and hideous noises, (things that cared not for *Christian's* Sword, as did *Apollyon* before) that he was forced to put
up his Sword, and betake himself to another Weapon, called
All Prayer: So he cried, in my hearing, *O Lord, I beseech thee,*
deliver my Soul. Thus he went on a great while, yet still the
flames would be reaching towards him: Also he heard doleful
voices, and rushings to and fro, so that sometimes he thought
he should be torn in pieces, or trodden down like mire in the
streets. This frightful sight was seen, and these dreadful
noises were heard by him for several miles together: And
coming to a place, where he thought he heard a Company of
Fiends coming forward to meet him, he stopt, and began to
muse what he had best to do: Sometimes he had half a
thought to go back; then again he thought he might be half-

Eph. 6. 18.
Psal. 116. 4.

Christian *put*
to a stand, but
for a while.

King David Noted for his vulnerability to the sin of lust; see 2 Samuel
11:1–12; **the mouth of Hell** A physical "Hell-mouth" was a prominent feature on the Renaissance stage; **hard by** Close by.

POOR MAN! WHERE ART THOU NOW? THY DAY IS NIGHT:
GOOD MAN, BE NOT CAST DOWN, THOU YET ART RIGHT.
THY WAY TO HEAV'N LIES BY THE GATES OF HELL:
CHEAR UP, HOLD OUT, WITH THEE IT SHALL GO WELL.

way through the Valley: He remembred also, how he had already vanquished many a danger; and that the danger of going back might be much more than for to go forward; so he resolved to go on: Yet the *Fiends* seemed to come nearer and nearer: But when they were come even almost at him, he cried out with a most vehement voice, *I will walk in the Strength of the Lord God:* So they gave back, and came no further.

One thing I would not let slip:° I took notice that now poor *Christian* was so confounded, that he did not know his own voice: And thus I perceived it: Just when he was come over-against the mouth of the burning Pit, one of the Wicked Ones got behind him, and stept up softly to him, and whisperingly suggested many grievous Blasphemies to him, which he verily thought had proceeded from his own mind.° This put *Christian* more to it than any thing that he met with before, even to think that he should now blaspheme him that he loved so much before; yet, if he could have helped it, he would not have done it: But he had not the discretion either to stop his ears, or to know from whence those Blasphemies came.

Christian *made believe that he spake* Blasphemies *when 'twas* Satan that *suggested them into his* mind.

When *Christian* had travelled in this disconsolate condition some considerable time, he thought he heard the voice of a man, as going before him, saying, *Though I walk through the Valley of the Shadow of Death, I will fear none Ill, for thou art with me.*

Psal. 23. 4.

Then was he glad; and that for these reasons:

First, Because he gathered from thence, that some who feared God were in this Valley as well as himself.

Secondly, For that he perceived God was with them, though in that dark and dismal state: And why not, thought he, with me? Though by reason of the impediment that attends this place, I cannot perceive it.

Job 9. 10.

---

let slip Pass by; from his own mind In *Grace Abounding*, Bunyan reports hearing a voice urging him to "sell" Christ (see Introduction), and blasphemy was a constant temptation for him.

Thirdly, For that he hoped (could he overtake them) to have Company by-and-by.

Amos 5. 8.

So he went on, and called to him that was before; but he knew not what to answer: For that he also thought himself to be alone. And by and by the Day broke: Then said *Christian, He hath turned the Shadow of Death into the Morning.*

Now Morning being come, he looked back, not out of desire to return, but to see, by the Light of the Day, what Hazards he had gone through in the Dark: So he saw more perfectly the Ditch that was on the one hand, and the Quag that was on the other; also how narrow the Way was which led betwixt them both; also how he saw the Hobgoblins, and Satyrs, and Dragons of the Pit, but all afar off: For after break of Day they came not nigh, yet they were discovered to him, according to that which is written, *He discovereth deep things out of Darkness, and bringeth out to Light the shadow of death.*

Christian
glad at break
of Day.

Job 12. 22.

Now was *Christian* much affected with his deliverance from all the dangers of his solitary Way; which dangers, though he feared them more before, yet he saw them more clearly now, because the light of the day made them conspicuous to him; and about this time the Sun was rising, and this was another Mercy to *Christian:* For you must note, that though the first part of the Valley of the Shadow of Death was dangerous, yet this second part, which he was yet to go, was, if possible, far more dangerous: For, from the place where he now stood, even to the end of the Valley, the Way was all along set so full of snares, traps, gins, and nets here, and so full of pits, pitfalls, deep holes, and shelvings down there, that had it now been dark, as it was when he came the first part of the Way, had he had a thousand Souls, they had in reason been cast away; but, as I said, just now the Sun was rising. Then said he, *His Candle shineth on my head, and by his Light I go through Darkness.*

The second
part of this
Valley very
dangerous.

Job 29. 3.

In this Light therefore he came to the end of the Valley. Now I saw in my dream, that at the end of this Valley lay blood, bones, ashes, and mangled bodies of men, even of Pilgrims that had gone this Way formerly: And while I was musing what should be the reason, I espied a little before me a

Cave, where two giants, *Pope* and *Pagan*,° dwelt in old Time;
by whose power and tyranny° the men, whose bones, blood,
ashes, *&c.* lay there, were cruelly put to death. But by this
place *Christian* went without much danger, whereat I somewhat wondered: But I have learnt since, that *Pagan* has been
dead many a day;° and as for the other, though he be yet alive,
he is, by reason of age, and also of the many shrewd brushes°
that he met with in his younger days, grown so crazy and stiff
in his joints,[53] that he can now do little more than sit in his
Cave's mouth, grinning at Pilgrims as they go by, and biting
his nails, because he cannot come at them.

So I saw that *Christian* went on his Way; yet, at the sight of
the *Old Man*,° that sat in the mouth of the Cave, he could not
tell what to think, 'specially because he spake to him, though he
could not go after him; saying, *You will never mend, till more of
you be burnt.*° But he held his peace, and set a good face on't,
and so went by, and catched no hurt. Then sang *Christian:*

> *O World of Wonders! (I can say no less)*
> *That I should be preserv'd in that Distress*
> *That I have met with here! O blessed be*
> *That Hand that from it hath deliver'd me!*
> *Dangers in darkness, Devils, Hell, and Sin,*
> *Did compass° me, while I this Vale was in:*
> *Yea Snares, and Pits, and Traps, and Nets did lie*
> *My Path about, that worthless, silly I*
> *Might have been catch'd, entangled, and cast down:*
> *But since I live, let* JESUS *wear the Crown.*

Pope and Pagan Bunyan regarded these as equally enemies of true religion;
tyranny The pagan tyranny of ancient Rome and the Catholic tyranny of
modern Rome; **Pagan has been dead many a day** Note that Bunyan does not
consider witchcraft, which was flourishing as he wrote, a form of paganism;
he would have seen it as Satanism; **shrewd brushes** Harsh blows; a reference
to the Reformation; **the Old Man** Giant Pope, but the term was used to refer
to the fleshly mind as a whole; **burnt** Keeble finds "an allusion to the 'fires of
Smithfield,' the execution of Protestants by burning during the reign of Mary
Tudor" (Keeble, ed., *The Pilgrim's Progress*, p. 271); **compass** Surround.

Now, as *Christian* went on his Way, he came to a little ascent, which was cast up on purpose, that Pilgrims might see before them: Up there, therefore, *Christian* went; and looking forward, he saw *Faithful* before him upon his Journey: Then said *Christian* aloud, *Ho, ho: Soho:*° *Stay, and I will be your Companion*. At that *Faithful* looked behind him; to whom *Christian* cried again, *Stay, stay, till I come up to you*. But *Faithful* answer'd, *No, I am upon my Life, and the Avenger of Blood is behind me.*

At this *Christian* was somewhat moved, and putting to all his strength, he quickly got up with *Faithful*, and did also overrun him; so the *last* was *first.*° Then did *Christian* vaingloriously smile,[54] because he had gotten the start of his Brother: But not taking good heed to his feet, he suddenly stumbled and fell, and could not rise again, until *Faithful* came up to help him.

Then I saw in my dream, they went very lovingly on together, and had sweet discourse of all things that had happened to them in their Pilgrimage; and thus *Christian* began.

Chr. My honoured and well beloved Brother *Faithful*, I am glad that I have overtaken you; and that God has so tempered° our Spirits, that we can walk as Companions in this so pleasant a path.

Faith. I had thought, dear Friend, to have had your Company quite from our town, but you did get the start of me: Wherefore I was forced to come thus much of the Way alone.

Chr. How long did you stay in the City of *Destruction*, before you set out after me on your Pilgrimage?

Faith. Till I could stay no longer; for there was great talk presently after you were gone out, that our City would, in a short time, with Fire from Heaven, be burned down to the ground.

Chr. What, did your Neighbours talk so?

Faith. Yes, 'twas for a while in everybody's mouth.

Christian overtakes Faithful.

Christian's Fall makes Faithful and he go lovingly together.

Their talk about the Country from whence they came.

Soho A hunting cry; Bunyan uses it as a greeting; **the last was first** Reference to Matthew 19:30; **tempered** Blended.

Chr. What and did no more of them but you come out to escape the danger?

Faith. Though there was, as I said, a great Talk thereabout, yet I do not think they did firmly believe it. For in the heat of the discourse, I heard some of them deridingly speak of you and of your desperate Journey (for so they called this your Pilgrimage:) But I did believe, and do still, that the end of our City will be with fire and brimstone from Above. And therefore I have made my escape.

Chr. Did you hear no talk of neighbour *Pliable?*

Faith. Yes, *Christian,* I heard that he followed you till he came at the Slough of *Despond;* where, as some said, he fell in: But he would not be known to have so done; but I am sure he was soundly bedaubed with that kind of dirt.

Chr. And what said the neighbours to him?

Faith. He hath, since his going back, been had greatly in derision, and that among all sorts of people; some do mock and despise him, and scarce will any set him on work.° He is now seven times worse than if he had never gone out of the City. *How* Pliable *was accounted of, when he got home.*

Chr. But why should they be so set against him, since they also despise the Way that he forsook?

Faith. O, they say, Hang him; he is a turncoat![55] he was not true to his Profession! I think God has stirred up even his enemies to hiss at him, and make him a proverb, because he hath forsaken the Way. *Jer. 29. 18, 19.*

Chr. Had you no talk with him before you came out?

Faith. I met him once in the streets, but he leered° away on the other side, as one ashamed of what he had done: So I spake not to him.

Chr. Well, at my first setting out, I had hopes of that man; but now I fear he will perish in the overthrow of the City. For it has happened to him according to the true proverb, *The dog is turned to his vomit again; and the sow that was washed, to her wallowing in the mire.* *2 Pet. 2. 22. The Dog and the Sow.*

---

set him on work Give him a job; **leered** Sneaked.

Faith. They are my fears of him too, but who can hinder that which will be?

Chr. Well, neighbour *Faithful* (said *Christian*) let us leave him, and talk of things that more immediately concern ourselves. Tell me now what you have met with in the Way as you came: For I know you have met with some things, or else it may be writ for a Wonder.

Faith. I escaped the *Slough* that I perceive you fell into, and got up to the Gate without° that danger; only I met with one whose name was *Wanton*,° that had like to have done me a mischief.

Faithful
assaulted by
Wanton.

Chr. 'Twas well you escaped her Net: *Joseph*° was hard put to it by her, and he escaped her as you did; but it had like to have cost him his Life. But what did she do to you?

Gen. 39. 11, 12, 13.

Faith. You cannot think (but that you know something) what a flattering tongue she had; she lay at me hard to turn aside with her, promising me all manner of Content.

Chr. Nay, she did not promise you the Content of a good Conscience.

Faith. You know what I mean; all carnal and fleshly content.

Prov. 22. 14.

Chr. Thank God you have escaped her: The abhorred of the Lord shall fall into her ditch.

Faith. Nay, I know not whether I did wholly escape her, or no.

Chr. Why, I trow, you did not consent to her desires?

Faith. No not to defile myself; for I remembered an old Writing that I had seen, which said, *Her steps take hold of Hell.* So I shut mine eyes, because I would not be bewitched° with her looks: Then she railed on me, and I went my way.

Prov. 5. 5.
Job 31. 1.

Chr. Did you meet with no other assault as you came?

Faith. When I came to the foot of the Hill called *Difficulty*, I met with a very aged Man, who asked me what I was? and whither bound? I told him, that I was a Pilgrim, going to the

He was
assaulted by
Adam the
First.

---

without On the other side of; **Wanton** Horny; **Joseph** In Genesis 39, Potiphar's wife attempts to seduce Joseph; **bewitched** Sexual temptation was often described as a kind of witchcraft.

Cœlestial City. Then said the old man, Thou lookest like an
honest fellow; wilt thou be content to dwell with me, for the
Wages° that I shall give thee? Then I asked him his name, and
where he dwelt? He said his name was *Adam the first*° and I   Eph. 4. 22.
dwell in the town of *Deceit*. I asked him then, What was his
Work? and what the Wages that he would give? He told me,
that his *Work* was *many delights;* and his *Wages,* that I should
be his Heir at last. I further asked him, what House he kept,
and what other Servants he had? So he told me, that his
House was maintained with all the dainties in the world; and
that his *servants* were those of his own begetting. Then I
asked, how many children he had? He said, that he had but
three daughters, *The Lust of the Flesh, The Lust of the Eyes*, and   1 John 2. 16.
The Pride of Life; and that I should marry them all, if I would.
Then I asked, how long Time he would have me live with
him? And he told me, As long as he lived himself.

    Chr. Well, and what conclusion came the old man and you
to at last?

    Faith. Why, at first I found myself somewhat inclinable to
go with the man, for I thought he spake very fair; but looking
in his forehead, as I talked with him, I saw there written,° *Put
off the Old Man with his Deeds.*

    Chr. And how then?

    Faith. Then it came burning hot into my mind, whatever
he said, and however he flattered, when he got me home to
his house, he would sell me for a Slave.° So I bid him forbear
to talk, for I would not come near the door of his house. Then
he reviled me, and told me, that he would send such a one
after me, that should make my Way bitter to my Soul. So I
turned to go away from him; but just as I turned myself to go
thence, I felt him take hold of my Flesh, and give me such a
deadly twitch back, that I thought he had pulled part of me

Wages As in Christian's encounter with Apollyon, wage-labor is used as a
figure for allegiance to the world; **Adam the first** The "old man." Paul describes Christ as the Second Adam in Romans 5:12–14; **there written** Faithful shows his ability to read the real significance of the Old Man, which is
the reverse of his apparent meaning; **a Slave** The Old Man, or flesh, is a child
of Hagar the bondwoman (see Introduction).

Rom. 7. 24. after himself: This made me cry, *O wretched Man!* So I went
on my Way up the Hill.

Now when I had got above half way up, I looked behind
me, and saw one coming after me,[56] swift as the wind; so he
overtook me just about the place where the Settle stands.

Chr. Just there, said *Christian*, did I sit down to rest me;
but being overcome with Sleep, I there lost this Roll out of my
bosom.

Faith. But, good brother, hear me out: So soon as the man
overtook me, he was but a word and a blow;° for down he
knocked me, and laid me for dead. But when I was a little
come to myself again, I asked him, Wherefore he served° me
so? He said, Because of my secret inclining to *Adam the First:*
And with that he struck me another deadly blow on the
breast, and beat me down backward; so I lay at his foot as
dead as before. So when I came to myself again, I cried him
mercy: But he said, I know not how to show mercy;° and with
that knocked me down again. He had doubtless made an end
of me, but that one came by, and bid him forbear.

Chr. Who was that, that bid him forbear?

Faith. I did not know him at first; but as he went by, I perceived the holes in his hands and in his side: Then I concluded that he was our Lord. So I went up the Hill.

The temper of Moses. *Chr.* That Man that overtook you, was *Moses.* He spareth
none, neither knoweth he how to shew mercy to those that
transgress his Law.

Faith. I know it very well; it was not the first time that he
has met with me. 'Twas he that came to me when I dwelt securely at home, and that told me he would burn my house
over my head, if I staid there.

Chr. But did you not see the House that stood there on the
top of that Hill, on the side of which *Moses* met you?

Faith. Yes, and the Lions too, before I came at it; but for the
Lions, I think they were asleep; for it was about Noon: And

---

but a word and a blow That is, he hit me as soon as he spoke to me; Moses'
words *are* blows; **served** Treated; **I know not how to show mercy** The purpose of the law is to diagnose sin, not to treat it.

because I had so much of the Day before me, I passed by the Porter, and came down the Hill.

Chr. He told me indeed, That he saw you go by; but I wish you had called at the House; for they would have shewed you so many rarities, that you would scarce have forgot them to the day of your death. But pray tell me, Did you meet nobody in the Valley of *Humility?*

Faith. Yes, I met with one *Discontent*, who would willingly have persuaded me to go back again with him: His reason was, For that the Valley was altogether without *Honour.*[57] He told me moreover, That there to go, was the way to disobey all my Friends, as *Pride, Arrogancy, Self-Conceit, Worldly-Glory*, with others, who, he knew, as he said, would be very much offended, if I made such a Fool of myself as to wade through this Valley.

Chr. Well, and how did you answer him?

Faith. I told him, That although all these that he named, might claim kindred of me, and that rightly, (for indeed they *were* my relations, *according to the Flesh*) yet since I became a Pilgrim, they have disowned me, as I also have rejected them; and therefore they were to me now, no more than if they had never been of my lineage; I told him moreover, That as to this Valley, he had quite misrepresented the thing; for before *Honour* is *Humility*, and a *Haughty Spirit* before a *Fall*. Therefore, said I, I had rather go through this Valley to the honour that was so accounted by the Wisest, than choose that which he esteemed most worthy our affections.

Chr. Met you with nothing else in that Valley?

Faith. Yes I met with *Shame;* but of all the men that I met with in my Pilgrimage, he, I think, bears the wrong name.° The other would be said Nay, after a little argumentation, (and somewhat else): But this bold-faced *Shame* would never have done.

Chr. Why, what did he say to you?

Faith. What! why he objected against *Religion* itself; he said, 'Twas a pitiful, low, sneaking business for a man to mind

Faithful assaulted by Discontent.

Faithful's answer to Discontent.

He is assaulted with Shame.

---

the wrong name Shame causes shame in others; he is himself shameless.

Religion; he said that a tender Conscience was an unmanly thing; and that for a man to watch over his Words and Ways, so as to tie up himself from that hectoring liberty° that the brave *Spirits of the Times*° accustomed themselves unto, would make him the ridicule of the Times. He objected also, That but *few* of the *Mighty, Rich,* or *Wise,* were ever of my opinion; nor any of *them* neither, before they were persuaded to be fools, and to be of a voluntary fondness° to venture the Loss of all, for nobody else knows what. He moreover objected the base and low estate° and condition of those that were chiefly the Pilgrims of the times in which they lived; also their Ignorance, and want of understanding in all Natural Science.[58] Yea, he did hold me to it at that rate also, about a great many more things than here I relate; as that it was a shame to sit whining and mourning under a sermon, and a shame to come sighing and groaning home: That it was a shame° to ask my neighbour Forgiveness for petty faults, or to make Restitution where I have taken from any. He said also, That Religion made a man grow strange to the Great, because of a few Vices, (which he called by finer names) and made him own and respect the Base,° because of the same Religious Fraternity:° And is not this, said he, a Shame?

Chr. And what did you say to him?

Faith. Say! I could not tell what to say at first. Yea, he put me so to it, that my blood came up in my face; even this *Shame* fetched it up,° and had almost beat me quite off. But at last I began to consider, That that which is highly esteemed among Men, is had in abomination with God. And I thought

Margin notes:
1 Cor. 1. 26.
ch. 3. 18.
Phil. 3. 7. 8.
John 7. 48.

Luke 16. 15.

---

tie up himself from that hectoring liberty Prevent himself from indulging in riotous behavior; a "hector" is a bully; **Spirits of the Times** Libertinism was much in vogue during the Restoration, particularly at court; **fondness** Silliness; **low estate** The pilgrims are again identified as the poor; **shame . . . shame . . . shame** See Mark 8:38. Shame sees shame everywhere, but he is unaware that this is because of his own shameful nature; **the Base** Bunyan regards true Christianity as the ideology of the lower class; **Fraternity** Term commonly applied to dissenting congregations; **Shame fetched it up** Faithful blushes for shame.

again, this *Shame* tells me what *men* are; but it° tells me nothing what *God* or the *Word of God* is. And I thought moreover, That at the Day of Doom we shall not be doomed to Death or Life, according to the hectoring spirits of the world, but according to the Wisdom and Law of the Highest. Therefore, thought I, what God says, is best, though all the men in the world are against it: Seeing then that God prefers his Religion; seeing God prefers a tender Conscience; seeing they that make themselves fools for the Kingdom of Heaven,° are wisest; and that the poor man that loveth Christ, is richer than the greatest man in the world that hates him; *Shame*, depart, thou art an Enemy to my Salvation; shall I entertain thee against my Sovereign Lord? How then shall I look him in the Face at his Coming? Should I now be *ashamed* of his Ways and Servants, how can I expect the   Mar. 8. 38. blessing? But indeed this *Shame* was a bold villain: I could scarce shake him out of my company: Yea, he would be haunting of me, and continually whispering me in the ear, with some one or other of the Infirmities that attend Religion; but at last I told him, it was but in vain to attempt further in this business; for those things that he disdained, in those did I see most Glory: And so at last I got past this importunate° one. And when I had shaken him off, then I began to sing:

> *The Tryals that those men do meet withal,*
> *That are obedient to the Heavenly Call,*
> *Are manifold and suited to the Flesh,*
> *And come, and come, and come again afresh;*
> *That now, or some time else, we by them may*
> *Be taken, overcome, and cast away.*
> *O let the Pilgrims, let the Pilgrims then*
> *Be vigilant, and quit° themselves like Men.*

---

it Faithful now perceives shame as one of his own abstract qualities, no longer as a personified character; **fools for the Kingdom of Heaven** Rejecting worldly wisdom; **importunate** Demanding; **quit** Acquit.

Chr. I am glad, my Brother, that thou didst withstand this villain so bravely; for of all, as thou sayest, I think he has the wrong name; for he is so bold as to follow us in the streets, and to attempt to put us to shame before all men, that is, to make us ashamed of that which is Good; but if he was not himself audacious, he would never attempt to do as he does; but let us still resist him; for notwithstanding all his bravados, he promoteth the Fool, and none else. The Wise shall inherit Glory, said *Solomon;* but Shame shall be the promotion of Fools.

Prov. 3. 35.

Faith. I think we must cry to Him for help against *Shame,* that would have us be valiant for Truth upon the earth.

Chr. You say true: But did you meet nobody else in that Valley?

Faith. No not I; for I had Sun-shine all the rest of the Way through that,° and also through the Valley of the Shadow of Death.

Chr. It was well for you; I am sure, it fared far otherwise with me; I had for a long season, as soon almost as I entered into that Valley, a dreadful Combat with that foul Fiend *Apollyon;* yea, I thought verily he would have killed me, especially when he got me down, and crushed me under him, as if he would have crushed me to pieces. For as he threw me, my Sword flew out of my hand; nay, he told me, he was *sure of me:* but I cried to God, and he heard me, and delivered me out of all my troubles. Then I entered into the Valley of the *Shadow of Death*, and had no Light for almost half the Way through it. I thought I should have been killed there over and over; but at last Day brake, and the Sun rose, and I went through that which was behind with far more ease and quiet.

Moreover I saw in my dream, that as they went on, *Faithful*, as he chanced to look on one side, saw a man whose name was *Talkative*,[59] walking at a distance besides them (for in this place there was room enough for them all to walk.)

---

through that That is, through that day.

He was a tall man,° and something more comely at a dis-   Talkative
tance, than at hand: To this man *Faithful* addressed himself   *described.*
in this manner.

Faith. Friend, Whither away? are you going to the Heavenly Country?

Talk. I *am* going to that same Place.

Faith. That is well; then I hope we may have your good
company?

Talk. With a very good will will I be your Companion.

Faith. Come on then, and let us go together, and let us   Faithful *and*
spend our time in discoursing of things that are profitable.   Talkative
enter into
Talk. To talk of things that are good, to me is very accept-   *discourse.*
able, with you, or with any other; and I am glad that I have
met with those that incline to so good a work: For to speak the
truth, there are but few that care thus to spend their time (as
they are in their Travels) but choose much rather to be speak-   Talkative's
ing of things to no profit; and this hath been a Trouble to me.   *dislike of his*
discourse.
Faith. That is indeed a thing to be lamented; for what thing
so worthy of the use of the tongue and mouth of men on
Earth, as are the things of the God of Heaven?

Talk. I like you wonderful well; for your sayings are full of
conviction; and I will add, What thing is so pleasant, and
what so profitable, as to talk of the Things of God?

What things so pleasant? (that is, if a man hath any delight
in things that are wonderful) for instance: If a man doth delight to talk of the History, or the Mystery of things; or if a
man doth love to talk of Miracles, Wonders, or Signs, where
shall he find things recorded so delightful, and so sweetly
penned, as in the Holy Scripture?

Faith. That's true; but to be profited by such things in our   Talkative's
talk, should be that which we design.   *fine discourse.*

Talk. That is it that I said; for to talk of such things is most
profitable; for by so doing, a man may get Knowledge of
many things; as of the vanity of Earthly things, and the ben-

---

a **tall man** A rare physical description of a Bunyan character. In *The Life and
Death of Mr. Badman* (1680) the title character is called "tall, and fair" (1988
ed., p. 66).

efit of things Above: (Thus in general) but more particularly; by this a man may learn the necessity of the New Birth; the insufficiency of our Works; the need of Christ's righteousness, &c. Besides, by this a man may learn what it is to repent, to believe, to pray, to suffer, or the like: By this also, a Man may learn what are the great Promises and consolations of the Gospel, to his own comfort. Farther, by this a Man may learn to refute false opinions, to vindicate the Truth, and also to instruct the Ignorant.

Faith. All this is true, and glad am I to hear these things from you.

Talk. Alas! the want of this is the cause that so few understand the need of Faith, and the necessity of a work of Grace in their soul, in order to Eternal Life; but ignorantly live in the works of the Law, by which a man can by no means obtain the Kingdom of Heaven.

Faith. But, by your leave, Heavenly knowledge of these is the Gift of God; no man attaineth to them by human industry, or only by the talk of them.°

*O brave
Talkative.*

Talk. All this I know very well.° For a man can receive nothing, except it be given him from Heaven; all is of Grace, not of works: I could give you an hundred Scriptures for the confirmation of this.

Faith. Well then, said *Faithful,* what is that one thing that we shall at this time found our discourse upon?

*O brave
Talkative.*

Talk. What you will: I will talk of things Heavenly, or things Earthly; things Moral, or things Evangelical; things Sacred, or things Prophane; things past, or things to come; things foreign, or things at home; things more essential, or things circumstantial; provided that all be done to our Profit.

*Faithful
beguiled by
Talkative.*

Faith. Now did *Faithful* begin to wonder; and stepping to *Christian,* (for he walked all this while by himself) he said to

---

But by your leave . . . by the talk of them This is Bunyan's argument against the Quakers; they deny man's utter sinfulness and thus obviate the need for imputed grace; **All this I know very well** Talkative's theology is unimpeachable.

him, (but softly,) What a brave Companion have we got? Surely this man will make a very excellent Pilgrim.

Chr. At this *Christian* modestly smiled, and said, This man, with whom you are so taken, will beguile, with this Tongue of his, twenty of them that know him not.

Faith. Do you know him then?

Chr. Know him! Yes, better than he knows himself.°

Faith. Pray what is he?

Chr. His name is *Talkative;* he dwelleth in our town; I wonder that you should be a stranger to him, only I consider that our Town is large.

Faith. Whose son is he? And whereabout doth he dwell?

Chr. He is the son of one *Say-well*, he dwelt in *Prating-Row;*° and he is known of all that are acquainted with him, by the name of *Talkative* in *Prating-Row;* and notwithstanding his fine tongue, he is but a sorry fellow.

Faith. Well, he seems to be a very pretty° man.

Chr. That is, to them that have not a thorough acquaintance with him; for he is best abroad, near home he is ugly enough: Your saying that he is a *pretty man*, brings to my mind what I have observed in the work of the Painter, whose pictures shew best at a distance; but very near, more unpleasing.

Faith. But I am ready to think you do but *jest*, because you smiled.°

Chr. God forbid that I should *jest*, (though I smiled) in this matter, or that I should accuse any falsely; I will give you a further discovery of him: This man is for any company, and for any *talk;* as he *talketh now* with you, so will he talk when he is on the *ale-bench:*[60] And the more Drink he hath in his crown, the more of these things he hath in his mouth: Religion hath no place in his heart, or house, or conversation; all he hath lieth in his *tongue,* and his religion is to make a noise therewith.

Faith. Say you so! then am I in this man greatly deceived.

Christian *makes a discovery of* Talkative, *telling* Faithful *who he was.*

---

better than he knows himself Talkative is ignorant of his own allegorical significance, while Christian is distinguished by his ability to read the other characters as allegorical figures; **Prating-Row** To "prate" is to chatter nonsense; **pretty** Charming; **you smiled** Christian is amused at Faithful's ingenuousness.

Mat. 23.
1 Cor. 4. 20.
Talkative
*talks, but does
not.*

*His House is
empty of
Religion.*

*He is a Stain
to Religion.*
Rom. 2. 24.
25.

*The Proverb
that goes of
him.*

*Men shun to
deal with
him.*

Chr. Deceived! you may be sure of it: Remember the proverb, *They say, and do not; but the Kingdom of God is not in word, but in power.* He talketh of Prayer, of Repentance, of Faith, and of the New Birth; but he knows but only to *talk* of them. I have been in his Family, and have observed him both at home and abroad; and I know what I say of him is the truth. His house is as empty of religion, as the white of an egg is of savour.° There is there neither Prayer, nor sign of Repentance for Sin: Yea, the brute in his kind,° serves God far better than he. He is the very stain, reproach, and shame of Religion to all that know him; it can hardly have a good word in all that end of the Town where he dwells, through him. Thus, say the common people that know him, *A Saint abroad, and a Devil at home.* His poor family finds it so, he is such a churl;° such a railer at, and so unreasonable with his servants, that they neither know how to do for, or speak to him. Men that have any dealings with him, say, 'Tis better to deal with a *Turk*° than with him, for fairer dealing they shall have at their hands. This *Talkative* (if it be possible) will go beyond them, defraud, beguile, and over-reach them. Besides, he brings up his sons to follow his steps; and if he findeth in any of them *a foolish Timourousness*, (for so he calls the first appearance of a tender conscience) he calls them Fools and blockheads; and by no means will employ them in much, or speak to their commendations before others. For my part, I am of opinion, that he has, by his wicked Life, caused many to stumble and fall; and will be, if God prevent not, the ruin of many more.

Faith. Well, my brother, I am bound to believe you; not only because you say you know him, but also because, like a Christian, you make your reports of men. For I cannot think that you speak these things of Ill-will, but because it is even so as you say.

Chr. Had I known him no more than you, I might perhaps

---

savour Taste; **the brute in his kind** The animal in his nature; **churl** Boor, lout, yokel; **a Turk** Famed for their alleged cruelty, the Ottoman Turks were still a clear and present threat to Christendom in the mid-seventeenth century.

have thought of him as at the first you did: Yea, had he received this report at their hands only that are enemies to Religion,° I should have thought it had been a slander. (A lot that often falls from bad mens mouths, upon good mens names and professions:) But all these things, yea, and a great many more as bad, of my own knowledge, I can prove him guilty of. Besides, good men are ashamed of him; they can neither call him *brother* nor *friend;* The very naming of him among them, makes them blush, if they know him.

Faith. Well, I see that *saying* and *doing* are two things, and hereafter I shall better observe this distinction.

Chr. They are two things indeed, and are as diverse, as are the Soul and the Body; for as the Body without the Soul is but a dead carcass, so *saying*, if it be alone, is but a dead carcass also. The Soul of Religion is the Practick° part: *Pure Religion and undefiled, before God and the Father, is this, To visit the fatherless and widows in their affliction, and to keep himself unspotted from the World.* This *Talkative* is not aware of; he thinks that *hearing* and *saying* will make a good Christian; and thus he deceiveth his own soul. Hearing is but as the sowing of the seed: Talking is not sufficient to prove that fruit° is indeed in the Heart and Life; and let us assure ourselves, that at the day of Doom, men shall be judged according to their Fruit: It will not be said then, *Did you believe?* But were you *Doers*, or *Talkers* only? And accordingly shall they be judged. The end of the world is compared to our harvest; and you know men at harvest regard nothing but fruit. Not that any thing can be accepted, that is not of Faith; but I speak this to shew you how insignificant the profession of *Talkative* will be at that Day.

Faith. This brings to my mind that° of *Moses*, by which he described the beast that is clean. He is such an one that parteth the hoof, and cheweth the cud; not that parteth the *hoof* only, or that cheweth the *cud* only. The hare cheweth the cud, but yet is unclean; because he parteth not the hoof. And

The carcass of Religion.

Jam. 1. 27.
See ver. 23, 24, 25, 26.

See Matt. 13. *and* ch. 25.

Lev. 11.
Deut. 14.
Faithful *convinced of the badness of* Talkative.

---

enemies to religion Bunyan and the Ranters shared common enemies, but he did not consider his enemy's enemy to be his friend; **Practick** Practical; **fruit** Fruition of faith; result; **that** That saying.

this truly resembleth° *Talkative;* he cheweth the cud, he seeketh Knowledge, he cheweth upon the Word; but he divideth not the hoof, he parteth not with the Way of Sinners; but as the hare, he retaineth the foot of a dog or bear, and therefore is unclean.

Chr. You have spoken, for ought I know,° the true Gospel sense of those texts. And I will add another thing: *Paul* calleth some men, yea, and those great *Talkers* too, *Sounding Brass,* and *Tinkling Cymbals;* that is, as he expounds them in another place, *Things without life, giving sound.* Things without life, that is, without the true Faith and Grace of the Gospel; and consequently, things that shall never be placed in the Kingdom of Heaven among those that are the Children of Life: Though their *sound* by their *talk,* be as it were the tongue or voice of an Angel.

1 Cor. 13. 1, 2, 3. ch. 14. 7. Talkative like to things that sound without Life.

Faith. Well, I was not so fond of his company at first, but I am as sick of it now. What shall we do to be rid of him?

Chr. Take my advice, and do as I bid you, and you shall find that he will soon be sick of your company too, except° God shall touch his heart and turn it.

Faith. What would you have me to do?

Chr. Why, go to him, and enter into some serious discourse about the *Power of Religion;* and ask him plainly, (when he has approved of it, for that he will) whether this thing be set up in his Heart, House, or Conversation.

Faith. Then *Faithful* stept forward again, and said to *Talkative, Come, what chear? How is it now?*

Talk. Thank you, well; I thought we should have had a great deal of talk by this time.

Faith. Well, if you will, we will fall to it now; and since you left it with me to state the question, let it be this: How doth the Saving Grace of God discover itself, when it is in the Heart of Man?

Talkative's false discovery of a Work of Grace.

Talk. I perceive then that our talk must be about the *Power of Things:* Well, 'tis a very good question, and I shall be willing to answer you. And take my answer in brief, thus: *First,*

---

resembleth Faithful understands Talkative through biblical typology; **for ought I know** As far as I can see; **except** Unless.

Where the Grace of God is in the heart, it causeth there a great Outcry against Sin. *Secondly,*

Faith. Nay, hold, let us consider of one at once: I think you should rather say, It shews itself by inclining the soul to abhor its Sin.°

Talk. Why, what difference is there between crying out against, and abhorring of Sin?

Faith. Oh! a great deal: A man may cry out against Sin, of Policy,° but he cannot abhor it but by virtue of a godly antipathy against it: I have heard many cry out against Sin in the Pulpit, who yet can abide it well enough in the Heart, House, and Conversation. *Joseph's* Mistress cried out with a loud voice, as if she had been very holy; but she would willingly, notwithstanding that, have committed uncleanness° with him. Some cry out against Sin, even as the mother cries out against her child in her lap, when she calleth it slut° and naughty girl, and then falls to hugging and kissing it. *The Crying out against Sin, no sign of Grace.*

Gen. 39. 15.

Talk. You lie at the Catch,[61] I perceive.

Faith. No, not I, I am only for setting things right. But what is the second thing whereby you would prove a discovery of a Work of Grace in the heart?

Talk. Great Knowledge of *Gospel-Mysteries.*

Faith. This sign should have been first; but first or last, it is also false; for Knowledge, great knowledge may be obtained in the mysteries of the Gospel, and yet no Work of Grace in the Soul. Yea, if a man have all Knowledge, he may yet be nothing; and so consequently be no child of God. When Christ said, *Do you know all these things?* And the disciples had answered, Yes: He added, *Blessed are ye, if ye do them.* He doth not lay the blessing in the *knowing* of them, but in the *doing* of them. For there is a knowledge that is not attended with doing: *He that knoweth his Master's will, and doth it not.* *Great Knowledge no sign of Grace.*

1 Cor. 13.

---

inclining the soul to abhor its Sin Talkative believes he can separate his sin from himself and "cry out against it" as something outside him. Faithful believes that his soul is irremediably sinful and that he must learn to "abhor" it; **of Policy** Out of self-interested calculation; **uncleanness** Adultery; **slut** Dirty, not necessarily in the sexual sense.

A man may know like an Angel, and yet be no Christian; therefore your sign is not true. Indeed, to *know*, is a thing that pleaseth Talkers and Boasters; but to *do*, is that which pleaseth God. Not that the heart can be good without knowledge; for without that, the heart is naught. There is therefore

Knowledge and knowledge.

knowledge and knowledge; knowledge that resteth in the bare speculation of things,° and knowledge that is accompanied with the grace of Faith and Love; which puts a man upon doing° even the Will of God from the Heart: The first of these will serve the *Talker*; but without the other, the true Christian

True Knowledge attended with Endeavours.

is not content. *Give me Understanding, and I shall keep thy Law; yea, I shall observe it with my whole Heart.* Psal. cxix. 34.

Talk. You lie at the Catch again; this is not for edification.

Faith. Well, if you please, propound another sign how this work of Grace discovereth itself where it is.

Talk. Not I, for I see we shall not agree.

Faith. Well, if you will not, will you give me leave to do it?

Talk. You may use your liberty.

One good sign of Grace.
John 16. 8.
Rom. 7. 24.
John 16. 9.
Mark 6. 16.
Ps. 38. 18.
Jer. 31. 19.
Gal. 2. 16.
Acts 4. 12.
Matt. 5. 6.
Rev. 21. 6.

Faith. A Work of Grace in the Soul discovereth itself, either to him that hath it, or to standers by.

To him that hath it, *thus;* It gives him Conviction of Sin, especially the defilement of his Nature,° and the Sin of Unbelief,° (for the sake of which he is sure to be damned, if he findeth not Mercy at God's hand, by faith in Jesus Christ.) This fight and sense of things worketh in him sorrow and shame for Sin: He findeth, moreover, revealed in him the Saviour of the World, and the absolute necessity of closing with him for Life, at the which he findeth hungrings and thirstings after him; to which hungrings, *&c.* the Promise is made. Now according to the strength or weakness of his faith in his Saviour, so is his Joy and Peace, so is his love to Holiness, so are his desires to know him more, and also to serve him in this World. But though, I say, it discovereth itself thus unto him,

---

knowledge ... of things Empiricism, a mode of inquiry much in fashion after the Restoration; **puts a man upon doing** Makes a man do; **defilement of his Nature** Man is sinful by nature, in essence; **Sin of Unbelief** According to Bunyan no one is born a Christian, and the first step on the way to becoming one is the realization that one is not a Christian.

yet it is but seldom that he is able to conclude, that this is a
Work of Grace, because his Corruptions now, and his abused
Reason, make his mind to misjudge in this matter; therefore
in him that hath this Work, there is required a very sound
judgment, before he can with steadiness conclude that this is
a Work of Grace. To others it is thus discovered:

1. By an *experimental confession* of his *Faith in Christ.* 2. By
a Life answerable° to that confession, to wit, *a life of Holiness:*
heart-holiness, family-holiness, (if he hath a family,) and by
conversation-holiness in the world; which in the general teach-
eth him inwardly to abhor his Sin, and himself for that, in secret; to suppress it in his family, and to promote holiness in
the world; not by *talk* only, as an hypocrite or talkative person may do, but by a practical subjection in Faith and Love to
the Power of the Word: And now, Sir, as to this brief description of the Work of Grace, and also the discovery of it, if you
have ought to object, object; if not, then give me leave to propound to you a second question.

Talk. Nay, my part is not now to object, but to hear: Let me
therefore have your second question.

Faith. It is this: Do you experience the first part of the description of it? And doth your Life and Conversation testify the
same? Or standeth your Religion in *Word* or *Tongue,* and not in
Deed and *Truth?* Pray, if you incline to answer me in this, say no
more than you know the God above will say *Amen* to; and also
nothing but what your Conscience can justify you in: *For not he
that commandeth himself, is approved, but whom the Lord commendeth.* Besides, to say, I am thus, and thus, when my conversation, and all my neighbours, tell me I lie, is great wickedness.

Talk. Then *Talkative* at first began to blush; but recovering
himself, thus he replied: You come now to Experience, to
Conscience, and God; and to appeal to him for justification
of what is spoken: This kind of discourse I did not expect: nor
am I disposed to give an answer to such questions, because I
count not myself bound thereto, unless you take upon you to

Marginal notes:
Rom. 10. 10.
Phil. 1. 27.
Matt. 5. 9.
John 14. 15.
Ps. 50. 23.
Job 42. 5, 6.
Ezek. 20. 43.

*Another good
sign of Grace.*

Talkative *not
pleased with*
Faithful's
Question.

---

answerable Both "corresponding" and "responsible."

be a *Catechizer;* and though you should so do, yet I may refuse to make you my Judge: But I pray will you tell me why
you ask me such questions?

    Faith. Because I saw you forward° to talk, and because I
knew not that you had ought else but Notion.[62] Besides, to
tell you all the truth, I have heard of you, that you are a man
whose Religion lies in Talk, and that your Conversation gives

this your mouth-profession the lie.° They say you are a Spot°
among Christians; and that Religion fareth the worse for your
ungodly conversation; that some already have stumbled at
your wicked ways, and that more are in danger of being destroyed thereby; your Religion, and an ale-house, and covetousness, and uncleanness, and swearing, and lying, and
vain company-keeping, *&c.*° will stand together. The proverb
is true of you, which is said of a whore, to wit, *That she is a
Shame to all Women,* so you are a shame to all professors.

    Talk. Since you are ready to take up Reports, and to judge
so rashly as you do, I cannot but conclude you are some pee-
vish or melancholy man, not fit to be discoursed with, and so
Adieu.

    Chr. Then came up *Christian,* and said to his brother, I
told you how it would happen; your Words and his Lusts
could not agree: He had rather leave your Company, than re-

form his Life; but he is gone, as I said, let him go, the Loss is
no man's but his own; he has saved us the trouble of going
from him; for he continuing (as I suppose he will do) as he is,
he would have been but a Blot in our Company: Besides, the
Apostle says, *From such withdraw thyself.*

    Faith. But I am glad we had this little discourse with him;
it may happen that he will think of it again; however, I have
dealt plainly with him, and so am clear° of his blood, if he
perisheth.

    Chr. You did well to talk so plainly to him as you did; there

----

forward Eager; **Conversation . . . the lie** Your behavior contradicts what you
say; **a Spot** A blemish; **an ale-house . . . vain company-keeping** Note that
the list includes physical places, abstract concepts, and practical actions;
clear Innocent.

is but little of this faithful dealing with men now a days, and
that makes Religion so stink in the nostrils of many as it doth;
for they are these talkative fools, whose Religion is only in
word, and are debauched and vain in their conversation, that
(being so much admitted into the fellowship of the godly) do
puzzle the world, blemish Christianity, and grieve the sincere.
I wish that all men would deal with such, as you have done;
then should they either be made more conformable to Religion, or the company of Saints would be too hot for them.
Then did *Faithful* say,

> *How* Talkative *at first lifts up his plumes!*
> *How bravely doth he speak! How he presumes*
> *To drive down all before him! But so soon*
> *As* Faithful *talks of* Heart-work, *like the Moon*
> *That's past the Full, into the Wane he goes;*
> *And so will all, but he that* Heart-work *knows.*

Thus they went on talking° of what they had seen by the
Way, and so made that Way easy, which would otherwise, no
doubt, have been tedious to them; For now they went
through a Wilderness.

Now when they were got almost quite out of this Wilderness, *Faithful* chanced to cast his eye back, and espied one
coming after them, and he knew him. Oh! said *Faithful* to his
brother, who comes yonder? Then *Christian* looked, and said,
It is my good friend *Evangelist;* Ay, and my good friend too,
said *Faithful*, for 'twas he that set me the Way to the Gate.
Now was *Evangelist* come up unto them, and thus saluted
them:

Evangelist. Peace be with you, dearly beloved; and, Peace be
to your helpers.°

Chr. Welcome, welcome, my good *Evangelist;* the sight of

Evangelist overtakes them again.

---

they went on talking Having purged themselves of empty words, the pilgrims are free to carry on a genuinely profitable discourse; **your helpers** No
other pilgrims are present; the "helpers" are interior.

They are glad at the sight of him.

thy countenance brings to my remembrance thy ancient°
kindness and unwearied labouring for my Eternal Good.

Faith. And a thousand times Welcome, said good *Faithful;*
thy company, O sweet *Evangelist,* how desirable is it to us
poor Pilgrims!

Evan. Then, said *Evangelist,* How hath it fared with you,
my Friends, since the time of our last parting? What have you
met with, and how have you behaved yourselves?

Then *Christian* and *Faithful* told him of all things that had
happened to them in the Way; and how, and with what difficulty, they had arrived to that place.

His Exhortation to them.

Evan. Right glad am I, said *Evangelist,* not that you met
with Trials, but that you have been Victors, and for that you
have (notwithstanding many weaknesses) continued in the
way to this very day.

I say, right glad am I of this thing, and that for mine own
sake and yours; I have sowed, and you have reaped; and the
Day is coming, when both he that soweth, and they that
reaped, shall rejoice together; that is, if you hold out; for in
due time ye shall reap, if you faint not. The Crown is before
you, and it is an uncorruptible one; so run, that you may obtain it. Some there be that set out for this Crown, and after
they have gone far for it, another comes in and takes it from
them: Hold fast therefore that you have, let no man take your
Crown: You are not yet out of the gunshot° of the Devil: You
have not resisted unto Blood,° striving against Sin: Let the
Kingdom be always before you, and believe stedfastly concerning things that are invisible: Let nothing that is on this
side the other World get within you: And above all, look well
to your own Hearts and to the Lusts thereof, for they are deceitful above all things, and desperately wicked; set your faces
like a flint; you have all power in Heaven and Earth on your
side.

John 4. 36.
Gal. 6. 9.
1 Cor. 9. 24,
25, 26, 27.

Rev. 3. 11.

They do thank him for his Exhortation.

Chr. Then *Christian* thanked him for his exhortation; but

---

ancient Former; **gunshot** Range; **resisted unto Blood** Evangelist is preparing the pilgrims for their imminent ordeal at Vanity Fair.

told him withal, that they would have him speak farther to them for their help the rest of the Way; and the rather, for that they well knew that he was a Prophet, and could tell them of things that might happen unto them, and also how they might resist and overcome them. To which request *Faithful* also consented. So *Evangelist* began as followeth:

Evan. My Sons, you have heard in the words of the truth of the Gospel, that you must through many Tribulations enter into the Kingdom of Heaven.[63] And again, That in every City, Bonds and Afflictions abide in you;° and therefore you cannot expect that you should go long on your Pilgrimage without them, in some sort or other: You have found some thing of the truth of these Testimonies upon you already, and more will immediately follow; for now, as you see, you are almost out of this Wilderness, and therefore you will soon come into a Town that you will by and by see before you; and in that Town you will be hardly° beset with enemies, who will strain° hard but they will kill you; and be you sure that one or both of you must seal the testimony which you hold, with Blood; but be you faithful unto Death, and the King will give you a Crown of Life. He that shall die there, although his death will be unnatural,° and his pains perhaps great, he will yet have the better of his fellow; not only because he will be arrived at the Cœlestial City soonest, but because he will escape many miseries that the other will meet with in the rest of his Journey. But when you are come to the Town, and shall find fulfilled what I have here related, then remember your Friend, and quit yourselves like men, and commit the keeping of your souls to your God (in well-doing), as unto a Faithful Creator.

Then I saw in my dream, that when they were got out of the Wilderness, they presently saw a Town before them, and the name of that Town is *Vanity*, and at the Town there is a Fair kept, called *Vanity-Fair*:[64] It is kept all the year long; it beareth the name of *Vanity-Fair*, because the Town where it

He predicteth what troubles they shall meet with in Vanity Fair, *and encourageth them to Steadfastness.*

He whose lot it will be there to suffer, will have the better of his brother.

---

in you Note that the "Bonds and Afflictions" are internal; hardly Sorely; strain Try; unnatural Monstrous, both ethically and physically.

Isa. 40. 17.
Eccles. 1.
ch. 2. 11, 17.

is kept, *is lighter than Vanity;* and also, because all that is there sold, or that cometh thither, is *Vanity.* As is the saying of the Wise, *All that cometh is Vanity.*

This Fair is no new erected business, but a thing of ancient standing: I will shew you the original° of it.

The Antiquity of this Fair.

Almost five thousand years agone,° there were Pilgrims walking to the Cœlestial City, as these two honest persons are; and *Beelzebub, Apollyon,* and *Legion,*° with their companions, perceiving by the path that the Pilgrims made, that their Way to the City lay through this Town of *Vanity,* they contrived here to set up a Fair; a Fair, wherein should be sold *all Sorts of Vanity,* and that it should last all the year long; therefore, at this Fair, are all such merchandizes sold, as houses, lands, trades, places, honours, preferments, titles, countries, king-doms, lusts, pleasures; and delights of all sorts, as whores, bawds, wives, husbands, children, masters, servants, lives, blood, bodies, souls, silver, gold, pearls, precious stones, and what not?[65]

The merchandize of this Fair.

And moreover, At this Fair there is at all times to be seen jugglings, cheats, games, plays, fools, apes, knaves, and rogues, and that of every kind.

Here are to be seen too, and that for nothing, thefts, mur-ders, adulteries, false-swearers, and that of a blood-red colour.

And as in other fairs of less moment,° there are the several rows and streets under their proper names, where such and such wares are vended: So here likewise, you have the proper places, rows, streets, (*viz.* Countries and Kingdoms) where the wares of this Fair are soonest to be found: Here is the *Britain* row, the *French* row, the *Italian* row, the *Spanish* row, the *German* row, where several sorts of vanities are to be sold. But as in other fairs, some one commodity is as the chief of

The Streets of this Fair.

---

original Origin; **five thousand years agone** Keeble believes that "Bunyan refers . . . to the age after Noah's flood (2348 B.C.), the period of the patri-archs, the first pilgrims" (Keeble, ed., *The Pilgrim's Progress,* p. 273); **Legion** Mark 5:9 reads: "And he asked him, What is thy name? And he answered, saying, My name is Legion: for we are many" (KJV); **less moment** Less sig-nificance.

Behold *Vanity-Fair!* the Pilgrims there
Are chain'd, and ston'd beside:
Even so it was our *Lord* pass'd here,
And on Mount *Calvary* dy'd.

all the fair, so the ware of *Rome*° and her merchandize is greatly promoted in this Fair: Only our *English* nation, with some others, have taken a dislike thereat.

Now, as I said, the Way to the Cœlestial City lies just through this Town, where this lusty Fair is kept; and he that will go to the City, and yet not go through this Town, must needs go out of the World. The Prince of Princes himself, when here, went through this Town to his own Country, and that upon a *Fair-day* too: Yea, and as I think, it was *Beelzebub*, the Chief Lord of this Fair, that invited him to buy of his Vanities; yea, would have made him Lord of the Fair, would he but have done him reverence as he went through the Town. Yea, because he was such a Person of Honour, *Beelzebub* had him from street to street, and shewed him all the Kingdoms of the World in a little time,° that he might, (if possible) allure that Blessed One, to cheapen and buy° some of his Vanities; but he had no mind to the merchandize, and therefore left the Town, without laying out so much as one farthing upon these Vanities. This Fair, therefore, is an ancient thing, of long standing, and a very great Fair.

Now these Pilgrims, as I said, must needs go through this Fair. Well, so they did; but behold, even as they entered into the Fair, all the people in the Fair were moved, and the Town itself, as it were, in a hubbub about them; and that for several reasons: For,

First, The Pilgrims were cloathed with such kind of Raiment as was diverse from the Raiment of any that traded in that Fair. The people, therefore, of the Fair made a great Gazing upon them: Some said they were fools; some they were bedlams;[66] and some they were outlandish men.°

Secondly, And as they wondered at their apparel, so they did likewise at their speech; for few could understand what

Marginal notes:

1 Cor. 5. 10.
Christ went through this Fair.
Mat. 4. 8.
Luke 4. 5, 6, 7.

Christ bought nothing in this Fair.

The Pilgrims enter the Fair.

The Fair in a hubbub about them.

The First cause of the hubbub.

1 Cor. 2. 7. 8.

The second cause of the hubbub.

---

the ware of Rome Luther protested against the Papacy's commodification of salvation through the sale of indulgences and the sacraments; **Beelzebub . . . a little time** Bunyan refers to the devil's temptation of Jesus in the wilderness, when he offers Him power over the entire world; **cheapen and buy** If Jesus had bought Satan's commodities He would have cheapened Himself; **outlandish men** Foreigners, aliens.

they said; they naturally spoke the language of *Canaan;* but they that kept the Fair were the men of this World: So that from one end of the Fair to the other, they seemed barbarians° each to the other.

Thirdly, But that which did not a little amuse the merchandizers,° was, that these Pilgrims set very light by all their wares; they cared not so much as to look upon them; and if they called upon them to buy, they would put their fingers in their ears, and cry, *Turn away mine eyes from beholding Vanity;*[67] and look upwards, signifying, That their trade and traffick was in Heaven.

Third cause of the hubbub.

One chanced mockingly, beholding the carriages° of the men, to say unto them, *What will ye buy?* But they looking gravely upon him, said, *We buy the Truth.°* At that, there was an occasion taken to despise the men the more; some mocking, some taunting, some speaking reproachfully, and some calling upon others to smite them. At last things came to an hubbub, and great stir in the Fair, insomuch that all order was confounded.° Now was word presently brought to the Great One of the Fair,° who quickly came down and deputed some of his most trusty Friends to take these men into examination, about whom the Fair was almost overturned.° So the men were brought to examination; and they that sat upon them,° asked them, Whence they came, whither they went, and what they did there in such an unusual Garb? The men told them, That they were Pilgrims and Strangers in the World, and that they were going to their own country, which was the Heavenly *Jerusalem;* and that they had given none occasion to the men of the Town, nor yet to the merchandizers,

Fourth cause of the hubbub.

Prov. 23. 23.
They are mocked.

The Fair in a hubbub.

They are examined.

They tell who they are, and whence they came.
Heb. 11. 13, 14, 15, 16.

---

barbarians Uncivilized foreigners; **merchandizers** A stronger term than "merchants," meaning "those who make everything into merchandise"; **carriages** Demeanors; **We buy the Truth** The pilgrims are interested in the logos. The Greek word used in the New Testament for God's "Word," it is the true source of all value; **all order was confounded** The very presence of the pilgrims turns the world upside down; **the Great One of the Fair** Both Satan and King Charles II; **almost overturned** The pilgrims pose a threat to Vanity Fair by their very existence; **sat upon them** Sat in judgment upon them, but with a semi-comic suggestion of physical oppression.

thus to abuse° them, and to let° them in their Journey: Except it was for that, when one asked them what they would buy, they said, they would *buy the Truth*. But they that were appointed to examine them, did not believe them to be any other than Bedlams and Mad, or else such as came to all things into a confusion in the Fair. Therefore they took them and beat them, and besmeared them with dirt, and then put them into the Cage, that they might be made a Spectacle to all the men of the Fair. There therefore they lay for some time, and were made the objects of any man's Sport, or Malice, or Revenge; the Great One of the Fair laughing still at all that befell them: But, the men being patient, and not rendring railing for railing, but contrariwise blessing, and giving good words for bad, and kindness for injuries done; some men in the Fair that were more observing, and less prejudiced than the rest,° began to check and blame the baser sort for their continual abuses done by them to the men: They therefore in angry manner let fly at them again, counting them as bad as the men in the Cage, and telling them that they seemed Confederates, and should be made partakers of their misfortunes.[68] The other replied, that for ought they could see, the men were quiet and sober, and intended nobody any harm: And that there were many that traded in their Fair, that were more worthy to be put into the Cage, yea, and Pillory too, than were the men that they had abused. Thus, after divers° words had passed on both sides, (the men behaving themselves all the while very wisely and soberly before them) they fell to some blows among themselves, and did harm one to another. Then were these two poor men brought before their examiners again, and there charged as being guilty of the late hubbub that had been in the Fair. So they beat them pitifully, and hanged irons upon them, and led them in chains up and down the Fair, for an example and a terror to others, lest any

They are taken for Madmen.
[They are not believed. 1st Edit.]
They are put in the Cage.

Their behavior in the Cage.

The men of the Fair do fall out among themselves about these two men.

They are made the Authors of this disturbance.

They are led up and down the Fair in chains, for a terror to others.

---

abuse The term was often used to mean "commodify" or "make merchandise of"; **let** Hinder; **some men . . . the rest** Alludes to the diversions among the Anglicans as to how much toleration should be extended to dissenters; **divers** Various.

should further speak in their behalf, or join themselves unto them. But *Christian* and *Faithful* behaved themselves yet more wisely, and received the ignominy and shame that was cast upon them, with so much meekness and patience, that it won to their side (though but few in comparison of the rest) several of the men in the Fair. This put the other Party yet into a greater rage, insomuch that they concluded the death of these two men. Wherefore they threatned, that neither Cage nor irons should serve their turn, but that they should die for the abuse they had done, and for deluding the men of the Fair.

Some men of the Fair won over to them. Their adversaries resolve to kill them.

Then were they remanded to the Cage again, until further order should be taken with them. So they put them in, and made their feet fast in the stocks.

They are again put into the Cage, and after brought to Tryal.

Here also they called again to mind what they had heard from their faithful friend *Evangelist*, and were the more confirmed in their ways and sufferings, by what he told them would happen to them. They also now comforted each other, that whose Lot it was to suffer, even he should have the best on't; therefore each man secretly wished that he might have that preferment: But committing themselves to the All-wise dispose of Him that ruleth all things, with much content they abode in the condition in which they were, until they should be otherwise disposed of.

Then a convenient time being appointed, they brought them forth to their Tryal, in order to their condemnation. When the time was come, they were brought before their enemies, and arraigned. The Judge's name was Lord *Hate-Good*: Their indictment was one and the same in substance, though somewhat varying in form; the contents whereof was this:

That they were Enemies to, and Disturbers of their Trade: That they had made Commotions and Divisions in the Town, and had won a Party[69] to their own most dangerous Opinions, in contempt of the Law of their Prince.

Their Indictment.

Then *Faithful* began to answer, That he had only set himself against that, which had set itself against Him that is higher than the Highest.° And, said he, as for Disturbance, I

Faithful's answer for himself.

---

he had . . . Highest Not the pilgrims but the "Great One" is the true rebel, as he is in revolt against God. John Milton applied the same argument to both Satan and King Charles I.

make none, being myself a man of Peace; the parties that were won to us, were won by beholding our Truth and Innocence, and they are only turned from the worse to the better. And as to the King you talk of, since he is *Beelzebub*, the Enemy° of our Lord, I defy him and all his angels.

Then proclamation was made, That they that had ought to say for their Lord the King against the Prisoner at the Bar, should forthwith appear, and give in their evidence. So there came in three witnesses, to wit, *Envy, Superstition*, and *Pick-thank*:[70] They were then asked, if they knew the Prisoner at the Bar; and what they had to say for their Lord the King against him.

Envy begins.   Then stood forth *Envy*, and said to this effect: My Lord, I have known this man a long time, and will attest upon my oath before this honourable Bench, that he is——

Judge. Hold—Give him his Oath.

So they sware him: Then he said, My Lord, this man, notwithstanding his plausible name, is one of the vilest men in our Country; he neither regardeth Prince nor People, Law nor Custom: but doth all that he can to possess all men with certain of his disloyal notions, which he in the general calls *Principles of Faith and Holiness.* And in particular, I heard him once myself affirm, *That Christianity and the Customs of our town of Vanity, were diametrically opposite, and could not be reconciled.* By which saying, my Lord, he doth, at once, not only condemn all our laudable° doings, but *us* in the doing of them.

Judge. Then did the Judge say to him, Hast thou any more to say?

Envy. My Lord, I could say much more, only I would not be tedious to the Court. Yet if need be, when the other gentlemen have given in their evidence, rather than any thing shall be wanting that will dispatch him, I will enlarge my testimony against him. So he was bid stand by.

Beelzebub, the Enemy Identifies Beelzebub with Satan; **laudable** With a pun on Archbishop Laud, the much-hated leading prelate under Charles I; Laud was executed by parliament in 1645.

Then they called *Superstition*, and bid him look upon the
Prisoner: They also asked, what he could say for their Lord
the King against him? Then they sware him; so he began:

Super. My Lord, I have no great acquaintance with this
man, nor do I desire to have further knowledge of him; however, this I know, That he is a very pestilent fellow,° from
some discourse that the other day I had with him in this
Town; for then talking with him, I heard him say, That our
Religion was naught, and such by which a man could by no
means please God. Which saying of his, my Lord, your Lord-
ship very well knows what necessarily thence will follow, to
wit, *that we still do worship in vain, are yet in our Sins, and fi-
nally shall be damned:* And this is that which I have to say.

Then was *Pickthank* sworn, and bid say what he knew in
the behalf of their Lord the King, against the Prisoner at the
Bar.

Pick. My Lord and you gentlemen all; this fellow I have
known of a long time, and have heard him speak things that
ought not to be spoke; for he hath railed on our noble Prince
Beelzebub, and hath spoke contemptibly of his honourable
Friends, whose names are, the Lord *Old-Man*, the Lord *Carnal-
Delight*, the Lord *Luxurious*, the Lord *Desire of Vain-Glory*,
my old Lord *Leachery*, Sir *Having Greedy*, with all the rest of
our nobility;° and he hath said moreover, That if all men were
of his mind, if possible, there is not one of these noblemen
should have any longer a being in this Town. Besides, he hath
not been afraid to rail on you, my Lord, who are now appointed to be his Judge, calling you an ungodly Villain, with
many other such-like vilifying terms, with which he hath be-
spattered most of the gentry° of our Town.

Marginal notes: *Superstition follows.* *Pickthank's testimony.* *Sins are all Lord and great ones.*

---

a very pestilent fellow When Bunyan's wife appealed to the High Court, Justice Chester called her husband "a pestilent fellow" (*Grace Abounding to the
Chief of Sinners and A Relation of the Imprisonment of Mr. John Bunyan*, p.
107). The trial at Vanity Fair is patterned after Bunyan's own trial; **the Lord
Old-Man . . . all the rest of our nobility** Bunyan comes close to suggesting
that all aristocrats are evil; **gentry** These occupied a rank below the aristocrats, and whereas Christian attacks "all" the nobility, he limits his ire to
"most" of the gentry.

[*Runagate* 1st edit.]

When this *Pickthank* had told his tale, the Judge directed his speech to the Prisoner at the Bar, saying, Thou Renegade, Heretick, and Traitor, hast thou heard what these honest gentlemen have witnessed against thee?

Faith. May I speak a few words in my own defence?

Judge. Sirrah, sirrah,° thou deservest to live no longer, but to be slain immediately upon the place; yet that all men may see our Gentleness towards thee, let us see what thou hast to say.

Faithful's defence of himself.

Faith. 1. I say then, in answer to what Mr. *Envy* hath spoken, I never said ought but this, That what rule, or laws, or custom, or people, were flat against the Word of God, are diametrically opposite to Christianity. If I have said amiss in this, convince me of my error, and I am ready here before you to make my recantation.

2. As to the second, to wit, Mr. *Superstition*, and his charge against me, I said only this, That in the worship of God there is required a Divine Faith: but there can be no Divine Faith without a Divine Revelation° of the Will of God. Therefore, whatever is thrust into the worship of God, that is not agreeable to Divine Revelation, cannot be done but by an human Faith, which Faith will not profit to eternal Life.

3. As to what Mr. *Pickthank* hath said, I say (avoiding terms,° as that I am said to rail, and the like) that the Prince of this Town, with all the rablement, his attendants, by this gentleman named, are more fit for being in Hell, than in this Town and Country; *and so the Lord have Mercy upon me.*

The Judge's speech to the Jury.

Then the Judge called to the Jury (who all this while stood by to hear and observe) Gentlemen of the Jury, you see this man about whom so great an uproar hath been made in this Town: You have also heard what these worthy gentlemen have witnessed against him: Also you have heard his Reply and

---

Sirrah Derogatory term used by a social superior toward an inferior; **Revelation** Statement of the Protestant doctrine of *sola scriptura*: the idea that only what is revealed in the Bible, as opposed to the traditions of the church, is valid in religious practice; **terms** Name-calling.

Now, *Faithful*, play the Man, speak for thy God;
Fear not the Wicked's malice, nor their rod:
Speak boldly, man, the Truth is on thy side;
Die for it, and to Life in triumph ride.

Confession: It lieth now in your breasts to hang him, or save his life; but yet I think meet to instruct you into our Law.

Exod. 1.
There was an act made in the days of *Pharaoh* the Great, servant to our Prince, that lest those of a contrary Religion should multiply, and grow too strong for him, their males should be thrown into the river. There was also an act made in the days
Dan. 3.
of *Nebuchadnezzar* the Great, another of his servants, that whoever would not fall down and worship his Golden Image,[71] should be thrown into a Fiery Furnace. There was also an act made in the days of *Darius*,° That whoso for some time called
Dan. 6.
upon any God but him, should be cast into the Lions Den. Now the substance of these Laws this Rebel has broken, not only in thought (which is not to be borne) but also in word and deed; which must therefore needs be intolerable.

For that of *Pharaoh*, his Law was made upon a supposition, to prevent mischief, no Crime being yet apparent; but here is a Crime apparent. For the second and third, you see he disputeth against our Religion; and for the Treason he hath confessed, he deserveth to die the Death.

Then went the Jury out, whose names were Mr. *Blind-man*,
The Jury and their names.
Mr. *No-good*, Mr. *Malice*, Mr. *Love-lust*, Mr. *Live-loose*, Mr. *Heady*, Mr. *High-mind*, Mr. *Enmity*, Mr. *Lyer*, Mr. *Cruelty*, Mr. *Hate-light*, and Mr. *Implacable*; who every one gave in his private verdict against him among themselves, and afterwards unanimously concluded to bring him in Guilty, before the Judge. And first among themselves, Mr. *Blind-man* the fore-
Every one's private Verdict.
man said, I see clearly° that this man is an Heretick. Then said Mr. *No-good*, Away with such a fellow from the earth. Ay, said Mr. *Malice*, for I hate the very looks of him. Then said Mr. *Love-lust*, I could never endure him. Nor I, said Mr. *Live-loose*, for he would always be condemning my Way. Hang him, hang him, said Mr. *Heady*. A sorry Scrub,° said Mr. *High-mind*. My heart riseth against him, said Mr. *Enmity*. He is a Rogue, said Mr. *Lyer*. Hanging is too good for him, said Mr. *Cruelty*. Let's

---

Darius Ruler of Persia mentioned in the book of Daniel; **I see clearly** Blind-man reveals his allegorical significance in the act of denying it; he is blind to his own nature; **Scrub** Stunted tree—hence, an insignificant person.

BRAVE *FAITHFUL*! BRAVELY DONE IN WORD AND DEED!
JUDGE, WITNESSES, AND JURY HAVE, INSTEAD
OF OVERCOMING THEE, BUT SHEWN THEIR RAGE,
WHEN THEY ARE DEAD, THOU'LT LIVE, FROM AGE TO AGE.

dispatch him out of the way, said Mr. *Hate-light*. Then said

They conclude to bring him in Guilty of Death.

Mr. *Implacable*, Might I have all the World given me, I could not be reconciled to him, therefore let us forthwith bring him in Guilty of Death. And so they did; therefore he was presently condemned to be had from the place where he was, to the place from whence he came, and there to be put to the most cruel Death that could be invented.

The cruel death of Faithful.

They therefore brought him out, to do with him according to their Law; and first they scourged him, then they buffeted him, then they lanced his flesh with knives: after that they stoned him with stones, then pricked him with their swords; and last of all, they burnt him to ashes at the Stake. Thus came *Faithful* to his end.

Chariot and horses take away Faithful.

Now I saw, that there stood behind the multitude a Chariot and a couple of horses waiting for *Faithful*, who (so soon as his adversaries had dispatched him) was taken up into it, and straitway was carried up through the clouds with Sound of Trumpet, the nearest way to the Cœlestial Gate. But as for

Christian still a Prisoner. [early edits. 'is still alive.']

Christian, he had some respite, and was remanded back to prison; so he there remained for a space: But he that over-rules all things, having the Power of their rage in his own Hand, so wrought it about, that *Christian* for that time escaped them,[72] and went his way. And as he went he sang, saying:

The Song that Christian made of Faithful after his death.

> Well, Faithful, *thou hast faithfully profest*
> Unto thy Lord, *with Him thou shalt be blest;*
> When faithless ones, *with all their vain delights,*
> Are crying out under their hellish plights:
> Sing, Faithful, *sing, and let thy Name survive;*
> For tho' they kill'd thee, *thou art yet alive.*

Christian has another companion.

Now I saw in my dream, that *Christian* went not forth alone; for there was one whose name was *Hopeful*, (being made so by the beholding of *Christian* and *Faithful* in their words and behaviour, in their sufferings at the Fair)° who joined himself

---

Hopeful . . . Fair The commonplace that "the blood of the martyrs is the seed of the church" originated with African church father Tertullian (c.155–after 220 A.D.).

unto him, and entring into a brotherly covenant, told him, that he would be his companion. Thus one died to make testimony to the Truth, and another rises out of his ashes to be a companion with *Christian* in his Pilgrimage. This *Hopeful* also told *Christian*, that there were many more of the men in the Fair that would take their time, and follow after.

There are more of the men of the Fair will follow.

So I saw, that quickly after they were got out of the Fair, they overtook one that was going before them, whose name was *By-ends;*° so they said to him, What countryman, Sir? and how far go you this Way? He told them, that he came from the town of *Fair-speech*, and he was going to the Cœlestial City, (but told them not his name.)

They overtake By-ends.

From *Fair-speech*, said *Christian*, is there any good that lives there?

Prov. 26. 25.

By-ends. Yes, (said *By-ends*,) I hope.

Chr. Pray, Sir, what may I call you?

By-ends. I am a Stranger to you, and you to me. If you be going this Way, I shall be glad of your company: If not, I must be content.

By-ends loth to tell his name.

Chr. This town of *Fair-speech* (said *Christian*,) I have heard of it, and, as I remember, they say it's a wealthy place.°

By-ends. Yes, I will assure you that it is, and I have very many Rich Kindred there.

Chr. Pray, who are your kindred there, if a man may be so bold?

By-ends. Almost the whole Town: And in particular my Lord *Turn-about*,° my Lord *Time-server*, my Lord *Fair-speech*, (from whose ancestors that town first took its name:) Also Mr. *Smooth-man*,° Mr. *Facing-both-ways*, Mr. *Any-thing*, and

---

By-ends According to Keeble, "incidental or secondary considerations" (Keeble, ed., *The Pilgrim's Progress*, p. 273), but "self-interest" seems a better definition; **a wealthy place** By-Ends, who appears just after Christian has left Vanity Fair, stands for the pursuit of self-interest in the ostensible service of religion; **Lord Turn-about** The names of his "kindred" indicate that By-Ends is an opportunist Latitudinarian like Edward Fowler (see Introduction); **Mr. Smooth-man** Jacob tricked his blind father, Isaac, into bestowing his brother Esau's birthright on him by putting goat's hair on his arms; in reality, he was a "smooth man."

the parson of our parish, Mr. *Two-tongues*, was my mother's own brother by father's side: And, to tell you the truth, I am become a Gentleman of good quality, yet my great grandfather was but a waterman, looking one way and rowing another, and I got most of my estate by the same occupation.

Chr. Are you a married man?

The wife and kindred of By-ends

By-ends. Yes, and my wife is a very vertuous woman, the daughter of a vertuous woman; she was my Lady *Feigning's* daughter, therefore she came of a very honourable family, and is arrived to such a pitch of breeding, that she knows how to carry it to all, even to prince and peasant. 'Tis true, we

Where By-ends differs from others in Religion.

somewhat differ in Religion from those of the stricter sort, yet but in two small points: First, We never strive against Wind and Tide. Secondly, We are always most zealous when Religion goes in his Silver Slippers; we love much to walk with him in the street, if the Sun shines and the People applaud him.

Then *Christian* stept a little aside to his fellow *Hopeful*, saying, It runs in my mind that this is one *By-ends* of *Fair-speech;* and, if it be he, we have as very a Knave in our company as dwelleth in all these parts. Then said *Hopeful*, Ask him, methinks he should not be ashamed of his Name. So *Christian* came up with him again, and said, Sir, You talk as if you knew something more, than all the world doth; and, if I take not my mark amiss, I deem I have half a guess of you: Is not your name Mr. *By-ends* of *Fair-speech?*

By-ends. That is not my name, but indeed it is a nick-name that is given me by some that cannot abide me,[73] and I must be content to bear it as a Reproach, as other good men have borne theirs before me.

Chr. But did you never give an occasion to men to call you by this name?

How By-ends got his name.

By-ends. Never! never! The worst that ever I did to give them an occasion to give me this name, that I had always the Luck to jump in my judgment with the present Way of the Times, whatever it was, and my Chance was to get thereby; but if things are thus cast upon me, let me count them a blessing; but let not the malicious load me therefore with reproach.

Chr. I thought indeed that you were the man that I had heard of; and, to tell you what I think, I fear this name belongs to you more properly than you are willing we should think it doth.°

By-ends. Well, if you will thus imagine, I cannot help it: You shall find me a fair company-keeper, if you will still admit me your associate.

Chr. If you will go with us, you must go against Wind and Tide; the which, I perceive, is against your opinion: You must also own Religion in his Rags as well as when in his Silver Slippers; and stand by him too when bound in Irons, as well as when he walketh the streets with Applause.

By-ends. You must not impose, nor lord it over my faith; leave me to my Liberty, and let me go with you.

Chr. Not a Step further, unless you will do in what I propound, as we.

Then said *By-ends*, I shall never desert my old Principles, since they are harmless and profitable. If I may not go with you, I must do as I did before you overtook me, even go by myself, until some overtake me that will be glad of my company.

Now I saw in my dream, that *Christian* and *Hopeful* forsook him, and kept their distance before him; but one of them looking back, saw three men following Mr. *By-ends*, and behold, as they came up with him, he made them a very low congee;° and they also gave him a compliment. The mens names were Mr. *Hold-the-World*, Mr. *Money-love*, and Mr. *Save-all*; men that Mr. *By-ends* had formerly been acquainted with; for in their minority they were school-fellows, and taught by one Mr. *Gripe-man*,° a school-master in *Love-gain*, which is a market-town in the county of *Coveting*, in the north.[74] This School-master taught them the Art of Getting,°

He desires to keep company with Christian.

By-ends and Christian part.

He has new companions.

I fear this name ... doth Christian is able to recognize the allegorical essence behind appearances; **congee** Bow; **Gripe-man** To "gripe" was to grab or clutch; the word was often used to mean oppressive covetousness, as in the many contemporary references to "griping usury"; **the Art of Getting** The new science of "political economy," known to us as "economics," was fashionable after the Restoration.

either by violence, cozenage,[75] flattery, lying, or by putting on a guise of Religion; and these four gentlemen had attained much of the Art of their Master, so that they could each of them have kept such a school themselves.

Well, when they had, as I said, thus saluted each other, Mr. *Money-love* said to Mr. *By-ends*, Who are they upon the road before us? For *Christian* and *Hopeful* were yet within view.

By-end's character of the Pilgrims.

By-ends. They are a couple of far country-men, that *after their mode* are going on Pilgrimage.

Money-love. Alas! why did they not stay, that we might have had their good company; for they, and we, and you, Sir, I hope, are all going on Pilgrimage?

By-ends. We are so, indeed; but the men before us are so rigid, and love so much their own notions, and do also so lightly esteem the opinions of others, that let a man be never so godly, yet if he jumps not with them in all things, they thrust him quite out of their company.

Mr. *Save-all.* That's bad; but we read of some that are *righteous over-much*, and such mens Rigidness prevails with them to judge and condemn all but themselves; but I pray *what*, and *how many* were the things wherein you differed?

By-ends. Why they, after their head-strong manner, conclude that it is their Duty to rush on their journey all weathers, and I am for waiting for Wind and Tide. They are for hazarding all for God at a clap, and I am for taking all advantages to secure my Life and Estate. They are for holding their notions, though all other men be against them; but I am for Religion, in what, and so far as the Times and my safety will bear it. They are for Religion when in Rags and Contempt, but I am for him when he walks in his Golden Slippers in the sunshine, and with Applause.

Mr. *Hold-the-World.* Ay, and hold you there still, good Mr. *By-ends;* for, for my part, I can count him but a Fool, that having the Liberty to keep what he has, shall be so unwise as to lose it. Let us be wise *as Serpents;*[76] it's best to make hay when the Sun shines; you see how the Bee lieth still all winter, and bestirs her only when she can have Profit with Pleasure. God sends sometimes rain, and sometimes sun-shine: If they be such fools to go through the first, yet let us be content to take fair weather along with us. For my part, I like that Religion best, that will stand with the security of God's good blessings unto us: For who can imagine, that is ruled by his Reason,° since God has bestowed upon us the good things of this Life, but that he would have us keep them for his Sake. *Abraham* and *Solomon* grew rich in Religion. And *Job* says, That a good man *shall lay up Gold as Dust.*[77] But he must not be such as the men before us, if they be as you have described them.

Mr. *Save-all.* I think that we are all agreed in this matter, and therefore there needs no more words about it.

Mr. *Money-love.* No, there needs no more words about this matter indeed; for he that believes neither Scripture nor Reason, (and you see we have both on our side) neither knows his own Liberty, nor seeks his own Safety.

Mr. *By-ends.* My brethren, we are, as you see, going all on Pilgrimage, and for our better diversion from things that are bad, give me leave to propound unto you this question:

Suppose a man, a Minister, or a Tradesman,° *&c.* should have an advantage lie before him, to get the good blessings of this life, yet so as that he can by no means come by them, except, in appearance at least, he becomes extraordinary zealous in some points of Religion that he meddled not with before; may he not use this Means to attain his End,° and yet be a right honest man?

Mr. *Money-love.* I see the bottom° of your question; and, with these gentlemen's good leave, I will endeavour to shape you an answer: And first, to speak to your question as it concerns a *Minister* himself. Suppose a Minister a worthy man, possess'd but of a very small benefice,° and has in his eye a

---

Reason Much beloved of the Latitudinarians, of whom Hold-the-World is representative; **a Minister, or a Tradesman** By-Ends blithely omits the distinction between the two lines of work; in the terminology of the day he is a "hireling," who views preaching the gospel as labor to be exchanged for money; **Means to attain his End** By-Ends betrays the significance of his name; **bottom** Import; **benefice** Living.

greater, more fat and plump by far; he has also now an opportunity of getting of it, yet so as by being more studious, by
preaching more frequently and zealously, and, because the
temper of the people requires it, by altering of some of his
Principles; for my part, I see no reason but a man may do this;
(provided he has a Call)° ay, and more a great deal besides,
and yet be an honest man. For why?

1. His desire of a greater benefice is lawful, (this cannot be
contradicted) since 'tis set before him by Providence; so then
he may get it if he can, making no question for Conscience
sake.

2. Besides, his desire after that benefice makes him more
studious, a more zealous Preacher, &c. and so makes him a
better man,[78] yea, makes him better improve his parts, which
is according to the Mind of God.

3. Now as for his complying with the temper of his people,
by dissenting, to serve them, some of his Principles, this argueth, 1. That he is of a Self-denying temper. 2. Of a sweet and
winning deportment. 3. And so more fit for the ministerial
function.

4. I conclude then, that a minister that changes a *small* for
a *great*, should not, for so doing, be judged as covetous; but
rather, since he is improved in his parts and industry hereby,
be counted as one that pursues his Call, and the opportunity
put into his hand to do Good.

And now to the second part of the question, which concerns the *Tradesman* you mentioned: Suppose such a one to
have but a poor employ in the world, but, by becoming Religious, he may mend his market,° perhaps get a rich wife, or
more and far better customers to his shop. For my part, I see
no reason but this may be lawfully done. For why?

1. To become *Religious* is a Vertue, by what Means soever a
man becomes so.

2. Nor is it unlawful to get a rich wife, or more custom to
my shop.

---

a **Call** An ironic qualification; **mend his market** Improve his market share.

3. Besides, the man that gets these by becoming religious, gets that which is good of them that are good, by becoming good himself; so then here is a good Wife, and good Customers, and good Gain, and all these by becoming Religious, which is good: Therefore, to become religious to get all these, is a good and profitable Design.

This answer thus made by this Mr. *Money-love* to Mr. *By-ends's* question, was highly applauded by them all; wherefore they concluded upon the whole, that it was most wholesome and advantageous. And because, as they thought, no man was able to contradict it, and because *Christian* and *Hopeful* were yet within call, they jointly agreed to assault them with the question as soon as they overtook them; and the rather,° because they had opposed Mr. *By-ends* before. So they called after them, and they stopt and stood still till they came up to them; but they concluded, as they went that not Mr. *By-ends*, but old Mr. *Hold-the-World* should propound the question to them, because, as they supposed, their answer to him would be without the remainder of that heat that was kindled betwixt Mr. *By-ends* and them, at their parting a little before.

So they came up to each other, and after a short salutation, Mr. *Hold-the-World* propounded the question to *Christian* and his fellow, and bid them to answer it if they could.

Chr. Then said *Christian*, Even a babe in Religion may answer ten thousand such questions. For, if it be unlawful to follow Christ for loaves, as it is, *John* 6. how much more abominable is it to make of him and Religion a Stalking-horse° to get and enjoy the World? Nor do we find any other than Heathens, Hypocrites, Devils, and Witches, that are of this opinion.

1. *Heathens;* for when *Hamor* and *Sechem* had a mind to the daughters and cattle of *Jacob*, and saw that there was no ways for them to come at them, but by becoming circum-

---

the rather Especially; Stalking-horse Facade to conceal true motives.

cised; they said to their companions, If every male of us be circumcised, as they are circumcised, shall not their cattle, and their substance, and every beast of theirs be ours? Their Daughters and their Cattle were that which they sought to obtain, and their Religion the stalking-horse they made use of to come at them. Read the whole story, *Gen.* 34. 20, 21, 22, 23.

2. The Hypocritical *Pharisees* were also of this Religion: Long Prayers were their Pretence; but to get widows houses was their Intent, and greater damnation was from God their Judgment, *Luke* 20. 46, 47.

3. *Judas* the Devil was also of this Religion; he was religious for the Bag,° that he might be possessed of what was therein; but he was lost, cast away, and the very Son of Perdition.

4. *Simon* the Witch° was of this Religion too; for he would have had the Holy Ghost, that he might have got Money therewith, and his sentence from *Peter's* mouth was according, *Acts* 8. 19, 20, 21, 22.

5. Neither will it out of my mind, but that that man that takes up Religion for the world, will throw away Religion for the World; for so surely as *Judas* designed° the world in becoming religious, so surely did he also sell religion and his Master for the same. To answer the question therefore affirmatively, as I perceive you have done; and to accept of, as authentick, such answer, is both Heathenish, Hypocritical, and Devilish; and your Reward will be according to your Works. Then they stood staring one upon another, but had not wherewith to answer *Christian*. *Hopeful* also approved of the soundness of *Christian's* answer, so there was a great Silence among them. Mr. *By-ends* and his company also staggered and kept behind, that *Christian* and *Hopeful* might out-go them. Then said *Christian* to his fellow, If these men cannot stand before the sentence of men, what will they do with the sentence of God? And if they are mute

---

the Bag "The bag in which Judas carried the 30 pieces of silver" (Sharrock, ed., *The Pilgrim's Progress*, p. 395); Simon the Witch A Samarian sorcerer who in Acts 8:18–19 tried to purchase the power of the Holy Spirit and gave his name to ecclesiastical corruption, or "simony"; designed Had designs on.

when dealt with by vessels of Clay, what will they do when they
shall be rebuked by the flames of a devouring Fire?

Then *Christian* and *Hopeful* out-went them again, and went
till they came at a delicate plain, called *Ease*, where they went
with much content; but that plain was but *narrow*, so they were
quickly got over it. Now at the further side of that plain was a
little hill called *Lucre*, and in that hill a *Silver-Mine*,[79] which
some of them that had formerly gone that way, because of the
rarity of it, had turned aside to see; but going too near the
brink of the pit, the ground, being deceitful under them, broke,
and they were slain: Some also had been maimed there, and
could not, to their Dying-day, be their own men° again.

The Ease that Pilgrims have, is but little in this life.

Lucre hill a dangerous hill.

Then I saw in my dream, that a little off the road, over
against the *Silver-Mine*, stood *Demas*° (gentleman-like)° to
call to passengers to come and see; who said to *Christian* and
his fellow, Ho! turn aside hither, and I will shew you a thing.

Demas at the hill Lucre.

He calls to Christian and Hopeful to come to him.

Chr. What thing so deserving, as to turn us out of the Way?

Demas. Here is a *Silver-Mine*, and some digging in it for
Treasure; if you will come, with a little pains, you may richly
provide for yourselves.

Hope. Then said *Hopeful*, Let us go see.

Chr. Not I, said *Christian*, I have heard of this place before
now, and how many have there been slain; and besides, that
treasure is a Snare to those that seek it; for it hindreth them
in their Pilgrimage.

Hopeful tempted to go, but Christian holds him back.

Then *Christian* called to *Demas*, saying, Is not the place
dangerous? Hath it not hindred many in their Pilgrimage?

Hos. 4. 18.

Demas. Not very dangerous,° except to those that are careless; but withal, he *blushed* as he spake.

Chr. Then said *Christian* to *Hopeful*, Let us not stir a Step;
but still keep on our Way.

---

their own men Independent, but implying that they are alienated from their
selves, having sold them; **Demas** Paul describes his desertion, "having loved
this present world," in 2 Timothy 4:10; **gentleman-like** Note Bunyan's constant insistence on the high social class of the bad characters; **Not very dangerous** A deliciously naturalistic qualification.

Hope. I will warrant you, when *By-ends* comes up, if he hath the same Invitation as we, he will turn in thither to see.

Chr. No doubt thereof, for his principles lead him that way, and a hundred to one but he dies there.

Demas. Then *Demas* called again, saying, But will you not come over and see?

Christian
roundeth up
Demas.
2 Tim. 4. 10.

Chr. Then *Christian* roundly° answered, saying, *Demas*, Thou art an Enemy to the right ways of the Lord of this Way, and hast been already condemned for thine own turning aside, by one of his Majesties Judges: And why seekest thou to bring us into the like condemnation? Besides, if we at all turn aside; our Lord the King will certainly hear thereof, and will there put us to shame, where we would stand with boldness before him.

Demas cried again, That he also was one of their Fraternity; and that if they would tarry a little, he also himself would walk with them.

Chr. Then said *Christian*, What is thy name?° Is it not the same by the which I have called thee?

Demas. Yes, my name is *Demas*, I am the son of *Abraham.*[80]

2 Kings 5. 20.
Matt. 26. 14,
15.
Ch. 27. 1, 2, 3,
5, 6.

Chr. I know you; *Gehazi*° was your great grandfather, and *Judas* your father, and you have trod their steps; it is but a devilish prank that thou usest: Thy father was hang'd for a Traitor, and thou deservest no better reward. Assure thyself, that when we come to the King, we will do him word of ° this thy behaviour. Thus they went their Way.

By-ends *goes
over to*
Demas.

By this time *By-ends* and his companions were come again within sight, and they at the first beck° went over to *Demas.* Now, whether they fell into the pit by looking over the brink thereof, or whether they went down to dig, or whether they were smothered in the bottom by the damps that commonly arise, of these things I am not certain; but this I observed, that they never were seen again in the Way. Then sang *Christian*:

---

roundly Bluntly; **What is thy name?** Christian knows that the name will reveal the nature; **Gehazi** A servant of Elisha, he begs a talent of silver from Namaan in 2 Kings 5:22; **do him word of** Tell him about; **beck** Call.

By-ends *and* Silver Demas *both agree;*
One calls, the other runs, that he may be
A Sharer in his Lucre, so these two
Take up in this World, and no further go.

Now I saw, that just on the other side of this plain, the Pilgrims came to a place where stood an old *Monument*, hard-by the highway side, at the sight of which they were both concerned, because of the strangeness of the form thereof, for it seemed to them as if it had been a *Woman* transformed into the shape of a Pillar; here therefore they stood looking and looking upon it, but could not for a time tell what they should make thereof: At last *Hopeful* espied written above upon the head thereof, a writing in an unusual hand; but he being no scholar, called to *Christian* (for he was learned) to see if he could pick out the meaning; so he came, and after a little laying of letters together, he found the same to be this, *Remember Lot's Wife*. So he read it to his fellow; after which they both concluded that that was the Pillar of Salt into which *Lot's* wife was turned, for her looking back with a *covetous heart*, while she was going from *Sodom*° for safety. Which sudden and amazing sight, gave them occasion of this discourse.

They see a strange Monument.

Gen 19. 26.

Chr. Ah, my brother! this is a seasonable° sight; it came opportunely to us after the invitation which *Demas* gave us to come over to view the hill *Lucre;* and had we gone over, as he desired us, and as thou wast inclined to do, my brother, we had, for ought I know, been made ourselves, like this Woman, a spectacle for those that shall come after, to behold.

Hope. I am sorry that I was so foolish, and am made to wonder that I am not now as *Lot's* wife; for wherein was the difference betwixt her Sin and mine? She only looked back, and I had a desire to go see; let Grace be adored, and let me be ashamed, that ever such a thing should be in mine heart.

Chr. Let us take notice of what we see here, for our help for time to come: *This* woman escaped one Judgment, for she fell

---

Sodom An emblem of all fleshly perversion, not necessarily sexual. Lot's wife's sin is covetousness, not lust; **seasonable** Timely.

not by the destruction of *Sodom;* yet she was destroyed by another; as we see, she is turned into a Pillar of Salt.

Hope. True, and she may be to us both *Caution*, and *Example; caution*, that we should shun her sin; or a sign of what Judgment will overtake such as shall not be prevented by this caution: So *Korah, Dathan*, and *Abiram*,° with the two hundred and fifty men that perished in their sin, did also become

Numb. 26. 9,
10.

a sign or *example* to beware. But above all, I muse° at one thing, to wit, how *Demas* and his fellows can stand so confidently yonder to look for that treasure, which this woman, but for looking behind her after, (for we read not that she stept one foot out of the Way) was turned into a Pillar of Salt; especially since the Judgment which overtook her did make her an example, within sight of where they are: For they cannot choose but see her, did they but lift up their eyes.

Chr. It is a thing to be wondred at, and it argueth that their heart is grown desperate in the case; and I cannot tell who to compare them to so fitly, as to them that pick pockets in the presence of the Judge, or that will cut purses under the Gal-

Gen. 13. 13.

lows. It is said of the men of *Sodom, that they were sinners exceedingly*, because they were sinners *before the Lord*, that is, in his Eyesight, and notwithstanding the Kindnesses that he had

Ver. 10.

shewed them; for the land of *Sodom* was now like the *Garden of Eden heretofore*. This therefore provoked him the more to Jealousy, and made their plague as hot as the fire of the Lord out of Heaven could make it. And it is most rationally to be concluded, That such, even such as these are, that shall sin in the Sight, yea, and that too in Despite° of such examples, that are set continually before them to caution them to the contrary, must be partakers of severest Judgments.

Hope. Doubtless thou hast said the truth; but what a Mercy is it, that neither thou, but especially I, am not made myself this example? This ministreth occasion to us to thank God, to fear before him, and always to remember *Lot's* wife.

Korah, Dathan, and Abiram Rebels against Moses, they were swallowed up by the earth and so "became a sign" (Numbers 26:10); **muse** Wonder; **Despite** Defiance.

I saw then, that they went on their way to a pleasant river;° *A River.* Psal. 65. 9. which *David* the King called *the river of God;* but *John, the river of the Water of Life.* Now their Way lay just upon the *Rev. 22. Ezek. 47.* bank of this River: Here therefore *Christian* and his companion walked with great delight; they drank also of the water of the River, which was pleasant and enlivening to their weary spirits. Besides, on the banks of this River, on either side, were green *Trees*, that bore all manner of fruit; and the leaves of the *Trees by the River.* trees were good for Medicine; with the fruit of these trees *The fruit and* they were also much delighted; and the leaves they eat to pre- *leaves of the* vent Surfeits,° and other diseases that are incident to° those *trees.* that heat their blood by Travels. On either side of the River was also a meadow, curiously beautified with lillies; and it *A Meadow in* was green all the year long. In this meadow they lay down and *which they lie* slept; for here they might *lie down safely.* When they awoke, *Psal. 23. 2.* they gathered again of the fruit of the trees, and drank again *Isa. 14. 30.* of the water of the River, and then lay down again to sleep. Thus they did several days and nights. Then they sang:

> *Behold ye, how these Crystal Streams do glide*
> *(To comfort Pilgrims) by the Highway side.*
> *The Meadows green, besides their fragrant smell,*
> *Yield dainties for them: And he that can tell*
> *What pleasant Fruit, yea, Leaves, these Trees do yield,*
> *Will soon sell all, that he may buy this Field.*

So when they were disposed to go on, (for they were not as yet at their Journey's end), they eat and drank, and departed.

Now I beheld in my dream, that they had not journied far, but the River and the Way for a time parted, at which they were not a little sorry, yet they durst not go out of the *Way.* Now the way from the River was rough, and their feet tender by reason of their travels. *So the Soul of the Pilgrims were* *Numb. 21. 4.*

---

a pleasant river The river has one meaning as an Old Testament type (Psalm 65:9) and another as a New Testament antitype (Revelation 22:1); see endnote 9 to part one; **Surfeits** Diseases caused by overeating; **incident to** Common among.

much discouraged, because of the way. Wherefore still as they went on, they wished for better Way. Now a little before them, there was on the Left Hand of the road a *Meadow*, and a Stile to go over into it, and that meadow is called *By-Path-Meadow*. Then said *Christian* to his fellow, If this meadow lieth along by our Wayside, let us go over into it. Then he went to the Stile to see, and behold a Path lay along by the Way on the other side of the fence. 'Tis according to my wish, said *Christian*, here is the easiest going;[81] come, good *Hopeful*, and let us go over.

Hope. But how if this Path should lead us out of the Way?

Chr. That's not likely, said the other; look, doth it not go along by the Wayside? So *Hopeful*, being persuaded by his fellow, went after him over the Stile. When they were gone over, and were got into the Path, they found it very easy for their feet; and withal, they looking before them, espied a man walking as they did, (and his name was *Vain Confidence*), so they called after him, and asked him, whither that Way led? He said, to the Cœlestial Gate: Look, said *Christian*, did not I tell you so? By this you may see we are right; so they followed, and he went before them. But behold, the Night came on, and it grew very dark; so that they that were behind lost the sight of him that went before.

He therefore that went before (*Vain-Confidence*° by name), not seeing the way before him, fell into a deep Pit, which was on purpose there made by the Prince of those grounds, to catch *vain-glorious* fools withal, and was dashed in pieces with his fall.

Now *Christian* and his fellow heard him fall. So they called to know the matter, but there was none to answer, only they heard a groaning. Then said *Hopeful*, Where are we now? Then was his fellow silent, as mistrusting that he had led him out of the Way; and now it began to rain, and thunder and lighten in a very dreadful manner; and the water rose amain.

Then *Hopeful* groaned in himself,° saying, *Oh that I had kept on my Way!*

Vain-Confidence Self-righteousness; **groaned in himself** His self is distinguished from his action.

Chr. Who could have thought that this Path should have led us out of the Way?

Hope. I was afraid on't at the very first, and therefore gave you that gentle caution. I would have spoke plainer, but that you are older than I.

Chr. Good brother, be not offended, I am sorry I have brought thee out of the way, and that I have put thee into such imminent Danger; pray, my brother, forgive me; I did not do it of an Evil Intent.

Hope. Be comforted, my brother, for I forgive thee; and believe too, that this shall be for our good.

Chr. I am glad I have with me a merciful brother: But we must not stand thus; let's try to go back again.

Hope. But, good brother, let me go before.

Chr. No, if you please, let me go first; that if there be any danger, I may be first therein, because by my means we are both gone out of the way.

Hope. No, said *Hopeful*, you shall not go first; for your mind being troubled, may lead you out of the Way again. Then for their Encouragement, they heard the Voice of one, saying, *Let thine Heart be towards the Highway; even the Way that thou wentest, turn again.* But by this time the Waters were greatly risen, by reason of which, the Way of going back was very dangerous. (Then I thought that it is easier going out of the way when we are in, than going in when we are out.) Yet they adventured to go back, but it was so dark, and the Flood was so high, that in their going back, they had like to have been drowned nine or ten times.

Neither could they, with all the skill they had, get again to the Stile that night. Wherefore at last, lighting° under a little shelter, they sat down there 'till the Day brake; but being weary, they fell asleep. Now there was, not far from the place where they lay, a castle, called *Doubting-Castle*, the owner whereof was *Giant Despair*, and it was in his grounds they now were sleeping; wherefore he getting up in the morning

Christian's Repentance for leading his brother out of the Way.

Jer. 31. 21.

They are in danger of drowning as they go back.

They sleep in the ground of Giant Despair.

---

lighting Alighting.

THE PILGRIMS NOW, TO GRATIFY THE FLESH,
WILL SEEK ITS *EASE;* BUT OH! HOW THEY AFRESH
DO THEREBY PLUNGE THEMSELVES NEW GRIEFS INTO!
WHO SEEK TO PLEASE THE FLESH, THEMSELVES UNDO.

early, and walking up and down in his fields,[82] caught *Christian* and *Hopeful* asleep in his grounds: Then with a *grim* and *surly* voice, he bid them awake, and asked them whence they were, and what they did in his grounds. They told him they were Pilgrims, and that they had lost their Way. Then said the *Giant*, You have this night trespassed on me, by trampling in and lying on my grounds, and therefore you must go along with me. So they were forced to go, because he was stronger than they. They also had but little to say, for they knew themselves in a Fault.° The *Giant* therefore drove them before him, and put them into his castle, in a very dark Dungeon,[83] nasty and stinking to the spirit of these two men: Here then they lay from *Wednesday* morning till *Saturday* night, without one bit of bread, or drop of drink, or Light, or any to ask how they did: They were therefore here in evil case,° and were far from Friends and Acquaintances. Now in this place *Christian* had double sorrow, because 'twas through his unadvised haste that they were brought into this distress.

He finds them in his ground, and carries them to Doubting-Castle.

The Grievousness of their Imprisonment. Psal. 88.

Now Giant *Despair* had a wife, and her name was *Diffidence:*° So when he was gone to bed, he told his wife what he had done, to wit, That he had taken a couple of Prisoners, and cast them into his *Dungeon*, for trespassing on his grounds. Then he asked her also, what he had best to do further to them. So she asked him what they were, whence they came, and whither they were bound? and he told her. Then she counselled him, that when he arose in the morning, he should beat them without any mercy: So when he arose, he getteth him a grievous crab-tree cudgel, and goes down into the *Dungeon* to them, and there first falls to rating° of them as if they were dogs, although they gave him never a word of distaste: Then he falls upon them, and beats them fearfully, in such sort, that they were not able to help themselves, or to turn them upon the floor. This done, he withdraws, and leaves them there to condole their misery, and to mourn under their distress: So all that day they spent the time in

On Thursday *Giant* Despair *beats his Prisoners.*

---

they knew themselves in a Fault That is, according to the property laws; **in evil case** In a bad way; **Diffidence** Distrust of God's mercy; **rating** Scolding.

nothing but sighs and bitter Lamentations.[84] The next night she talking with her husband about them further, and understanding that they were yet alive, did advise him to counsel them to make away themselves: So when morning was come, he goes to them in a surly manner, as before, and perceiving them to be very sore with the stripes that he had given them the day before, he told them, That since they were never like°

On Friday *Giant* Despair *counsels them to kill themselves.*

to come out of that place, their only way would be forthwith to make an end of themselves, either with Knife, Halter, or Poison: For why, said he, should you choose Life, seeing it is attended with so much Bitterness? But they desired him to let them go; with that he looked ugly upon them, and rushing to them had doubtless made an end of them himself, but that he

The Giant sometimes has Fits.

fell into one of his fits (for he sometimes in Sun-shine weather fell into fits)[85] and lost, for a time, the use of his hand: Wherefore he withdrew, and left them as before, to consider what to do. Then did the Prisoners consult between themselves, whether 'twas best to take his counsel or no; and thus they began to discourse:

Christian *begins to despair.* Job 7. 15.

Chr. Brother, said *Christian*, what shall we do? The life that we now live is miserable! For my part, I know not whether 'tis best to live thus, or to die out of hand. *My Soul chooseth Strangling rather than Life*, and the Grave is more easy for me than this Dungeon! Shall we be ruled by the Giant?

Hopeful *comforts him.*

Hope. Indeed our present condition is dreadful, and death would be far more welcome to me, than *thus* for ever to abide: But yet let us consider, the Lord of the Country to which we are going, hath said, Thou shalt do no Murder, no not to another man's person; much more then are we forbidden to take his counsel, to kill ourselves. Besides, he that kills another, can but commit murther upon his body: But for one to kill *himself*, is to kill Body and Soul at once. And moreover, my brother, thou talkest of ease in the grave, but hast thou forgotten the Hell, whither for certain the Murderers go? For no Murderer hath Eternal Life, &c. And let us consider again,

---

like Likely.

that all the Law is not in the hand of *Giant Despair;* others, so far as I can understand, have been taken by him, as well as we; and yet have escaped out of his hands. Who knows, but that God, who made the world, may cause that *Giant Despair* may die, or that, at some time or other, he may forget to lock us in; or but he may in short time have another of his fits before us, and may lose the use of his limbs? And if ever that should come to pass again, for my part I am resolved to pluck up the heart of a Man, and to try my utmost to get from under his hand. I was a fool that I did not try to do it before; but however, my brother, let's be patient, and endure a while, the time may come that may give us a happy release: But let us not be our own murderers. With these words *Hopeful* at present did moderate the mind of his brother; so they continued together (in the Dark) that day in their sad and doleful condition.

Well, towards evening the *Giant* goes down into the Dungeon again, to see if his prisoners had taken his counsel; but when he came there, he found them alive; and truly alive was all;° for now, what for want of bread and water, and by reason of the Wounds they received when he beat them, they could do little but breathe. But I say, he found them alive; at which he fell into a grievous rage, and told them, that seeing they had disobeyed his counsel, it should be worse with them than if they had never been born.

At this they trembled greatly, and I think that *Christian* fell into a Swoon;° but coming a little to himself again, they renewed their discourse about the *Giant's* counsel, and whether yet they had best take it or no. Now *Christian* again seemed to be for doing it, but *Hopeful* made his second reply as followeth.   *Christian still dejected.*

Hope. My Brother, said he, remembrest thou not, how valiant thou hast been heretofore? *Apollyon* could not crush thee, nor could all that thou didst hear, or see, or feel, in the valley of the Shadow of Death; what hardship, terror, and   Hopeful *comforts him again, by calling former things to remembrance.*

---

alive was all Barely alive; I think . . . Swoon The narrator is not omniscient.

amazement hast thou already gone through, and art thou now nothing but Fear?° Thou seest that I am in the Dungeon with thee, a far weaker man by nature than thou art; also this *Giant* has wounded me as well as thee, and hath also cut off the bread and water from my mouth, and with thee I mourn without the Light. But let's exercise a little more patience, remember how thou playedst the Man at *Vanity Fair*, and was neither afraid of the chain nor cage, nor yet of bloody Death; wherefore let us (at least to avoid the Shame that becomes not a Christian to be found in) bear up with patience as well as we can.

Now night being come again, and the *Giant* and his wife being in bed, she asked him concerning the prisoners, and if they had taken his counsel: To which he replyed; They are sturdy rogues,° they choose rather to bear all hardships, than to make away themselves. Then said she; Take them into the castle-yard to-morrow, and shew them the *Bones* and *Skulls* of those that thou hast already dispatch'd, and make them believe e're a week comes to an end, thou also wilt tear them in pieces, as thou hast done their fellows before them.

So when the morning was come, the *Giant* goes to them again, and takes them into the castle-yard, and shews them as his wife had bidden him: These, said he, were Pilgrims as you are, once, and they trespassed in my grounds, as you have done; and when I thought fit, I tore them in pieces, and so within ten days I will do you; go, get you down to your Den° again; and with that he beat them all the way thither. They lay *On* Saturday therefore all day on *Saturday* in a lamentable case, as before. *the Giant threatned,* Now, when night was come, and when Mrs. *Diffidence* and *that shortly he* her husband the *Giant* were got to bed, they began to renew *would pull* their discourse of their prisoners; and withal, the old *Giant* *them in* wondered that he could neither by his Blows nor Counsel *pieces.* bring them to an end. And with that his wife replied; I fear,

---

nothing but Fear Hopeful thinks allegorically; he does not ask whether Christian *feels* fear, but whether he *is* Fear; **sturdy rogues** Several commentators note that the English poor law provided for the relief of the incapacitated, but for the punishment of "sturdy beggars"; **Den** Prison.

said she, that they live in hope that some will come to relieve them, or that they have picklocks about them, by the means of which they hope to escape. And say'st thou so, my dear,° said the *Giant;* I will therefore search them in the morning.

Well, on *Saturday* about midnight they began to *pray*, and continued in Prayer till almost break of day.

Now, a little before it was Day, good *Christian*, as one half amazed, brake out in this passionate speech; What a Fool, quoth he, am I, thus to lie in a stinking dungeon, when I may as well walk at liberty? I have a key in my bosom, called *Promise*,[86] that will I am persuaded open any lock in *Doubting-Castle*. Then said *Hopeful*, That's good news, good brother, pluck it out of thy bosom and try.

A Key in Christian's bosom called Promise, opens any lock in Doubting-Castle.

Then *Christian* pulled it out of his bosom, and began to try at the dungeon door, whose bolt (as he turned the Key) gave back, and the door flew open with ease, and *Christian* and *Hopeful* both came out. Then he went to the outward door that leads into the *castle-yard*, and with his key opened that door also. After he went to the Iron Gate, for that must be opened too, but that lock went very hard, yet the Key did open it. Then they thrust open the gate to make their escape with speed; but that gate as it opened made such a creaking, that it waked *Giant Despair*, who hastily rising to pursue his prisoners, felt his limbs to fail, for his fits took him again, so that he could by no means go after them. Then they went on, and came to the King's Highway again, and so were safe, because they were out of his jurisdiction.

Now, when they were gone over the Stile, they began to contrive with themselves what they should do at that Stile, to prevent those that should come after from falling into the hands of *Giant Despair*. So they consented to erect there a pillar,[87] and to engrave upon the side thereof this sentence; 'Over this Stile is the way to *Doubting-Castle*, which is kept by *Giant Despair*, who despiseth the King of the Cœlestial Country, and seeks to destroy his holy Pilgrims.' Many therefore

A Pillar erected by Christian and his fellow.

---

my dear Despair and Diffidence are a happy couple, and as such virtually unique in Bunyan's fiction.

Mountains delectable they now ascend,
Where Shepherds be, which to them do commend
Alluring things, and things that Cautions are,
Pilgrims are steady kept, by Faith and Fear.

that followed after, read what was written, and escaped the danger. This done, they sang as follows:

> *Out of the Way we went, and then we found*
> *What 'twas to tread upon forbidden ground.*
> *And let them that come after have a care,*
> *Lest heedlessness makes them as we to fare,*
> *Lest they for trespassing, his Pris'ners are,*
> *Whose Castle's* Doubting, *and whose name's* Despair.

They went then till they came to the *Delectable Mountains;°* which mountains belong to the Lord of that Hill, of which we have spoken before; so they went up to the mountains, to behold the Gardens and Orchards, the Vineyards, and Fountains of water; where also they drank and washed themselves, and did freely eat of the vineyards. Now there was on the tops of those mountains, Shepherds° feeding their Flocks, and they stood by the Highway side. The Pilgrims therefore went to them, and leaning upon their staves, (as is common with weary Pilgrims, when they stand to talk with any by the way) they asked, *Whose Delectable Mountains are these? And whose be the Sheep that feed upon them?*

Shepherd. These mountains are *Emmanuel's Land,* and they are within sight of his City; and the Sheep also are his, and he laid down his Life for them.

Chr. Is this the Way to the Cœlestial City?

Shep. You are just in your Way.

Chr. How far is it thither?

Shep. Too far for any, but those that shall get thither indeed.

Chr. Is the Way safe or dangerous?

Shep. Safe for those for whom it is to be safe,[88] *but Transgressors shall fall therein.*

Chr. Is there in this place any Relief, for Pilgrims that are weary, and faint in the Way?

The Delectable Mountains. They are refreshed in the mountains.

Talk with the Shepherds.

John 10. 11.

Hos. 14. 9.

---

the Delectable Mountains See endnote 48 to part one; **Shepherds** Pastors.

Heb. 13. 1, 2.

Shep. The Lord of these mountains hath given us a Charge *not to be forgetful to entertain strangers*, therefore the Good of the place is even before you.

I saw also in my dream, That when the Shepherds perceived they were Way-fairing men, they also put questions to them, (to which they made answer as in other places) as, Whence came you? And how got you into the Way? And by what Means have you so persevered therein? For, but few of them that begin to come hither, do shew their face on these mountains. But when the Shepherds heard their answers, being pleased therewith, they looked very lovingly upon them, and said, *Welcome to the Delectable Mountains.*

The Shepherds welcome them. The names of the Shepherds.

The Shepherds, I say, whose names were *Knowledge, Experience, Watchful,* and *Sincere,* took them by the hand, and had them to their tents, and made them partake of that which was ready at present. They said, moreover, We would that you should stay here a while, to be acquainted with us, and yet more to solace yourselves with the good of these Delectable Mountains. They then told them, That they were content to stay; so they went to their Rest that night, because it was very late.

Then I saw in my dream, That in the morning the Shepherds called up *Christian* and *Hopeful* to walk with them upon the Mountains: So they went forth with them, and walked a while, having a pleasant prospect on every side. Then said the Shepherds one to another, Shall we shew these Pilgrims some

They are shewn wonders. The Mountain of Error.

Wonders?° So when they had concluded to do it, they had them first to the Top of an Hill, called *Error,* which was very steep on the furthest side, and bid them look down to the bottom. So *Christian* and *Hopeful* looked down, and saw at the bottom several men dashed all to pieces by a Fall that they had from the top. Then said *Christian,* What meaneth this? The Shepherds answered, Have you not heard of them that were

2 Tim. 2. 17, 18.

made to err, by hearkning to *Hymeneus* and *Philetus,*[89] as concerning the Faith of the Resurrection of the body? They answered, Yes. Then said the Shepherds, Those that you see lie

---

Wonders Signs.

dashed in pieces at the bottom of this mountain are they; and they have continued to this day unburied, (as you see) for an Example for others to take heed how they clamber too high, or how they come too near to the brink of this Mountain.

Then I saw that they had them to the top of another mountain, and the name of that is *Caution*, and bid them look afar off: Which when they did, they perceived, as they thought, several men walking up and down among the Tombs that were there: And they perceived that the men were blind, because they stumbled sometimes upon the Tombs, and because they could not get out from among them. Then said *Christian, What means this?* *Mount* Caution.

The Shepherds then answered, Did you not see a little below these mountains a Stile that led into a Meadow, on the left hand of this Way? They answered, Yes. Then said the Shepherds, From that Stile there goes a path that leads directly to *Doubting-Castle,* which is kept by Giant *Despair,* and these men (pointing to them among the Tombs) came once on Pilgrimage, as you do now, even till they came to that same Stile. And because the right Way was rough in that place, they chose to go out of it into that Meadow, and there were taken by Giant *Despair,* and cast into *Doubting-Castle;* where, after they had a while been kept in the Dungeon, he at last did put out their Eyes, and led them among those Tombs, where he has left them to wander to this very day, that the saying of the Wise Man° might be fulfilled, *He that wandereth out of the Way of* Prov. 21. 16. *Understanding, shall remain in the Congregation of the Dead.* Then *Christian* and *Hopeful* looked one upon another, with tears gushing out, but yet said nothing to the Shepherds.°

Then I saw in my dream, That the Shepherds had them to another place in a bottom,° where was a door in the side of an Hill, and they opened the door, and bid them look in: They looked in therefore, and saw that within it was very dark and

---

the Wise Man Solomon, reputed author of the book of Proverbs; **said nothing to the Shepherds** According to Offor, Bunyan's purpose here is "probably to guard pilgrims against the Popish doctrine of auricular confession" (*Works*, vol. 3, p. 145); **bottom** Valley.

smoky; they also thought that they heard there a rumbling noise, as of fire, and a Cry of some tormented, and that they smelt the scent of brimstone. Then said *Christian, What means this?* The Shepherds told them, This is a by-way to Hell, a way that Hypocrites° go in at; namely, such as sell their Birth-right with *Esau;*[90] such as sell their Master, with *Judas;* such as blaspheme the Gospel, with *Alexander;*° and that Lie and dissemble, with *Ananias* and *Sapphira*[91] his wife.

A By-way to Hell.

Then said *Hopeful* to the Shepherds, I perceive that these had on them, even every one, a shew° of Pilgrimage, as we have now, had they not?

Shep. Yes, and held it a long time too.

Hope. How far might they go on Pilgrimage in their day, since they notwithstanding were thus miserably cast away.

Shep. Some further, and some not so far as these Mountains.

Then said the Pilgrims one to another, *We had need cry to the* Strong *for strength.*

Shep. Ay, and you will have need to use it, when you have it, too.

By this time the Pilgrims had a desire to go forwards, and the Shepherds a desire they should; so they walked together towards the end of the mountains. Then said the Shepherds one to another, Let us here shew to the Pilgrims the Gates of the Cœlestial City, if they have skill to look through our *Perspective-Glass.*° The Pilgrims then lovingly accepted the motion: So they had them to the top of an high hill, called *Clear,* and gave them the Glass to look.

The Shepherds Perspective-Glass.

The hill Clear.

Then they essayed° to look, but the Remembrance of that last thing that the Shepherds had shewed them, made their hands shake; by means of which impediment, they could not look steadily through the Glass; yet they thought they saw

---

Hypocrites Greek for "actors," always used pejoratively in the New Testament; **Alexander** In 1 Timothy 1:20, Paul refers to him among former disciples "whom I have delivered unto Satan, that they may learn not to blaspheme" (KJV); **shew** Appearance; **Perspective-Glass** Telescope; **essayed** Attempted.

something like the Gate, and also some of the Glory of the   *The fruits of Servile Fear.*
place. Then they went away and sang this song:

> *Thus by the Shepherds Secrets are reveal'd,*
> *Which from all other men are kept conceal'd:*
> *Come to the Shepherds then, if you would see*
> *Things deep, Things hid, and that Mysterious be.*

When they were about to depart, one of the Shepherds
gave them a *Note of the Way*. Another of them bid them *Be-*   *A two-fold*
ware of the Flatterer. The third bid them *Take Heed that they*   *Caution.*
sleep not upon the Inchanted Ground. And the fourth bid them
God Speed. So I awoke from my Dream.[92]

And I slept, and dreamed again, and saw the same two Pilgrims going down the mountains along the highway towards
the City. Now a little below these mountains on the Left
Hand,° lieth the country of *Conceit;* from which country   *The country*
there comes into the Way in which the Pilgrims walked, a lit-   *of* Conceit,
                                                                 out of which
tle crooked lane. Here therefore, they met with a very brisk°   *came*
lad, that came out of that country; and his name was *Igno-*   *Ignorance.*
rance. So *Christian* asked him *From what Parts he came, and*
whither he was going.

Ignor. Sir, I was born in the country that lieth off there, a   Christian *and*
little on the Left Hand, and am going to the Cœlestial City.   Ignorance
                                                                 have some
Chr. But how do you think to get in at the Gate? for you   *talk together.*
may find some difficulty there.

Ignor. As other good people do,[93] said he.

Chr. But what have you to shew at that Gate, that the Gate
should be opened to you?

Ignor. I know my Lord's Will, and have been a good liver;   *The Grounds*
I pay every man his own; I Pray, Fast, pay Tithes, and give   *of* Ignorance's
                                                                 Hope.
Alms, and have left my country, for whither I am going.

---

brisk Lively, showy. Recalling, in *Grace Abounding*, his period of merely formal, hypocritical religion, Bunyan describes himself as "a brisk talker . . . in
the matters of religion" (p. 14).

Chr. But thou camest not in at the Wicket-Gate that is at the Head of this Way; thou camest in hither through that same crooked lane, and therefore I fear, however thou mayest think of thyself, when the reckoning-day shall come, thou wilt have laid to thy charge, that thou art a Thief and a Robber, instead of getting admittance into the City.

He telleth every one he is but a Fool.

Ignor. Gentlemen, ye be utter Strangers to me, I know you not; be content to follow the Religion of your country, and I will follow the Religion of mine.[94] I hope all will be well; and as for the Gate that you talk of, all the world knows that that is a great way off our Country; I cannot think that any men in all our parts, do so much as know the way to it; nor need they matter whether they do or no, since we have, as you see, a fine pleasant green lane, that comes down from our country the next way into it.

Prov. 26. 13.
Eccles. 10. 3.

How to carry it to a Fool.

When *Christian* saw that the man was wise in his own conceit,° he said to *Hopeful* whisperingly, *There is more hopes of a Fool than of him.* And said moreover, *When he that is a Fool walketh by the Way, his wisdom faileth him, and he saith to every one, that he is a Fool.* What, shall we talk further with him, or out-go him at present, and so leave him to think of what he hath heard already; and then stop again for him afterwards, and see if by Degrees we can do any good of him? Then said *Hopeful,*

> Let Ignorance *a little while now muse*
> *On what is said, and let him not refuse*
> *Good Counsel to embrace, lest he remain*
> *Still ignorant of what's the chiefest Gain.*
> *God saith, Those that no Understanding have,*
> *(Altho' he made them) them he will not save.*

Hope. He further added, It is not good, I think, to say all to him at once; let us pass him by, if you will, and talk to him anon,° *even as he is able to bear it.*

---

wise in his own conceit Ignorance is considered wise in his home town of Conceit; **anon** Immediately.

So they both went on, and *Ignorance* he came after. Now when they had passed him a little way, they entered into a very dark lane, where they met a man whom seven devils had bound with seven strong cords, and were carrying of him back to the door that they saw on the side of the Hill: Now good *Christian* began to tremble, and so did *Hopeful* his companion: Yet, as the devils led away the man, *Christian* looked to see if he knew him; and he thought it might be one *Turn-away* that dwelt in the town of *Apostasy*.° But he did not perfectly see his face; for he did hang his head like a thief that is found. But being gone past, *Hopeful* looked after him, and espied on his back a paper, with this inscription, *Wanton Professor*,° *and damnable Apostate*. Then said *Christian* to his fellow, Now I call to remembrance that which was told me, of a thing that happened to a good man hereabout. The name of the man was *Little-Faith*, but a good man, and he dwelt in the town of *Sincere*. The thing was this: At the entering in of this passage, there comes down from *Broad-way-gate*, a lane called *Dead-man's-lane*; so called, because of the Murders that are commonly done there: And this *Little-Faith* going on Pilgrimage, as we do now, chanced to sit down there and slept: Now there happened at that time to come down that *Lane* from *Broad-way-gate*, three sturdy Rogues, and their names were *Faint-heart, Mistrust, and Guilt*, (three brothers) and they espying *Little-Faith* where he was, came galloping up with speed: Now the good man was just awakened from his sleep, and was getting up to go on his Journey. So they came up all to him, and with threatning language bid him *stand*.° At this *Little-Faith* looked as white as a clout,° and had neither power to fight nor fly. Then said *Faint-Heart*, Deliver thy purse; but he making no haste to do it, (for he was loth to lose his Money)[95] *Mistrust* ran up to him, and thrusting his hand into his pocket, pull'd out thence a bag of silver. Then he cried out, Thieves, thieves.

Matt. 12. 45.
Prov. 5. 22.

The Destruction of one Turn-away.

Christian telleth his companion a story of Little-Faith.

Broad-way-gate. Dead-man's-lane.

Little-Faith robbed by Faint-Heart, Mistrust, and Guilt.

They got away his Silver and knocked him down.

Apostasy To commit apostasy—to turn away from true religion having once known it—is worse than ignorance; **Wanton Professor** Wayward religious man; **stand** Freeze, as in the highwayman's demand: "Stand and deliver"; **clout** Either "cloud" or "cloth."

With that *Guilt*, with a great club that was in his hand, struck *Little-Faith* on the head, and with that blow fell'd him flat to the ground; where he lay bleeding as one that would bleed to death. All this while, the Thieves stood by: But at last, they hearing that some were upon the road, and fearing lest it should be one *Great Grace*,° that dwells in the city of *Good-Confidence*, they betook themselves to their heels, and left this good man to shift° for himself. Now after a while, *Little-Faith* came to himself, and getting up, made shift° to scrabble on his Way. This was the story.

Hope. But did they take from him all that ever he had?

Chr. No: The place where his Jewels were, they never ran-sack'd; so those he kept still: But, as I was told, the good man was much afflicted for his loss; for the thieves got most of his spending-money.[96] That which they got not, (as I said) were Jewels; also he had a little odd money left, but scarce enough to bring him to his Journey's end; nay, (if I was not mis-informed,) he was forced to beg as he went, to keep himself alive; for his Jewels he might not sell:° But beg and do what he could, *he went* (as we say) *with many a hungry belly*, the most part of the rest of the Way.

Hope. But is it not a wonder they got not from him his Certificate,° by which he was to receive his admittance at the Cœlestial Gate?

Chr. 'No,' ('tis a wonder) but they got not that; though they missed it not through any good cunning of his: for he being dismay'd with their coming upon him, had neither power nor skill to hide any thing, so 'twas more by good Providence than by his Endeavour, that they miss'd of that good thing.

Hope. But it must needs be a Comfort to him, that they got not this Jewel from him.

Chr. It might have been great comfort to him, had he used it as he should: But they that told me the story, said, that he made but little use of it all the rest of the Way; and that because

Little-Faith lost not his best things.

1 Pet. 4. 18.

Little-Faith forced to beg to his Journey's end.

['No' only in 1st edit.]
He kept not his best things by his own Cunning.
2 Tim. 1. 14.
2 Pet. 2. 9.

Great Grace Even a little faith will be rewarded by God's freely given grace; **shift** Care; **made shift** Managed; **he might not sell** Faith can be neither earned nor lost by human effort, only granted by God; **his Certificate** Of election.

of the Dismay that he had in their taking away of his money: Indeed he forgot it a great part of the rest of his Journey; and besides when, at any time it came into his mind, and he began to be comforted therewith, then would fresh thoughts of his Loss come again upon him, and those thoughts would swallow up all.

Hope. Alas, poor man! This could not but be a great grief unto him! *He is pitied by both.*

Chr. Grief! Ay, a grief indeed. Would it not have been so to any of us, had we been used as he, to be robbed and wounded too, and that in a strange place, as he was? 'Tis a wonder he did not die with grief, poor heart; I was told that he scattered almost all the rest of the Way with nothing but doleful and bitter complaints: Telling also to all that overtook him, or that he overtook in the Way as he went, where he was robbed, and how; who they were that did it, and what he lost; how he was wounded, and that he hardly escaped with his life.

Hope. But 'tis a wonder that his Necessities did not put him upon *selling* or *pawning* some of his Jewels, that he might have wherewith to relieve himself in his Journey.

Chr. Thou talkest like one upon whose head is the Shell° to this very day: For What should he *Pawn* them? or to whom should he sell them? In all that country where he was robbed, his Jewels were not accounted of; nor did he want that Relief which could from thence be administered to him; besides, had his Jewels been missing at the Gate of the *Cœlestial City*, he had (and that he knew well enough) been excluded from an Inheritance there, and that would have been worse to him than the appearance and villany of ten thousand thieves. *Christian snubs his fellow for unadvised speaking.*

Hope. Why art thou so tart,° my brother; *Esau* sold his birth-right, and that for a mess of pottage, and that birth-right was his greatest Jewel; and if he, why might not *Little-Faith* do so too? *Heb. 12. 16.*

Chr. Esau did sell his birth-right indeed, and so do many *A discourse about Esau and Little-Faith.*

---

whose head is the Shell Hard-headed, stubborn; also hiding one's head like a snail, hence blind, and also extremely youthful and naive, like a baby bird emerging from the shell; **tart** Sharp.

besides, and by so doing exclude themselves from the chief blessing, as also that caitiff° did; but you must put a difference betwixt *Esau* and *Little-Faith*, and also betwixt their estates. *Esau's* birth-right was Typical,° but *Little-Faith's* Jewels were not so. *Esau's* belly was his God, but *Little-Faith's* belly

Esau *was ruled by his Lusts.*
Gen. 25. 32.

was not so. *Esau's* Want lay in his appetite, *Little-Faith's* did not so: Besides, *Esau* could see no further than to the fulfilling of his Lusts; *For I am at the point to die, said he, and what good will this birth-right do me?* But *Little-Faith*, though it was his lot to have but a *little faith*, was by his little faith° kept from such extravagancies, and made to see and prize his Jew-

Esau *never had Faith.*

els more, than to sell them as *Esau* did his birth-right. You read not any where that *Esau* had Faith, no, not so much as a little; therefore no marvel if where the Flesh only bears sway, (as it will in that man where no faith is to resist) if he sells his birth-right, and his Soul and all, and that to the Devil of Hell;° for it is with such, as it is with the ass, *who in her occa-*

Jer. 2. 24.

sions cannot be turned away. When their minds are set upon their lusts, they will have them, whatever they cost; but *Little-*

Little-Faith *could not live upon* Esau's *pottage.*

Faith was of another temper, his mind was on things Divine; his livelihood° was upon things that were Spiritual and from above; therefore, to what end should he that is of such a temper, sell his Jewels, (had there been any that would have bought them) to fill his mind with empty things? Will a man give a penny to fill his belly with Hay? or can you persuade

A comparison between the turtle-dove *and the* crow.

the *turtle-dove* to live upon carrion like the *crow?*° Though *faithless* ones can for carnal lusts, pawn, or mortgage, or sell what they have, and themselves outright to boot;[97] yet they that have Faith, *Saving faith*, though but a little of it, cannot do so. Here therefore, my brother, is thy mistake.

Hope. I acknowledge it; but yet your severe Reflexion had almost made me angry.

---

caitiff Rogue; **Typical** Symbolic; **by his little faith** The person is separated from his allegorical qualities; **the Devil of Hell** The Faust legend was a powerful, popular myth in seventeenth-century England; **livelihood** What he needed to live; **turtle-dove . . . crow** The elect and the reprobate are different species.

Chr. Why, I did but compare thee to some of the birds that are of the brisker sort, who will run to and fro in trodden paths with the shell upon their heads:° But pass by that, and consider the matter under debate, and all shall be well betwixt thee and me.

Hope. But, *Christian*, these three fellows, I am persuaded in my heart, are but a company of Cowards: Would they have run else, think you, as they did, at the noise of one that was coming on the road? Why did not *Little-Faith* pluck up a greater heart? He might, methinks, have stood one brush° with them, and have yielded when there had been no Remedy.

Hopeful swaggers.

Chr. That they are Cowards, many have said, but few have found it so in the time of Trial. As for a great heart,° *Little-Faith* had none; and I perceive by thee, my brother, hadst thou been the man concerned, thou art but for a brush, and then to yield. And verily, since this is the height of thy stomach,° now they are at a distance from us, should they appear to thee, as they did to him, they might put thee to second thoughts.

No great heart for God where there is but little Faith.

We have more Courage when out, than when we are in.

But consider again, they are but journey-men thieves,° they serve under the King of the bottomless Pit; who, if need be, will come in to their aid himself, and his voice is *as the Roaring of a Lion.* I myself have been engaged as this *Little-Faith* was, and I found it a terrible thing. These three villains set upon me, and I beginning like a *Christian* to resist, they gave but a call, and in came their Master; I would (as the saying is), have given my life for a penny;° but that, as God would have it, I was cloathed with Armour of Proof.° Ay, and yet, though I was so harnessed, I found it hard work to quit myself like a Man; no man can tell what in that combat attends us, but he that hath been in the Battle himself.

Psal. 5. 8.
[Prov. 28. 15?]
Christian tells his own Experience in this case.

---

birds . . . with the shell upon their heads Like a newborn bird; see the footnote to "whose head is the Shell" on page 145; **brush** Bout; **a great heart** This is rectified in the second part of *The Pilgrim's Progress*, where "Greatheart" is a character; **stomach** Courage; **but journey-men thieves** Only hired thieves; **my life for a penny** He was tempted to "sell" himself; **Armour of Proof** Impenetrable armor.

Hope. Well, but they ran, you see, when they did but suppose that one *Great-Grace* was in the way.

Chr. True, they have often fled, both they and their Master, when *Great-Grace* hath but appeared; and no marvel, for he is the *King's Champion:* But I tro,° you will put some difference between *Little-Faith* and the *King's Champion.* All the King's subjects are not his Champions, nor can they, when tried, do such feats of War as he. Is it meet to think, that a little child should handle *Goliah* as *David* did? Or, that there should be the strength of an *ox* in a *wren?* Some are strong, some are weak; some have great Faith, some have little; this man was one of the weak, and therefore he went to the walls.°

The King's Champion.

Hope. I would it had been *Great-Grace* for their sakes.

Chr. If it had been he, he might have had his hands full: For I must tell you, that though *Great-Grace* is excellent good at his weapons, and has and can, so long as he keeps them at sword's point, do well enough with them; yet, if they get within him, even *Faint-heart, Mistrust,* or the other, it shall go hard, but they will throw up his heels.° And when a man is down, you know, what can he do?°

Whoso looks well upon *Great-Grace's* face, shall see those scars and cuts there, that shall easily give demonstration of what I say. Yea, once I heard he should say, (and that when he was in the combat) *We despaired even of Life.* How did these sturdy rogues and their fellows make *David* groan, mourn, and roar? Yea, *Heman°* and *Hezekiah°* too, though Champions in their day, were forced to bestir them,° when by these assaulted; and yet notwithstanding they had their Coats soundly brushed° by them. *Peter,* upon a time, would go try what he could do; but though some do say of him,[98] that he

---

tro Believe; **went to the walls** Pews for the sick and infirm were placed along the walls of churches, hence the saying "the weakest go to the wall"; **throw up his heels** Knock him over; **And when . . . what can he do** At times Bunyan's colloquial style sounds startlingly contemporary; **Heman** A follower of David, mentioned in 1 Chronicles 25:1; **Hezekiah** King of Judah, described in 2 Kings and 2 Chronicles as an iconoclastic reformer and successful warrior; **to bestir them** To exert themselves; **brushed** Beaten.

is the Prince of the Apostles, they handled him so, that they made him at last afraid of a sorry Girl.°

Besides, their King is at their whistle;° he is never out of hearing; and if at any time they be put to the worst, he, if possible,° comes in to help them: And of him it is said, *The Sword of him that layeth at him cannot hold; the Spear, the Dart, nor the Habergeon;° he esteemeth Iron as Straw, and Brass as rotten Wood. The Arrow cannot make him fly; Sling-stones are turned, with him, into stubble; Darts are counted as stubble; he laugheth at the shaking of a Spear.* What can a man do in this case? 'Tis true, if a man could at every turn have *Job's* horse, and had Skill and Courage to ride him, he might do notable things. *For his neck is clothed with Thunder; he will not be afraid as the grass-hopper; the Glory of his nostrils is terrible; he paweth in the Valley, rejoyceth in his Strength, and goeth out to meet the Armed Men. He mocketh at Fear, and is not affrighted, neither turneth back from the Sword. The Quiver rattleth against him, the glittering Spear, and the Shield. He swalloweth the ground with fierceness and rage, neither believeth he that it is the sound of the Trumpet. He saith among the Trumpets, Ha, ha; and he smelleth the Battle afar off, the Thundering of the captains and the Shoutings.*

But for such footmen° as thee and I are, let us never desire to meet with an Enemy, nor vaunt° as if we could do better, when we hear of others that they have been foiled, nor be tickled at the thoughts of our own Manhood, for such commonly come by the worst when tried. Witness *Peter*, of whom I made mention before; he would swagger, ay, he would; he would, as his vain mind prompted him to say, do better, and stand more for his Master than all men; but, who so foiled and run down by these villains as he?

When therefore we hear that such Robberies are done on the King's Highway, two things become us to do: First, to go

Job 41. 26.
Leviathan's sturdiness.

Job 39. 19.
The excellent mettle that is in Job's horse.

---

a sorry Girl In Matthew 26 Peter denies being a follower of Jesus when he is accused by a serving maid; **at their whistle** He will come when they call him; **if possible** That is, if God permits it; **Habergeon** Coat of chain mail; **footmen** Foot soldiers, but also servants and travelers; **vaunt** Boast.

out harnessed, and to be sure to take a Shield with us; for it was for want of that, that he that laid so lustily at *Leviathan*[99] could not make him yield; for indeed, if that be wanting, he fears us not at all. Therefore, he that had Skill, hath said,

Eph. 6. 16.

Above all, take the Shield of Faith, wherewith ye shall be able to quench all the fiery Darts of the Wicked.

'Tis good to
have a
Convoy.

'Tis good also that we desire of the King a *Convoy*,° yea that he will go with us himself. This made *David* rejoyce when in the valley of the Shadow of Death; and *Moses* was

Exod. 33. 15.

rather for dying where he stood, than to go one Step without

Psal. 3. 5, 6, 7,
8. & 27. 1, 2,
3.

his God. O, my brother, if he will but go along with us, what need we be afraid of ten thousands that shall set themselves against us? but without him, *the proud Helpers fall under the*

Isa. 10.4.

Slain.

I, for my part, have been in the fray before now; and though (through the Goodness of him that is best) I am, as you see, alive, yet I cannot boast of my manhood. Glad shall I be, if I meet with no more such brunts;° though I fear we are not got beyond all danger. However, since the Lion and the Bear have not as yet devoured me, I hope God will also deliver us from the next uncircumcised *Philistine.*[100] Then sang *Christian:*

> *Poor* Little-Faith! *Hast been among the Thieves?*
> *Wast robb'd? Remember this; Whoso believes,*
> *And gets more Faith, shall then a Victor be*
> *Over ten thousand; else scarce over three.*

So they went on, and *Ignorance* followed. They went then till they came at a place where they saw a way put itself into

A way and a
Way.

their Way, and seemed withal to lie as strait as the Way which they should go; and here they knew not which of the two to take, for both seemed strait before them; therefore here they stood still to consider. And as they were thinking about the Way, behold a man black of Flesh, but covered with a very

The Flatterer
finds them.

light Robe,[101] came to them, and asked them why they stood

Convoy Escort; brunts Blows.

there? They answered, They were going to the Cœlestial City, but knew not which of these Ways to take. Follow me, said the man, it is thither that I am going. So they followed him in the Way that but now came into the road, which by Degrees turned, and turned them *so* from the City, that they desired to go to, that in a little time their faces were turned away from it; yet they followed him. But, by and by, before they were aware, he led them both within the compass of a Net, in which they were both so entangled, that they knew not what to do; and with that, the *White robe fell off the black man's back:* Then they saw where they were. Wherefore there they lay crying some time, for they could not get themselves out.

Chr. Then said *Christian* to his fellow, Now do I see myself in an Error. Did not the Shepherds bid us beware of the Flatterers? As is the saying of the Wise Man, so we have found it this day: *A man that flattereth his neighbour, spreadeth a Net for his feet.*

Hope. They also gave us a Note of Directions about the Way, for our more sure finding thereof; but therein we have also forgotten to read, and have not kept ourselves from the paths of the Destroyer. Here *David* was wiser than we; for, saith he, *Concerning the works of men, by the Word of thy Lips, I have kept me from the paths of the Destroyer.* Thus they lay bewailing themselves in the Net. At last they espied a Shining One° coming toward them with a Whip of small cord in his hand. When he was come to the place where they were, he asked them whence they came, and what they did there. They told him, that they were poor Pilgrims going to *Zion,* but were led out of their Way by a black man, cloathed in white, who bid us, said they, follow him, for he was going thither too. Then said he with the Whip, It is *Flatterer,* a false Apostle, that hath transformed himself into an Angel of Light.° So he rent° the Net, and let the men out. Then said he to them, Follow me, that I may set you in your Way again; so he led them back to the Way which they had left to follow the *Flatterer.* Then he

Christian and his fellow deluded.

They are taken in a Net.

They bewail their condition.

Prov. 29. 5.

Psal. 17. 4.

A Shining One comes to them with a Whip in his hand.

Prov. 29. 5.
Dan. 11. 32.
2 Cor. 11. 13, 14.

---

a Shining One Either an angel or a glorified soul; **an Angel of Light** Satan too can appear as such according to Paul (2 Corinthians 11:14); **rent** Tore.

*They are
examined,
and
convicted of
Forgetfulness.*
asked them, saying, Where did you lie the last night? They said, With the Shepherds, upon the *Delectable Mountains*. He asked them then, If they had not of those Shepherds a *note of direction* for the Way? They answered, Yes. But, did you, said he, when you were at a stand, pluck out and read your Note?

*Deceivers fine
spoken.*
Rom. 6. 18.
Deut. 25. 2.
2 Chron. 6.
26, 27.
Rev. 3. 19.
They answered, No. He asked them, Why? They said, They forgot. He asked moreover, If the Shepherds did not bid them beware of the *Flatterer?* They answered, Yes. But we did not imagine, said they, *that this fine-spoken man° had been he.*

Then I saw in my dream, That he commanded them to *lie down;* which when they did, he chastized them sore, to teach

*They are
whipt and
sent on their
Way.*
them the good Way wherein they should walk: And as he chastized them, he said, *As many as I love, I rebuke and chasten, be zealous, therefore, and repent.* This done, he bids them go on their Way, and take good heed to the other directions of the Shepherds. So they thanked him for all his Kindness, and went softly along the right Way, singing;

> *Come hither, you that walk along the Way,*
> *See how the Pilgrims fare, that go astray:*
> *They catched are in an intangling Net,*
> *'Cause they good Counsel lightly did forget:*
> *'Tis true, they rescu'd were, but yet you see*
> *They're scourg'd to boot: Let this your Caution be.*

Now, after a while, they perceived afar off, one coming softly, and alone, all along the highway to meet them. Then said *Christian* to his fellow, Yonder is a man with his back toward *Zion*, and he is coming to meet us.

The Atheist
meets them.
Hope. I see him, let us take heed to ourselves now, lest he should prove a *Flatterer* also. So he drew nearer and nearer, and at last came up unto them. His name was *Atheist*, and he asked them whither they were going.

Chr. We are going to the Mount *Zion*.

---

this fine-spoken man The Flatterer confirms his identity in the act of concealing it.

Then *Atheist* fell into a very great Laughter.

Chr. What is the meaning of your laughter?

Atheist. I laugh to see what ignorant° persons you are, to take upon you so tedious a journey, and yet are like to have nothing but your Travel° for your pains.

Chr. Why, man? Do you think we shall not be received?

Atheist. Received! There is no such place as you dream of in all this World.

Chr. But there is in the World to come.

Atheist. When I was at home in mine own country, I heard as you now affirm, and from that hearing went out to see, and have been seeking this City these twenty years, but find no more of it than I did the first day I set out.

Chr. We have both heard, and believe that there is such a place to be found.

Atheist. Had not I, when at home, believed, I had not come thus far to seek: but finding none, (and yet I should, had there been such a place to be found, for I have gone to seek it further than you)° I am going back again, and will seek to refresh myself with the things that I then cast away, for hopes of that which I now see is not.

Chr. Then said *Christian* to *Hopeful*, his fellow, *Is it true which this man hath said?*

Hope. Take heed, he is one of the *Flatterers*; remember what it hath cost us once already for our hearkening to such kind of fellows. What! No Mount *Zion*? Did we not see° from the *Delectable Mountains*, the Gate of the City? Also, are we not now to walk by Faith? Let us go on, said *Hopeful*, lest the man with the Whip overtake us again.

You should have taught *me* that Lesson, which I will round you in the ears withal: *Cease, my Son, to hear the Instruction that causeth to err from the Words of Knowledge:* I say, my brother, cease to hear him, and let us Believe to the saving of the soul.

He laughs at them.

They reason together.

Jer. 22. 13.
Eccl. 10. 15.

The Atheist *takes up his content in this* World.
Christian *proveth his brother.*
Hopeful's *gracious Answer.*
2 Cor. 5. 7.

Remembrance *of former* Chastisements, *is a Help against present* Temptations.

Prov. 19. 27.
Heb. 10. 39.

---

ignorant Atheist considers himself learned—he espouses the materialist worldview of Baconian empiricism; **Travel** With a pun on "travail" (labor); **I have . . . you** Atheist is aware only of the world of experience; **Did we not see** The pilgrims experience the world as an allegory.

Chr. My brother, I did not put the question to thee, for that I doubted of the Truth of our belief myself, but to prove° thee, and to fetch from thee a Fruit of the honesty of thy heart. As for this man, I know that he is blinded by the God of this world.° Let thee and I go on, knowing that we have belief of the Truth, and no Lie is of the truth.

Hope. Now do I rejoice in hope of the Glory of God: So they turned away from the man; and he laughing at them, went his way.

I saw then in my dream, that they went till they came into a certain Country, whose air naturally tended to make one drowzy, if he came a Stranger into it. And here *Hopeful* began to be very dull and heavy of sleep; wherefore he said unto *Christian*, I do now begin to grow so drowzy, that I can scarcely hold up mine eyes: Let us lie down here, and take one nap.

*They are
come to the
Enchanted
ground.*
*Hopeful
begins to be
drowzy.*

Chr. By no means, (said the other) lest sleeping we never awake more.

Hope. Why, my brother? Sleep is sweet to the labouring man; we may be refreshed if we take a nap.

Chr. Do you not remember, that one of the Shepherds bid us beware of the Enchanted ground?° He meant by that, that we should beware of Sleeping; wherefore let us not sleep as do others; but let us watch and be sober.

Hope. I acknowledge myself in fault; and had I been here alone, I had by sleeping run the danger of Death. I see it is true, that the Wise Man saith, *Two are better than one.* Hitherto hath thy company been my mercy; *And thou shalt have a good reward for thy labour.*

Chr. Now then, said *Christian*, to prevent drowziness in this place, let us fall into good discourse.

Hope. With all my heart, said the other.

*To prevent
Drowziness
they fall to
good
discourse.*
*Good
discourse
preventeth
drowziness.*

Chr. Where shall we begin?

Hope. Where God began with us, but do you begin if you please.

---

prove Test; **the God of this world** Satan; **the Enchanted ground** Offor cites a note from T. Scott's edition (1797): "The Enchanted Ground may represent worldly prosperity" (*Works*, vol. 3, p. 153).

Chr. I will sing you first this song.

> *When Saints do sleepy grow, let them come hither,*
> *And hear how these two Pilgrims talk together,*
> *Yea, let them learn of them in any wise*
> *Thus to keep ope' their drowzy slumb'ring eyes;*
> *Saints Fellowship if it be manag'd well,*
> *Keeps them awake, and that in spite of Hell.*

The dreamer's note.

Chr. Then *Christian* began, and said, I will ask you a question. How came you to think at first of doing as you do now?

Hope. Do you mean, how came I at first to look after the Good of my Soul?[102]

Chr. Yes, that is my meaning.

Hope. I continued a great while in the delight of those things which were seen and sold at our Fair; things which I believe now would have (had I continued in them still) drowned me in perdition and destruction.

Chr. What things were they?

Hope. All the treasures and riches of the World. Also I delighted much in rioting, revelling, drinking, swearing, lying, uncleanness, sabbath-breaking, and what not, that tended to destroy the Soul. But I found at last, by hearing and considering of things that are Divine, which indeed I heard of you, as also of beloved *Faithful,* that was put to death for his faith and good living in *Vanity-Fair, That the end of these things is Death.°* And that for these things sake, the wrath of God cometh upon the children of disobedience.

Chr. And did you presently° fall under the power of this conviction?

Hope. No, I was not willing presently to know the Evil of Sin, nor the Damnation that follows upon the commission of it; but endeavoured, when my mind at first began to be shaken with the Word, to shut mine eyes against the light thereof.

They begin at the beginning of their Conversion.

Hopeful's life before Conversion.

Rom. 6. 21, 22, 23.
Eph. 5. 6.

Hopeful at first shuts his eyes against the Light.

---

the end of these things is Death Everything earthy is transient, thus unreal, and to take it for reality is sinful; **presently** Both "currently" and "immediately."

Chr. But what was the Cause of your carrying of it thus to the first workings of God's blessed Spirit upon you?

Reasons of his resisting the Light.

Hope. The causes were, 1. I was ignorant that this was the work of God upon me. I never thought that by awakenings for Sin, God at first begins the Conversion of a Sinner. 2. Sin was yet very sweet to my Flesh, and I was loth to leave it. 3. I could not tell how to part with mine old Companions, their presence and actions were so desirable unto me. 4. The hours in which Convictions were upon me, were such troublesome and such Heart-affrighting hours, that I could not bear, no not so much as the Remembrance of them upon my heart.

Chr. Then, as it seems, sometimes you got rid of your Trouble.

Hope. Yes, verily, but it would come into my mind again, and then I should be as bad, nay worse than I was before.

Chr. Why, what was it that brought your Sins to mind again?

Hope. Many things; as,

When he had lost his Sense of Sin, what brought it again.

1. If I did but meet a Good man in the streets; or,

2. If I have heard any read in the Bible; or,

3. If mine head did begin to ache; or,

4. If I were told that some of my neighbours were sick; or,

5. If I heard the bell toll for some that were dead, or,

6. If I thought of Dying myself; or,

7. If I heard that sudden Death happened to others.

8. But especially when I thought of myself, that I must quickly come to Judgment.

Chr. And could you at any time, with ease, get off the Guilt of Sin, when by any of these ways it came upon you?

Hope. No, not latterly;° for then they got faster hold of my Conscience; and then, if I did but think of going back to Sin, (though my mind was turned against it) it would be double Torment to me.

---

latterly Toward the end.

Chr. And how did you do then?

Hope. I thought I must endeavour to mend my Life; for else, thought I, I am sure to be damned.

Chr. And did you endeavour to mend?

Hope. Yes; and fled from, not only my Sins, but sinful company too, and betook me to religious duties; as Praying, Reading, weeping for Sin, speaking Truth to my neighbours, *&c.* These things I did, with many others, too much here to relate.

Chr. And did you think yourself well then?

Hope. Yes, for a while;° but at the last my Trouble came tumbling upon me again, and that over the neck of all my reformations.°

Chr. How came that about, since you were now reformed?

Hope. There were several things brought it upon me, especially such sayings as these: *All our Righteousnesses are as filthy rags. By the Works of the Law, no man shall be justified. When ye have done all things, say, We are unprofitable:* With many more such like. From whence I began to reason with myself thus: If all my Righteousnesses are filthy rags; if by the Deeds of the Law no man can be justified; and if when we have done *all* we are yet unprofitable, then 'tis but a folly to think of Heaven by the Law. I further thought thus: If a man runs a hundred pounds into the shop-keeper's Debt,[103] and after that shall pay for all that he shall fetch; yet his old Debt stands still in the Book uncross'd, for the which the shop-keeper may sue him, and cast him into Prison, till he shall pay the debt.

Chr. Well, and how did you apply this to yourself?

Hope. Why, I thought thus with myself; I have by my Sins run a great way into GOD's Book,° and that my now Reforming will not pay off that score;° therefore I should think still, under all my present amendments, But how shall I be freed

---

for a while This is Hopeful's phase of "works righteousness," when he believes he can be saved by his own actions; tumbling . . . my reformations Note that Hopeful has personified both his "Trouble" and his "reformations"; the allegorical mode comes naturally to him; God's Book Not the Bible, but the account book kept by the shopkeeper-God who terrified Hopeful; score Bill.

from that Damnation that I have brought myself in danger of by my former Transgressions?

Chr. A very good application; but pray go on.

His espying bad things in his best Duties troubled him.

Hope. Another thing that hath troubled me even since my late amendments is, that if I look narrowly° into the best of what I do now, I still see Sin, new Sin, mixing itself with the best of that I do; so that now I am forced to conclude, that notwithstanding my former fond Conceits of myself and duties, I have committed Sin enough in one duty to send me to Hell,° tho' my former life had been faultless.

Chr. And what did you do then?

This made him break his mind to Faithful, *who told him the way to be saved.*

Hope. Do! I could not tell what to do, till I brake my mind to *Faithful,* for he and I were well acquainted. And he told me, that unless I could obtain the Righteousness° of a man that never had sinned; neither mine own, nor all the Righteousness of the World could save me.

Chr. And did you think he spake true?

Hope. Had he told me so when I was pleased and satisfied with mine own amendments, I had called him Fool for his pains; but now, since I see mine own Infirmity, and the Sin that cleaves to my best performance, I have been forced to be of his opinion.

Chr. But did you think, when at first he suggested it to you, that there was such a man to be found, of whom it might justly be said, That he never committed Sin?

At which he started at present.

Hope. I must confess the words at first sounded strangely, but after a little more talk and company with him, I had full conviction about it.

Chr. And did you ask him, What man this was, and how you must be justified by him?

Heb. 10.
Rom. 4.
Col. 1.
1 Pet. 1.

Hope. Yes, and he told me it was the Lord Jesus, that dwelleth on the right hand of the Most High: And thus, said he, you must be justified by him, even by trusting to what he hath done by himself in the days of his flesh, and suffered

---

narrowly Closely; I have . . . Hell The Calvinist doctrine of total depravity, which grew from Luther's conviction that our works cannot save us; Righteousness The imputed righteousness of Christ.

when he did hang on the Tree. I asked him further, how *that* Man's righteousness could be of that efficacy, as to justify another before GOD? And he told me, He was the Mighty GOD, and did what he did, and died the Death also, not for himself, but for me; to whom His doings, and the worthiness of them, should be imputed,° if I believed on him.

A more particular Discovery of the Way to be saved.

Chr. And what did you do then?

Hope. I made my objections against my believing, for that I thought he was not willing to save me.

He doubts of Acceptation.

Chr. And what said *Faithful* to you then?

Hope. He bid me go to him and see; then I said it was Presumption; he said No, for I was Invited to come. Then he gave me a Book of Jesus his inditing,° to encourage me the more freely to come; and he said concerning that Book, That every jot and tittle° thereof stood firmer than Heaven and earth. Then I asked him what I must do when I came: And he told me, I must entreat upon my knees, with all my heart and soul, the Father to reveal him to me. Then I ask'd him further, how I must make my supplication to him? And he said, Go, and thou shalt find him upon a Mercy-Seat,° where he sits all the year long, to give Pardon and Forgiveness to them that come. I told him, that I knew not what to say when I came. And he bid me say to this effect:

Mat. 11. 28.
He is better instructed.

Mat. 24. 35.
Psal. 95. 6.
Dan. 6. 10.
Jer. 29. 12, 13.

Ex. 25. 22.
Lev. 16. 2.
Num. 7. 8, 9.
Heb. 4. 16.

He is bid to Pray.

> *God be merciful to me a Sinner, and make me to know and believe in Jesus Christ; for I see, that if his Righteousness had not been, or I have not Faith in that Righteousness, I am utterly cast away. Lord, I have heard that thou art a merciful God, and hast ordained that thy Son Jesus Christ should be the Saviour of the World; and moreover, that thou art willing to bestow upon such a poor sinner as I am, (and I am a sinner indeed) Lord, take therefore this opportunity, and magnify thy Grace in the Salvation of my soul, through thy Son Jesus Christ. Amen.*

---

imputed Through faith in the efficacy of His sacrifice, the righteousness of Christ is bestowed upon us; **inditing** Writing; **jot and tittle** Iota; **Mercy-Seat** A physical part of the Jewish temple mentioned in the Old Testament, and read by Christians as a type of Christ's mercy.

Chr. And did you do as you were bidden?

He prays.

Hope. Yes; over and over, and over.

Chr. And did the Father reveal his Son to you?

Hope. Not at the first, nor second, nor third, nor fourth, nor fifth; no, nor at the sixth time neither.

Chr. What did you do then?

Hope. What! why I could not tell what to do.

He thought to leave off praying. Durst not leave off praying, and why.

Chr. Had you not thoughts of leaving off Praying?

Hope. Yes; an hundred times twice told.

Chr. And what was the reason you did not?

Hope. I believed that that was true, which had been told me, *to wit*, That without the Righteousness of this Christ, all the World could not save me; and therefore thought I with myself, if I leave off, I die, and I can but die at the Throne of

Habb. 2. 3.

Grace. And withal this came into my mind, *If it tarry, wait for it, because it will surely come, and will not tarry.* So I continued Praying, until the Father shewed me his Son.

Chr. And how was he revealed unto you?

Eph. 1. 18, 19.

Hope. I did not see him with my bodily eyes, but with the eyes of mine Understanding; and thus it was. One day I was very sad, I think sadder than at any one time of my Life; and

Christ is revealed to him, and how.

this sadness was through a fresh sight of the greatness and vileness of my Sins. And as I was then looking for° nothing but *Hell*, and the everlasting Damnation of my Soul, suddenly, as I thought, I saw° the Lord Jesus looking down from

Acts 16. 30, 31.

Heaven upon me, and saying, *Believe on the Lord Jesus Christ, and thou shalt be saved.*

But I replied, Lord I am a great, a very great Sinner: And

2 Cor. 12. 9.

he answered, *My Grace is sufficient for thee.* Then I said, but Lord, what is Believing? And then I saw from that saying, *He*

John 6. 35.

that cometh to me shall never hunger, and he that believeth on me shall never thirst that Believing and Coming was all one; and that he that came, that is, ran out in his heart and affections after Salvation by Christ, he indeed believed in Christ.

---

looking for Expecting; **I saw** This is not a vision, as Hopeful has just explained, but an understanding.

Then the water stood in mine eyes, and I asked further, But Lord, may such a great Sinner as I am, be indeed accepted of thee, and be saved by thee? And I heard him say, *and him that* John 6. 37. *cometh to me, I will in no wise° cast out.* Then I said, But how, Lord, must I consider of thee in my coming to thee, that my Faith may be placed aright upon thee? Then he said, *Christ* 1 Tim. 1. 15. *Jesus came into the World to save Sinners. He is the end of the* Rom. 10. 4. *Law for Righteousness to every one that believes. He dyed for* Chap. 4. *our Sins, and rose again for our Justification: He loved us, and* Heb. 7. 24, 25. *washed us from our Sins in his own blood: He is Mediator between God and us.*[104] *He ever liveth to make Intercession for us.* From all which I gathered, that I must look for Righteousness in his Person, and for Satisfaction for my Sins by his Blood; that what he did in Obedience to his Father's Law, and in submitting to the Penalty thereof, was not for himself, but for him that will accept it for his Salvation, and be thankful. And now was my heart full of joy, mine eyes full of tears, and mine affections running over with love to the Name, People, and Ways of Jesus Christ.

Chr. This was a Revelation of Christ to your soul indeed; But tell me particularly what effect this had upon your spirit?[105]

Hope. It made me see that all the World, notwithstanding all the righteousness thereof, is in a state of Condemnation. It made me see that God the Father, though he be just, can justly justify the coming Sinner: It made me greatly ashamed of the Vileness of my former life, and confounded me with the sense of mine own Ignorance;° for there never came thought into my heart before now, that showed me so the beauty of Jesus Christ: It made me love a Holy Life, and long to do something for the honour and glory of the name of the Lord Jesus; Yea, I thought that had I now a thousand gallons of blood in my body, I could spill it all for the sake of the Lord Jesus.

---

in no wise In no way; **mine own Ignorance** Anticipating that character's imminent reappearance.

I then saw in my dream, that *Hopeful* looked back and saw *Ignorance*, whom they had left behind, coming after. Look, said he to *Christian*, how far yonder youngster loitereth behind?

Chr. Ay, ay, I see him; he careth not for our company.

Hope. But I trow it would not have hurt him, had he kept pace with us hitherto.

Chr. That's true, but I warrant you he thinketh otherwise.

Hope. That I think he doth; but however, let us tarry for him. So they did.

Young Ignorance comes up again. Their talk.

Then *Christian* said to him, Come away man, why do you stay so behind?

Ignorance. I take my pleasure in walking alone,° even more a great deal than in company, unless I like it the better.

Then said *Christian* to *Hopeful*, (but softly) Did I not tell you he cared not for our company: But however, said he, come up, and let us talk away the time in this solitary place. Then directing his speech to *Ignorance*, he said, Come how do you? How stands it between God and your Soul now?

Ignorance's Hope, and the Ground of it.

Ignor. I hope well, for I am always full of good motions, that come into my mind, to comfort me as I walk.

Chr. What good motions?° Pray tell us.

Ignor. Why, I think of GOD and Heaven.

Chr. So do the Devils and damned souls.

Ignor. But I think of them, and desire them.

Prov. 13. 4.

Chr. So do many that are never like to come there. The soul of the Sluggard desires, and hath nothing.

Ignor. But I think of them, and leave all for them.

Chr. That I doubt; for leaving of all is a hard matter; yea, a harder matter than many are aware of. But why or by what, art thou persuaded that thou hast left all for GOD and Heaven?

Ignor. My Heart tells me so.°

---

alone Ignorance does not see the necessity of church membership; **motions** Thoughts; **My Heart tells me so** Like the Quakers, Ignorance believes the testimony of his "inner light."

Chr. The Wise Man says, *He that trusts his own heart, is a fool.* Prov. 28. 26.

Ignor. This is spoken of an evil heart, but mine is a good one.°

Chr. But how dost thou prove that?

Ignor. It comforts me in hopes of heaven.

Chr. That may be through its *Deceitfulness;* for a man's Heart may minister comfort to him in the Hopes of that thing for which he yet has no Ground to hope.

Ignor. But my Heart and Life agree together, and therefore my Hope is well grounded.

Chr. Who told thee that thy Heart and Life agree together?

Ignor. My Heart tells me so.

Chr. Ask my Fellow, if I be a Thief? Thy Heart tells thee so! Except the Word of GOD beareth witness in this matter, other testimony is of no value.

Ignor. But is it not a good Heart that has good Thoughts? And is not that a good Life, that is according to God's Commandments?

Chr. Yes, that is a good Heart that hath good Thoughts; and that is a good Life that is according to God's Commandments: But it is one thing indeed to have these, and another thing only to think so.

Ignor. Pray what count you good thoughts, and a life according to God's commandments?

Chr. There are good thoughts of divers kinds; some respecting ourselves, some God, some Christ, and some other things.

Ignor. What be good thoughts respecting ourselves?

Chr. Such as agree with the Word of God.

What are good thoughts.

Ignor. When do our thoughts of ourselves agree with the Word of God?

Chr. When we pass the same Judgment upon ourselves which the Word passes. To explain myself: The Word of God saith of persons in a Natural Condition, *There is none Righteous, there is none that doth good;* it saith also, *That every imagination of the heart of a man is only Evil, and that contin-*

Rom. 3.
Gen. 6. 5.

---

mine is a good one The Quakers believed in the essential goodness of man.

ually; and again, *The imagination of man's heart is Evil from his youth.* Now then, when we think thus of ourselves, having *Sense*° thereof, then are our thoughts good ones, because according to the Word of God.

Ignor. I will never believe that my heart is thus bad.

Chr. Therefore thou never hadst one good thought concerning thyself in thy life.° But let me go on. As the Word passeth a judgment upon our *Heart,* so it passeth a judgment upon our *Ways,* and when our thoughts of our *Hearts* and *Ways* agree with the judgment which the Word giveth of both, then are both good, because agreeing thereto.

Ignor. Make out your meaning.

Chr. Why, the Word of God saith, That man's ways are crooked ways, not good, but perverse: It saith, They are naturally out of the good Way, that they have not known it. Now when a man thus thinketh of his ways, I say, when he doth sensibly, and with Heart-humiliation thus think, then hath he good thoughts of his own ways, because his thoughts now agree with the judgment of the Word of God.

Ignor. What are good thoughts concerning God?

Chr. Even (as I have said concerning ourselves) when our thoughts of God do agree with what the Word saith of him; and that is, when we think of his Being and Attributes as the Word hath taught; of which I cannot now discourse at large: But to speak of him with reference to us, then we have right thoughts of God, when we think that he knows us better than we know ourselves, and can see Sin in us when and where we can see none in ourselves: When we think He knows our inmost thoughts, and that our heart, with all its depths, is always open unto his eyes: Also when we think that all our Righteousness stinks in his nostrils,° and that therefore he cannot abide to see us stand before him in any Confidence, even of all our best performances.°

Psal. 125. 5.
Prov. 2. 15.
Rom. 3.

Sense Understanding; **thou never hadst one good thought . . . life** For Christian, the only good thoughts about one's self are bad thoughts; **our Righteousness stinks in his nostrils** A strikingly anthropomorphic image of God; **performances** Actions, but with the sense of empty shows, as in a performance of a play.

Ignor. Do you think that I am such a Fool as to think God can see no further than I? Or, that I would come to God in the best of my Performances?

Chr. Why, how dost thou think in this matter?

Ignor. Why, to be short, I think I must believe in Christ for Justification.

Chr. How! Think thou must believe in Christ, when thou seest not thy need of him! Thou neither seest thy original nor actual Infirmities,° but hast such an opinion of thyself, and of what thou dost, as plainly renders thee to be one that did never see a necessity of Christ's personal Righteousness° to justify thee before God. How then dost thou say, I believe in Christ?

Ignor. I believe well enough for all that.

Chr. How dost thou believe?

Ignor. I believe that Christ died for sinners, and that I shall be justified before God from the Curse, through his gracious acceptance of my obedience to his law. *Or thus,* Christ makes my Duties, that are religious, acceptable to his Father by virtue of his Merits, and so shall I be justified. *The Faith of* Ignorance.

Chr. Let me give an answer to this confession of thy Faith.

1. Thou believest with a *fantastical* Faith; for this faith is no where described in the Word.

2. Thou believest with a *false* Faith, because it taketh Justification from the Personal Righteousness of Christ, and applies it to thy own.

3. This Faith maketh not Christ a justifier of thy person, but of thy actions;[106] and of thy person, for thy actions sake, which is false.

4. Therefore this Faith is deceitful, even such as will leave thee under Wrath in the day of God Almighty; For true *Justifying Faith* puts the soul (as sensible of its lost condition by the Law) upon flying for refuge unto Christ's Righteousness:

---

original or actual Infirmities Neither the sin that naturally comes with being human nor the particular sins Ignorance himself has committed; **Christ's personal Righteousness** The Quakers believed Christ was resurrected in their own flesh, not in the personal figure of Jesus of Nazareth.

which righteousness of *his* is not an act of Grace, by which he maketh, for Justification, *thy* Obedience accepted with God; but *his* Personal Obedience to the Law, in doing and suffering for us what that requireth at our hands. This righteousness, I say, true Faith accepteth; under the skirt of which, the soul being shrouded, and by it presented as spotless before God, it is accepted, and acquit from Condemnation.

Ignor. What! would you have us trust to what Christ in his own Person has done without us? This conceit would loosen the reins of our Lust,[107] and tolerate us to live as we list: For, what matter how we live, if we may be justify'd by Christ's Personal Righteousness, from all, when we believe it.

Chr. Ignorance is thy Name; and as thy name is, so art thou;° even this thy answer demonstrateth what I say. *Ignorant* thou art of what *Justifying Righteousness* is, and as ignorant how to secure thy Soul through the Faith of it from the heavy Wrath of GOD. Yea, thou also art ignorant of the true effects of Saving Faith in this righteousness of Christ, which is to bow and win over the heart to God in Christ, to love his Name, his Word, Ways, and People, and not as thou ignorantly imaginest.

Hope. Ask him if ever he had Christ revealed to him from Heaven?

Ignor. What! You are a man for Revelations! I believe that what both you and all the rest of you° say about that matter, is but the fruit of distracted brains.

Hope. Why man! Christ is so hid in God from the natural apprehensions of all Flesh, that he cannot by any man be savingly known, unless God the Father reveals him to them.

Ignor. That is your Faith, but not mine; yet mine, I doubt not, is as good as yours, though I have not in my head so many Whimsies as you.

Chr. Give me leave to put in a word: You ought not so slightly to speak of this matter; For this I will boldly affirm,

Ignorance jangles with them.

He speaks reproachfully of what he knows not.

---

so art thou Christian's usual trump card of identifying the character's allegorical significance by the manner in which they deny it; **all the rest of you** Indicating that Christian represents an entire denomination.

(even as my good companion hath done) that no man can Matt. 11. 27.
know Jesus Christ but by the revelation of the Father; yea,
and Faith too, by which the soul layeth hold upon Christ, (if 1 Cor. 12. 3.
it be right) must be wrought by the exceeding greatness of his
mighty Power; the working of which Faith, I perceive, poor Eph. 1. 18, 19.
Ignorance! thou art ignorant of. Be awakened then, see thine
own wretchedness, and fly to the Lord Jesus; and by his righteousness, which is the righteousness of GOD, (for he himself
is GOD) thou shalt be delivered from Condemnation.

Ignor. You go so fast, I cannot keep pace with you: Do you *The Talk broke up.*
go on before; I must stay a while behind. Then they said,

> *Well, Ignorance, wilt thou yet foolish be*
> *To slight good Counsel, ten times given thee?*
> *And if thou yet refuse it, thou shalt know,*
> *E're long, the Evil of thy doing so.*
> *Remember, man, in time; stoop, do not fear;*
> *Good Counsel taken well saves; therefore hear.*
> *But if thou yet shalt slight it, thou wilt be*
> *The Loser, Ignorance, I'll warrant thee.*

Then *Christian* addressed himself thus to his fellow:

Chr. Well, come my good *Hopeful*, I perceive that thou and
I must walk by ourselves again.

So I saw in my dream, that they went on apace before, and
Ignorance he came hobbling after. Then said *Christian* to his
companion, It pities me much for this poor man;° it will certainly go ill with him at last.

Hope. Alas! there are abundance in our town in his condition, whole families, yea, whole streets, (and that of Pilgrims
too;)° and if there be so many in our parts, how many, think
you, must there be in the place where he was born?

It pities me much for this poor man Christian rarely sympathizes with the
unregenerate; the young Bunyan may have been tempted by Ignorance's
ideas himself; **and that of Pilgrims too** It is possible for true pilgrims to
share Ignorance's erroneous theology.

Chr. Indeed the Word saith, *He hath blinded their eyes, lest they should see,* &c.

But now we are by ourselves, What do you think of such men? Have they at no time, think you, Convictions of Sin, so consequently fears that their state is dangerous?

Hope. Nay, do you answer that question yourself, for you are the elder man.

Chr. Then I say, sometimes (as I think) they may; but they being naturally ignorant, understand not that such convictions tend to their Good; and therefore they do desperately seek to stifle them, and presumptuously continue to flatter themselves in the way of their own hearts.°

The good Use of Fear.

Hope. I do believe, as you say, that Fear tends much to men's good, and to make them right at their beginning to go on Pilgrimage.

Job 28. 28.
Psal. 111. 10.
Prov. 1. 7.
ch. 9. 10.

Chr. Without all doubt it doth, if it be right; for so says the Word, *The Fear of the Lord is the beginning of Wisdom.*

Hope. How will you describe right fear?

Right Fear.

Chr. True or right fear is discovered by three things:

1. By its rise, It is caused by saving Convictions for Sin.

2. It driveth the soul to lay fast hold of Christ for Salvation.

3. It begetteth and continueth in the soul a great Reverence of God, his Word and Ways, keeping it tender, and making it afraid to turn from them, to the right hand or to the left, to any thing that may dishonour God, break its peace, grieve the Spirit, or cause the enemy to speak reproachfully.

Hope. Well said; I believe you have said the truth. Are we now almost got past the Enchanted ground?

Chr. Why, art thou weary of this discourse?

Hope. No, verily, but that I would know where we are.

Why ignorant persons do stifle Convictions.
1. *In general.*

Chr. We have not now above two miles further to go thereon. But let us return to our matter. Now the Ignorant know not that such convictions that tend to put them in Fear, are for their Good, and therefore they seek to stifle them.

---

the way of their own hearts Both "as their own hearts incline them," and "about the nature of their own hearts."

Hope. How do they seek to stifle them?

Chr. 1. They think that those fears are wrought by the Devil; (tho' indeed they are wrought of God;) and thinking so, they resist them, as things that directly tend to their overthrow. 2. They also think that these fears tend to the spoiling of their Faith, (when, alas for them, poor men that they are, they have none at all) and therefore they harden their hearts against them. 3. They presume they ought not to fear, and therefore in despite of them wax° presumptuously confident. 4. They see that those fears tend to take away from them their pitiful old Self-holiness, and therefore they resist them with all their might.

2. In particular.

Hope. I know something of this myself; before I knew myself, it was so with me.

Chr. Well, we will leave, at this time, our neighbour *Ignorance* by himself, and fall upon another profitable question.

Talk about one Temporary.

Hope. With all my heart, but you shall still begin.

Chr. Well then, did you not know, about ten years ago,° one *Temporary*° in your parts, who was a forward man in religion then?

Hope. Know him! yes, he dwelt in *Graceless*, a town about two miles off of *Honesty*, and he dwelt next door to one *Turnback*.

Where he dwelt.

Chr. Right, he dwelt under the same roof with him. Well, that man was much awakened once; I believe that then he had some sight of his Sins, and of the Wages that were due thereto.

He was towardly once.

Hope. I am of your mind, for (my house not being above three miles from him) he would oft times come to me, and that with many tears. Truly I pitied the man, and was not altogether without Hope of him: But one may see, it is not every one that cries, *Lord, Lord,*———

Chr. He told me once, That he was resolved to go on Pil-

---

wax Grow; ten years ago Before the Restoration, suggesting that this section was written around 1670; **Temporary** A turncoat. Offor cites Mason: "one who is doctrinally acquainted with the Gospel, but a stranger to its sanctifying power" (*Works*, vol. 3, p. 160).

grimage, as we do now; but all of a sudden he grew acquainted with one *Saveself*, and then he became a stranger to me.

Hope. Now, since we are talking about him, let us a little enquire into the Reason of the sudden backsliding of him and such others.

Chr. It may be very profitable, but do you begin.

Hope. Well then, there are, in my judgment, four reasons for it.

1. Though the Consciences of such men are awakened, yet their Minds are not changed: Therefore, when the power of Guilt weareth away, that which provoked them to be religious ceaseth: Wherefore they naturally turn to their own course again; even as we see the dog that is sick of what he hath eaten, so long as his sickness prevails, he vomits and casts up all: Not that he doth this of a free mind (if we may say a dog has a mind) but because it troubleth his stomach; but now, when his sickness is over, and so his stomach eased, his desires being not at all alienated° from his vomit, he turns him about and licks up all; and so it is true which is written, *The dog is turned to his own vomit again.* This I say; being hot for Heaven by virtue only of the sense and fear of the torments of Hell; as their sense of hell and the fears of damnation chills and cools, so their desires for Heaven and Salvation cool also: So then it comes to pass, that when their Guilt and Fear is gone, their desires for Heaven and happiness die, and they return to their course again.

Reasons why towardly ones go back.

2 Pet. 2. 22.

2. Another reason is, they have slavish fears that do overmaster them; I speak now of the fears that they have of men:° *For the fear of men bringeth a Snare.* So then though they seem to be hot for Heaven so long as the flames of Hell are about their ears, yet when that terror is a little over, they betake themselves to second thoughts, namely, that 'tis good to be wise, and not to run (for they know not what) the hazard of losing all, or at least of bringing themselves into unavoidable and unnecessary Troubles, and so they fall in with the World again.

Prov. 29. 25.

---

alienated Just as Temporary was not truly alienated from the world; **fears that they have of men** Many dissenters conformed to the Anglican Church for fear of the penal laws known as the Clarendon Code.

3. The Shame that attends Religion lies also as a block in their way; they are proud and haughty, and Religion in their eye is low and contemptible: Therefore when they have lost their sense of Hell, and Wrath to come, they return again to their former course.

4. Guilt, and to meditate Terror, are grievous to them; they like not to see their misery before they come into it, though perhaps the Sight of it first, if they loved° that sight, might make them fly whither the righteous fly and are safe; but because they do, as I hinted before, even shun the thoughts of guilt and terror, therefore when once they are rid of their awakenings about the terrors and wrath of God, they harden their hearts gladly, and chuse such ways as will harden them more and more.

Chr. You are pretty near the business, for the bottom of all is, for want of a change in their Mind and Will. And therefore they are but like the felon that standeth before the Judge; he quakes and trembles, and seems to repent most heartily; but the bottom of all is, the fear of the halter;° not that he hath any detestation of the offence, as it is evident, because, let but this man have his liberty, and he will be a thief, and so a rogue still; whereas, if his mind was changed, he would be otherwise.

Hope. Now I have shewed you the Reasons of their going back, do you shew me the Manner thereof.

Chr. So I will willingly.

1. They draw off their thoughts, all that they may, from the remembrance of God, Death, and Judgment to come.

How the Apostate goes back.

2. Then they cast off by *degrees* private duties, as Closet-Prayer, Curbing their Lusts, Watching, Sorrow for Sin, and the like.

3. Then they shun the company of lively and warm Christians.

4. After that they grow cold to publick duty, as Hearing, Reading, Godly Conference, and the like.

---

loved "Valued," rather than "enjoyed"; **halter** Noose.

5. Then they begin to pick holes, as we say, in the coats of some of the Godly,° and that devilishly, that they may have a seeming colour to throw Religion (for the sake of some infirmity they have spied them) behind their backs.

6. Then they begin to adhere to, and associate themselves with carnal, loose, and wanton men.

7. Then they give way to carnal and wanton discourses in secret; and glad are they if they can see such things in any that are counted honest, that they may the more boldly do it through their Example.

8. After this, they begin to play with little Sins openly.

9. And then being hardened, they shew themselves as they are. Thus being launched again into the gulph of misery, unless a Miracle of Grace prevent it, they everlastingly perish in their own deceivings.

Now I saw in my dream, that by this time the Pilgrims were got over the Enchanted ground, and entering into the Country of *Beulah*,[108] whose air was very sweet and pleasant, the Way lying directly through it, they solaced themselves there for a season. Yea, here they heard continually the singing of birds, and saw every day the flowers appear in the earth, and heard the voice of the turtle in the land. In this country the Sun shineth night and day; wherefore this was beyond the valley of the *Shadow of Death*, and also out of the reach of Giant *Despair*, neither could they from this place so much as see *Doubting-Castle*. Here they were within sight of the City they were going to; also here met them some of the inhabitants thereof: For in this land the *Shining Ones* commonly walked, because it was upon the borders of Heaven. In this land also the contract between the Bride and the Bridegroom was renewed:° Yea, here, *as the Bridegroom rejoyceth over the Bride, so did their God rejoyce over them.* Here they had no want of corn and wine; for in this place they met with abundance of what they had sought in all their Pilgrimage.

Isa. 62. 4.
Cant. 2. 10, 11,
12.

Angels.

Isa. 62. 5.
Ver. 8.

---

to pick holes . . . the Godly To criticize the holiness of others; the contract . . . was renewed Several biblical texts describe the Church as the bride of Christ.

Here they heard voices from out of the City, loud voices, saying, *Say ye to the Daughter of Zion, Behold thy Salvation*   Ver. 11.
cometh! Behold his Reward is with him! Here all the inhabitants of the Country called them, *The holy People, the Re-*   Ver. 12.
deemed of the Lord, Sought out, &c.

Now, as they walked in this land, they had more Rejoycing
than in parts more remote from the Kingdom to which they
were bound; and drawing near to the City, they had yet a
more perfect View thereof: It was builded of Pearls and precious Stones; also the streets thereof were paved with Gold, so
that by reason of the natural glory of the City, and the reflection of the Sun-beams upon it, *Christian* with desire fell sick;
Hopeful also had a fit or two of the same disease: Wherefore
here they lay by it a while, crying out because of their pangs;
If you see my Beloved tell him that I am sick of Love.

But being a little strengthned, and better able to bear their
sickness, they walked on their Way, and came yet nearer and
nearer, where were orchards, vineyards and gardens, and their
gates opened into the High-way. Now as they came up to
these places, behold the gardener stood in the Way, to whom
the Pilgrims said, Whose goodly vineyards and gardens are   Deut. 23. 24.
these? He answered, They are the KING'S, and are planted here
for his own delight, and also for the solace of Pilgrims: So the
gardener had them into the vineyards, and bid them refresh
themselves with dainties; He also shewed them *there* the
King's walks and the arbours, where he delighted to be: And
here they tarried and slept.

Now I beheld in my dream, that they talked more in their
sleep at this time, than ever they did in all their Journey; and
being in a muse thereabout, the gardener said even to me,°
Wherefore musest thou at the matter? It is the nature of the
fruit of the grapes of these vineyards to go down so sweetly,
as to cause the lips of them that are asleep to speak.

So I saw that when they awoke, they addressed themselves
to go up to the City. But as I said, the reflection of the Sun

---

even to me The narrator comes into more prominence toward the end of
the journey.

Rev. 21. 18.
2 Cor. 3. 18.

upon the City (for the City was pure gold) was so extremely glorious, that they could not as yet with open face behold it; but through an *instrument*° made for that purpose. So I saw that as they went on, there met them two Men[109] in raiment that shone like gold, also their faces shone as the light.

These men asked the Pilgrims whence they came? and they told them. They also asked them where they had lodged, what difficulties and dangers, what comforts and pleasures they had met with in the Way? And they told them. Then said the men that met them, You have but two Difficulties more to meet with, and then you are in the City.

Christian then and his Companion asked the men to go along with them, so they told them they would: But, said they, you must obtain it by your own Faith. So I saw in my dream that they went on together till they came within Sight of the Gate.

Now I further saw, that betwixt them and the Gate was a River,° but there was no bridge to go over, and the river was very deep. At the sight therefore of this River, the Pilgrims were much astounded, but the men that went with them, said, You must go through, or you cannot come at the Gate.

Death is not welcome to Nature, though by it we pass out of this world into Glory.
1 Cor. 15. 51, 52.

The Pilgrims then began to enquire if there was no other Way to the Gate; to which they answered, Yes, but there hath not any, save two, to wit, *Enoch* and *Elijah*,° been permitted to tread that path, since the foundation of the World, nor shall until the last Trumpet shall sound. The Pilgrims then (especially *Christian*) began to despond in his mind, and looked this way and that, but no way could be found by them, by which they might escape the River. Then they asked the Men if the Waters were all of a depth? They said, No; yet they could not help them in that case; *For*, said they, *you shall find it deeper or shallower, as you believe in the King of the Place.*

Angels help us not comfortably through Death.

---

instrument In 2 Corinthians 3:18 Paul describes "beholding as in a glass the glory of the Lord" (KJV); **a River** Of death. The biblical type is the River Jordan; after crossing it the Israelites entered the promised land; **Enoch and Elijah** In Genesis 5:22–24 Enoch and Elijah are translated to heaven without out dying.

They then addressed themselves to the Water, and entring, *Christian* began to sink, and crying out to his good friend *Hopeful*, he said, I sink in deep Waters; the Billows go over my head, all the Waves go over me. *Selah.*°

Then said the other, Be of good cheer, my Brother, I feel the bottom, and it is good. Then said *Christian*, Ah! my friend, the sorrows of Death have compassed me about, I shall not see the Land that flows with milk and honey. And with that a great darkness and horror fell upon *Christian*, so that he could not see before him. Also here he in a great measure lost his senses, so that he could neither remember nor orderly talk of any of those sweet refreshments that he had met with in the Way of his Pilgrimage. But all the words that he spake still tended to discover, that he had Horror of Mind, and Heart-Fears that he should die in that River, and never obtain Entrance in at the Gate. Here also, as they that stood by perceived,° he was much in the troublesome thoughts of the Sins that he had committed, both since and before he began to be a Pilgrim. 'Twas also observed, that he was troubled with apparitions of Hobgoblins and evil Spirits;° for ever and anon he would intimate so much by words. *Hopeful* therefore here had much ado to keep his brother's head above water, yea sometimes he would be quite gone down, and then e're a while he would rise up again half dead. *Hopeful* also would endeavour to comfort him, saying, Brother, I see the Gate, and Men standing by to receive us; but *Christian* would answer, 'Tis you, 'tis you they wait for; you have been *Hopeful* ever since I knew you. And so have you,° said he to *Christian*. Ah, brother! said *he*, surely if I was right,

Christian's Conflict at the hour of Death.

Selah This word, which occurs frequently in the Bible, is not a word but a form of punctuation designating a pause for consideration. In Bunyan's time a similar function was performed by marginal drawings of pointing fingers; **they that stood by perceived** Death was a public event in Bunyan's *milieu*, and the dying person's behavior was studied closely for clues about their soul's destination; **Hobgoblins and evil Spirits** In *Grace Abounding*, Bunyan tells us: "I have in my bed been greatly afflicted with the apprehensions of devils, and wicked spirits" (p. 8); **so have you** As they cross the river, and leave the world, the characters slough off the allegorical significances that designate their alienated condition; now Christian is called "hopeful."

he would now rise to help me, but for my Sins he hath brought me into the snare, and hath left me. Then said *Hopeful*, My Brother, you have quite forgot the text, where it is said

Psal. 73. 4, 5.

of the Wicked, *There is no Bands° in their Death, but their Strength is firm, they are not troubled as other men, neither are they plagued like other men.* These troubles and distresses that you go through in these Waters, are no sign that God hath forsaken you, but are sent to try you, whether you will call to mind that which heretofore you have received of his Goodness, and live upon him in your Distresses.

Christian
delivered from
his Fears in
Death.

Then I saw in my dream, That *Christian* was as in a muse a while. To whom also *Hopeful* added these words, *Be of good cheer, Jesus Christ maketh thee whole:* And with that *Christian* brake out with a loud voice, Oh, I see him again! and he tells

Isa. 43. 2.

me, When thou passest through the Waters, I will be with thee; and through the Rivers, they shall not overflow thee. Then they both took courage, and the Enemy° was after that as still as a stone, until they were gone over. *Christian* therefore presently found Ground to stand upon, and so it followed, that the rest of the River was but shallow: Thus they got over. Now upon the bank of the River on the other side, they saw the two shining men again, who there waited for

The Angels do
wait for them
so soon as
they are
passed out of
this World.

them: Wherefore being come up out of the River, they saluted them, saying, *We are Ministring Spirits sent forth to minister to those that shall be Heirs of Salvation;* Thus they went along toward the Gate. Now you must note, that the City stood upon a mighty Hill, but the Pilgrims went up that Hill with ease, because they had these two men to lead them up by the arms; also they had left their *mortal Garments°* behind them in the

They have put
off Mortality.

River; for though they went in with them, they came out without them. They therefore went up here with much agility and speed, though the Foundation upon which the City was framed was higher than the Clouds; They therefore went up

---

Bands Pains, concerns; the wicked die peacefully because they are oblivious to the afterlife; **the Enemy** We have met no external "enemy" here; the word refers to Christian's temptation to despair, stimulated by Satan; **mortal Garments** Not their bodies, but their bodies' mortality.

through the region of the air, sweetly talking as they went, being comforted, because they safely got over the River, and had such glorious Companions to attend them.

The talk that they had with the Shining Ones was about the Glory of the place, who told them, that the Beauty and Glory of it was inexpressible. There, said they, is *Mount Sion,* *the heavenly Jerusalem, the innumerable Company of Angels,* *and the Spirits of just men made Perfect.* You are going now, said they, to the Paradise of GOD, wherein you shall see the *Tree of Life,* and eat of the never-fading Fruits thereof; and when you come there you shall have white Robes given you, and your walk and talk shall be every day with the KING, even all the days of Eternity. There you shall not see again such things as you saw when you were in the lower region upon the earth, to wit, Sorrow, Sickness, Affliction, and Death, *for* *the former things are passed away.* You are going now to *Abra-* *ham, Isaac,* and *Jacob,* and to the Prophets, men that God hath taken away from the Evil to come,° and that are now resting upon their beds, each one walking° in his Righteous-ness. The men then asked, What must we do in the Holy Place? To whom it was answered, You must there receive the Comfort of all your Toil, and have Joy for all your Sorrow; you must reap what you have sown, even the fruit of all your Prayers and Tears, and Sufferings for the King by the Way. In that place you must wear Crowns of Gold, and enjoy the per-petual sight and vision of the *Holy One, for there you shall see* *him as he is.*° There also you shall serve him continually with Praise, with Shouting, and Thanksgiving, whom you desired to serve in the World, though with much difficulty because of the Infirmity of your Flesh. There your eyes shall be delighted with seeing, and your ears with hearing the pleasant Voice of the *Mighty One.* There you shall enjoy your Friends again,

Heb. 12. 22, 23, 24.

Rev. 2. 7.

& 3. 4.

Rev. 22. 7.

Isa. 57. 1, 2. & 65. 16, 17.

Gal. 6. 7.

1 John 3. 2.

---

the Evil to come The Apocalypse; **resting . . . walking** Bunyan forces the fig-ural interpretation on the reader; they could not rest and walk at the same time if these verbs were taken literally; **as he is** In essence, rather than in the mediated form that Christ is manifest in the world. See 1 Corinthians 13:12: "For now we see through a glass, darkly; but then face to face" (KJV).

that are gone thither before you; and there you shall with joy receive even every one that follows into the Holy Place after you. There also you shall be cloathed with Glory and Majesty, and put into an equipage° fit to ride out with the *King of Glory*. When he shall come with Sound of Trumpet in the Clouds, as upon the wings of the Wind, you shall come with him; and when he shall sit upon the Throne of Judgment, you shall sit by him; yea, and when he shall pass Sentence upon all the workers of Iniquity, let them be Angels or men; you also shall have a voice in that Judgment, because they were his and your Enemies. Also when he shall again return to the City, you shall go too with sound of Trumpet, and be ever with him.

Now while they were thus drawing towards the Gate, behold a company of the Heavenly Host came out to meet them; to whom it was said by the other two Shining Ones, These are the men that have loved our Lord, when they were in the World, and that have left all for his Holy Name, and he hath sent us to fetch them, and we have brought them thus far on their desired Journey, that they may go in and look their Redeemer in the face with Joy. Then the Heavenly Host gave a great shout, saying, *Blessed are they that are called to the Marriage Supper of the Lamb.* There came out also at this time, to meet them, several of the King's Trumpeters, cloathed in white and shining raiment, who with melodious noises and loud, made even the Heavens to echo with their sound. These Trumpeters saluted *Christian* and his fellow with ten thousand Welcomes from the world; and this they did with shouting and Sound of Trumpet.

This done, they compassed them round on every side; some went before, some behind, and some on the right-hand, some on the left, (as 'twere to guard them through the upper regions) continually sounding as they went with melodious noise, in notes on high; so that the very sight was to them that could behold it, as if Heaven itself was come down to meet

Margin notes:
1 Thes. 4. 13, to 17.
Jude 14.
Dan. 7. 9, 10.
1 Cor. 6. 2, 3.

Rev. 19. 9.

---

put into an equipage Furnished with equipment.

Now, now look how the holy Pilgrims ride,
Clouds are their Chariots, Angels are their Guide;
Who would not here for him all Hazards run?
That thus provides for *His,* when this world's done.

them. Thus therefore they walked on together; and as they walked ever and anon these Trumpeters, even with joyful sound, would, by mixing their musik with looks and gestures, still signify to *Christian* and his brother how welcome they were into their company, and with what gladness they came to meet them: And now were these two men, as 'twere, in Heaven before they came at it; being swallowed up with the sight of Angels, and with hearing their melodious notes. Here also they had the City itself in view, and they thought they heard all the bells therein to ring, to welcome them thereto; but above all, the warm and joyful thoughts that they had about their own dwelling there with such Company, and that for ever and ever; Oh! by what tongue or pen can their glorious Joy be expressed! Thus they came up to the Gate.

Now, when they were come up to the Gate, there was written over it in letters of Gold, *Blessed are they that do his Commandments, that they may have right to the Tree of Life, and may enter in through the Gates into the City.*

Rev. 22. 14.

Then I saw in my dream, that the shining men bid them call at the Gate, the which when they did, some from above looked over the Gate; to wit, *Enoch, Moses*, and *Elijah, &c.* to whom it was said, These Pilgrims are come from the City of *Destruction*, for the Love that they bear to the King of this place; and then the Pilgrims gave in unto them each man his Certificate,[110] which they had received in the beginning; those therefore were carried in to the King, who when he had read them, said, Where are the men? to whom it was answered, They are standing without the Gate. The King then commanded to open the Gate, *that the Righteous Nation*, said he, *that keepeth Truth, may enter in.*

Isa. 26. 2.

Now I saw in my dream, that these two men went in at the Gate; and lo, as they entered, they were transfigured:° and they had raiment put on that shone like Gold. There was also that met them, with Harps and Crowns, and gave them to them, the harps to praise withal, and the crowns in token of

---

transfigured Transformed into a source of radiance; Jesus is "transfigured" in front of the disciples in Matthew 17:2.

honour. Then I heard in my dream, that all the bells in the City rang again for joy; and that it was said unto them, *Enter ye into the Joy of our Lord.* I also heard° the men themselves say, that they sang with a loud voice, saying, *Blessing, Honour, Glory, and Power, be to Him that sitteth upon the Throne, and to the Lamb, for ever and ever.*

Rev. 5. 13, 14.

Now, just as the Gates were opened to let in the men, I looked in after them; and behold the City shone like the Sun, the streets also were paved with Gold, and in them walked many men with Crowns on their heads, Palms in their hands, and Golden Harps to sing praises withal.

There were also of them that had wings, and they answered one another without intermission, saying, *Holy, Holy, Holy is the Lord:* and after that, they shut up the Gates: which when I had seen, I wished myself among them.°

Now, while I was gazing upon all these things, I turned my head to look back, and saw *Ignorance* coming up to the River-side; but he soon got over, and that without half the Difficulty which the other two men met with. For it happened that there was then in that place one *Vain-Hope*, a ferry-man, that with his boat helped him over: so he, as the other, I saw did ascend the Hill, to come up to the Gate, only he came alone; neither did any man meet him with the least encouragement. When he was come up to the Gate, he looked up to the Writing that was above, and then began to knock, supposing that Entrance should have been quickly administred to him: But he was asked by the men that looked over the top of the Gate, Whence come you? And what would you have? He answered, I have eat and drank in the Presence of the King, and he has taught in our streets. Then they asked him for his Certificate, that they might go in and shew it to the King; so he fumbled in his bosom for one, and found none.[111] Then, said they, Have you none? but the man answered never a word. So they

Ignorance *comes up to the River, and* Vain-Hope *ferrys him over.*

I also heard The narrator repeatedly asserts his presence now that Christian has been transfigured, since human beings no longer have direct access to his experience; **I wished myself among them** The story does not end happily, but on a melancholy note of exclusion.

told the King, but he would not come down to see him, but commanded the two shining Ones that conducted *Christian* and *Hopeful* to the City, to go out and take *Ignorance* and bind him hand and foot, and have him away. Then they took him up, and carried him through the air to the door that I saw in the side of the Hill, and put him in there. *Then I saw that there was a* Way to Hell, *even from the* Gates of Heaven, *as well as from the* City of *Destruction*. So I awoke, and behold it was a Dream.°

---

behold it was a Dream This does not diminish, but rather augments, the truth of the vision.

The Conclusion.

N *ow, Reader, I have told my Dream to thee,*
   See if thou canst Interpret° it to me,
   Or to Thyself, or Neighbour; but take heed
Of mis-interpreting; for that, instead
Of doing Good, will but thyself abuse:°
By mis-interpreting, Evil ensues.

   Take heed also that thou be not extreme
In playing with the out-side° *of my dream:*
Nor let my Figure or similitude°
Put thee into a Laughter, or a Feud;
Leave this for Boys and Fools; but as for thee,
So thou the Substance° *of my matter see.*

   Put by° the curtains, look within my vail,
Turn up° my metaphors, and do not fail;
There, if thou seekest them, such things thou'lt find
As will be helpful to an honest mind.

   What of my dross° *thou findest here, be bold*
To throw away, but yet preserve the Gold.
What if my Gold° *be wrapped up in ore?°*
None throws away the Apple for the Core.
But if thou shalt cast all away as vain,
I know not but 'twill make me dream again.

The End of the First Part.

Interpret The book's purpose has been to teach the skill of allegorical interpretation. This is the "progress" achieved by Christian and, Bunyan hopes, the reader; **abuse** Misinterpret, idolize, sell; **the out-side** The apparent, external, fleshly, and literal meaning; **Figure or similitude** The outward trappings in which Bunyan has dressed his message; **Substance** Essence; **Put by** Draw; **Turn up** Look under; **dross** The waste product in the purification of gold; **Gold** Bunyan alludes to the ethical significance of gold as the most perfect of all metals, not to its financial significance as the incarnation of exchange value; **ore** Unpurified mixture of minerals, including gold.

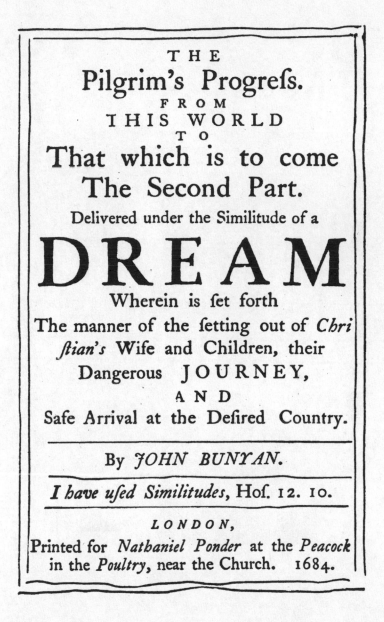

THE
Pilgrim's Progreſs.
FROM
THIS WORLD
TO
That which is to come
The Second Part.

Delivered under the Similitude of a

DREAM

Wherein is ſet forth
The manner of the ſetting out of *Chri
ſtian's* Wife and Children, their
Dangerous JOURNEY,
AND
Safe Arrival at the Deſired Country.

By *JOHN BUNYAN.*

I have uſed Similitudes, Hoſ. 12. 10.

LONDON,
Printed for *Nathaniel Ponder* at the *Peacock*
in the *Poultry,* near the Church. 1684.

The Author's Way of sending forth his Second Part of the Pilgrim

Go now, my little Book, to every place,
Where my first Pilgrim *has but shewn his Face:*
Call at their door: If any say, Who's there?
Then answer thou, Christiana[1] is here.
If they bid thee Come in, *then enter thou,*
With all thy boys: And then as thou know'st how;
Tell who they are, also from whence they came;
Perhaps they'll know them by their looks or name:
But if they should not, ask them yet again,
If formerly they did not entertain
One Christian *a Pilgrim? If they say,*
They did, and were delighted in his Way,
Then let them know, that those related were
Unto him: Yea, his Wife and Children are.[2]

    Tell them that they have left their House and Home;
Are turned Pilgrims, seek a World to come:
That they have met with Hardships in the Way,
That they do meet with Troubles night and day:
That they have trod on Serpents, fought with Devils,
Have also overcome a many evils.
Yea, tell them also of the next, who have
Of° Love to Pilgrimage, *been stout and brave*
Defenders of that Way, and how they still
Refuse° this World, to do their Father's will.

    Go tell them also of those dainty things,
That Pilgrimage *unto the* Pilgrim *brings:*
Let them acquainted be too, how they are

Of Out of; **Refuse** Both "reject" and "turn into refuse."

187

Beloved of their King, under his Care;
What goodly Mansions for them he provides,
Tho' they meet with rough Winds and swelling Tides,
How brave a Calm they will enjoy at last,
Who to their Lord, and by his Ways hold fast.
      Perhaps with heart and hand they will embrace
Thee, as they did my firstling,° and will grace
Thee, and thy fellows, with such cheer and fare,
As shew will, they of Pilgrims Lovers are.

1. Objection.

But how, if they will not believe of me
That I am truly thine; 'cause some there be
That counterfeit° the Pilgrim and his Name,
Seek, by Disguise, to seem the very same,
And by that means have brought themselves into
The hands and houses of I know not who.

Answer.

'Tis true, some have of late to counterfeit
My Pilgrim, to their own, my Title set;
Yea, others half my Name and Title too
Have stitched to their Book, to make them do;
But yet they by their Features do declare
Themselves not mine to be, whose e'er they are.
      If such thou meet'st with, then thine only way
Before them all, is, to Say out thy Say,
In thine own native Language, which no man
Now useth,° nor with ease dissemble can.
If, after all, they still of you shall doubt,
Thinking that you, like Gipsies,° *go about*
In naughty wise,° the Country to defile,

---

firstling Firstborn; **counterfeit** In 1682 Thomas Sherman had published his own *Second Part of the Pilgrim's Progress*, and numerous imitations of Bunyan's work were circulating; **In thine . . . Now useth** The plainspoken Puritanism Bunyan espouses was deeply unfashionable in Restoration England; **Gipsies** Bunyan himself was a tinker, a profession usually practiced by gypsies in his day; **In naughty wise** In a wicked manner.

Or that you seek good people to beguile
With things unwarrantable, send for me,
And I will testify you Pilgrims *be;*
Yea, I will testify that only you
My Pilgrims *are; and that alone will do.*

2. Object.

But yet, perhaps, I may enquire for him,
Of those that wish him damned life and limb.°
What shall I do, when I at such a door
For *Pilgrims* ask, and they shall rage the more?

Answer.

Fright not thyself, my Book, for such bugbears°
Are nothing else but Ground for groundless fears,
My Pilgrim's *Book has travell'd Sea and Land,*
Yet could I never come to understand°
That it was slighted or turn'd out of door
By any Kingdom, were they Rich or Poor.
   In France° *and* Flanders, *where men kill each other,*
My Pilgrim *is esteem'd a Friend, a Brother.*
   In Holland *too, 'tis said, as I am told,*
My Pilgrim *is with some worth more than Gold.°*
   Highlanders *and* Wild Irish° *can agree,*
My Pilgrim *should familiar with them be.*
'Tis in New England° *under such advance,*
Receives there so much loving countenance,°
As to be trim'd, new-cloath'd, and deck'd with gems
That it may shew its features and its limbs,
Yet more, so comely doth my Pilgrim *walk,*
That of him Thousands daily sing and talk.

Of those . . . life and limb The radical theology of *The Pilgrim's Progress* had
not endeared Bunyan to the authorities; **bugbears** Boogeymen; **understand**
Hear; **In France** The following lines boast of the many translations and
widespread popularity of the first part; **In Holland . . . Gold** The Dutch, like
the Scots, were reputed misers; **Highlanders and Wild Irish** The most
"primitive" people in Bunyan's experience; **New England** Bunyan's book
was strongly influential in New England, whose inhabitants had long styled
themselves "pilgrims"; **countenance** Regard.

If you draw nearer Home, it will appear,
My Pilgrim *knows no ground of° shame or fear;*
City and Country will him entertain
With, Welcome, Pilgrim, *yea, they can't refrain,*
From smiling, if my Pilgrim *be but by,*
Or shews his head in any Company.

 Brave Gallants° do my Pilgrim *hug and love,*
Esteem it much, yea, value it above
Things of a greater bulk, yea, with delight,
Say, my Lark's *leg is better than a* Kite.°

 Young Ladies, and young Gentlewomen too,
Do no small kindness to my Pilgrim *shew;*
Their cabinets, their bosoms, and their hearts,
My Pilgrim *has, 'cause he to them imparts*
His pretty riddles, in such wholsome strains,
As yields them Profit double to their Pains
Of reading; yea, I think I may be bold
To say, some prize him far above their Gold.[3]

 The very Children that do walk the street,
If they do but my Holy Pilgrim *meet,*
Salute him will, will wish him well, and say,
He is the only stripling[4] *of the day.*

 They that have never seen him, yet admire
What they have heard of him, and much desire
To have his Company, and hear him tell
Those Pilgrim *stories, which he knows so well.*

 Yea, some who did not love him at the first,
But call'd him Fool *and* Noddy,° *say they must,*
Now they have seen and heard him, him commend;
And to those whom they love, they do him send.

 Wherefore, my Second Part, *thou need'st not be*
Afraid to shew thy head; none can hurt thee,
That wish but well to him that went before,
'Cause thou com'st after with a second store,

---

ground of Cause for; **Brave Gallants** Dashing young men; **my Lark's . . .
Kite** A dainty, apparently trivial dish is preferable to a hearty but indigestible repast; **Noddy** Twit.

Of things as good, as rich, as profitable,
For Young, for Old; for Stagg'ring, and for Stable.

3. Object.

But some there be that say, *He laughs too loud;*
And some do say, *His Head is in a Cloud.*°
Some say, *His Words and Stories are so dark,*
They know not how by them to find his mark.

Answer.

One may (I think) say, Both his laughs and cries
May well be guess'd at by his wat'ry eyes.
Some things are of that nature; as to make
One's Fancy checkle,° *while his Heart doth ake;*°
When Jacob *saw his* Rachel *with the sheep,*
He did at the same time both kiss and weep.°
Whereas some say, A Cloud is in his Head,
That doth but shew how Wisdom's covered
With its own mantles,° *and to stir the mind*
To a search after what it fain would find.
Things that seem to be hid in words obscure,
Do but the Godly mind the more allure,
To study what those sayings should contain,
That speak to us in such a cloudy strain.
I also know a dark Similitude
Will on the Fancy more itself intrude,
And will stick faster in the Heart and Head,
Than things from Similies not borrowed.°
Wherefore, my Book, let no discouragement
Hinder thy travels: Behold; thou art sent
To Friends, not foes, to Friends that will give place°
To thee, thy Pilgrims, and thy Words embrace.
Besides, what my first Pilgrim left conceal'd,

His Head is in a Cloud Compare the endnote to "Dark Clouds bring Waters" on page 342; **checkle** Chuckle; **ake** Ache; **When Jacob . . . weep** Genesis 29:11: "And Jacob kissed Rachel, and lifted up his voice, and wept" (KJV); **mantles** Cloaks; **I also know . . . borrowed** The truth can be approached only through linguistic mediation: "Similies" and analogies; **place** Honor.

Thou, my brave Second Pilgrim *hast reveal'd;*
What Christian *left lock'd up, and went his Way,*
Sweet Christiana *opens with her Key.*[5]

4. Object.

But some love not the method of your first;
Romance° they count it, throw't away as dust.
If I should meet with such, What should I say?
Must I slight them as they slight me, or nay?

Answer.

My Christiana, *if with such thou meet,*
By all means in all Loving wise them greet;
Render them not reviling for revile;
But if they frown, I prithee° on them smile:
Perhaps 'tis Nature,° or some ill report,
Has made them thus despise, or thus retort.
Some love no cheese, some love no fish, and some
Love not their Friends, nor their own house or Home.
Some start° at pig, slight° chicken, love not fowl,
More than they love a cuckow, or an owl.
Leave such, my Christiana, *to their Choice,*
And seek those, who to find thee will rejoice;
By no means strive,° but in all humble wise,°
Present thee to them in thy Pilgrim's guise.
Go then, my little Book, and shew to all
That entertain, and bid thee Welcome shall,
What thou shalt keep close,° shut up from the rest,
And wish what thou shall shew them, may be blest
To them for good, may make them chuse to be
Pilgrims better by far, than thee or me.
Go then, I say, tell all men who thou art,
Say, I am Christiana, *and my part*
Is now with my four Sons to tell you what
It is for men to take a Pilgrim's *lot.*

Romance Fiction; **prithee** Ask you to; **Nature** That is, their own nature; **start**
Recoil; **slight** Criticize; **strive** Fight; **wise** Manner; **close** Secret.

Go also, tell them who and what they be,
That now do go on Pilgrimage with thee:
Say, Here's my neighbour Mercy, *she is one,*
That has long time with me a Pilgrim gone:
Come, see her in her Virgin face, and learn
'Twixt idle ones,° and Pilgrims, *to discern.*
Yea, let young Damsels learn of her to prize
The World which is come, in any wise:
When little tripping° maidens follow God,
And leave all doting° Sinners to his Rod;
'Tis like those days wherein the young ones cry'd
Hosanna, *to whom old ones did deride.°*

   Next tell them of old Honest, *who you found*
With his white hairs treading the Pilgrim's ground
Yea, tell them how plain-hearted this man was,
How after° his good Lord he bare his Cross:
Perhaps with some gray head this may prevail
With Christ to fall in Love, and Sin bewail.

   Tell them also, how Master Fearing *went*
On Pilgrimage, and how the time he spent
In solitariness, with fears and cries;
And how, at last, he won the Joyful Prize.
He was a good man, tho' much down in spirit;
He is a good man, and doth Life inherit.

   Tell them of Master Feeble-mind *also,*
Who, not before, but still behind would go;
Shew them also how he had like° been slain,
And how one Great-Heart *did his life regain:*
This man was true of Heart, tho' weak in Grace,
One might true Godliness read in his face.

   Then tell them of Master Ready-to-halt,
A man with Crutches, but much without fault.
Tell them how Master Feeble-mind *and he*
Did love, and in Opinions much agree.

---

idle Lazy, vain, with a pun of "idol"; **tripping** Skipping; **doting** Foolish; **old ones did deride** Children were attracted to Jesus; the elders of his society were not; **after** Both "behind" and "after the fashion of"; **like** Likely.

And let all know, tho' Weakness was their chance,
Yet sometimes one would Sing, the other Dance.
  Forget not Master Valiant-for-the-Truth,
That man of courage, tho' a very Youth:
Tell every one his spirit was so stout,
No man could ever make him face about;
And how Great-Heart *and he could not forbear,*
But put down Doubting-Castle, *slay* Despair.
  Overlook not Master Despondency,
Nor Much-afraid *his daughter, tho' they lie*
Under such mantles, as may make them look
(With some) as if their God had them forsook.
They softly went, but sure, and at the End
Found that the Lord of Pilgrims *was their Friend.*
When thou hast told the World of·all these things,
Then turn about, my Book, and touch these strings;°
Which, if but touched, will such musick make,
They'll make a Cripple dance, a Giant quake.
  Those Riddles that lie couch'd° within thy breast,
Freely propound expound: And for the rest
Of thy mysterious lines, let them remain
For those whose nimble Fancies° shall them gain.
  Now may this little Book a blessing be
To those that love this little Book, and me:
And may its Buyer have no cause to say,
His money is but lost or thrown away;
Yea, may this Second Pilgrim *yield that Fruit*
As may with each good Pilgrim's *fancy suit;*
And may it persuade some that go astray,
To turn their Foot and Heart to the right Way.

Is the Hearty Prayer of

THE AUTHOR,

JOHN BUNYAN.

---

touch these strings The strings of a lyre, a classical emblem of poetic inspiration; **couch'd** Contained; **nimble Fancies** Quick minds. Despite Bunyan's claims to universal appeal, some especially "mysterious" meanings will be accessible only to skilled readers.

The Pilgrims Progress

In the Similitude of a Dream.
THE SECOND PART.

*C*ourteous Companions, some time since, to tell you my
Dream that I had of *Christian* the *Pilgrim*, and of his
dangerous Journey towards the Cœlestial Country,
was pleasant to me, and profitable to you. I told you then also
what I saw concerning his *Wife* and *Children*, and how unwilling they were to go with him on Pilgrimage; insomuch
that he was forced to go on his Progress without them; for he
durst not run the danger of that destruction, which he feared
would come, by staying with them in the City of *Destruction*:
Wherefore, as I then shewed you, he left them and departed.

Now, it hath so happened, through the multiplicity of
business,° that I have been much hindred and kept back from
my wonted Travels into those parts whence he went, and so
could not, till now, obtain an opportunity to make further
enquiry after whom he left behind, that I might give you an
account of them. But having had some concerns that way of
late, I went down again thitherward. Now having taken up
my lodgings in a Wood, about a mile off the place, as I slept,
I dreamed again.

And as I was in my dream, behold an aged gentleman
came by where I lay; and because he was to go some part of
the Way that I was travelling, methought I got up and went
with him. So as we walked, and as Travellers usually do, I was
as if we fell into discourse, and our talk happened to be about
Christian, and his Travels: For thus I began with the old man.

Sir, said I, what Town is that, there below, that lieth on the
Left Hand of our Way?

---

the multiplicity of business Part two was written when Bunyan was at liberty to preach and to practice his tinker's trade.

Then said Mr. *Sagacity*,° for that was his name, it is the City of *Destruction*, a populous place, but possess'd with a very ill-condition'd and idle sort of people.

I thought that was that City, *quoth I:* I went once myself thro' that Town; and therefore I know that this report you give of it is true.

Sag. Too true; I wish I could speak truth in speaking better of them that dwell therein.

Well Sir, quoth I, then I perceive you to be a well-meaning man, and so one that takes pleasure to hear and tell of that which is Good: Pray, did you never hear what happen'd to a man some time ago in this Town, (whose name was *Christian*) that went on Pilgrimage up towards the higher Regions?

Sag. Hear of him! Ay; and I also heard of the molestations, troubles, wars, captivities, cries, groans, frights, and fears that he met with and had in his Journey; besides, I must tell you, all our Country rings of him; there are but few houses that have heard of him and his doings, but have sought after, and got the Records of his Pilgrimage; yea, I think I may say, that his hazardous Journey has got many well-wishers to his ways:

Christians are well spoken of when gone, tho' called Fools while they are here. For tho' when he was here, he was *Fool* in every man's mouth, yet now he is gone, he is highly commended of all; for, 'tis said, he lives bravely where he is: Yea, many of them that are resolved never to run his hazards, yet have their mouths water at his gains.

They may, *quoth I,* well think, if they think any thing that is true, that he liveth well where he is; for he now lives at, and in the Fountain of Life, and has what he has without labour and sorrow, for there is no grief mixed therewith. 'But pray; what talk have the people about him?'

[Edit. 1728.]

Rev. 3. 4. Chap. 6. 11. *Sag.* Talk! The people talk strangely about him: Some say, that he now walks in white, that he has a chain of Gold about his neck, that he has a crown of Gold, beset with Pearls, upon his head: Others say, that the shining Ones that sometimes shewed themselves to him in his Journey, are become his

---

Mr. Sagacity The wisdom Bunyan has acquired from contemplation of Christian's pilgrimage.

companions, and that he is as familiar with them in the place where he is, as here one neighbour is with another. Besides, 'tis confidently affirmed concerning him, that the King of the place where he is, has bestowed upon him already, a very rich and pleasant dwelling at Court, and that he every day eateth and drinketh, and walketh and talketh with him, and receiveth of the smiles and favours of him that is Judge of all there. Moreover, it is expected of some, that his Prince, the Lord of that country, will shortly come into these parts,° and will know the reason, if they can give any, why his neighbours set so little by him, and had him so much in derision, when they perceived that he would be a Pilgrim.

Zech. 3. 7.
Luke 14. 15.

Jude 14, 15.

For they say, that now he is so in the affections of his Prince, and that his Sovereign is so much concern'd with the indignities that were cast upon *Christian*, when he became a Pilgrim, that he will look upon all as if done unto himself; and no marvel, for 'twas for the Love that he had to his Prince, that he ventured as he did.

Christian's King will take Christian's part.

Luke 10. 16.

I dare say, *quoth I*, I am glad on't; I am glad for the poor man's sake, for that° now he has Rest from his labour, and for that he now reapeth the benefit of his tears with Joy; and for that he has got beyond the gun-shot of his enemies, and is out of the reach of them that hate him. I also am glad, for that a rumour of these things is noised abroad° in this country; who can tell but that it may work some good effect on some that are left behind? But, pray, Sir, while it is fresh in my mind, do you hear any thing of his Wife and Children? Poor hearts, I wonder in my mind what they do!

Rev. 14. 13.
Psal. 126. 5, 6.

Sag. Who! *Christiana* and her Sons! They are like to do as well as did *Christian* himself; for though they all play'd the fool at the first, and would by no means be persuaded by either the tears or entreaties of *Christian*, yet second thoughts have wrought wonderfully with them, so they have pack'd up, and are also gone after him.

Good tidings of Christian's Wife and Children.

---

come into these parts The second coming of Christ; for that Because; noised abroad Spread around.

Better and better, *quoth I:* But, what! Wife and Children and all?

Sag. 'Tis true, I can give you an account of the matter, for I was upon the spot at the instant, and was throughly acquainted with the whole affair.

Then, *said I,* a man it seems may report it for a Truth?

Sag. You need not fear to affirm it; I mean, that they are all gone on Pilgrimage, both the good woman and her four boys. And being we are, as I perceive, going some considerable way together, I will give you an account of the whole matter.

This *Christiana* (for that was her name from the day that she with her children betook themselves to a Pilgrim's life,) after her husband was gone *over the River,* and she could hear of him no more, her thoughts began to work in her mind. First, for that she had lost her husband, and for that the loving bond of that relation was utterly broken betwixt them. For you know, said he to me, Nature can do no less but entertain the living with many a heavy cogitation in the remembrance of the loss of loving relations. This therefore of her husband did cost her many a tear. But this was not all, for *Christiana* did also begin to consider with herself, Whether her unbecoming behaviour towards her husband[6] was not one Cause that she saw him no more; and that in such sort he was taken away from her. And upon this, came into her mind by *swarms,* all her unkind, unnatural, and ungodly carriage° to her dear friend; which also clogg'd her conscience, and did load her with Guilt. She was moreover much broken° with calling to remembrance the restless groans, the brinish° tears, and self-bemoanings of her husband, and how she did harden her heart against all his entreaties, and loving persuasions (of her and her Sons) to go with him; yea, there was not any thing that *Christian* either said to her, or did before her, all the while that his Burden did hang on his back, but it returned upon her like a Flash of Lightning, and rent the caul

Part I. page 176.

Mark this, you that are churls to your godly relations.

---

carriage Actions, bearing; **broken** "Breaking" the heart with guilt was a precondition of conversion; **brinish** Salty.

of her heart[7] in sunder;° especially that bitter out-cry of his, *Part I. pages* 13, 14.
What shall I do to be saved? did ring in her ears most dolefully.

Then said she to her children, Sons, we are all undone. I
have sinned away your father, and he is gone; he would have
had us with him, but I would not go myself; I also hindred
you of Life. With that the boys fell all into tears, and cried out
to go after their father. Oh! said *Christiana*, that it had been
but our lot to go with him, then had it fared well with us, beyond what 'tis like to do now. For tho' I formerly foolishly
imagin'd concerning the Troubles of your father, that they
proceeded of a foolish fancy that he had, or for that he was   *James* 1. 23, 24,
over-run with melancholy humours; yet now 'twill not out of   25.
my mind, but that they sprang from another cause, to wit, for   [1st Edit. 'Light
that the Light of Life was given him; by the help of which, as   *of Light.*']
I perceive, he has escaped the Snares of Death. Then they all
wept again, and cry'd out, *Oh, Wo worth the day!*°

The next night, *Christiana* had a dream; and behold, she   *Christiana's
saw as if a broad Parchment was opened before her, in which   dream.*
were recorded the Sum of her ways, and the crimes, as she
thought, look'd *very black upon her.* Then she cry'd out aloud
in her sleep, *Lord have Mercy upon me, a Sinner;* and the little   *Luke* 18. 13.
children heard her.

After this, she thought she saw two very ill-favour'd° Ones
standing by her bed-side and saying, *What shall we do with*   *Mark this,
this Woman? For she cries out for Mercy waking and sleeping: If*   *this is the
she be suffer'd° to go on as she begins, we shall lose her as we*   *Quintessence
have lost her Husband.* Wherefore we must, by one way or   *of Hell.*
other, seek to take her off from the thoughts of what shall be
hereafter, else all the world cannot help it but she will become
a Pilgrim.

Now she awoke in a great sweat, also a trembling was upon
her; but after a while she fell to sleeping again. And then she
thought she saw *Christian* her husband in a place of Bliss   *Help against
among many *Immortals*, with a *Harp* in his hand, standing   Discouragement.*

---

in sunder Asunder; **Wo worth the day!** Both "woe to the day" and "it was a
woeful day"; **ill-favour'd** Ugly. The marginal note indicates that these are
devils; **suffer'd** Allowed.

and playing upon it before one that sat on a Throne, with a Rainbow about his head. She saw also as if he bowed his head with his face to the paved-work° that was under the Prince's feet, saying, *I heartily thank my Lord and King for bringing me into this Place.* Then shouted a Company of them that stood round about and harped with their harps: But no man living could tell what they said, but *Christian* and his Companions.

Next morning, when she was up, had pray'd to God, and talked with her children a while, one knocked hard at the door; to whom she spake out, saying, *If thou comest in God's name, come in.* So he said, *Amen;* and open'd the door and saluted her with *Peace be to this House.* The which, when he

Convictions seconded with fresh tidings of God's Readiness to pardon.

had done, he said, *Christiana,* knowest thou wherefore I am come? Then she blushed and trembled, also her heart began to wax warm with desires to know whence he came, and what his errand was to her. So he said unto her, My name is *Secret,*[8] I dwell with those that are high. It is talked of where I dwell, as if thou hadst a desire to go thither; also there is a report that thou art aware of the Evil thou hast formerly done to thy husband, in hardning of thy heart against his Way, and in keeping of these thy babes in their Ignorance. *Christiana,* the Merciful One has sent me to tell thee, That he is a God ready

[1st edit. 'To multiply to pardon offences.' See Isa. 55. 7, margin.]

to forgive, and that he taketh Delight to multiply the pardon of offences. He also would have thee know, that he inviteth thee to come into his Presence, to his Table, and that he will feed thee with the fat of his house, and with the heritage of *Jacob* thy father.°

There is *Christian* thy husband, *that was,* with Legions more, his companions, ever beholding that Face that doth minister Life to beholders: And they will all be glad when they shall hear the sound of thy feet step over thy Father's threshold.

Christiana at this was greatly abashed in herself, and bowed her head to the ground, this *Visiter* proceeded, and said, *Christiana,* here is also a Letter for thee, which I have

---

paved-work Pavement; Jacob thy father Luke 1:33 describes Israel as the "House of Jacob"; for Bunyan the modern Israelites were members of godly congregations such as his own.

brought from thy husband's King; so she took it and opened Song 1. 11, 12. it, but it smelt after the manner of the best perfume. Also it was written in letters of Gold. The contents of the letter was; *That the King would have her do as did* Christian *her husband, for that was the way to come to his City, and to dwell in his Presence with Joy for ever.* At this the good woman was quite over- come: So she cried out to her Visiter, *Sir, will you carry me and my Children with you, that we also may go and worship this King?*

Christiana quite overcome.

Then said the Visiter, *Christiana! the Bitter is before the Sweet.* Thou must through 'Troubles, as did he that went be- fore thee, enter this Cœlestial City. Wherefore I advise thee to do as did *Christian* thy husband: Go to the *Wicket-Gate* yon- der over the Plain, for that stands in the head of the Way up which thou must go, and I wish thee all good speed. Also I ad- vise, that thou put this Letter in thy bosom: That thou read therein to thyself, and to thy Children, until you have got it by root-of-heart:° For it is one of the songs that thou must sing while thou art in this House of thy Pilgrimage:° Also this thou must deliver in at the *further* Gate.

Further instructions to Christiana.

Psal. 119. 54.

Now I saw in my dream, that this old gentleman, as he told me this story, did himself seem to be greatly affected there- with. He moreover proceeded, and said: So *Christiana* called her Sons together, and began thus to address herself unto them: My Sons, I have, as you may perceive, been of late under much exercise in my Soul, about the death of your fa- ther; not for that I doubt at all of his happiness; for I am sat- isfied now that he is well. I have also been much affected° with the thoughts of mine own State and yours, which I ver- ily believe is by Nature° miserable. My carriage also to your father in his distress, is a great load° to my conscience: For I harden'd both my own heart and yours against him, and re- fused to go with him on Pilgrimage.

Christiana prays well for her Journey.

---

by root-of-heart Keeble notes this "conflation of "by rote" and "by heart" (Keeble, ed., *The Pilgrim's Progress*, p. 278); **House of thy Pilgrimage** A de- liberately mixed metaphor, emphasizing the symbolic nature of the journey; **affected** Moved; **by Nature** According to the flesh; **load** Burden. Christiana has acquired a corresponding burden to Christian's in part one.

The thoughts of these things would now kill me outright, but that for a dream which I had last night, and but that for the Encouragement that this Stranger has given me this morning. Come, my children, let us pack up, and be gone to the Gate that leads to the Cœlestial Country, that we may see your father, and be with him and his companions in Peace, according to the laws of that land.

Then did her Children burst out into tears, for joy that the heart of their mother was so inclined: So their Visiter bid them farewell; and they began to prepare to set out for their Journey.

But while they were thus about to be gone, two of the women that were *Christiana's* neighbours,° came up to her house, and knocked at the door: To whom she said as before, *If you come in God's name, come in.* At this the women were stunn'd; for this kind of language they used not to hear, or to perceive to drop from the lips of *Christiana.* Yet they came in: But behold, they found the good woman a preparing to be gone from her house.

Christiana's
new language
stuns her old
neighbours.

So they began, and said, Neighbour, pray what is your meaning by this?

Christiana answered, and said to the eldest of them, whose name was Mrs. *Timorous,* I am preparing for a Journey. (This *Timorous* was daughter to him° that met *Christian* upon the Hill of *Difficulty,* and would ha' had him gone back for fear of the Lions.)

Part I. page
51.

Tim. For what Journey, I pray you?

Christ. Even to go after my good Husband; and with that she fell a weeping.

Timorous
comes to visit
Christiana
with Mercy,
one of her
neighbours.

Tim. I hope not so, good neighbour; pray, for your poor children's sake, do not so unwomanly cast away yourself.°

Christ. Nay, my children shall go with me, not one of them is willing to stay behind.

Christiana's neighbours As with Obstinate and Pliable in part one, Christiana's recognition of these two characters' allegorical identities betokens the beginning of her psychological pilgrimage; **him** This character from part one was also called "Timorous"; **cast away yourself** Christiana must cast off her "old man" and be born again.

Tim. I wonder in my very heart, what or who has brought you into this mind.

Christ. Oh, neighbour, knew you but as much as I do, I doubt not but that you would go with me.

Tim. Prithee, what new Knowledge hast thou got, that so worketh off thy mind from thy Friends, and that tempteth thee to go no body knows where?

Christ. Then *Christiana* reply'd, I have been sorely afflicted since my husband's departure from me; but especially since he went *over the River*. But that which troubleth me most, is my churlish° carriage to him, when he was under his distress. Besides I am *now*, as he was *then;* nothing will serve° me, but going on Pilgrimage. I was a dreaming last night, that I saw him. O that my Soul was with him! He dwelleth in the Presence of the King of the Country; he sits and eats with him at his table; he is become a companion of *Immortals*, and has a House now given him to dwell in, to which the best palaces on Earth, if compared, seem to me to be but as a dunghill. The Prince of the Place has also sent for me, with promise of entertainment, if I shall come to him; his Messenger was here even now, and has brought me a Letter, which invites me to come. And with that she pluck'd out her Letter, and read it, and said to them, what now will you say to this?

Tim. Oh! the Madness that has possessed thee and thy husband! to run yourselves upon such Difficulties! You have heard, I am sure, what your husband did meet with, even in a manner° at the first step that he took on his Way, as our neighbour *Obstinate* can yet testify, for he went along with him; yea, and *Pliable* too, until they, like wise men, were afraid to go any further. We also heard over and above, how he met with the Lions, *Apollyon*, the Shadow of Death, and many other things. Nor is the Danger that he met with at *Vanity-Fair* to be forgotten by thee. For if he, tho' a man, was so hard put to it, what canst thou, being but a poor woman,

Death.

2 Cor. 5. 1, 2, 3, 4.

Part I. *pages* 17 to 20.

The reasonings of the Flesh.

---

churlish Rude; serve Both "satisfy" and "be of use to"; in a manner That is, in a manner of speaking; a signal that the "step" is figurative.

do? Consider also, that these four sweet babes are thy children, thy flesh, and thy bones. Wherefore, though thou shouldest be so rash as to cast away thyself; yet for the sake of the fruit of thy body, keep thou at home.

But *Christiana* said unto her, tempt me not, my neighbour: I have now a price put into my hand to get gain,° and I should be a Fool of the greatest size, if I should have no heart to strike in with° the opportunity. And for that you tell me of all these Troubles that I am like to meet with in the Way, they are so far off from being to me a Discouragement, that they

*A pertinent
Reply to
fleshly
Reasonings.*

shew I am in the right. *The Bitter must come before the Sweet*, and that also will make the Sweet the sweeter. Wherefore since you came not to my house *in God's name*, as I said; I pray you to be gone, and not to disquiet° me farther.

Then *Timorous* also reviled her, and said to her fellow, Come, neighbour *Mercy*, let's leave her in her own hands, since she scorns our counsel and company. But *Mercy* was at a stand,° and could not so readily comply with her neighbour,

*Mercy's
bowels yearn
over
Christiana.*

and that for a twofold reason, 1st, Her bowels° yearned over *Christiana:* So she said within herself, if my neighbour will be gone, I will go a little way with her, and help her. 2dly, Her bowels yearned over her own Soul, (for what *Christiana* had said, had taken some hold upon her mind:) Wherefore she said within herself again, I will yet have more talk with this *Christiana*, and if I find Truth and Life in what she shall say, myself with my heart shall also go with her. Wherefore *Mercy* began thus to reply to her neighbour *Timorous*.

Mercy. Neighbour, I did indeed come with you to see

*Timorous
forsakes her,
but* Mercy
cleaves to her.

Christiana this morning; and since she is, as you see, a taking of her last farewell of her Country, I think to walk this sunshine morning, a little way with her, to help her on the Way. But she told her not of her second reason, but kept that to herself.

Tim. Well, I see you have a mind to go a fooling too; but

---

price . . . gain A principal sum that I can invest gainfully; **strike in with** Seize; **disquiet** Disturb; **at a stand** At a loss; **bowels** Conventional synecdoche for compassion.

take heed in time and be wise; while we are out of danger, we are out; but when we are in, we are in. So Mrs. *Timorous* returned to her house, and *Christiana* betook herself to her journey. But when *Timorous* was got home to her house, she sends for some of her neighbours, to wit, Mrs. *Bat's-eyes*, Mrs. *Inconsiderate*, Mrs. *Light-mind*, and Mrs. *Know-nothing*. So when they were come to her house, she falls to telling of the story of *Christiana*, and of her intended Journey. And thus she began her tale.

Timorous acquaints her friends, what the good Christiana intends to do.

Tim. Neighbours, having had little to do this morning, I went to give *Christiana* a visit; and when I came at the door, I knocked, as you know 'tis our custom; and she answered, *If you come in God's name, come in*. So in I went, thinking all was well: But when I came in, I found her preparing herself to depart the town, she and also her children. So I asked her, what was her meaning by that? and she told me in short, that she was now of a mind to go on Pilgrimage, as did her Husband. She told me also a dream that she had, and how the King of the Country where her Husband was, had sent her an inviting Letter to come thither.

Then said Mrs. *Know-nothing*, And what do you think she will go?

Mrs. Know-nothing.

Tim. Ay, go she will, whatever comes on't; and methinks I know it by this; for that which was my great argument to persuade her to stay at home, (to wit, the Troubles she was like to meet with in the Way) is one great argument with her, to put her forward on her Journey. For she told me in so many words, *The Bitter goes before the Sweet:* Yea, and forasmuch as it so doth, it makes the sweet the sweeter.

Mrs. *Bat's-eyes*. Oh, this blind and foolish woman, said she; will she not take warning by her Husband's afflictions? For my part, I see,° if he was here again, he would rest him content in a whole skin,° and never run so many hazards for nothing.

Mrs. Bat's-eyes.

I see Mrs. Bat's-eyes reveals the propriety of her name in the act of denying it; **he would . . . skin** He would be glad to be alive, but Bat's-eyes refers to worldly, not eternal, life.

Mrs.
Inconsiderate.

Mrs. *Inconsiderate* also replied, saying, Away with such fantastical fools from the town; a good riddance, for my part, I say, of her; should she stay where she dwells, and retain this her mind, who could live quietly by her; for she will either be dumpish° or unneighbourly, or talk of such matters as no wise body can abide: Wherefore, for my part, I shall never be sorry for her departure; let her go, and let better come in her room; 'twas never a good world since these whimsical fools dwelt in it.

Mrs. Light-
mind.
*Madam
Wanton, she
that had like
to have been
too hard for*
Faithful *in
time past,
Part* I. *page*
82.

Then Mrs. *Light-mind* added as followeth; Come, put this kind of talk away. I was yesterday at Madam *Wanton's*,[9] where we were as merry as the maids. For who do you think should be there, but I and Mrs. *Love-the-Flesh*,° and three or four more, with Mr. *Lechery*, Mrs. *Filth*, and some others: So there we had musick, and dancing, and what else was meet to fill up° the Pleasure. And I dare say, my Lady herself is an admirable well-bred° gentlewoman, and Mr. *Lechery* is as pretty a fellow. By this time *Christiana* was got on her Way, and *Mercy* went along with her: So as they went, her Children being there also, *Christiana* began to discourse. And *Mercy*, said *Christiana*, I take this as an unexpected favour, that thou shouldest set foot out of doors with me, to accompany me a little in my Way.

Discourse
between
Mercy *and
good*
Christiana.

Mercy
inclines to go.

Mercy. Then said young *Mercy*, (for she was but young) If I thought it would be to purpose to go with you, I would never go near the town any more.

Christiana
*would have
her Neighbour
with her.*

Christ. Well, *Mercy*, said *Christiana*, cast in thy lot with me, I well know what will be the end of our Pilgrimage; my Husband is where he would not but be for all the Gold in the *Spanish* Mines.[10] Nor shalt thou be rejected, tho' thou goest but upon *my Invitation.* The King who hath sent for me and my Children, is one that delighteth in *Mercy.* Besides, if thou

---

dumpish Grumpy; **Mrs. Love-the-flesh** Note that the female vices are married women; **meet to fill up** "Suitable to complete," with hints of drinking and sex; **well-bred** Sin is once again associated with the upper classes; Mrs. Light-mind's snobbery parallels her sexual lust; both are manifestations of worldliness.

wilt, I will hire thee, and thou shalt go along with me as my servant. Yet we will have all things in common[11] betwixt thee and me, only go along with me.

Mercy. But how shall I be ascertained° that I also shall be entertained?° Had I this Hope but from one that can tell, I would make no stick° at all, but would go, being helped by him that can help, tho' the Way was never so tedious.

Christ. Well, loving *Mercy,* I will tell thee what thou shalt do; go with me to the *Wicket-Gate,* and there I will further enquire for thee; and if there thou shalt not meet with encouragement, I will be content that thou shalt return to thy place; I also will pay thee for thy kindness which thou shewest to me and my Children, in thy accompanying of us in our Way as thou doest.

Mercy. Then will I go thither, and will take what shall follow; and the Lord grant that my lot may there fall, even as the King of Heaven shall have his heart upon me.

Christiana then was glad at her heart, not only that she had a companion, but also for that she had prevailed with this poor maid to fall in love with her own Salvation.[12] So they went on together, and *Mercy* began to weep. Then said *Christiana,* Wherefore weepeth my Sister so?

Mercy. Alas! said she, who can but lament, that shall but rightly consider what a state and condition my poor relations are in, that yet remain in our sinful town: And that which makes my grief the more heavy, is because they have no instructor, nor any to tell them what is to come.

Christ. Bowels become Pilgrims; and thou dost for thy friends, as my good *Christian* did for me when he left me; he mourned for that I would not heed nor regard him, but his Lord and ours did gather up his tears, and put them into his bottle,° and now both I and thou, and these my sweet Babes, are reaping the fruit and benefit of them. I hope, *Mercy,* these tears of thine will not be lost; for the Truth hath said, *that they*

Mercy doubts of Acceptance.

Christiana *allures her to the Gate, which is* Christ, *and promiseth there to enquire for her.*

Mercy prays.

Christiana *glad of* Mercy's *company.*

Mercy *grieves for her carnal Relations.*

Christian's *Prayers were answered for his Relations, after he was dead.*

---

ascertained Made certain; entertained Welcomed; stick Delay; his bottle God suckles Christiana, as she suckles her "sweet Babes."

Psal. 126. 5, 6. *that sow in Tears, shall reap in Joy and singing. And he that goeth forth and weepeth, bearing precious seed, shall doubtless come again with rejoycing, bringing his Sheaves with him.*

Then said Mercy,

Let the most Blessed be my Guide,
If't be his blessed Will,
Unto his Gate, into his Fold,
Up to his Holy Hill:

And let him never suffer° me
To swerve or turn aside
From his Free Grace, and Holy Ways,
Whate'er shall me betide.

And let him gather them of mine,
That I have left behind;
Lord, make them pray they may be thine,
With all their Heart and Mind.

Part I. page 20, 21. Their own Carnal Conclusions instead of the Word of Life.

Now my old Friend proceeded, and said,—But when *Christiana* came to the Slough of *Despond*, she began to be at a stand; for, said she, This is the place in which my dear Husband had like to have been smothered with mud. She perceived also, that notwithstanding the command of the King to make this place for Pilgrims good, yet it was rather worse than formerly:[13] So I asked if that was true? Yes, said the old Gentleman, too true: For that many there be, that pretend to be the King's Labourers, and that say, they are for mending the King's Highway, that bring *dirt* and *dung* instead of stones, and so mar instead of mending. Here *Christiana* therefore, with her boys, did make a stand: But said *Mercy*, Come let us venture, only let us be wary. Then they looked well to the Steps, and made a shift to get staggeringly over.

Mercy the boldest at the Slough of Despond.

---

suffer Allow.

Yet *Christiana* had like to have been in,° and that not once nor twice. Now they had no sooner got over, but they thought they heard words, that said unto them, *Blessed is she that be-* Luke 1. 45. *lieveth, for there shall be a Performance of the things that have been told her from the Lord.*

Then they went on again, and said *Mercy* to *Christiana*, had I as good ground° to hope for a loving reception at the Wicket-Gate, as you, I think no Slough of *Despond* would discourage me.

Well, said the other, you know *your* sore,° and I know *mine;* and, good friend, we shall all have enough evil before we come at our Journey's end.

For can it be imagined, that the people that design to attain such excellent Glories *as we do*, and that are so envied that happiness *as we are;* but that we shall meet with what Fears and Scares, with what troubles and afflictions they can possibly assault us with, that hate us.°

And now Mr. *Sagacity*[14] left me to dream out my dream by myself. Wherefore, methought I saw *Christiana* and *Mercy*, and the Boys, go all of them up to the Gate: To which, when they were come, they betook themselves to a short debate, about *how* they must manage their calling at the Gate; and what should be said to him that did open to them. So it was concluded, since *Christiana* was the eldest, that she should knock for entrance, and that she should speak to him that did open, for the rest. So *Christiana* began to knock, and as her poor Husband did, she *knocked*, and *knocked* again. But instead of any that answered, they all thought that they heard as if a Dog° came barking upon them; a Dog, and a great one too, and this made the Women and Children afraid, nor durst they for a while to knock any more, for fear the Mastiff should fly upon them. Now therefore they were greatly tum-

Prayer should be made with Consideration and Fear, as well as in Faith and Hope.

Part I. *page* 31.

The Dog, the Devil, an enemy to Prayer.

---

in Sunk; **ground** Note the convergence of the literal and figural senses; **sore** Pain, weakness; **that hate us** The persecuting civil and ecclesiastical authorities, a reminder that *The Pilgrim's Progress* is a partisan text addressed specifically to dissenters; **a Dog** The practical effects of Satan's influence. See Psalm 22:20: "Deliver . . . my darling from the power of the dog" (KJV).

Christiana
and her
Companions
perplexed
about Prayer.

bled up and down in their minds,° and knew not what to do; Knock they durst not, for fear of the Dog; Go back they durst not, for fear that the Keeper of that Gate° should espy them as they so went, and should be offended with them: At last they thought of knocking again, and knocking more vehemently than they did at the first. Then said the Keeper of the Gate, Who is there? So the Dog left off to bark, and he opened unto them.

Then *Christiana* made low obeisance,° and said, Let not our Lord be offended with his hand-maidens, for that we have knocked at his Princely Gate. Then said the Keeper, Whence come ye? And what is that you would have?

Christiana answered, We are come from whence *Christian* did come, and upon the same errand as he; to wit, to be, if it shall please you, graciously° admitted, by this Gate, into the Way that leads to the Cœlestial City: And I answer, my Lord, in the next place, that I am *Christiana*, once the Wife of *Christian*, that now is gotten above.

With that the Keeper of the Gate did marvel, saying, What is she become now a Pilgrim, that but a while ago abhorred that Life? Then she bowed her head, and said, Yes, and so are these my sweet Babes also.

Then he took her by the hand and let her in, and said also, *Suffer the little Children to come unto me,*° and with that he shut up the Gate. This done, he called to a Trumpeter that was above, over the Gate, to entertain *Christiana* with Shouting, and Sound of Trumpet, for Joy. So he obeyed and sounded, and filled the air with his melodious notes.

How
Christiana *is*
entertained at
the Gate.

Luke 15. 7.

Now all this while poor *Mercy* did stand without, trembling and crying, for fear that she was rejected. But when *Christiana* had gotten admittance for herself and her Boys, then she began to make intercession for *Mercy*.

Christiana's
Prayer for her
friend Mercy.

Christ. And she said, My Lord, I have a companion of mine that stands yet without, that is come hither upon the same ac-

---

tumbled up and down in their minds The pilgrims are described as inhabitants of their own minds; **the Keeper of that Gate** Christ; **obeisance** Curtsy; **graciously** By grace; **Suffer . . . unto me** Jesus' words at Mark 10:14.

count as myself: One that is much dejected in her mind, for that° she comes, as she thinks, without sending for; whereas I was sent to by my husband's King to come.

Now *Mercy* began to be very impatient, for each minute was as long to her as an hour; wherefore she prevented *Christiana* from a fuller interceding for her, by knocking at the Gate herself. And she knocked then so loud, that she made *Christiana* to start. Then said the Keeper of the Gate, Who is there? And *Christiana* said, It is my friend. *The Delays make the hungering Soul the ferventer.*

So he opened the Gate and looked out, but *Mercy* was fallen down without in a swoon, for she fainted, and was afraid that no Gate would be opened to her. *Mercy faints.*

Then he took her by the hand, and said, *Damsel*, I bid thee arise.

O, Sir, said she, I am faint; there is scarce life left in me. But he answered, that one once said, *When my soul fainted within me, I remembered the Lord, and my Prayer came in unto thee, into thy Holy Temple.* Fear not, but stand upon thy feet, and tell me wherefore thou art come. *Jonah 2. 7.*

Mercy. I am come for *that* unto which I was never invited, as my friend *Christiana* was.[15] Hers was from the King, and mine was but from her: Wherefore I fear I presume. *The Cause of her fainting.*

Did she desire thee to come with her to this place?

Mercy. Yes; and as my Lord sees, I am come. And if there is any Grace and Forgiveness of Sins to spare, I beseech that I thy poor hand-maid may be partaker thereof.

Then he took her again by the hand, and led her gently in, and said, I pray for all them that believe on me, by what Means soever they come unto me. Then said he to those that stood by, fetch something and give it *Mercy* to smell on, thereby to stay her fainting: So they fetch'd her a bundle of myrrh;° and a while after, she was revived. *Mark this.*

And now was *Christiana* and her Boys, and *Mercy*, received of the Lord at the head of the Way, and spoke kindly unto by him. Then said they yet further unto him, we are sorry for

---

for that Because; **myrrh** A healing herb, among the gifts presented to the infant Christ.

our Sins, and beg of our Lord his Pardon and further infor-
mation what we must do.

Song 1. 2.
John 20. 20.

I grant Pardon, said he, by word and deed; by word, in the
Promise of Forgiveness; by deed, in the Way I obtained it.
Take the first from my lips with a kiss, and the other as it shall
be revealed.

Now I saw in my dream, that he spake many good words

Christ
Crucified seen
afar off.

unto them, whereby they were greatly gladded. He also had
them up to the top of the Gate, and shewed them by what
Deed° they were saved; and told them withal, that that sight
they would have again as they went along in the Way, to their
comfort.

Talk between
the
Christians.

So he left them awhile in a summer parlour below, where
they entred into talk by themselves; and thus *Christiana*
began: O Lord! how glad am I, that we are got in hither!

Mercy. So you well may; but I of all have cause to leap for
Joy.

Christ. I thought one time as I stood at the Gate, (because
I had knocked and none did answer) that all our labour had
been lost, 'specially when that ugly cur made such a heavy
barking against us.

Mercy. But my worst fears was, after I saw that you was
taken into his favour, and that I was left behind: Now,
thought I, 'tis fulfilled which is written; *Two Women shall be*

Mat. 24. 41.

grinding together, the one shall be taken, and the other left. I
had much ado to forbear crying out, *Undone! Undone!*

And afraid I was to knock any more; but when I looked up
to what was written over the Gate, I took courage. I also

Part I. p. 31.

thought that I must either knock again, or die: So I knocked,
but I cannot tell how; for my spirit now struggled betwixt Life
and Death.

Christiana
thinks her
Companion
prays better
than she.
Mat. 11. 12.

Christ. Can you not tell how you knocked? I am sure your
knocks were so earnest, that the very sound of them made me
start; I thought I never heard such knocking in all my life; I
thought you would ha' come in by violent hands, or ha' took
the Kingdom by storm.

Deed The Crucifixion.

Mercy. Alas! to be in my case, who that so was, could but ha' done so? You saw that the Door was shut upon me, and that there was a most cruel *Dog* thereabout.° Who, I say, that was so faint-hearted as I, that would not ha' knocked with all their might? But pray, what said my Lord unto my rudeness? was he not angry with me?

Christ. When he heard your lumbring° noise, he gave a wonderful innocent smile: I believe what you did, pleased him well enough, for he shewed no sign to the contrary. But I marvel in my heart why he keeps such a Dog; had I known that afore, I fear I should not have had heart enough to ha' ventured myself in this manner. But now we are in, we are in, and I am glad with all my heart.

Christ pleased with loud and restless Prayer. If the soul at first did know all it should meet with in its journey to Heaven, it would hardly ever set out.

Mercy. I will ask, if you please, next time he comes down, why he keeps such a filthy cur in his yard; I hope he will not take it amiss.

Ay do, said the Children, and persuade him to hang him, for we are afraid he will bite us when we go hence.

The Children are afraid of the Dog.

So at last he came down to them again, and *Mercy* fell to the ground on her face, before him, and worshipped, and said, Let my Lord accept the Sacrifice of Praise which I now offer unto him with the calves of my lips.°

So he said unto her, *Peace be to thee, stand up.* But she continued upon her face, and said, *Righteous art thou, O Lord, when I plead with thee, yet let me talk with thee of thy Judgments:* Wherefore dost thou keep so cruel a Dog in thy yard, at the sight of which, such women and children, as we, are ready to fly from thy Gate for fear?

Jer. 12. 1, 2.

Mercy expostulates about the Dog.

He answered and said, That Dog has another *Owner;* he also is kept close in another man's ground, only my Pilgrims hear his barking:° He belongs to the Castle which you see

Devil.

Part I. p. 32.

You saw . . . a most cruel Dog thereabout The experience of being shut out from salvation and threatened by the "dog" impels Mercy to seek admission more emphatically; **lumbring** Heavy, sad, burdened; **the calves of my lips** Sacrifices. See Hosea 14:2: "So will we render the calves of our lips" (KJV), in which the verbal praise of God replaces the sacrificial calves; **only my Pilgrims hear his barking** The unregenerate are unaware of Satan's power and influence in the world.

there at a distance, but can come up to the walls of this place. He has frighted many an honest Pilgrim from *worse* to *better*, by the great Voice of his Roaring. Indeed, he that owneth him, doth not keep him of any good-will to me or mine, but with intent to keep the Pilgrims from coming to me, and that they may be afraid to knock at this Gate for entrance. Sometimes also he has broken out, and has *worried* some that I love; but I take all at present patiently. I also give my Pilgrims timely help, so they are not delivered up to his power, to do them what his doggish nature would prompt him to. But what! my purchased° one, I tro,° hadst thou known never so much before-hand, thou wouldest not have been afraid of a dog.

*A Check to
the carnal fear
of the
Pilgrims.*

The Beggars that go from door to door, will, rather than they will lose a supposed alms, run the hazard of the bawling, barking, and biting too of a Dog: and shall a *dog*, a dog in another man's yard, a dog, whose barking I turn to the Profit of Pilgrims, keep any from coming to me? I deliver them from the Lions, and my darling from the power of the Dog.

*Christians
when wise
enough,
acquiesce in
the Wisdom of
their Lord.*

Mercy. Then said *Mercy*, I confess my Ignorance: I spake what I understood not; I acknowledge that thou doest all things well.

Christ. Then *Christiana* began to talk of their Journey, and to enquire after the Way. So he fed them, and washed their feet,° and set them in the Way of his steps, according as he had dealt with her Husband before. So I saw in my dream, that they walked on in their Way, and had the weather very comfortable to them.

Part I, *p.* 35.

Then *Christiana* began to sing, saying,

> *Blest be the Day that I began*
> *A Pilgrim for to be;*
> *And blessed also be that man*
> *That thereto mov-ed me.*

---

purchased Redeemed; **tro** Warrant; **washed their feet** As Jesus does for the disciples in John 13.

'Tis true, 'twas long ere I began
To seek to live for ever:
But now I run fast as I can;
'Tis better late, than never.

Our Tears to Joy, our Fears to Faith,
Are turned as we see;
Thus our Beginning (as one saith)
Shews what our End will be.

Now there was on the other side of the Wall, that fenced in the Way up which *Christiana* and her companions was to go, a garden, and that garden belonged to him whose was that *barking Dog*, of whom mention was made before. And some of the fruit-trees° that grew in that garden, shot their branches over the Wall; and being mellow,° they that found them did gather them up and oft eat of them to their hurt. So *Christiana's* boys, as boys are apt to do, being pleased with the trees, and with the fruit that did hang thereon, did plash° them and began to eat. Their mother did also chide them for so doing, but still the boys went on.

The Devil's Garden.

The Children eat of the Enemy's Fruit.

Well, said she, my Sons, you transgress, for that fruit is none of ours; but she did not know that they did belong to the Enemy: I'll warrant you, if she had, she would have been ready to die for fear. But that passed, and they went on their Way. Now, by that they were gone about two bows-shot° from the place that let them into the Way, they espied two very ill-favoured Ones coming down apace to meet them. With that *Christiana*, and *Mercy* her friend, covered themselves with their veils, and kept also on their Journey: The Children also went on before; so that at last they met together. Then they that came down to meet them, came just up to the Women, as if they would embrace° them; but *Christiana* said, Stand back, or go peaceably by as you should. Yet these two, as men

Two Ill-favoured Ones.

They assault Christiana.

---

fruit-trees Alluding to the fruit of the tree of knowledge in the garden of Eden; **mellow** Ripe; **plash** "Bend down," or possibly "crush"; **bows-shot** The distance an arrow can be shot from a bow; **embrace** Sexually assault.

The Pilgrims struggle with them.

that are deaf, regarded not *Christiana's* words, but began to lay hands upon them; at that *Christiana* waxing very wroth,° spurned° at them with her feet. *Mercy* also, as well as she could, did what she could to shift them. *Christiana* again said to them, Stand back, and be gone, for we have no money to lose, being Pilgrims as ye see, and such too as live upon the Charity of our friends.

Ill-Fav. Then said one of the two men, we make no assault upon you for money, but are come out to tell you, that if you will but grant one small request which we shall ask, we will make Women of you° for ever.

Christ. Now *Christiana* imagining what they should mean, made answer again, *We will neither hear, nor regard, nor yield to what you shall ask. We are in haste, and cannot stay, our business is a business of Life and Death:* So again, she and her companions made a fresh essay to go past them: But they letted° them in their Way.

Ill-Fav. And they said, We intend no hurt to your lives, 'tis another thing we would have.

She cries out.

Christ. Ay, quoth *Christiana*, you would have us Body and Soul, for I know 'tis for that you are come; but we will die rather upon the spot, than suffer ourselves to be brought into such snares as shall hazard our well-being hereafter. And with that they both shrieked out, and cried, *Murder, Murder:* And so put themselves under those laws that are provided for the protection of Women.° But the men still made their approach upon them, with design to prevail against them. They therefore cried out again.

'Tis good to cry out when we are assaulted.

Now, they being, as I said, not far from the Gate, in at which they came, their Voice was heard from where they was, thither: Wherefore some of the house came out, and knowing that it was *Christiana's* tongue, they made haste to her relief. But by that° they was got within sight of them, the women

---

waxing very wroth Becoming very angry; **spurned** Kicked; **make Women of you** Both "enrich" and "rape"; the ill-favored ones offer money in exchange for sex; **letted** Hindered; **those laws . . . Women** The law will prove incapable of saving them; **by that** By that time.

were in a very great scuffle, the children also stood crying by. Then did he that came in for their relief call out to the Ruffi-ans, saying, What is that thing you do? Would you make my Lord's people to transgress? He also attempted to take° them, but they did make their escape over the Wall into the garden of the man to whom the great Dog belonged; so the Dog be-came their protector. This *Reliever* then came up to the women, and asked them how they did. So they answered, we thank thy Prince, pretty well, only we have been somewhat af-frighted; we thank thee also, for that thou camest in to our help, for otherwise we had been overcome.

The Reliever comes.

The ill Ones fly to the Devil for relief.

Reliever. So after a few more words, this *Reliever* said, as followeth: I marvelled much when you was entertained at the Gate above, being ye knew that ye were but weak women,[16] that you petitioned not the Lord there for a Conductor:° then might you have avoided these troubles and dangers; for he would have granted you one.

The Reliever talks to the women.

Christ. Alas! said *Christiana*, We were so taken with our present blessing, that dangers to come were forgotten by us; besides, who could have thought, that so near the King's Palace, there should have lurked such naughty° ones? Indeed, it had been well for us, had we asked our Lord for one; but since our Lord knew 'twould be for our profit, I wonder he sent not one along with us.

Mark this.

Rel. It is not always necessary to grant things not asked for, lest by so doing, they become of little esteem; but when the Want° of a thing is felt, it then comes under, in the eyes of him that feels it, that estimate,° that properly is its due, and so conse-quently will be hereafter used. Had my Lord granted you a Con-ductor, you would not neither so have bewailed that oversight of yours, in not asking for one, as now you have occasion to do. So all things work for good, and tend to make you more wary.

We lose for want of asking.

Christ. Shall we go back again to my Lord, and confess our folly, and ask one?

Rel. Your confession of your folly I will present him with:

---

take Capture; **Conductor** But women, like the congregation in general, need pastoral guidance; **naughty** Wicked; **Want** Lack; **estimate** Price, appraisal.

To go back again, you need not; for in all places where you shall come, you will find no want at all; for in every of my Lord's lodgings, which he has prepared for the reception of his Pilgrims, there is sufficient to furnish them against all attempts whatsoever: But as I said, he will be enquired of by them to do it for them; and it is a poor thing that is not worth asking for. When he had thus said, he went back to his place, and the Pilgrims went on their Way.

Ezek. 36. 37.

Mercy. Then said *Mercy*, What a sudden blank° is here? I made account° we had been past all danger, and that we should never sorrow more.

The mistake of Mercy.

Christ. Thy *innocency*, my Sister, said *Christiana* to *Mercy*, may excuse thee much; but as for me, my fault is so much the greater, for that I saw this danger before I came out of the doors, and yet did not provide for it where provision might ha' been had. I am much therefore to be blamed.

Christiana's Guilt.

Mercy. Then said *Mercy*, How knew you this before you came from home? Pray open° to me this riddle?

Christ. Why, I will tell you: Before I set foot out of doors, one night, as I lay in my bed, I had a dream about this; for methought I saw two men, as like these as ever the world they could look, stand at my bed's feet, plotting how they might prevent my Salvation. I will tell you their very words: They said, ('twas when I was in my Troubles)° What shall we do with this woman? For she cries out waking and sleeping for Forgiveness; if she be suffered to go on as she begins, we shall lose her as we have lost her Husband. This you know might ha' made me take heed, and have provided when Provision might ha' been had.

Christiana's dream repeated.

Mercy. Well, said *Mercy*, As by this neglect we have an occasion ministred unto us, to behold our own imperfections: So our Lord has taken occasion thereby to make manifest the Riches of his Grace; for he, as we see, has followed us with

Mercy makes good use of their neglect of duty.

---

blank Check, obstacle; **made account** Calculated; **open** Interpret; **Troubles** Spiritual tribulation.

unasked kindness, and has delivered us from their hands that were stronger than we, of his mere good Pleasure.°

Thus now when they had talked away a little more time, they drew nigh to a house which stood in the Way, which house was built for the relief of Pilgrims, as you will find more fully related in the First Part of these Records of the *Pilgrims Progress:* So they drew on towards the House, (the house of the *Interpreter*) and when they came to the door, they heard a great talk in the house, they then gave ear, and heard, as they thought, *Christiana* mentioned by name; for you must know, that there went along even before her, a talk of her and her Children's going on Pilgrimage. And this thing was the more pleasing to them, because they had heard that she was *Christian's* wife; that woman who was some time ago so unwilling to hear of going on Pilgrimage. Thus, therefore, they stood still, and heard the good people within commending her, who they little thought stood at the door. At last, *Christiana* knocked, as she had done at the Gate before. Now when she had knocked, there came to the door a young damsel, and opened the door, and looked, and behold, two women were there.

Damsel. Then said the damsel to them, With whom would you speak in this place?

Christ. Christiana answered, We understand that this is a privileged place for those that are become Pilgrims, and we now at this door are such: Wherefore we pray that we may be partakers of that for which we at this time are come; for the day, as thou seest, is very far spent, and we are loth, to night, to go any further.

Damsel. Pray what may I call your name, that I may tell it to my Lord within?

Christ. My name is *Christiana;* I was the wife of that Pilgrim that some years ago did travel this Way, and these be his four children. This maiden also is my companion, and is going on Pilgrimage too.

Part I. *p.* 35, *&c.*

Talk in the Interpreter's house about Christiana's going on Pilgrimage.

She knocks at the Door.

The Door is opened to them by Innocent.

---

mere good Pleasure Pure grace

Joy in the house of the Interpreter, that Christiana is turned Pilgrim.

Innocent. Then ran *Innocent* in (for that was her name) and said to those within, Can you think who is at the Door? There is *Christiana* and her Children, and her Companion, all waiting for entertainment here. Then they leaped for joy, and went and told their Master. So he came to the door, and looking upon her, he said, Art thou that *Christiana* whom *Christian* the good man left behind him, when he betook himself to a Pilgrim's life?

Christ. I am that woman that was so hard-hearted as to slight my Husband's troubles, and that left him to go on in his Journey alone, and these are his four children; but now I also am come, for I am convinced that no Way is right but this.

Mat. 21. 29.

Interp. Then is fulfilled that which is written of the Man that said to his son, Go work to day in my vineyard; and he said to his Father, I will not; but afterwards repented and went.

Christ. Then said *Christiana*, So be it, *Amen.* God make it a true saying upon me, and grant that I may be found at the last of him in peace, without spot, and blameless.

Interp. But why standest thou thus at the door? Come in, thou daughter of *Abraham;°* we was talking of thee but now, for tidings have come to us before, how thou art become a Pilgrim. Come, children, come in; come, maiden, come in; so he had them all into the house.

So when they were within, they were bidden sit down and rest them; the which, when they had done, those that attended upon the Pilgrims in the house, came into the room

Old Saints glad to see the young ones walk in God's ways.

to see them. And one smiled, and another smiled, and they all smiled, for joy that *Christiana* was become a Pilgrim: They also looked upon the boys; they stroked them over the faces with the hand, in token of their kind reception of them: They also carried it° lovingly to *Mercy*, and bid them all welcome into their Master's house.

The Significant Rooms.

After a while, because supper was not ready, the *Interpreter* took them into his *Significant Rooms*, and shewed them what *Christian*, *Christiana's* Husband, had seen some time before.

---

daughter of Abraham Chosen one; **carried it** Behaved.

Here therefore they saw the Man in the Cage, the Man and his Dream, the Man that cut his Way through his Enemies, and the Picture of the biggest of them all, together with the rest of those things that were then so profitable to *Christian*.

This done, and after these things had been somewhat digested by *Christiana* and her company, the *Interpreter* takes them apart again, and has them first into a room, where was a Man that could look no way but downwards, with a muckrake° in his hand: There stood also one over his head, with a Cœlestial Crown in his hand, and proffered to give him that Crown for his muckrake; but the man did neither look up, nor regard, but raked to himself the straws, the small sticks, and dust of the floor.

The Man with the muckrake, expounded.

Then said Christiana, I persuade myself, that I know somewhat the meaning of this: For this is a Figure° of a man of this World: Is it not, good Sir?

Interp. Thou hast said the right, said he, and his muckrake doth shew his Carnal mind. And whereas thou seest him rather give heed to rake up straws and sticks, and the dust of the floor, than to what he says that calls to him from above, with the Cœlestial Crown in his hand; it is to shew, that Heaven is but as a Fable to some, and that things here are counted the only things substantial.° Now, whereas, it was also shewed thee, that the man could look no way but downwards:[17] It is to let thee know, that earthly things, when they are with power upon men's minds, quite carry their hearts away from God.

Christ. Then said *Christiana*, Oh! deliver me from this muckrake.

Christiana's Prayer against the muckrake. Prov. 30. 8.

Interp. That Prayer, said the *Interpreter*, has lain by 'till it is almost rusty;° *Give me not Riches,* is scarce the prayer of one

---

muckrake "A traditional image for avarice" (Sharrock, ed., *The Pilgrim's Progress*, p. 401). Christian was not shown this image; Bunyan suggests that avarice is a greater problem now than it was before; **Figure** Symbol; **substantial** Real. The Interpreter describes the growth of philosophical materialism, which he presents as a by-product of avarice; **almost rusty** From lack of use; Bunyan emphasizes the contemporary prevalence of avarice.

of ten thousand. Straws and sticks, and dust, with most, are the great things now looked after.

With that *Mercy* and *Christiana* wept, and said, It is, alas! too true.

When the *Interpreter* had shewed them this, he has them into the very best room in the house; (a very brave room it was) so he bid them look round about, and see if they could find any thing profitable there. Then they looked round and round; for there was nothing to be seen but a very great Spi-
Of the Spider.   der[18] on the wall; and that they over-looked.

Mercy. Then said *Mercy*, Sir, I see nothing: But *Christiana* held her peace.

Interp. But said the *Interpreter*, look again; she therefore looked again, and said, Here is not any thing but an ugly spider, who hangs by her hands upon the wall. Then said he, is there but one spider in all this spacious room? Then the water stood in *Christiana's* eyes, for she was a woman quick of ap-
Talk about the Spider.   prehension: and she said, Yes Lord, there is here more than one. Yea, and Spiders, whose venom is far more destructive than that which is in her. The *Interpreter* then looked pleasantly upon her, and said. Thou hast said the Truth. This made *Mercy* blush, and the boys to cover their faces; for they all began now to understand the riddle.

Then said the *Interpreter* again, *The Spider taketh hold with*
The *Interpretation.* Prov. 30. 28.   *her hands,* as you see, *and is in King's Palaces.* And wherefore is this recorded, but to shew you, that how full of the venom of Sin soever you be, yet you may, by the hand of Faith, lay hold of and dwell in the best room° that belongs to the King's House above.

Christ. I thought, said *Christiana*, of something of this; but I could not imagine it all. I thought, that we were like *spiders*, and that we looked like ugly creatures, in what fine room soever we were: But that by this *spider*, this venomous and ill-favoured creature, we were to learn *how to act Faith,* came not into my mind; and yet she has taken hold with her hands, as

---

the best room Heaven, where sinners are welcomed, once they acknowledge their sin.

I see, and dwells in the best room in the house: God has made nothing in vain.

Then they seemed all to be glad; but the water stood in their eyes: Yet they looked one upon another, and also bowed before the *Interpreter.*

He had them then into another room, where was a Hen and chickens, and bid them observe a while. So one of the chickens went to the trough to drink, and every time she drank, she lifted up her head, and her eyes towards Heaven. See, said he, what this little chick doth, and learn of her to acknowledge whence your mercies come, by receiving them with looking up. Yet again, said he, observe and look; so they gave heed, and perceived that the Hen did walk in a four-fold method towards her chickens. 1. She had a *common call*, and that she hath all day long. 2. She had a *special call*, and that she had but sometimes. 3. She had a *brooding note.* And, 4. She had an *out-cry.* *Of the Hen and chickens.*

Mat. 23. 37.

Now, said he, compare this Hen to your King, and these chickens to his obedient ones. For answerable to° her, himself has his methods, which he walketh in towards his People; by his common Call, he gives nothing; by his special Call, he always has something to give; he has also a brooding Voice, for them that are under his Wing; and he has an Out-cry, to give the alarm when he seeth the enemy come. I chose, my darlings, to lead you into the room where such things are, because you are women, and they are easy for you.

Christ. And, Sir, said *Christiana*, pray let us see some more: So he had them into the slaughter-house, where was a butcher killing a sheep:° And behold the sheep was quiet, and took her death patiently. Then said the *Interpreter*, You must learn of this sheep to suffer, and to put up wrongs without murmurings and complaints. Behold how quietly she takes her death, and without objecting, she suffereth her skin to be pulled over her ears. Your King doth call you his Sheep. *Of the Butcher and the Sheep.*

---

answerable to Corresponding to; **sheep** The Bible describes Christ as the "lamb of God"; the lamb that God gave to Abraham to sacrifice in place of his son Isaac was a type of Christ.

*Of the
Garden.*

After this, he led them into his Garden, where was great variety of flowers: And he said, Do you see all these? So *Christiana* said, Yes. Then said he again, Behold the flowers are divers° in *stature*, in *quality*, and *colour*, and *smell*, and *virtue;* and some are better than some: Also where the gardener has set them, there they stand, and quarrel not one with another.

Of the Field.

Again, he had them into his Field, which he had sowed with wheat and corn: But when they beheld the tops of all was cut off, only the straw remained, he said again, This ground was dunged, and ploughed, and sowed, but what shall we do with the crop? Then said *Christiana*, burn some and make muck of the rest. Then said the *Interpreter* again, Fruit,° you see, is that thing you look for, and for want of that you condemn it to the Fire, and to be trodden under foot of men: Beware that in this you condemn not yourselves.

Of the Robin
and the
Spider.

Then as they were coming in from abroad, they espied a little *Robin* with a great *spider* in his mouth: So the *Interpreter* said, look here: So they looked, and *Mercy* wondered; but *Christiana* said, What a disparagement° is it to such a little pretty bird as the *Robin-red-breast* is, he being also a bird above many, that loveth to maintain a kind of sociableness with man; I had thought they had lived upon crums of bread, or upon other such harmless matter; I like him worse than I did.

The *Interpreter* then replyed, This *Robin* is an emblem, very apt to set forth° some professors by; for to sight they are, as this *Robin*, pretty of note, colour and carriage: They seem also to have a very great love for professors that are sincere; and above all other to desire to sociate° with them, and to be in their company, as if they could live upon the good man's crums: They pretend also, that therefore it is, that they frequent the house of the godly, and the appointments of the Lord: But when they are by themselves, as the *Robin*, they can catch and gobble up *spiders*,° they can change their diet, drink iniquity, and swallow down Sin like water.

---

divers Diverse, indicating the variety among human beings; **Fruit** The external manifestations of inner faith; **disparagement** Discredit; **set forth** Represent; **sociate** Associate; **spiders** Sins.

So when they were come again into the house, because supper as yet was not ready, *Christiana* again desired that the *Interpreter* would either shew or tell of some other things that are profitable.

Pray, and you will get at that which yet lies unrevealed.

Then the *Interpreter* began° and said: *The fatter the Sow is, the more she desires the mire; the fatter the Ox is, the more gamesomely he goes to the slaughter; and the more healthy the lusty° man is, the more prone he is unto Evil.*

There is a desire in Women to go neat and fine, and it is a comely thing to be adorned with that, that in God's sight is of great Price.

'Tis easier watching a night or two, than to sit up a whole Year together: So 'tis easier for one to begin to profess well, than to hold out as he should to the End.

Every Ship-master, when in a Storm, will willingly cast that over-board that is of the smallest value in the vessel; but who will throw the Best out first? None but he that feareth not God.

One Leak will sink a Ship, and one Sin will destroy a Sinner.

He that forgets his friend, is ungrateful unto him; but he that forgets his Saviour, is unmerciful to himself.

He that lives in Sin, and looks for happiness hereafter, is like him that soweth cockle,° and thinks to fill his barn with wheat or barley.

If a man would live well, let him fetch his last day to him, and make it always his Company-keeper.

Whispering and change of thoughts, proves that Sin is in the World.

If the World, which God sets light by, is counted a thing of that worth with men, what is Heaven that God commendeth?

If the Life that is attended with so many Troubles, is so loth to be let go by us, what is the Life above?

Every body will cry up the Goodness of men; but who is there, that is, as he should, affected with the Goodness of God?

We seldom sit down to meat, but we eat, and leave: So there

---

the Interpreter began The following series of metaphors recalls the book of Proverbs, as well as the parables of Jesus; lusty Strong; cockle A species of weed.

is in *Jesus Christ*, more Merit and Righteousness, than the whole World has need of.

When the *Interpreter* had done, he takes them out into his Garden again, and had them to a Tree, whose inside was all rotten and gone, and yet it grew and had leaves. Then said *Mercy*, What means this? This tree, said he, whose outside is fair, and whose inside is rotten, it is, to which many may be compared that are in the Garden of God: Who with their mouths speak high in behalf of God, but indeed will do nothing for him; whose leaves are fair, but their Heart good for nothing but to be tinder for the Devil's tinder-box.°

Now supper was ready, the table spread, and all things set on the board; so they sat down and did eat, when one had given thanks. And the *Interpreter* did usually entertain those that lodged with him with musick at meals; so the minstrels played. There was also one that did sing, and a very fine voice he had. His Song was this:

> *The Lord is only my support,*
> *And he that doth me feed;*
> *How can I then want any thing.*
> *Whereof I stand in Need?*

When the song and musick was ended, the *Interpreter* asked *Christiana*, What it was that at first did move her thus to betake herself to a Pilgrim's life? *Christiana* answered, *First*, the loss of my Husband came into my mind, at which I was heartily grieved; but all that was natural° affection. Then, after that came the troubles and Pilgrimage of my Husband into my mind, and also how like a churl° I had carried it to him as to that. So Guilt took hold of my mind, and would have drawn me into the pond;° but that opportunely I had a dream of the well-being of my Husband, and a Letter sent me

---

tinder-box Used to strike a light; **natural** Pertaining to the flesh; **churl** Brute. Christian's empathy with her husband replaces her selfish grief at having lost him; **So Guilt . . . into the pond** Note the elision of the mental and physical dimensions.

by the King of that country where my Husband dwells to
come to him. The dream and the Letter together so wrought
upon my mind, that they forced me to this Way.

Interp. But met you with no Opposition before you set out
of doors?

Christ. Yes, a neighbour of mine, one Mrs. *Timorous*, (she
was akin° to him that would have persuaded my Husband to
go back, for fear of the Lions.) She also befooled me,° for, as
she called it, my intended desperate° adventure; she also
urged what she could to dishearten me to it, the hardship and
troubles that my Husband met with in the Way; but all this I
got over pretty well. But a dream that I had of two ill-look'd
Ones, that I thought did plot how to make me miscarry in my
Journey, that hath troubled me much: Yea, it still runs in my
mind, and makes me afraid of every one that I meet, lest they
should meet me to do me a mischief, and to turn me out of
the Way. Yea, I may tell my Lord, tho' I would not every body
know it, that between this and the Gate by which we got into
the Way, we were both so sorely assaulted, that we were made
to cry out *Murder;* and the two that made this assault upon
us, were like the two that I saw in my dream.

Then said the *Interpreter*, Thy beginning is Good, thy latter end shall greatly increase. So he addressed himself to
Mercy, and said unto her, And what moved thee to come
hither, Sweet-heart?

A Question put to Mercy.

Mercy. Then *Mercy* blushed and trembled, and for a while
continued silent.

Interp. Then said he, Be not afraid, only believe, and speak
thy mind.

Mercy. So she began, and said, Truly, Sir, my want of experience is that, that makes me covet to be in silence, and that
also that fills me with Fears of coming short at last. I cannot
tell of Visions and Dreams,° as my friend *Christiana* can: Nor

Mercy's Answer.

---

akin Related; **befooled me** Called me a fool; **desperate** Hopeless; **I cannot
tell of Visions and Dreams** Mercy has not received Christian's direct inspiration, but this is no bar to her salvation.

know I what it is to mourn for my refusing of the counsel of those that were good relations.

Interp. What was it then, dear heart, that hath prevailed with thee to do as thou hast done?

Mercy. Why, when our friend here was packing up to be gone from our Town; I and another went accidentally° to see her. So we knocked at the Door, and went in. When we were within, and seeing what she was doing, we asked what was her meaning? She said, she was sent for to go to her Husband; and then she up and told us how she had seen him in a dream, dwelling in a curious Place, among *Immortals*, wearing a Crown, playing upon a Harp, eating and drinking at his Prince's Table, and singing Praises to him for bringing him thither, *&c*. Now methought while she was telling these things unto us, my heart burned within me. And I said in my heart, If this be true, I will leave my Father and my Mother, and the land of my nativity, and will, if I may, go along with *Christiana*.

So I asked her further of the Truth of these things, and if she would let me go with her; for I saw now, that there was no dwelling, but with the danger of Ruin, any longer in our town. But yet I came away with a heavy heart, not for that I was unwilling to come away, but for that so many of my relations were left behind. And I am come with all the desire of my heart, and will go if I may, with *Christiana*, unto her Husband and his King.

Interp. Thy setting out is Good, for thou hast given credit to the Truth; thou art a *Ruth*,[19] who did for the love that she bore to *Naomi*, and to the Lord her God, leave Father and Mother, and the land of her nativity, to come out and go with a People that she knew not heretofore, *Ruth* 2. 11, 12. *The* LORD *recompence thy work, and a full reward be given thee of the* LORD GOD *of Israel, under whose Wings thou art come to trust.*

They address themselves for bed.

Now supper was ended, and preparations was made for bed, the women were laid singly alone, and the boys by them-

---

accidentally By chance.

selves. Now when *Mercy* was in bed, she could not sleep for joy, for that now her doubts, of missing° at last, were removed further from her than ever they were before; so she lay blessing and praising God, who had such favour for her.

Mercy's good night's rest.

In the morning they arose with the sun, and prepared themselves for their departure; but the *Interpreter* would have them tarry a while, for said he, you must orderly° go from hence. Then said he to the damsel that at first opened unto them, Take them and have them into the Garden to the *Bath*[20] and there wash them, and make them clean from the Soil, which they have gathered by travelling. Then *Innocent* the damsel took them, and had them into the Garden, and brought them to the *Bath*; so she told them, that there they must wash and be clean, for so her Master would have the women to do, that called at his house as they were going on Pilgrimage. They then went in and washed, yea, they and the boys and all; and they came out of that *Bath*, not only sweet and clean, but also much enlivened and strengthened in their joints. So when they came in, they looked fairer a deal, than when they went out to the washing.

The Bath of Sanctification.

They wash in it.

When they were returned out of the Garden from the *Bath*, the *Interpreter* took them, and looked upon them, and said unto them, *Fair as the Moon*. Then he called for the *Seal*, wherewith they used to be *sealed* that were washed in his *Bath*. So the *Seal* was brought, and he set his Mark upon them, that they might be known in the places whither they were yet to go: Now the Seal was the contents and sum of the Passover which the children of *Israel* did eat, when they came out from the land of *Egypt;* and the Mark was set between their eyes. This *Seal* greatly added to their beauty, for it was an ornament to their faces. It also added to their gravity, and made their countenance more like them of Angels.

They are sealed.

Exod. 13. 8, 9, 10.

Then said the *Interpreter* again to the damsel that waited upon these Women, Go into the vestry,° and fetch out Gar-

---

missing Missing her aim, missing out on salvation; **orderly** In proper order, having received the sacrament of baptism; **vestry** The storehouse and dressing-room in a church.

They are clothed.

ments for these people: So she went and fetched out White Raiment, and laid it down before him; so he commanded them to put it on. *It was fine Linen white and clean.* When the women were thus adorned, they seemed to be a terror one to the other; for that they could not see that Glory each one on herself, which they could see in each other. Now therefore they began to esteem each other better than themselves. For

True Humility.

you are fairer than I am, said one; and you are more comely than I am, said another. The children also stood amazed, to see into what fashion they were brought.

The *Interpreter* then called for a man-servant of his, one *Great-heart*,[21] and bid him take *Sword*, and *Helmet*, and *Shield*, and take these my daughters, said he, and conduct them to the house called *Beautiful*, at which place they will rest next. So he took his weapons and went before them; and the *Interpreter* said, God speed. Those also that belonged to the family, sent them away with many a good wish. So they went on their Way, and sang;

> *This place has been our second stage,*
> *Here we have heard, and seen*
> *Those good things, that from Age to Age*
> *To others hid have been.*

> *The Dunghill-raker, Spider, Hen,*
> *The Chicken too, to me,*
> *Hath taught a lesson, let me then*
> *Conformed to it be.*

> *The Butcher, Garden, and the Field,*
> *The Robin, and his bait,*
> *Also the rotten Tree doth yield*
> *Me argument of weight;*

> *To move me for to Watch and Pray,*
> *To strive to be sincere;*
> *To take my Cross up day by day,*
> *And serve the Lord with fear.*

Now I saw in my dream, that they went on, and *Great-* *Part* I. *page* 4.
heart went before them; so they went and came to the place
where *Christian's* Burden fell off his back, and tumbled into a
Sepulchre. Here then they made a pause; and here also they
blessed God. Now, said *Christiana*, it comes to my mind, what
was said to us at the Gate, to wit, that we should have Pardon
by *Word* and *Deed;* by word, that is, by the Promise; by *Deed*,
to wit, in the Way it was obtained. What the Promise is, of
that I know something: But what is it to have Pardon by deed,
or in the Way that it was obtained? Mr. *Great-heart*, I suppose
you know; therefore, if you please, let us hear your discourse
thereof.

Great-heart. Pardon by the Deed done, is pardon obtained A Comment
by some one for another that hath need thereof: Not by the *upon what*
person pardoned, but in the Way, *saith another*, in which I *was said at*
have obtained it. So then to speak to the question more at *the Gate, or a*
large, the pardon that you and *Mercy*, and these boys have *at-* *Discourse of*
tained, was *obtained* by another;° to wit, by him that let you *our being*
in at the Gate: and he hath obtained it in this double way; he *justified by*
Christ.
has performed Righteousness to cover you, and spilt Blood to
wash you in.

Christ. But if he parts with his Righteousness to us, what
will he have for himself?

Great-heart. He has more Righteousness than you have
Need of, or than he needeth himself.

Christ. Pray make that appear.°

Great-heart. With all my heart; but first I must premise,
that he of whom we are now about to speak, is One that has
not his fellow: He has two Natures in one Person, plain to be
distinguish'd, impossible to be *divided.* Unto each of these natures a righteousness belongeth, and each righteousness is essential to that nature. So that one may as easily cause the
nature to be extinct, as to separate its Justice or Righteousness
from it. Of *these* righteousnesses therefore we are not made
partakers, so as that they, or any of them, should be put upon

---

obtained by another Righteousness is imputed by Christ, not earned by
human works; **appear** Clear.

us, that we might be made Just, and lively° thereby. Besides these, there is a righteousness which this Person has, as these two natures are joined in one. And this is not the righteousness of the *God-head*, as distinguished from the *Manhood;* nor the righteousness of the *Manhood*, as distinguished from the *God-head*, but a righteousness which standeth° in the Union of both natures; and may properly be called the righteousness that is essential to his being prepared of God to the capacity of the Mediatory Office,° which he was to be entrusted with. If he parts with his first righteousness, he parts with his *God-head:* If he parts with his second righteousness, he parts with the Purity of his *Manhood:* If he parts with his third, he parts with that Perfection that capacitates him to the office of Mediation. He has therefore another righteousness, which standeth in *Performance*, or obedience to a revealed Will: And that is it that he puts upon° Sinners, and that by which their Sins are covered. Wherefore he saith, *As by one man's Disobedience, many were made Sinners: So by the Obedience of one, shall many be made Righteous.*

Rom. 5. 19.

Christ. But are the other righteousnesses of no Use to us?

Great-heart. Yes; for though they are essential to his Natures and Office, and so cannot be communicated unto another, yet it is by virtue of them, that the righteousness that justifies, is for that purpose efficacious. The *righteousness* of his *God-head* gives Virtue° to his obedience; the *righteousness* of his *Manhood* giveth Capability to his obedience to justify, and the righteousness that standeth in the union of these two Natures to his Office, giveth Authority to that righteousness to do the work for which it was ordained.

So then here is a righteousness that Christ, as God, has no need of; for he is God without it: Here is a righteousness, that Christ, as Man, has no need of, to make him so, for he is perfect Man without it. Again, here is a righteousness, that Christ, as God-man, has no need of; for he is perfectly so

---

lively Alive; **standeth** Consists; **Mediatory Office** Christ is the mediator between God and man; **puts upon** Imputes to; **Virtue** Power.

without it. Here then is a righteousness, that Christ, as God, as man and as God-man, has no need of, with reference to himself, and therefore he can spare it a justifying righteousness, that he for himself wanteth not, and therefore he giveth it away: Hence it is called *the Gift of Righteousness*. This righteousness, since Christ Jesus the Lord has made himself under the Law, *must* be given away; for the Law doth not only bind him that is under it, *to do justly*, but to use Charity.° Where- Rom. 5. 17. fore he must, he ought by the Law, if he hath two Coats, to give one to him that hath none. Now our Lord indeed hath two Coats, one for himself, and one to spare: Wherefore he freely bestows one upon those that have none; and thus, *Christiana* and *Mercy*, and the rest of you that are here, doth your Pardon come by *Deed*, or by the work of another man. Your Lord Christ is he that has worked, and has given away what he wrought° for, to the next poor beggar he meets.

But again, in order to pardon by *Deed*, there must something be paid to God as a Price, as well as something prepared to cover us withal. Sin has delivered us up to the just Curse of a righteous Law: Now from this curse we must be justified by way of Redemption, a Price being paid for the harms we have done; and this is by the Blood of your Lord, who came and stood in your place and stead, and died your Death for your Transgressions: Thus has he ransomed you from your transgressions, by Blood, and covered your polluted and deformed Souls with Righteousness: For the sake of which, God passeth Rom. 4. 24. by you,° and will not hurt you, when he comes to judge the Gal. 3. 13. world.

Christ. This is brave:° Now I see that there was something Christiana to be learned by our being pardoned by *Word* and *Deed*. *affected with* Good *Mercy*, let us labour to keep this in mind; and, my chil- *this Way of* dren, do you remember it also. But, Sir, was not this it that *Redemption.* made my good *Christian's* Burden fall from off his shoulder, and that made him give three leaps for Joy?

Charity Charity is part of the law, since it is enjoined by the law; **wrought** Worked; **God passeth by you** The Jewish feast of Passover is the Old Testament type of redemption by Christ; **brave** Splendid.

How the Strings that bound Christian's Burden to him were cut.

Great-heart. Yes, 'twas the Belief of this that cut out those strings, that could not be cut by other means; and 'twas to give him a proof of the virtue of this, that he was suffer'd° to carry his Burden to the Cross.

Christ. I thought so; for tho' my heart was lightful and joyous before, yet it is ten times more lightsome and joyous now. And I am persuaded by what I have felt, tho' I have felt but little as yet, that if the most burdened man in the world was here, and did see and believe as I now do, 'twould make his heart the more merry and blithe.

How Affection to Christ is begot in the Soul.

Great-heart. There is not only Comfort, and the Ease of a Burden brought to us, by the sight and consideration of these, but an endeared Affection begot in us by it: For who can (if he doth but once think that Pardon comes not only by Promise, but thus)° but be affected with the way and means of Redemption, and so with the Man that hath wrought it for him?

Christ. True; methinks it makes my heart bleed to think that he should bleed for me. Oh! thou loving One: Oh! thou blessed One. Thou deservest to have me; thou hast bought° me: Thou deservest to have me all; thou hast paid for me ten

Part I. page 45.
Cause of Admiration.

thousand times more than I am worth. No marvel that this made the water stand in my Husband's eyes, and that it made him trudge so nimbly on: I am persuaded he wished me with him; but vile wretch that I was, I let him come all alone. O *Mercy*, that thy Father and Mother were here; yea, and Mrs. *Timorous* also: Nay, I wish now with all my heart, that here was Madam *Wanton* too. Surely, surely, their hearts would be affected; nor could the Fear of the one, nor the powerful Lusts of the other, prevail with them to go home again, and to refuse to become good Pilgrims.

To be affected with Christ, and with what he has done, is a thing Special.

Great-heart. You speak now in the warmth of your affections:° Will it, think you, be always thus with you? Besides, this is not communicated to every one, nor to every one that did see your JESUS bleed. There was that° stood by, and that

---

suffer'd Allowed; not only by Promise, but thus Another dig at the Quakers, who denied the efficacy of the historical Crucifixion; bought Redeemed; affections Passions; There was that There were some who.

saw the Blood run from the Heart to the ground, and yet were so far off this, that instead of lamenting, they laugh'd at him; and instead of becoming his Disciples, did harden their hearts against him: So that all that you have, my daughters, you have by a peculiar° impression made by a divine contemplating upon what I have spoken to you. Remember that 'twas told you, that the *Hen*, by her common call, gives no meat to her Chickens.° This you have therefore by a special Grace.

Now I saw still in my dream, That they went on until they were come to the place, that *Simple*, and *Sloth*, and *Presump tion*, lay and slept in, when *Christian* went by on Pilgrimage: And behold they were hanged up in irons a little way off on the other side.

Simple, Sloth and Presumption hanged, and why.

Mercy. Then said *Mercy* to him that was their Guide and conductor, What are those three men? And for what are they hanged there?

Great-heart. These three men were men of very bad quali- ties; they had no mind to be Pilgrims themselves, and whoso- ever they could, they hinder'd; they were for *sloth* and *folly* themselves, and whosoever they could persuade with, they made so too; and withal taught them to presume that they should do well at last. They were asleep when *Christian* went by, and now you go by, they are hanged.

Their Crimes.

Mercy. But could they persuade any one to be of their opinion?

Great-heart. Yes, they turned several out of the Way. There was *Slow-pace* that they persuaded to do as they; they also prevailed with one *Short-wind*, with one *No-heart*, with one *Linger-after-Lust*, and with one *Sleepy-head*, and with a young woman, her name was *Dull*, to turn out of the Way and be- come as they. Besides, they brought up an ill report of your Lord, persuading others that he was a task-Master.° They also brought up an Evil report of the good Land, saying, it was not

Whom they prevailed upon to turn out of the Way.

---

peculiar Special; the Hen . . . Chickens That is, there is no general salvation offered to the human race as a whole; a task-Master Luther protests against those who depict Christ as a harsh, judgmental master in his *Commentary on Galatians* (1535).

BEHOLD HERE, HOW THE SLOTHFUL ARE A SIGN°
HUNG UP, 'CAUSE HOLY WAYS THEY DID DECLINE:
SEE HERE TOO, HOW THE CHILD DOTH PLAY THE MAN,
AND *WEAK* GROWS *STRONG*, WHEN *GREAT-HEART* LEADS THE VAN.

---

the Slothful are a sign Such editorial pointers grow more common as the pilgrimage progresses.

half so good as some pretended it was. They also began to vil-
lify his Servants, and to count the very best of them meddle-
some, troublesome busy-bodies: Further, they would call the
Bread of God *Husks;* the *Comforts* of his Children *Fancies;* the
travel and labour of Pilgrims, *Things to no Purpose.*

Christ. Nay, said *Christiana,* if they were such, they shall
never be bewailed by me; they have but what they deserve;
and I think it is well that they hang so near the highway, that
others may see and take Warning. But had it not been well if
their crimes had been engraven in some plate of Iron or
Brass, and left here, even where they did their mischiefs, for a
caution to other bad men?

Great-heart. So it is, as you may well perceive, if you will go
a little to the Wall.

Mercy. No, no; let them hang,²² and their names rot, and
their Crimes live for ever against them: I think it a high
favour that they were hanged afore we came hither; Who
knows else what they might ha' done to such poor women as
we are? Then she turned it into a Song, saying,

> Now then you three hang there, and be a Sign²³
> To all that shall against the Truth combine.
> And let him that comes after, fear this End,
> If unto Pilgrims he is not a Friend.
> And thou, my Soul, of all such men beware,
> That unto Holiness opposers are.

Thus they went on, till they came at the foot of the Hill
Difficulty, where again their good Friend, Mr. *Great-heart,*
took an occasion to tell them of what happened there when
Christian himself went by. So he had them first to the Spring;
Lo, saith he, *this is the Spring that* Christian *drank of* before he
went up this Hill, and then 'twas clear and good, but now 'tis
dirty° with the feet of some that are not desirous that Pilgrims here should quench their thirst: Thereat *Mercy* said,

Part I. *p.* 50.

Ezek. 34. 18.
'Tis difficult
getting of
good Doctrine
in erroneous
Times.

---

now 'tis dirty True doctrine has been polluted by the erroneous religion in
fashion during the Restoration.

And why so envious trow?° But, said the Guide, it will do, if taken up and put into a Vessel that is sweet and good;° for then the dirt will sink to the bottom, and the water come out by itself more clear. Thus therefore *Christiana* and her companions were compelled to do. They took it up and put it into an earthen pot, and so let it stand till the dirt was gone to the bottom, and then they drank thereof.

Next he shewed them the two *by-ways* that were at the foot of the Hill, where *Formality°* and *Hypocrisy* lost themselves. And, said he, these are dangerous paths: Two were here cast away when *Christian* came by; and although as you see these ways are since stopped up with *Chains, Posts,* and a *Ditch,* yet there are that will choose to adventure here, rather than take the pains to go up this Hill.

By-paths, tho' barred up, will not keep all from going in them.

Christ. The Way of transgressors is hard. 'Tis a wonder that they can get into those ways without danger of breaking their necks.

Prov. 13. 15.

Great-heart. They will venture, yea, if at any time any of the King's servants doth happen to see them, and doth call upon them, and tell them, that they are in the wrong ways, and do bid them beware the danger; then they will railingly° return them answer, and say, *As for the Word that thou hast spoken unto us in the Name of the King, we will not hearken unto thee; but we will certainly do whatsoever thing goeth out of our own mouths,* &c. Nay, if you look a little farther, you shall see that these ways are made cautionary enough, not only by these *Posts,* and *Ditch,* and *Chain,* but also by being hedged up: Yet they will choose to go there.

Jer. 44. 16, 17.

Christ. They are Idle; they love not to take pains; up-hill Way is unpleasant to them: So it is fulfilled unto them as it is Written, *The way of the Slothful Man is a Hedge of Thorns.* Yea, they will rather choose to walk upon a Snare, than to go up this Hill, and the rest of this Way to the City.

The reason why some do choose to go in By-ways.
Prov. 15. 19.

---

trow Do you think; a Vessel that is sweet and good Titus 1:15: "Unto the pure all things are pure" (KJV); Formality In part one, this character is called "Formalist"; railingly Angrily.

Then they set forward, and began to go up the Hill, and up the Hill they went; but before they got to the top, *Christiana* began to *pant*, and said, I dare say; this is a breathing Hill;° no marvel if they that love their Ease more than their Souls, choose to themselves a smoother way. Then said *Mercy*, I must sit down; also the least° of the children began to cry. Come, come, said *Great-heart*, sit not down here, for a little above is the Prince's *Arbour*. Then took he the little boy by the hand, and led him up thereto.

The Hill puts the Pilgrims to it.

When they were come to the *Arbour*, they were very willing to sit down, for they were all in a pelting° heat. Then said *Mercy, How sweet is Rest to them that labour?* And how good is the Prince of Pilgrims to provide such resting places for them? Of *this Arbour* I have heard much; but I never saw it before: But here let us beware of Sleeping; for as I have heard, for that it cost poor *Christian* dear.

They sit in the Arbour Part I. p. 50. Mat. 11. 28.

Then said Mr. *Great-heart* to the little ones, Come, my pretty boys, how do you do? What think you now of going on Pilgrimage? Sir, said the least, I was almost beat out of heart;° but I thank you for lending me a hand at my need; and I remember now what my mother has told me, namely, that the Way to Heaven is as a ladder, and the Way to Hell is as down a hill. But I had rather go up the ladder to Life, than down the hill to Death.

The little boy's answer to the Guide, and also to Mercy.

Then said *Mercy*, But the proverb is, *To go down the hill is easy:* But *James*[24] said, (for that was his name) The Day is coming, when in my opinion, *going down the Hill will be the hardest of all.* 'Tis a good boy, said his Master, thou hast given her a right answer. Then *Mercy* smiled, but the little boy did blush.

Which is hardest, up hill or down hill.

Christ. Come, said *Christiana*, will you eat a bit; a little to sweeten your mouths while you sit here to rest your legs? For I have here a piece of pomegranate, which Mr. *Interpreter* put into my hand just when I came out of his doors; he gave me

They refresh themselves.

---

a breathing Hill A hill that makes one breathe heavily; **the least** The youngest; **pelting** Sweating; **beat out of heart** Disheartened, exhausted.

also a piece of an honey-comb, and a little bottle of spirits;° I thought he gave you something, said *Mercy*, because he called you aside. Yes, so he did, said the other; but, *Mercy*, it shall be still as I said it should, when at first we came from home; thou shalt be a sharer in all the good that I have, because thou so willingly didst become my companion. Then she gave to them, and they did eat, both *Mercy* and the boys. And said *Christiana* to Mr. *Great-heart*, Sir, will you do as we? But he answered, You are going on Pilgrimage, and presently I shall return; much good may what you have do to you; at home I eat the same every day. Now, when they had eaten and drank, and had chatted a little longer, their Guide said to them, The day wears away, if you think good, let us prepare to be going. So they got up to go, and the little boys went before; But *Christiana* forgat to take her bottle of spirits with her; so she sent her little boy back to fetch it. Then said *Mercy*, I think this is a *losing* place. Here *Christian* lost his *Roll;* and here *Christiana* left her bottle behind her; Sir, what is the Cause of this? So their Guide made answer, and said, the cause is *Sleep*, or *Forgetfulness;* some *sleep* when they should keep *awake*, and some *forget* when they should *remember;* and this is the very cause, why often at the resting places, some Pilgrims, in some things, come off losers. Pilgrims should watch, and re-member what they have already received under their greatest enjoyments; but for want of doing so, ofttimes their rejoicing ends in tears, and their sun-shine in a Cloud; witness the story of *Christian* at this place.

When they were come to the place where *Mistrust* and *Timorous* met *Christian* to persuade him to go back for fear of the Lions, they perceived as it were a Stage,° and before it, towards the road, a broad plate,° with a copy of verses written thereon, and underneath, the reason of raising up of that Stage in that place, rendered. The Verses were these:

Christiana
*forgets her
bottle of
Spirits.*

Mark this.

Part I. *p.* 53, 54.

---

spirits Figural rather than literal; the term "spirits" came to be applied to liquor via the experiments of alchemists, who tried to "spiritualize" matter; **Stage** "Platform," but also "point in a journey"; **plate** Plaque.

> *Let him that sees this Stage, take heed*
> *Unto his Heart and Tongue:*
> *Lest if he do not, here he speed*
> *As some have long agone.*

The words underneath the verses were, *This Stage was built to punish such upon, who, through* Timorousness *or* Mistrust, *shall be afraid to go further on* Pilgrimage: *Also on this Stage, both* Mistrust *and* Timorous *were burnt through the tongue with a hot Iron,** *for endeavouring to hinder* Christian *on his Journey.*

Then said *Mercy*, This is much like to the saying of the Beloved, *What shall be given unto thee? Or what shall be done unto thee, thou false tongue? sharp arrows of the Mighty, with coals of juniper.* Psal. 120, 3, 4.

So they went on, till they came within sight of the Lions.[25] *Part* I. *p.* 55. Now Mr. *Great-heart* was a strong man, so he was not afraid of a Lion: But yet, when they were come up to the place where the Lions, were the boys that went before, were glad to cringe behind, for they were afraid of the Lions, so they stept back, and went behind. At this, their Guide smiled, and said; How now, my boys, do you love to go before when no danger doth approach; and love to come behind so soon as the Lions appear? *An Emblem of those that go on bravely when there is no danger, but shrink when Troubles come.*

Now, as they went up, Mr. *Great-heart* drew his Sword, with intent to make a Way for the Pilgrims in spite of the Lions. Then there appeared one that, it seems, had taken upon him to back the Lions; and he said to the Pilgrims Guide, What is the cause of your coming hither? Now the name of that man was *Grim*, (or *Bloody-Man*,)[26] because of his slaying of Pilgrims, and he was of the race of the *Giants*. *Of* Grim *the Giant, and of his backing the Lions.*

Great-heart. Then said the Pilgrims Guide, These women and children are going on Pilgrimage, and this is the Way they must go, and go it they shall, in spite of thee and the Lions.

Grim. This is not their way, neither shall they go therein. I

---

burnt . . . a hot Iron A common punishment for blasphemers; the persecuted turn persecutors.

am come forth to withstand them, and to that end will back the Lions.

Now, to say the truth, by reason of the fierceness of the Lions, and of the *grim* carriage of him that did back them, this Way had of late lain much unoccupied, and was almost all grown over with grass.

Christ. Then said *Christiana*, though the High-ways have been unoccupied heretofore,° and tho' the Travellers have been made in times past to walk through By-paths, it must

Judges 5. 6, 7.   not be so now I am risen, *Now I am risen a Mother in Israel.*

Grim. Then he swore *by the Lions*, but it should,° and therefore bid them turn aside, for they should not have passage there.

Great-heart. But their Guide made first his approach unto *Grim*, and laid so heavily at him with his Sword, that he forced him to a retreat.

A Fight *betwixt* Grim *and* Great-heart.   *Grim.* Then said he, (that attempted to back the Lions) Will you slay me upon mine own ground?°

Great-heart. 'Tis the King's high-way° that we are in, and in this Way it is that thou hast placed thy Lions; but these women, and these children, tho' weak, shall hold on their Way in spite of thy Lions. And with that he gave him again a downright[27] blow, and brought him upon his knees. With this blow he also broke his helmet, and with the next he cut off an arm. Then did the Giant roar so hideously, that his voice frighted

The Victory.   the women, and yet they were glad to see him lie sprawling upon the ground. Now the Lions were chained, and so of themselves could do nothing.[28] Wherefore, when old *Grim*, that intended to back them, was dead, Mr. *Great-heart* said to the Pilgrims, Come now, and follow me, and no hurt shall happen to you from the Lions. They therefore went on, but the

They pass by *the Lions.*   women trembled as they passed by them; the boys also looked as if they would die, but they all got by without further hurt.

---

heretofore Up until now; **but it should** That it should be so; **upon mine own ground** Like Giant Despair, Grim insists on his property rights; **the King's high-way** Great-heart stresses the separation of church and state; the civil authority has no power over the conscience.

Now, then, they were within sight of the *Porter's* Lodge, and they soon came up unto it; but they made the more haste after this to go thither, because 'tis dangerous travelling there in the night. So when they were come to the Gate, the Guide knocked, and the Porter cry'd, *Who is there?* but as soon as the Guide had said, *It is I*, he knew his voice, and came down; (for the Guide had oft before that come thither as a *Conductor of Pilgrims*) when he was come down, he opened the Gate, and seeing the Guide standing just before it, (for he saw not the women, for they were behind him) he said unto him, How now, Mr. *Great-heart*, what is your business here so late to-night? I have brought, said he, some Pilgrims hither, where, by my Lord's commandment, they must lodge: I had been here some time ago, had I not been opposed by the Giant that did use to back the Lions; but I, after a long and tedious combat with him, have cut him off, and have brought the Pilgrims hither in safety.

They come to the Porter's Lodge.

Porter. Will you not go in, and stay till morning?

Great-heart. No, I will return to my Lord to-night.

Christ. Oh, Sir, I know not how to be willing you should leave us in our Pilgrimage, you have been so faithful and so loving to us, you have fought so stoutly for us, you have been so hearty in counselling of us, that I shall never forget your favour towards us.

Great-heart attempts to go back.
The Pilgrims implore his company still.

Mercy. Then said *Mercy*, O that we might have thy company to our Journey's end! How can such poor women[29] as we, hold out in a Way so full of troubles as this Way is, without a Friend and Defender?

James. Then said *James*, the youngest of the boys, Pray, Sir, be persuaded to go with us, and help us, because we are so weak, and the Way so dangerous as it is.

Great-heart. I am at my Lord's commandment: If he shall allot me to be your Guide quite through, I will willingly wait upon you; but here you failed at first; for when he bid me come thus far with you, then you should have begged me of him to have gone quite through° with you, and he would have

Help lost for want of asking for.

---

quite through All the way.

granted your request. However at present I must withdraw, and so, good *Christiana, Mercy,* and my brave children, Adieu.

Part I. *p.* 55.
Christiana makes herself known to the Porter; he tells it to a damsel.
Then the Porter, Mr. *Watchful,* asked *Christiana* of her country, and of her kindred, and she said, *I came from the City of* Destruction; *I am a widow woman, and my husband is dead, his name was* Christian *the Pilgrim.* How, said the Porter, was he your husband? Yes, said she, and these are his Children; and this, pointing to *Mercy,* is one of my town's-women. Then the Porter rang his bell, as at such times he is wont, and there came to the door one of the damsels, whose name was *Humble-mind.* And to her the Porter said, Go tell it within, that *Christiana,* the Wife of *Christian,* and her Chil-

Joy at the noise of the Pilgrims coming.
dren are come hither on Pilgrimage. She went in therefore, and told it. But, oh, what a noise for Gladness was there, when the damsel did but drop that word out of her mouth!

So they came with haste to the Porter, for *Christiana* stood still at the door. Then some of the most grave said unto her, *Come in,* Christiana, *come in, thou Wife of that good Man; come in, thou blessed woman, come in, with all that are with thee.* So she went in, and they followed her that were her children and her companions. Now, when they were gone in, they were had into a very large room, where they were bidden to sit down: So they sat down, and the Chief of the House° was

Christians' Love is kindled at the sight of one another.
called to see and welcome the guests. Then they came in, and understanding who they were, did salute each other with a kiss, and said, Welcome, ye vessels of the Grace of God; Welcome to us your faithful Friends.

Now, because it was somewhat late, and because the Pilgrims were weary with their Journey, and also made faint with the sight of the fight, and of the terrible Lions, therefore they desired, as soon as might be, to prepare to go to Rest.

Exod. 12. 3–8.
John 1. 29.
Nay, said those of the Family, refresh yourselves with a morsel of meat: For they had prepared for them a Lamb, with the accustomed Sauce belonging thereto. For the Porter had heard before of their coming, and had told it to them within. So

---

Chief of the House Pastor of the church.

when they had supped, and ended their Prayer with a Psalm, they desired they might go to rest. But let us, said *Christiana*, if we may be so bold as to choose, be in that chamber that was my Husband's, when he was here; so they had them up *Part* I. *p.* 63. thither, and they lay all in a room. When they were at rest, *Christiana* and *Mercy* entered into discourse about things that were convenient.°

Christ. Little did I think once, that when my Husband *Christ's* went on Pilgrimage, that I should ever ha' followed him. *Bosom is for all Pilgrims.*

Mercy. And you as little thought of lying in his bed, and in his chamber to rest, as you do now.

Christ. And much less did I ever think of seeing his face with comfort, and of worshipping the Lord the King with him, and yet now I believe I shall.

Mercy. Hark! Don't you hear a noise?

Christ. Yes, 'tis, as I believe, a noise of musick, for Joy that we are here.

Mercy. Wonderful! musick in the house, musick in the *Musick.* Heart, and musick also in Heaven, for Joy that we are here.

Thus they talked awhile, and then betook themselves to sleep. So in the morning, when they were awake, *Christiana* said to *Mercy*, *Mercy did*

Christ. What was the matter that you did laugh in your *laugh in her* sleep to-night? I suppose you was in a dream. *sleep.*

Mercy. So I was, and a sweet dream it was; but are you sure I laughed?

Christ. Yes; you laughed heartily; but prithee, *Mercy*, tell me thy dream.

Mercy. I was a dreamed° that I sat all alone in a solitary *Mercy's* place, and was bemoaning of the hardness of my heart. *dream.*

Now I had not sat there long, but methought many were gathered about me to see me, and to hear what it was that I said. So they hearkened, and I went on bemoaning the hard-

---

convenient Appropriate; **I was a dreamed** Note that Mercy makes herself the object of the sentence: The dream is something that happens to her, rather than something she does.

ness of my heart. At this some of them laughed at me, some called me fool, and some began to thrust me about.° With that, methought I looked up, and saw one coming with Wings towards me. So he came directly to me, and said, *Mercy*, What aileth thee? Now when he had heard me make my complaint, he said, *Peace be to thee:* He also wiped mine eyes with his handkerchief, and *clad* me in *Silver and Gold*. He put a Chain about my neck, and Ear-Rings in mine ears, and a beautiful Crown upon my head. Then he took me by the hand, and said, *Mercy*, Come after me. So he went up, and I followed, till we came at a Golden Gate. Then he knocked, and when they within had opened, the Man went in, and I followed him up to a Throne, upon which one sat; and he said to me, *Welcome, Daughter*. The place looked bright and twinkling, like the Stars, or rather like the Sun, and I thought that I saw your Husband there; so I awoke from my dream. But did I laugh?

Christ. Laugh! ay, and well you might, to see yourself so well. For you must give me leave to tell you, that it was a good dream; and that as you have begun to find the First Part true, so you shall find the Second at last. *God speaks once, yea twice, yet Man perceiveth it not, in a Dream, in a Vision of the night, when deep Sleep falleth upon men, in slumbering upon the bed.* We need not, when abed, to lie awake to talk with God, he can visit us while we sleep, and cause us then to hear his Voice. Our heart oft-times wakes when we sleep, and God can speak to that, either by words, by proverbs, by signs and similitudes, as well as if one was awake.

Mercy. Well, I am glad of my dream, for I hope, e're long, to see it fulfilled, to the making me laugh again.

Christ. I think it is now high time to rise, and to know° what we must do.

Mercy. Pray, if they invite us to stay a while, let us willingly accept of the proffer.° I am the willinger to stay a while here, to grow better acquainted with these maids; methinks *Pru-*

Marginal notes:

What her dream was.

Ezek. 16. 10, 11, 12.

Job 33. 14, 15.

Mercy glad of her Dream.

---

thrust me about Push me around; know Find out; proffer Offer.

dence, *Piety* and *Charity*, have very comely and sober counte-
nances.

Christ. We shall see what they will do. So when they were
up and ready, they came down, and they asked one another of
their rest, and if it was comfortable or not?

Mercy. Very good, said *Mercy*, it was one of the best night's
lodgings that ever I had in my life.

Then said *Prudence* and *Piety*, if you will be persuaded to
stay here a while, you shall have what the house will afford.

Char. Ay, and that with a very good will, said *Charity*. So
they consented and staid there about a month or above, and
became very profitable one to another. And because *Prudence*
would see how *Christiana* had brought up her children, she
asked leave of her to Catechise them: So she gave her free consent. Then she began at the youngest, whose name was *James*.

They stay here some time.

Prudence desires to Catechise Christiana's children.

Prudence. And she said, Come, *James*, canst thou tell me
who made thee?

James. God the Father, God the Son, and God the Holy
Ghost.

James catechised.

Prud. Good boy. And canst thou tell who saves thee?

Jam. God the Father, God the Son, and God the Holy
Ghost.

Prud. Good boy still. But how doth God the Father save
thee?

Jam. By his Grace.

Prud. How doth God the Son save thee?

Jam. By his Righteousness, Death, and Blood, and Life.

Prud. And how doth God the Holy Ghost save thee?

Jam. By his *Illumination*, by his *Renovation*, and by his
Preservation.

Then said *Prudence* to *Christiana*, You are to be commended for thus bringing up your children. I suppose I need
not ask the rest these Questions, since the youngest of them
can answer them so well. I will therefore now apply myself to
the youngest next.

Prud. Then she said, Come, *Joseph*, (for his name was
Joseph) will you let me catechise you?

Joseph catechised.

Joseph. With all my heart.

Prud. What is Man?

Jos. A reasonable Creature, made so by God, as my brother said.

Prud. What is supposed by this word *Saved?*

Jos. That Man, by Sin, has brought himself into a state of Captivity and Misery.

Prud. What is supposed by his being saved by the Trinity?

Jos. That Sin is so great and mighty a Tyrant, that none can pull us out of its clutches, but God; and that God is so good and loving to Man, as to pull him indeed out of this miserable state.

Prud. What is God's design in saving of poor men?

Jos. The glorifying of his Name, of his Grace, and Justice, &c. and the everlasting Happiness of his Creature.

Prud. Who are they that must be saved?

Jos. Those that accept of his Salvation.°

Prud. Good boy, *Joseph*, thy mother has taught thee well, and thou hast hearkened to what she has said unto thee.

Then said *Prudence* to *Samuel*, who was the eldest but one:

Prud. Come, *Samuel*, are you willing that I should catechise you also?

Samuel. Yes, forsooth,° if you please.

Prud. What is Heaven?

Sam. A Place and State° most blessed, because God dwelleth there.

Prud. What is Hell?

Sam. A Place and State most woful, because it is the dwelling-place of Sin, the Devil, and Death.

Prud. Why wouldst thou go to Heaven?

Sam. That I may see God, and serve him without weariness; that I may see Christ, and love him everlastingly; that I may have that fulness of the Holy Spirit in me, that I can by no means here enjoy.

Prud. A very good boy also, and one that has learned well.

Samuel
catechised.

Those that accept of his Salvation Joseph's answer is more Lutheran than Calvinist; he does not refer to the doctrine of election; **forsooth** Truly; **A Place and State** Both a physical location and a psychological condition.

Then she addressed herself to the eldest, whose name was Matthew catechised. *Matthew;* and she said to him, Come, *Matthew,* shall I also catechise you?

Matthew. With a very good will.

Prud. I ask then, if there was ever any thing that had a Being antecedent to, or before God?

Matt. No, for God is Eternal; nor is there any thing, excepting Himself, that had a being, until the beginning of the first day. *For in six days the Lord made Heaven and Earth, the Sea, and all that in them is.*

Prud. What do you think of the Bible?

Matt. It is the Holy Word of God.

Prud. Is there nothing written therein, but what you understand?

Matt. Yes, a great deal.°

Prud. What do you do when you meet with places therein that you do not understand?

Matt. I think God is wiser than I. I pray also that he will please to let me know all therein that he knows will be for my good.

Prud. How believe you as touching the Resurrection of the Dead?

Matt. I believe they shall rise, the same that was buried; the same in *Nature,* tho' not in Corruption.° And I believe this upon a double account. *First,* Because God has promised it. *Secondly,* because he is able to perform it.

Then said *Prudence* to the boys, You must still hearken to your Mother, for she can learn you more. You must also dili- Prudence's conclusion upon the catechising of the boys. gently give ear to what good talk you shall hear from others; for your sakes do they speak good things. Observe also, and that with carefulness, what the Heavens and the Earth do teach you; but especially be much in the meditation of that Book that was the cause of your Father's becoming a Pilgrim.°

---

a great deal The ambiguity of Scripture is part of its meaning; **Corruption** Both spiritual sin and physical decay; **Observe also . . . a Pilgrim** Prudence urges them to study creation empirically—to read the "Book of the Creatures"—but to subordinate it to the study of Scripture.

I, for my part, my children, will teach you what I can while you are here, and shall be glad if you will ask me questions that tend to Godly edifying.

Mercy has a Sweet-heart.

Now, by that these Pilgrims had been at this place a week, *Mercy* had a visiter that pretended some good will unto her, and his name was Mr. *Brisk,*° a man of some breeding,° and that pretended to Religion, but a man that stuck very close to the World. So he came once or twice, or more, to *Mercy*, and offered love unto her. Now *Mercy* was of a fair countenance, and therefore the more alluring.

Mercy's temper.

Her Mind also was, to be always busying of herself in doing, for when she had nothing to do for herself, she would be making of hose and garments for others, and would bestow them upon them that had need. And Mr. *Brisk* not knowing where, or how she disposed of what she made, seemed to be greatly taken, for that he found her never idle. I will warrant her a good housewife, quoth he to himself.

Mercy enquires of the Maids concerning Mr. Brisk.

Mercy then revealed the business to the maidens that were of the house, and enquired of them concerning him, for they did know him better than she. So they told her, that he was a very busy° young man, and one that pretended to religion; but was, as they feared, a stranger to the Power of that which is Good.

Nay then, said *Mercy*, I will look no more on him; for I purpose never to have a Clog° to my Soul.

Prudence then replied, That there needed no great matter of discouragement to be given to him, her continuing so as she had begun to do for the Poor, would quickly cool his courage.

Talk betwixt Mercy and Mr. Brisk.

So, the next time he comes, he finds her at her old work, a making of things for the Poor. Then said he, What, always at it? Yes, said she, either for myself or for others: And what

---

Mr. Brisk Sharrock comments: "He behaves like a Restoration gallant, and the word suggests gallantry" (Sharrock, ed., *The Pilgrim's Progress*, p. 404); **some breeding** Mr. Brisk is a gentleman; **busy** Active, plausible. A more successful wooing of an innocent religious girl by a worldly hypocrite features in Bunyan's *The Life and Death of Mr. Badman* (1680); **Clog** Fetter.

canst thou *earn* a day, quoth he? I do these things, said she, *That I may be rich in good works, laying up in store a good foundation against the time to come, that I may lay hold on Eternal Life.* Why, Prithee, what dost thou with them? said he. Cloathe the naked, said she. With that his countenance fell.° So he forbore to come at° her again. And when he was asked the reason why, he said, that Mercy *was a pretty lass, but troubled with ill conditions.*°

1 Tim. 6. 17, 18, 19.

He forsakes her, and why.

When he had left her, *Prudence* said, Did I not tell thee, that Mr. *Brisk* would soon forsake thee? yea, he will raise up an ill report of thee: For notwithstanding his pretence to Religion, and his seeming love to *Mercy*, yet *Mercy* and he are of tempers so different, that I believe they will never come together.

Mercy in the practice of Mercy rejected, while Mercy in the name of Mercy is liked.

Mercy. I might have had husbands before now, tho' I spoke not of it to any; but they were such as did not like my conditions, tho' never did any of them find fault with my person.° So they and I could not agree.

Prud. Mercy in our days is little set by, any further than as to its name: The practice, which is set forth° by the conditions, there are but few that can abide.

Mercy. Well, said *Mercy*, if nobody will have me, I will die a maid, or my conditions shall be to me as a Husband. For I cannot change my Nature; and to have one that lies cross to° me in this, that I purpose never to admit of as long as I live. I had a sister named *Bountiful*, married to one of these churls; but he and she could never agree; but because my sister was resolved to do as she had begun, that is, to shew kindness to the Poor, therefore her husband first cried her down at the Cross,[30] and then turned her out of his doors.

Mercy's Resolution.

How Mercy's sister was served by her husband.

Prud. And yet he was a Professor,° I warrant you.

Mercy. Yes, such a one as he was, and of such as he the world is now full; but I am for none of them all.

---

his countenance fell Brisk's interest in Mercy was purely economic; **forbore to come at** Refrained from coming to; **conditions** Both "a disagreeable state of mind" and "poor financial circumstances"; **person** Body; **set forth** Represented; **lies cross to** Contradicts; **a Professor** A practitioner of religion.

Matthew *falls sick.*

Now *Matthew*, the eldest son of *Christiana*, fell sick, and his sickness was sore upon him, for he was much pained in his bowels, so that he was with it, at times, pulled as t'were both ends together. There dwelt also, not far from thence, one Mr. *Skill*, an ancient and well-approved Physician. So *Christiana* desired it, and they sent for him, and he came: When he was entred the room, and had a little observed the boy, he concluded that he was sick of the gripes.° Then he said to his mother, What *diet* has *Matthew* of late fed upon? Diet, said *Christiana*, nothing but what is wholsome. The Physician answered, This boy has been tampering with something that lies in his maw° undigested, and that will not away without Means.° And I tell you he must be purged, or else he will die.

Gripes of Conscience.

The Physician's Judgment.

Samuel *puts his mother in mind of the Fruit his brother did eat.*

Sam. Then said *Samuel*, Mother, mother, what was that which my brother did gather up and eat, so soon as we were come from the Gate that is at the head of this Way? You know that there was an orchard on the left-hand, on the other side of the Wall, and some of the trees hung over the Wall, and my brother did plash° and did eat.

Christ. True, my child, said *Christiana*, he did take thereof and did eat; naughty boy as he was, I did chide him, and yet he would eat thereof.

Skill. I knew he had eaten something that was not wholsome food, and that food, to wit, that fruit, is even the most hurtful of all. It is the fruit of *Beelzebub's* orchard. I do marvel that none did warn you of it; many have died thereof.

Christ. Then *Christiana* began to cry, and she said, O naughty boy, and O careless mother, what shall I do for my Son?

Skill. Come, do not be too much dejected; the boy may do well again, but he must purge and vomit.

Christ. Pray, Sir, try the utmost of your skill with him, whatever it costs.

Heb. 10, 1, 2, 3, 4.

Skill. Nay, I hope I shall be reasonable.° So he made him a

---

the gripes Indigestion; **maw** Throat; **Means** A material cause **reasonable** With regard to both method and price.

purge, but it was too weak;° 'twas said, it was made of the
Blood of a Goat, the Ashes of a Heifer, and with some of the
Juice of Hysop, &c. When Mr. *Skill* had seen that that purge
was too weak, he made him one to the purpose: 'Twas made
Ex Carne, & Sanguine Christi,° (you know Physicians give
strange medicines to their patients) and it was made up into
pills,[31] with a Promise or two, and a proportionate quantity
of Salt. Now he was to take them three at a time fasting, in
half a quarter of a pint of the tears of Repentance. When this
potion was prepared, and brought to the boy, he was loth to
take it, tho' torn with the gripes, as if he should be pull'd in
pieces, Come, come, said the Physician, you must take it. It
goes against my stomach,° said the boy. *I must have you take
it*, said his mother. I shall vomit it up again, said the boy. Pray,
Sir, said *Christiana* to Mr. *Skill*, how does it taste? It has no ill
taste, said the doctor; and with that she touched one of the
pills with the tip of her tongue. Oh, *Matthew*, said she, this
potion is sweeter than honey. If thou lovest thy Mother, if
thou lovest thy Brothers, if thou lovest *Mercy*, if thou lovest
thy Life, take it. So with much ado, after a short prayer for the
blessing of God upon it, he took it, and it wrought kindly°
with him. It caused him to purge, it caused him to sleep, and
rest quietly; it put him into a fine heat, and breathing sweat,
and did quite rid him of his gripes.

So in a little time he got up, and walked about with a Staff,
and would go from room to room, and talk with *Prudence*,
Piety and *Charity*, of his distemper, and how he was healed.

So when the boy was healed, *Christiana* asked Mr. *Skill*, saying, Sir, what will content you for your pains and care to and of
my child? And he said, You must pay the *Master of the College of
Physicians*,° according to Rules made in that case and provided.

Christ. But, Sir, said she, what is this pill good for else?

Marginal notes:

Potion prepared.

Joh. 6. 54, 55, 56, 57.
Mark 9. 49.
The Latin *I borrow.*
Heb. 9. 14.

The boy loth to take the Physick.

Zech. 12. 10.

The Mother tastes it, and persuades him.

A Word of God in the hand of his Faith.

Heb. 13. 11, 12, 13, 14, 15.

---

too weak The animal sacrifices described in the Old Testament are incapable
of purging sin; **Ex Carne, & Sanguine Christi** From the body and blood of
Christ (Latin); **stomach** Fleshly nature; **wrought kindly** Worked naturally;
the Master of the College of Physicians An unlikely title for Christ; the
metaphor is becoming strained.

This pill an
Universal
Remedy.

Skill. It is an universal pill;° 'tis good against all the diseases that *Pilgrims* are incident° to; and when it is well prepared, it will keep good, time out of mind.

Christ. Pray, Sir, make me up twelve boxes of them: For if I can get these, I will never take other physick.

Skill. These *pills* are good to prevent diseases, as well as to *cure* when one is sick. Yea, I dare say it, and stand to it, that if a man will but use this physick as he should, *it will make him*

John 6. 50.

live for ever. But good *Christiana*, thou must give these pills *no other way,*° but as I have prescribed: For if you do, they will

In a glass of
the tears of
Repentance.

do no good. So he gave unto *Christiana* physick for herself, and her boys, and for *Mercy*, and bid *Matthew* take heed how he eat any more *green plums*, and kissed them, and went his way.

It was told you° before, that *Prudence* bid the boys, that if at any time they would, they should ask her some Questions that might be profitable, and she would say something to them.

Of Physick.

Matt. Then *Matthew* who had been sick, asked her, Why for the most part Physick should be bitter to our palates?

Prud. To shew how unwelcome the word of God, and the effects thereof, are to a Carnal Heart.

Of the Effects
of Physick.

Matt. Why does Physick, if it does good, purge, and cause that we vomit?

Prud. To shew that the Word, when it works effectually, cleanseth the Heart and Mind. For look what the one doth to the body, the other doth to the soul.

Of Fire, and
of the Sun.

Matt. What should we learn by seeing the flame of our fire go upwards?° And by seeing the beams and sweet influences of the Sun strike downwards?

Prud. By the going up of the fire, we are taught to ascend to Heaven, by fervent and hot desires. And by the Sun his sending his heat, beams, and sweet influences downwards, we

---

universal pill Panacea; **incident** Susceptible; **no other way** The sacrament will not be efficacious unless accompanied by inward repentance; **you** The reader is addressed directly; **What should we learn . . . upwards?** Note that Matthew assumes that the world of appearances has ulterior significance.

are taught, that the Saviour of the World, tho' high, reaches down with his Grace and Love to us below.

Matt. Where have the Clouds their water?   *Of the Clouds.*

Prud. Out of the Sea.

Matt. What may we learn from that?

Prud. That Ministers should fetch their doctrine from God.

Matt. Why do they empty themselves upon the Earth?

Prud. To shew that Ministers should give out what they know of God to the world.

Matt. Why is the Rain-Bow caused by the Sun?   *Of the Rain-*

Prud. To shew that the covenant of God's Grace is con-   *Bow.*
firmed to us in Christ.

Matt. Why do the springs come from the Sea to us,   *Of the*
through the Earth?   *Springs.*

Prud. To shew, that the Grace of God comes to us through the Body of Christ.

Matt. Why do some of the springs rise out of the top of high Hills?

Prud. To shew, that the Spirit of Grace shall spring up in *some* that are great and mighty, as well as in *many* that are poor and low.

Matt. Why doth the fire fasten upon the candle-wick?   *Of the*

Prud. To shew that unless Grace doth kindle upon the   *Candle.*
heart, there will be no true Light of Life in us.

Matt. Why is the wick, and tallow,° and all spent, to maintain the light of the candle?

Prud. To shew that Body and Soul, and all should be at the service of, and spend themselves to maintain in good condition, that Grace of God that is in us.

Matt. Why doth the *Pelican*° pierce her own breast with   *Of the*
her bill?   *Pelican.*

Prud. To nourish her young ones with her blood, and thereby to shew that Christ the Blessed so loveth his young, his People, as to save them from Death by his Blood.

---

tallow Grease; **the Pelican** A conventional emblem for Christ.

Of the Cock.

Matt. What may one learn by hearing the cock to crow?

Prud. Learn to remember *Peter's* Sin,[32] and *Peter's* Repentance. The cock's crowing shews also, that Day is coming on; let then the crowing of the cock put thee in mind of that last and terrible Day of Judgment.

The Weak may sometimes call the Strong to Prayers.

Now about this time their month was out; wherefore they signified to those of the House, that 'twas convenient for them to up and be going. Then said *Joseph* to his mother, it is convenient that you forget not to send to the house of Mr. *Interpreter,*° to pray him to grant that Mr. *Great-heart* should be sent unto us, that he may be our conductor the rest of our Way. Good boy, said she, I had almost forgot. So she drew up a petition, and prayed Mr. *Watchful* the Porter, to send it by some fit° man, to her good friend Mr. *Interpreter;* who when it was come, and he had seen the contents of the petition, said to the messenger, Go tell them that I will send him.

They provide to be gone on their way.

When the Family where *Christiana* was, saw that they had a purpose to go forward, they called the whole house together, to give thanks to their King for sending of them such profitable guests as these; which done, they said to *Christiana*, And shall we not shew thee something, according as our custom is to do to Pilgrims, on which thou may'st meditate, when thou art upon the Way? So they took *Christiana*, her children, and *Mercy*

Eve's Apple.

into the closet, and shew'd them one of the *Apples* that *Eve* did eat of,° and that she also did give to her husband; and that for the eating of which, they were both turned out of Paradise, and

A sight of Sin is amazing.
Gen. 3. 6.
Rom. 7. 24.

asked her what she thought that was? Then *Christiana* said, 'Tis Food or Poison, I know not which. So they opened the matter to her, and she held up her hands and wondered.

Then they had her to a place, and shewed her *Jacob's Ladder.*°

---

the house of Mr. Interpreter Great-heart lives at the Interpreter's house: Courage springs from biblical methods of interpretation; fit Suitable; one of the Apples that Eve did eat of Christiana is shown the biblical correlative of the bad fruit eaten by her son. A series of biblical emblems follow, making Bunyan's point that his allegorical method accords with Scripture; Jacob's Ladder In Genesis 28:12 Jacob "dreamed, and behold a ladder set up on the earth, and the top of it reached to heaven: and behold the angels of God ascending and descending on it" (KJV).

Now at that time there were some Angels ascending upon it. So *Christiana* look'd and look'd to see the Angels go up, and so did the rest of the company. Then they were going into another place, to shew them something else; but *James* said to his mother, Pray bid them stay here a little longer, for this is a curious sight. So they turned again, and stood feeding their eyes with this *so pleasant a prospect*. After this they had them into a place where did hang up a *Golden Anchor,*° so they bid *Christiana* take it down; for, said they, you shall have it with you, for it is of absolute necessity that you should, that you may lay hold of that within the veil, and stand stedfast in case you should meet with turbulent weather: So they were glad thereof. Then they took them, and had them to the Mount upon which *Abraham* our Father had offered up *Isaac* his Son, and shewed them the *Altar*, the *Wood*, the *Fire*, and the *Knife*, for they remain to be seen to this very Day. When they had seen it, they held up their hands, and blest themselves, and said, Oh! What a man for Love to his Master, and for denial to himself was *Abraham!* After they had shewed them all these things, *Prudence* took them into the dining-room, where stood a pair of excellent virginals,° so she played upon them, and turned what she had shewed them into this excellent Song, saying,

margin notes:
Jacob's Ladder.
A sight of Christ is taking.
Gen. 28. 12.
Golden Anchor.
John 1. 51.
Heb. 6. 19.
Of Abraham *offering up* Isaac.
Gen. 22. 9.
Prudence's *Virginals.*

> Eve's *Apple we have shew'd you;*
>   *Of that be you aware.*
> *You have seen* Jacob's *Ladder too,*
>   *Upon which Angels are.*
>
> *An* Anchor *you received have,*
>   *But let not these suffice,*
> *Until with* Abra'm *you have gave*
>   *Your Best, a Sacrifice.*

Now about this time one knocked at the door: So the Porter opened, and behold Mr. *Great-heart* was there; but

---

Golden Anchor Hebrews 6:19: "Which hope we have as an anchor of the soul, both sure and steadfast, and which entereth into that within the veil" (KJV); **virginals** Harpsichords.

Mr. Great-
heart *come
again.*
when he was come in, what Joy was there! For it came now
fresh again into their minds, how but a while ago he had slain
Old *Grim* (*Bloody-man,*) the Giant, and had delivered them
from the Lions.

Then said Mr. *Great-heart* to *Christiana*, and to *Mercy*, My

*He brings a
token from his
Lord with
him.*
Lord has sent each of you a bottle of wine,° and also some
parched corn, together with a couple of pomegranates: He
has also sent the boys some figs and raisins, to refresh you in
your Way.

Then they addressed themselves to their Journey; and *Prudence* and *Piety* went along with them. When they came at the
Gate, *Christiana* asked the Porter, if any of late went by. He
said, No, only one some time since, who also told me, that of

Robbery.
late there had been a great robbery committed on the King's
high-way as you go: But, he saith, the thieves are taken, and
will shortly be tried for their lives. Then *Christiana* and *Mercy*
were afraid; but *Matthew* said, mother, fear nothing, as long
as Mr. *Great-heart* is to go with us, and to be our conductor.

Christiana
*takes her leave
of the Porter.*
Then said *Christiana* to the Porter, Sir, I am much obliged
to you for all the kindnesses that you have shewed me since I
came hither; and also for that you have been so loving and
kind to my children; I know not how to gratify° your kindness: Wherefore, pray, as a token of my respects to you, accept
of this small mite:° So she put a gold angel° in his hand, and

*The Porter's
blessing.*
he made her a low obeysance,° and said, Let thy Garments be
always white, and let thy head want no ointment. Let *Mercy*
live and not die, and let not her Works be few. And to the boys
he said, Do you fly youthful lusts, and follow after Godliness
with them that are grave and wise; so shall you put gladness
into your mother's heart, and obtain praise of all that are
sober-minded: So they thanked the Porter, and departed.

Now I saw in my dream, that they went forward until
they were come to the brow of the Hill, where *Piety*

---

bottle of wine Representing courage, as the word "bottle" does in modern
Cockney; **gratify** Show gratitude for; **mite** Mark 12:42: "And there came a
certain poor widow, and she threw in two mites, which make a farthing"
(KJV); **angel** A coin; **obeysance** Bow.

bethinking herself,° cried out, Alas! I have forgot what I intended to bestow upon *Christiana* and her companions. I will go back and fetch it; so she ran and fetched it. While she was gone, *Christiana* thought she heard in a grove a little way off on the right hand, a most curious melodious note, with words much like these:

> *Thro' all my Life thy Favour is*
> *So frankly shew'd to me,*
> *That in thy House for evermore*
> *My dwelling-place shall be.*

And listening still, she thought she heard another answer it, saying,

> *For why? The Lord our God is good;*
> *His Mercy is for ever sure:*
> *His Truth at all times firmly stood,*
> *And shall from Age to Age endure.*

So *Christiana* asked *Prudence* what 'twas that made those curious notes. They are, said she, our Country birds; they sing these notes but seldom, except it be at the Spring, when the flowers appear, and the Sun shines warm, and then you may hear them all day long. I often, said she, go out to hear them; we also oft-times keep them tame in our House. They are very fine company for us when we are melancholy; also they make the woods and groves and solitary places, places desirous° to be in. *Song* 2. 11, 12.

By this time *Piety* was come again; so she said to *Christiana*, Look here, I have brought thee a *Scheme*° of all those things that thou hast seen at our House, upon which thou may'st look when thou findest thyself forgetful, and call those things again to remembrance for thy edification and comfort. *Piety bestoweth something on them at parting.*

Now they began to go down the Hill into the Valley of *Hu-* *Part* I. p. 66.

---

bethinking herself Remembering, but note how Piety's self is objectified; **desirous** Desirable; **Scheme** Outline.

miliation. It was a steep hill, and the Way was slippery; but they were very careful, so they got down pretty well. When they were down in the Valley, *Piety* said to *Christiana*, this is the place where *Christian* your Husband met with the foul fiend *Apollyon*, and where they had that great Fight that they had: I know you cannot but have heard thereof; but be of good courage, as long as you have here Mr. *Great-heart* to be your Guide and conductor, we hope you will fare the better. So when these two had committed the Pilgrims unto the conduct of their Guide, he went forward and they went after.

Mr. Great-heart at the Valley of Humiliation.

Great-heart. Then said Mr. *Great-heart*, We need not be so afraid of this Valley, for here is nothing to hurt us, unless we procure it to° ourselves. 'Tis true, *Christian* did here meet with *Apollyon*, with whom he had also a sore Combat; but that *fray* was the fruit of those slips that he got in his going down the Hill: For they that get *Slips there*, must look for *Combats here;* and hence it is, that this Valley has got so hard a name.° For the common People, when they hear that some frightful thing has befallen such an one in such a place, are of an opinion that that place is haunted with some foul fiend, or evil spirit; when, alas! it is for the fruit of their doing,° that such things do befal them there.

The Reason why Christian was so beset here.

This Valley of *Humiliation* is of itself as fruitful a place, as any the crow flies over; and I am persuaded, if we could hit upon° it, we might find somewhere hereabout something that might give us an account why *Christian* was so hardly beset° in this place.

Then *James* said to his mother, Lo, yonder stands a Pillar, and it looks as if something was written thereon; let us go and see what it is. So they went and found there written, *Let*

A Pillar with an Inscription on it.

Christian's Slips, before he came hither, and the Battles that he met with in this place, be a warning to those that come after. Lo, said their Guide, Did I not tell you that there was something

---

procure it to Bring it on; **name** "Name," but also "reputation"; **the fruit of their doing** Now Great-heart begins to distance Christiana from allegorical understanding, portraying the foul fields as mere projections of the human mind's own fears; **hit upon** Find; **hardly beset** Roughly attacked.

hereabouts that would give intimation of the reason why *Christian* was so hard beset in this place: Then turning to *Christiana*, he said, No disparagement to *Christian* more than to many others whose hap° and lot it was. For 'tis easier going *up* than *down* this Hill, and that can be said but of few hills in all these parts of the World. But we will leave the good man, he is at rest, he also had a brave Victory over his enemy: Let Him grant that dwelleth above, that we fare no worse when we come to be tryed than he.

But we will come again to this Valley of *Humiliation*. It is the best and most fruitful piece of ground in all those parts. It is a fat ground,° and, as you see, consisteth much in meadows; and if a man was to come here in the summer time, as we do now, if he knew not any thing before thereof, and if he also delighted himself in the sight of his eyes, he might see that, that would be delightful to him. Behold how green this Valley is, also how beautified with *Lillies*. I have also known many labouring men that have got good estates° in this Valley of *Humiliation*. (For God resisteth the Proud, but gives *more, more*° Grace to the humble;) for indeed it is a very fruitful soil, and doth bring forth by handfuls. Some also have wished, that the next° way to their Father's House were here, that they might be troubled no more with either hills or mountains to go over; but the Way is the Way, and there's an end.°

This Valley a brave place.

Song 2. 1.
Jam. 4. 6.
1 Pet. 5. 5.

Men thrive in the Valley of Humiliation.

Now as they were going along, and talking, they espied a boy feeding his father's sheep. The boy was in very mean° cloaths, but of a very fresh and well-favoured countenance; and as he sat by himself, he sung. Hark, said Mr. *Great-heart*, to what the Shepherd's boy saith; so they hearkened, and he said,

> He that is down, needs fear no Fall;
> He that is low, no Pride:

Phil. 4. 12, 13.

---

hap Chance; **fat ground** Fertile land; **many laboring . . . estates** The literal poor are the figural rich in the eyes of God; **more, more** Repetition for emphasis; **next** Quickest; **there's an end** Both "that's all there is to it" and "it has an end"; **mean** Humble.

He that is humble, ever shall
Have God to be his Guide.

I am content with what I have,
Little be it or much:
And, Lord, Contentment still I crave,
Because thou savest such.

Heb. 13. 5.

Fulness to such, a Burden is,
That go on Pilgrimage:
Here little, and hereafter Bliss,
Is best from Age to Age.

Then said their Guide, Do you hear him? I will dare to say, that this boy lives a merrier life, and wears more of that herb call'd *Heart's-Ease°* in his bosom, than he that is clad in silk and velvet; but we will proceed in our discourse.

In this Valley our Lord formerly had his country house, he loved much to be here: He loved also to walk in these meadows, for he found the Air was pleasant: Besides, here a man shall be free from the noise, and from the hurryings of this life: all states° are full of noise and confusion, only the Valley of *Humiliation* is that empty and solitary place. Here a man shall not be so let and hindered in his contemplation, as in other places he is apt to be. This is a Valley that no body° walks in, but those that love a Pilgrim's life; and tho' *Christian* had the hard hap to meet here with *Apollyon*, and to enter with him a brisk° encounter, yet I must tell you, that in former times men have met with Angels here, have found Pearls here, and have in this place found the Words of Life.

Did I say our Lord had here in former days his country-house, and that he loved here to walk? I will add, in this place, and to the People that live and trace° these grounds, he has left a yearly revenue to be faithfully paid them at certain sea-

Christ, when in the Flesh, had his country house in the Valley of Humiliation.

Hos. 12. 4, 5.

---

that **Herb** call'd **Heart's-Ease** *Viola tricoloris herba*, also known as "Johnny Jump-up"; **states** Countries, conditions, estates; **no body** "Nobody" and also "no body"; **brisk** Stiff; **trace** Wander.

sons for their maintenance by the way, and for their farther
encouragement to go on their Pilgrimage.

Mat. 11. 29.

Samuel. Now as they went on, *Samuel* said to Mr. *Great-
heart:* Sir, I perceive that in this Valley, my father and *Apollyon*
had their Battle; but whereabout was the Fight, for I perceive
this Valley is large?

Great-heart. Your father had that Battle with Apollyon, at
a place yonder before us, in a narrow passage, just beyond
Forgetful Green. And indeed that place is the most dangerous
place in all these parts. For if at any time the Pilgrims meet
with any brunt,° it is when they forget what Favours they have
received, and how unworthy they are of them: This is the
place also where others have been hard put to it; but more of
the place when we are come to it; for I persuade myself, that
to this day there remains either some sign of the Battle, or
some monument to testify that such a battle there was fought.

Forgetful Green.

Mercy. Then said *Mercy*, I think I am as well in this Valley
as I have been any where else in all our Journey: The place,
methinks, suits with my spirit. I love to be in such places
where there is no rattling with coaches, nor rumbling with
wheels: Methinks here one may, without much molestation,
be thinking what he is, whence he came, what he has done,
and to what the King has called him: Here one may think and
break at heart, and melt in one's spirit, until one's eyes become like the *Fish-Pools of Heshbon.* They that go rightly
through this Valley of *Bacha*,° make it a Well, the rain that
God sends down from Heaven upon them that are here also,
filleth the Pools. This Valley is that from whence also the King
will give to their vineyards, and they that go through it, shall
sing, (as *Christian* did, for all° he met with *Apollyon.*)

Humility a sweet Grace.

Song 7. 4.
Psal. 84. 5, 6, 7.
Hos. 2. 15.

Great-heart. 'Tis true, said their Guide, I have gone
through this Valley many a time, and never was better than
when here.

An Experiment of it.

I have also been a conduct to several Pilgrims, and they
have confessed the same: *To this man will I look, saith the*

---

brunt Blow; **Valley of Bacha** The images are now almost entirely biblical,
rather than iconic; **for all** Despite the fact that.

King, even to him that is Poor, and of a contrite Spirit, and that trembles at my Word.

Now they were come to the place where the afore-mentioned Battle was fought: Then said the Guide to *Christiana,* her children and *Mercy,* This is the place, on this ground *Christian* stood, and up there came *Apollyon* against him; and *The Place where Christian and the* Fiend *did fight: Some signs of the Battle remain.* look, did not I tell you, here is some of your husband's blood upon these stones to this day: Behold, also, how here and there are yet to be seen upon the place, some of the shivers° of *Apollyon's* broken darts: See also how they did beat the ground with their feet as they fought, to make good their places against each other; how also with their by-blows,° they did split the very stones in pieces, verily *Christian* did here play the man, and shewed himself as stout° as could, had he been there, even *Hercules*° himself. When *Apollyon* was beat, he made his retreat to the next valley, that is called, *The Valley of the Shadow of Death,* unto which we shall come anon.

A Monument of the Battle. Lo, yonder also stands a monument, on which is engraven this Battle, and *Christian's* Victory, to his Fame, throughout all Ages: So, because it stood just on the Way-side before them, they stept to it, and read the writing, which word for word was this:

Hard-by° *here was a Battle fought,*
A Monument of Christian's Victory.
Most strange, and yet most true;
Christian and Apollyon fought
Each other to subdue.

The Man so bravely play'd the Man,
He made the Fiend to fly:
Of which a Monument I stand,
The same to testify.

Part I. p. 74.   When they had passed by this place, they came upon the borders of the Shadow of Death, and this Valley was longer

---

shivers Splinters; **by-blows** Follow-throughs; **stout** Brave; **Hercules** The strongest and most popular hero of pagan Greece is no match for a single Christian; **Hard-by** Nearby.

than the other, a place also most strangely haunted with evil things, as many are able to testify: But these women and children went the better through it, because they had Day-light, and because Mr. *Great-heart* was their conductor.

When they were entered upon this Valley, they thought that they heard a groaning, as of dead men; a very great groaning. They thought also they did hear words of Lamentation, spoken as of some in extreme torment. These things made the boys to quake, the women also looked pale and wan; but their Guide bid them be of good comfort.

Groanings heard.

So they went on a little further, and they thought that they felt the ground begin to shake under them, as if some hollow place was there; they heard also a kind of hissing, as of serpents, but nothing as yet appeared. Then said the boys, Are we not yet at the end of this doleful place? But the Guide also bid them be of good courage, and look well to their feet, lest haply, said he, you be taken in some snare.

The Ground shakes.

Now *James* began to be sick, but I think° the cause thereof was fear; so his Mother gave him some of that Glass of Spirits that she had given her at the *Interpreter's* house, and three of the Pills that Mr. *Skill* had prepared, and the boy began to revive. Thus they went on, till they came to about the middle of the Valley; and then *Christiana* said, Methinks I see something yonder upon the road before us, a thing of such a shape,[33] such as I have not seen. Then said *Joseph*, Mother, what is it? An ugly thing, child; an ugly thing, said she. But mother, what is it like? said he. 'Tis like I cannot tell what, said she. And now it was but a little way off: Then said she, It is nigh.

James sick with Fear.

A Fiend appears.

The Pilgrims are afraid.

Well, said Mr. *Great-heart*, let them that are most afraid, keep close to me: So the *Fiend* came on, and the conductor met it; but when it was just come to him, it vanished to all their sights: Then remembered they what had been said some time ago; *Resist the Devil, and he will fly from you.*

They went therefore on, as being a little refreshed; but they

---

I think The narrator's uncertainty contributes to the growing naturalism of the narrative.

Great-heart
encourages
them.

A Lion.

1 Pet. 5. 8, 9.

A Pit and
darkness.

Christiana
now knows
what her
Husband felt.

Great-heart's
reply.

had not gone far, before *Mercy*, looking behind her, saw, as she thought, something 'most like a Lion,[34] and it came a great padding pace after; and it had a hollow voice of roaring; and at every roar that it gave, it made all the Valley echo, and their hearts to ake, save the heart of him that was their Guide. So it came up, and Mr. *Great-heart* went behind, and put the Pilgrims all before him. The Lion also came on apace, and Mr. *Great-heart* addressed himself to give him battle. But when he saw that it was determined, that resistance should be made, he also drew back, and came no further.

Then they went on again, and their conductor did go before them, till they came at a place where was cast up a Pit, the whole breadth of the Way, and before they could be prepared to go over that, a great mist and a darkness fell upon them, so that they could not see. Then said the Pilgrims, Alas! Now what shall we do? But their Guide made answer, Fear not, stand still, and see what an end will be put to this also; so they staid there, because their path was marr'd.° They then also thought that they did hear more apparently° the noise and rushing of the Enemies; the fire also, and the smoke of the Pit, was much easier to be discerned. Then said *Christiana* to *Mercy*, Now I see what my poor Husband went through; I have heard much of this place, but I never was here afore now; poor man, he went here all alone in the night; he had night almost quite through the Way; also these Fiends were busy about him, as if they would have torn him in pieces. Many have spoke of it, but none can tell what the Valley of *the shadow of Death* should mean, untill they come in it themselves. *The heart knows its own bitterness, and a stranger intermeddleth not with its joy.* To be here, is a fearful thing.

Great-heart. This is like doing business in great waters, or like going down into the deep; this is like being in the heart of the Sea, and like going down to the bottoms of the mountains: Now it seems as if the Earth, with its bars,° were about us for ever. *But let them that walk in darkness, and have no*

---

marr'd Ruined; **apparently** Distinctly; **bars** "Obstacles," but also "prison bars."

light, trust in the name of the LORD, *and stay upon*° *their God.* For my part, as I have told you already, I have gone often through this Valley, and have been much harder put to it than now I am; and yet you see I am alive. I would not boast, for that I am not mine own Saviour. But I trust we shall have a good deliverance. Come, let us pray for Light to him that can lighten our darkness, and that can rebuke, not only these, but all the Satans° in Hell.

So they cried and prayed, and God sent light and deliver- *They pray.* ance, for there was now no let in their Way; no not there, where but now they were stopt with a Pit. Yet they were not got through the Valley; so they went on still, and behold great stinks and loathsome smells, to the great annoyance° of them. Then said *Mercy* to *Christiana*, There is not such pleasant being here as at the Gate, or at the *Interpreter's*, or at the house where we lay last.

O but, said one of the boys, it is not so bad to go through *One of the boys reply.* here, as it is to *abide* here always; and for ought I know, one reason why we must go this way to the House prepared for us, is, that our home might be made the sweeter to us.

Well said, *Samuel*, quoth the Guide, thou hast now spoke like a man. Why, if ever I get out here° again, said the boy, I think I shall prize light and good way, better than ever I did in all my life. Then said the Guide, We shall be out by and by.

So on they went, and *Joseph* said, Cannot we see to the end of this Valley as yet? Then said the Guide, Look to your feet, for you shall presently be among snares: So they looked to their feet, and went on; but they were troubled much with the snares. Now when they were come among the snares, they es- *Heedless is slain, and Takeheed preserved.* pied a man cast into the Ditch on the left hand, with his flesh all rent and torn. Then said the Guide, That is one *Heedless*, that was a going this Way; he has lain there a great while: There was one *Takeheed* with him, when he was taken and slain; but *he* escaped their hands. You cannot imagine how

---

stay upon Wait for; **Satans** Enemies. Bunyan's use of the plural draws attention to Satan's emblematic nature; **annoyance** Disgust; **out here** Out of here.

many are killed hereabouts, and yet men are so foolishly venturous, as to set out lightly on Pilgrimage, and to come without a Guide. Poor *Christian!* it was a wonder that he here
escaped; but he was beloved of his God: Also he had a good
heart of his own,° or else he could never ha' done it. Now they

Part I. p. 79.   drew towards the end of the Way, and just there where *Chris-*

Maul a Giant.   *tian* had seen the Cave when he went by, out thence came
forth *Maul* a giant.[35] This *Maul* did use to spoil young Pilgrims with Sophistry, and he called *Great-heart* by his name,

He quarrels
with Great-
heart.
  and said unto him, How many times have you been forbidden to do these things? Then said Mr. *Great-heart*, What
things? What things? quoth the Giant; you know what things;
but I will put an end to your trade. But, pray, said Mr. *Great-*
heart, before we fall to it, let us understand wherefore we
must fight. (Now the women and children stood trembling,
and knew not what to do.) Quoth the Giant, You rob the
country, and rob it with the worst of thefts.° These are but
generals, said Mr. *Great-heart;* come to particulars, man.

God's
Ministers
counted as
Kidnappers.
  Then said the Giant, Thou practisest the craft of a *Kidnap-*
per, thou gatherest up women and children, and carriest
them into a strange country, to the weakning of my Master's
kingdom. But now *Great-heart* replyed, I am a servant of the
God of Heaven; my business is to persuade Sinners to *Repen-*

The Giant
and Mr.
Great-heart
must fight.
  tance: I am commanded to do my endeavour to turn men,
women, and children, from Darkness to Light, and from the
Power of Satan to God; and if this be indeed the ground of
thy quarrel, let us fall to it as soon as thou wilt.

Then the Giant came up, and Mr. *Great-heart* went to meet
him; and as he went, he drew his Sword, but the Giant had a
club. So without more ado they fell to it, and at the first blow
the Giant struck Mr. *Great-heart* down upon one of his knees;

Weak folks
Prayers do
sometimes
help Strong
folks Cries.
  with that the women and children cried out: So Mr. *Great-*
heart recovering himself laid about him in full lusty manner,
and gave the Giant a wound in his arm; thus he fought for the
space of an hour, to that height of heat, that the breath came

---

a good heart of his own And therefore did not need an external Great-heart
to guide him; **the worst of thefts** That is, of souls.

out of the Giant's nostrils, as the heat doth out of a boiling cauldron.

Then they sat down to rest them, but Mr. *Great-heart* betook him to prayer; also the women and children did nothing but sigh and cry all the time that the battle did last.

When they had rested them, and taken breath, they both fell to it again, and Mr. *Great-heart* with a full blow fetch'd° the Giant down to the ground: Nay, hold, and let me recover, quoth he. So Mr. *Great-heart* fairly° let him get up: So to it they went again, and the Giant missed but little of all-to-breaking° Mr. *Great-heart's* skull with his club. *The Giant struck down.*

Mr. *Great-heart* seeing that, runs to him in the full heat of his spirit, and pierced him under the fifth rib; with that the Giant began to faint, and could hold up his club no longer. Then Mr. *Great-heart* seconded his blow, and smit° the head of the Giant from his shoulders. Then the women and children rejoiced, and Mr. *Great-heart* also praised God, for the deliverance he had wrought. *He is slain, and his head disposed of.*

When this was done, they amongst them erected a *Pillar*, and fastened the Giant's head thereon, and wrote underneath in letters that passengers might read:

> *He that did wear this Head, was one*
>   *That Pilgrims did misuse;*
> *He stopt their Way, he spared none,*
>   *But did them all abuse:*
> *Until that I,* Great-heart *arose,*
>   *The Pilgrims Guide to be;*
> *Until that I, did him oppose,*
>   *That was their Enemy.*

Now I saw that they went to the ascent that was a little way off cast up to be a prospect for *Pilgrims*, (that was the place from whence *Christian* had the first sight of *Faithful* his brother.) Wherefore here they sat down, and rested, they also *Part* I. *p.* 80.

---

fetch'd Knocked; **fairly** Sportingly; **all-to-breaking** All but breaking; **smit** Smote.

here did eat and drink, and make merry; for that they had gotten deliverance from this so dangerous an enemy. As they sat thus and did eat, *Christiana* ask'd the Guide, *If he had caught no hurt in the Battle?* Then said Mr. *Great-heart*, No, save a little on my flesh; yet that also shall be so far from being to my detriment, that it is at present a proof of my love to my Master and you, and shall be a means, by Grace, to increase my reward at last.

But was you not afraid, good Sir, when you see him come out with his Club?

It is my duty, said he, to distrust mine own ability, that I may have reliance on Him that is stronger than all. But what did you think, when he fetch'd you down to the ground at the first blow? Why, I thought, quoth° he, that so my Master himself was served, and yet he it was that conquered at the last.

Matt. When you all have thought what you please, I think God has been wonderful good unto us, both in bringing us out of this Valley, and in delivering us out of the hand of this Enemy; for my part, I see no reason why we should distrust our God any more, since he has *now*, and in *such* a place as this, given us such testimony of his love as this.

Then they got up, and went forward: Now a little before them stood an oak, and under it when they came to it, they found an old Pilgrim fast asleep; they knew that he was a Pilgrim by his *Clothes*, and his *Staff*, and his *Girdle*.

So the *Guide*, Mr. *Great-heart*, awaked him, and the old gentleman, as he lift up his eyes, cried out, What's the matter? Who are you? And what is your business here?

Great-heart. Come, man, be not so hot, here is none but Friends: Yet the old man gets up, and stands upon his guard, and will know of them what they were. Then said the *Guide*, my name is *Great-heart*, I am the guide of these Pilgrims, which are going to the Cœlestial Country.

Honest. Then said Mr. *Honest*, I cry you mercy;° I fear'd that you had been of the company of those that some time

2 Cor. 4.
Discourse of the Fights.

Matthew *here* admires God's Goodness.

Old Honest asleep under the Oak.

One Saint sometimes takes another for his Enemy.

---

quoth Said; **I cry you mercy** I beg your pardon (but note that Honest is literally addressing Mercy).

ago did rob *Little-Faith* of his money; but now I look better about me, I perceive you are honester people.°

Great-heart. Why what would, or could you ha' done, to ha' help'd yourself, if we indeed had been of that company?

Hon. Done! Why, I would have fought as long as breath had been in me; and had I so done, I am sure you could never have given me the worst on't; for a *Christian* can never be overcome, unless he shall yield of himself.

Great-heart. Well said, father *Honest*, quoth the Guide; for by this I know thou art a cock of the right kind,° for thou hast said the truth.

Hon. And by this also I know that thou knowest what true Pilgrimage is; for all others do think, that we are the soonest overcome of any.

Great-heart. Well, now we are so happily met, pray let me crave your name, and the name of the place you came from?

Hon. My name I cannot,° but I came from the town of *Stupidity*; it lieth about four degrees beyond the City of *Destruction*.

Great-heart. Oh! Are you that country-man then? I deem I have half a guess of you,° your name is old *Honesty*, is it not? So the old Gentleman blush'd, and said, Not *Honesty* in the *abstract*,° but *Honest* is my name, and I wish that my *nature* shall agree to what I am called.°

Hon. But, Sir, said the old gentleman, how could you guess that I am such a man, since I came from such a place?

Great-heart. I had heard of you before, by my Master; for he knows all things that are done on the Earth: But I have often wondered that any should come from your place, for your town is worse than is the City of *Destruction* itself.

Talk between Great-heart and he.

Whence Mr. Honest came.

Stupified Ones are worse than those merely Carnal.

---

you are honester people Hinting that Honest is a projection of the pilgrims' own honesty; **a cock of the right kind** A good fighter, an honest man; **My name I cannot** Honest is too honest to describe himself as "honest"; **I deem I have half a guess of you** I reckon I know who you are; **in the abstract** The shift from abstract noun to adjective shows how the characters gradually grow independent of their allegorical referents as the journey nears its end; **I wish . . . called** In contrast to the bad characters, who often deny any connection between their name and their nature.

Hon. Yes, we lie more off from the Sun, and so are more cold and senseless; but was a man in a mountain of Ice, yet if the Sun of Righteousness will arise upon him, his frozen heart shall feel a thaw; and thus it hath been with me.

Great-heart. I believe it, Father *Honest*, I believe it; for I know the thing is true.

Then the old gentleman saluted all the *Pilgrims* with a holy kiss of Charity, and asked them of their names, and how they had fared since they set out on their Pilgrimage.

Old Honest
and
Christiana
talk.

Christ. Then said *Christiana*, My name I suppose you have heard of; good *Christian* was my husband, and these four were his children. But can you think how the old gentleman was taken,° when she told him who she was! He skipped, he smiled, and blessed them with a thousand good wishes, saying:

Hon. I have heard much of your husband, and of his travels and wars, which he underwent in his days. Be it spoken to your comfort, the name of your husband rings all over these parts of the world; his Faith, his Courage, his Enduring, and his Sincerity under all,° has made his name famous. Then he

*He also talks
with the boys;
Old Mr.
Honest's
blessing on
them.*
Mat. 10. 3.
Psal. 99. 6.
Gen. 39.
Acts 1. 14.
[1. 13.]

turned him to the boys, and asked them of their names, which they told him: And then said he unto them, *Matthew*, be thou like *Matthew*° the publican, not in Vice but in Virtue. *Samuel*, said he, be thou like *Samuel* the prophet, a man of Faith and Prayer. *Joseph*, said he, be thou like *Joseph* in *Potiphar's* house, Chaste, and one that flies from temptation. And *James*, be thou like *James the Just*, and like *James* the brother of our Lord. Then they told him of *Mercy*, and how she had left her town and her kindred to come along with *Christiana*, and with her sons. At that the old honest man

*He blesseth
Mercy.*

said, *Mercy* is thy name: By *Mercy* shalt thou be sustain'd,° and carried through all those difficulties that shall assault

---

taken Delighted; **under all** Under all circumstances; **be thou like Matthew** In a further movement away from iconic to biblical images, the boys are now explicitly likened to their biblical namesakes; **Mercy is thy name . . . sustain'd** The quality of mercy is now distinguished from the individual who bears its name; Mercy is no longer an allegorical personification of mercy, but an independent character.

thee in thy Way, till thou shalt come thither, where thou shalt look the *Fountain of Mercy*° *in the face with comfort.*

All this while the Guide, Mr. *Great-heart*, was very much pleased, and smiled upon his companion.

Now, as they walked along together, the Guide asked the old gentleman, If he did not know one Mr. *Fearing*,° that came on Pilgrimage out of his parts?

Talk of one Mr. Fearing.

Hon. Yes, very well, said he. He was a man that had the Root of the matter in him,° but he was one of the most troublesome Pilgrims that I ever met with in all my days.

Great-heart. I perceive you knew him, for you have given a very right character° of him.

Hon. Knew him! I was a great companion of his; I was with him most an end;° when he first began to think of what would come upon us hereafter, I was with him.

Great-heart. I was his Guide from my Master's house to the gate of the Cœlestial City.

Hon. Then you knew him to be a troublesome one.

Great-heart. I did so; but I could very well bear it; for men of my calling° are oftentimes intrusted with the conduct of such as he was.

Hon. Well then, pray let us hear a little of him, and how he managed himself under your conduct.

Great-heart. Why, he was always afraid that he should come short of whither he had a desire to go. Every thing frightned him that he heard any body speak of, that had but the least appearance of opposition in it. I hear that he lay roaring at the *Slough of Despond*, for above a month together; nor durst he, for all he saw several go over before him, venture, tho' they many of them offered to lend him their hand. *He would not go back again neither.* The Cœlestial City, he said he should die if he came not to it, and yet was dejected at

Mr. Fearing's *troublesome* Pilgrimage.

His behaviour *at the* Slough of Despond.

---

the Fountain of Mercy Christ, Mercy's end and origin; Mr. Fearing Rather than an abstract noun, Bunyan uses the present participle of a verb; the Root of the matter in him Job 19:28: "Why persecute we him, seeing the root of the matter is found in me?" (KHV); a very right character A very accurate description; most an end In the utmost extremity; men of my calling Pastors.

every difficulty, and stumbled at every straw that any body cast in his Way. Well, after he had lain at the *Slough of Despond* a great while, as I have told you, one Sun-shine morning, I do not know how, he ventured, and so got over: But when he was over, he would scarce believe it. He had, I think, a *Slough of Despond* in his mind,° a *Slough* that he carry'd every where with him, or else he could never have been as he was. So he came up to the Gate, you know what I mean, that stands at the head of this Way, and there also he stood a good *His behaviour* while before he would adventure° to knock. When the Gate *at the Gate.* was opened, he would give back and give place to others, and say, that he was not worthy: For all he got before some to the Gate, yet many of them went in before him. There the poor man would stand shaking and shrinking; I dare say it would have pitied one's heart to have seen him: *Nor would he go back again.* At last he took the hammer that hang'd on the Gate in his hand, and gave a small rap or two; then one opened to him, but he shrunk back as before. He that open'd, stept out after him, and said, Thou trembling one, what wantest thou? With that he fell to the ground. He that spoke to him wonder'd to see him so faint. So he said to him, Peace to thee, up, for I have set open the Door to thee, come in, for thou art blest. With that he gat° up, and went in trembling; and when that he was in, he was ashamed to shew his face. Well, after he had been entertained there a while, as you know how the manner is, he was bid go on his Way, and also told the Way *His behaviour* he should take. So he came till he came to our house, but as *at the* he behaved himself at the Gate, so he did at my master the *In-* *Interpreter's* *terpreter's* door. He lay thereabout in the cold a good while, *door.* before he would adventure to call. *Yet he would not go back.* And the nights were long and cold then. Nay, he had a Note of *Necessity*° in his bosom to my Master to receive him, and grant him the comfort of his House, and also to allow him a

---

a Slough of Despond in his mind The allegorical is translated into the psychological; **adventure** Dare. The word, or the equivalent "venture," is used repeatedly in the discussion of Fearing; **gat** Got; **a Note of Necessity** Certificate of election.

stout and valiant conduct, because he was himself so *chicken-hearted* a man; and yet for all that, he was afraid to call at the door. So he lay up and down thereabouts, till, poor man, he was almost starv'd; yea, so great was his dejection, that tho' he saw several others for knocking got in, yet he was afraid to venture. At last I think, I looked out of the window, and perceiving a man to be up and down about the door, I went out to him, and asked what he was; but poor man the water stood in his eyes: So I perceived what he wanted. I went therefore in, and told it in the House, and we shewed the thing to our Lord: So he sent me out again, to entreat him to come in; but I dare say, I had hard work to do it. At last he came in, and I will say that for my Lord, he carry'd it wonderful lovingly to him. There were but a few good bits at the table, but some of it was laid upon his trencher.° Then he presented the *Note*, and my Lord looked thereon, and said, his desire should be granted. So when he had been there a good while, he seemed to get some heart, and to be a little more comfortable. For my Master, you must know, is one of very tender bowels, especially to them that are afraid; wherefore he carried it so towards him, as might tend most to his encouragement. Well, when he had had a sight of the things of the place, and was ready to take his Journey to go to the City, my Lord, as he did to *Christian* before, gave him a bottle of Spirits, and some comfortable things to eat. Thus we set forward, and I went before him, but the man was but of few words, only he would sigh aloud.

How he was entertained there.

He is a little encouraged at the Interpreter's house.

When we were come to where the three fellows were hanged, he said, that he doubted° that that would be his end also: Only he seemed glad when he saw the *Cross* and the *Sepulchre*. There I confess he desired to stay a little to look; and he seemed for a while after to be a little cheary. When we came at the Hill *Difficulty* he made no stick at that, nor did he much fear the Lions: For you must know, that his trouble *was not about such things as those*, his fear was about his acceptance at last.

He was greatly afraid when he saw the Gibbet, cheary when he saw the Cross.

---

trencher Plate; **doubted** Feared.

I got him in at the House *Beautiful*, I think before he was willing; also when he was in, I brought him acquainted with the damsels that were of the place, but he was ashamed to make himself much for company; he desired much to be alone, yet he always loved good talk, and often would get behind the *Screen* to hear it: He also loved much to see *ancient* things, and to be *pondering* them in his mind. He told me afterward, that he loved to be in those two houses from which he came last, to wit, at the Gate, and that of the *Interpreter*, but that he durst not be so bold to ask.

Dumpish at the House Beautiful.

When we went also from the House *Beautiful*, down the Hill, into the Valley of *Humiliation*, he went down as well as ever I saw a man in my life, for he cared not how mean° he was, so he might be happy at last. Yea, I think there was a kind of Sympathy betwixt that Valley and him:° For I never saw him better in all his Pilgrimage than when he was in that Valley.

He went down into, and was very pleasant in the Valley of Humiliation.

Here he would lie down, embrace the ground, and kiss the very flowers that grew in this Valley. He would now be up every morning by break of day, tracing° and walking to and fro in this Valley.

Lam. 3. 27, 28, 29.

But when he was come to the entrance of the Valley of the *Shadow of Death*, I thought I should have lost my man; not for that he had any inclination *to go back*, that he always abhorred, but he was ready to die for Fear. O, the *Hobgoblins* will have me, the *Hobgoblins* will have me, cried he; and I could not beat him out on't.° He made such a noise, and such an out-cry here, that had they but heard him, 'twas enough to encourage them to come and fall upon us.

Much perplexed in the Valley of the Shadow *of Death.*

But this I took very great notice of, that this Valley was as quiet° while he went through it, as ever I knew it before or since. I suppose those Enemies here had now a special check° from our Lord, and a command not to meddle until Mr. *Fearing* was passed over it.

---

mean Humble; **Sympathy betwixt that Valley and him** Bunyan continues to reveal his rhetorical tricks; the Valley is explicitly declared a sympathetic landscape; **tracing** Roaming; **beat him out on't** Get it out of his head; **quiet** The enemies are all in Fearing's mind; **check** Prohibition.

It would be too tedious to tell you of all; we will therefore only mention a passage or two more. When he was come at *Vanity-Fair*, I thought he would have fought with all the men in the fair; I feared there we should both have been knock'd o' the head,° so hot was he against their Fooleries; upon the inchanted ground he was also very wakeful. But when he was come at the *River*, where was no bridge, there again he was in a heavy case:° Now, now, he said, he should be drowned for ever, and so never see that Face with comfort, that he had come so many miles to behold.

His behaviour at Vanity-Fair.

And here also I took notice of what was very remarkable; The water of that river was lower at this time, than ever I saw it in all my life; so he went over at last, not much above wet-shod.° When he was going up to the Gate, Mr. *Great-heart* began to take his leave° of him, and to wish him a good reception above, so he said, *I shall, I shall:* Then parted we asunder, and I saw him no more.

His Boldness at last.

Hon. Then it seems he was well at last.

Great-heart. Yes, yes, I never had doubt about him, he was a man of a choice spirit, only he was always kept very low, and that made his life so burdensome to himself, and so troublesome to others. He was above many, tender of° Sin; he was so afraid of doing injuries to others, that he often would deny himself of that which was lawful, because he would not offend.

Psal. 88.
Rom. 14. 21.
1 Cor. 8. 13.

Hon. But what should be the reason that such a good man should be all his days so much in the dark?

Great-heart. There are two sorts of reasons for it; one is, The wise God will have it so, some must *pipe*,[36] and some must *weep:* Now Mr. *Fearing* was one that played upon *this bass.*° He and his fellows sound the *sackbut*,° whose notes are

Reasons why good men are so in the Dark.

When he was come . . . knock'd o' the head Fearing is not fearful of worldly opposition, and he finds his most hated opponents in the Fair; **heavy case** Sad mood, bad situation; **wet-shod** Just getting his shoes wet. Once again, the threat is illusory; **Mr. Great-heart began to take his leave** As Owens notes, "Bunyan seems to forget that Great-heart is the narrator here" (Owens, ed., *The Pilgrim's Progress*, p. 317); **tender of** Sensitive to; **bass** Low, heavy note; **sackbut** Trumpet, but used in the Scriptures for a stringed instrument.

278 The Pilgrim's Progress

more doleful than the notes of other musick are; though indeed some say, the bass is the ground° of musick: And for my part, I care not at all for that profession, that begins not in heaviness of mind. The first string that the musician usually touches, is the *bass*, when he intends to put all in tune; God also plays upon this string first, when he sets the soul in tune for himself. Only here was the imperfection of Mr. *Fearing*, he could play upon no other musick but this, till towards his latter end.

I make bold to talk thus Metaphorically,° for the ripening of the wits of young readers, and because in the book of the Revelations,° the Saved are compared to a company of musicians that play upon their *Trumpets and Harps*, and sing their songs before the Throne.

Hon. He was a very zealous man, as one may see by what relation you have given of him; difficulties, Lions, or Vanity-Fair, he feared not at all; 'twas only Sin, Death, and Hell, that was to him a terror; because he had some doubts about his interest in° that Cœlestial Country.

Great-heart. You say right: *Those* were the things that were his troublers, and they, as you have well observed, arose from the weakness of his mind thereabout, not from weakness of spirit as to the practical part of a Pilgrim's Life. I dare believe, that as the proverb is, *He could have bit a Fire-brand, had it stood in his Way:* But the things with which he was oppressed, no man ever yet could shake off with ease.

Christ. Then said *Christiana*, This relation of Mr. *Fearing* has done me good: I thought nobody had been like me; but I see there was some semblance 'twixt this good man and I, only we differ in two things. His troubles were so great, they brake° out, but mine I kept within. His also lay so hard upon him, they made him that he could not knock at the houses provided for entertainment; but my trouble was always such, as made me knock the louder.

Matt. 11. 16, 17, 18.

Rev. 8. 14. 2, 3.

A Close about him.

Christiana's Sentence.

---

ground Foundation; **Metaphorically** Bunyan makes his method increasingly clear; **Revelations** Once again Bunyan cites biblical authority for his figures; **interest in** Right to; **brake** Broke.

Mercy. If I might also speak my mind, I must say, that something of him has also dwelt in me. For I have ever been more afraid of the *Lake*, and the loss of a place in *Paradise*, than I have been of the loss of other things. O, thought I, may I have the happiness to have a habitation *there*, 'tis enough, though I part with all the World to win it. Mercy's *Sentence.*

Matt. Then said *Matthew, Fear°* was one thing that made me think that I was far from having that within me that accompanies Salvation; but if it was so with such a good man as he, why may it not also go well with me? Matthew's *Sentence.*

James. No fears, no Grace, said *James;* though there is not always Grace where there is the fear of Hell, yet to be sure there is no Grace where there is no fear of God. James's *Sentence.*

Great-heart. Well said, *James,* thou hast hit the mark; for the fear of God is the beginning of Wisdom;° and to be sure they that want the *beginning,* have neither *middle* nor *end.* But we will here conclude our discourse of Mr. *Fearing,* after we have sent after him this farewel.

> *Well, Master* Fearing, *thou didst fear*
> *Thy God, and wast afraid*
> *Of doing any thing, while here,*
> *That would have thee betray'd.*
> *And didst thou fear the Lake and Pit?*
> *Would others did so too!*
> *For, as for them that want thy wit,*
> *They do themselves undo.*

Their Farewell about him.

Now I saw, that they still went on in their talk. For after Mr. *Great-heart* had made an end with Mr. *Fearing,* Mr. *Honest* began to tell them of another, but his name was Mr. *Self-will.°* He pretended himself to be a *Pilgrim,* said Mr. *Honest;* Of Mr. Self-will.

Fear Matthew no longer refers to the symbol Mr. Fearing, but to the quality he represents, the "something of him" that Christiana has found in herself; **the fear of God is the beginning of Wisdom** Psalm 111:10, Proverbs 9:10; **Mr. Self-will** An antinomian.

but I persuade myself, he never came in at the Gate that stands at the head of the Way.

Great-heart. Had you ever any talk with him about it?

Old Honest *had talked with him.*

Hon. Yes, more than once or twice; but he would always be like himself, *self-willed.*[37] He neither cared for man, nor Argument, nor yet Example; what his mind prompted him to, that he would do, and nothing else could he be got° to.

Great-heart. Pray what principles did he hold? for I suppose you can tell.

Self-will's Opinion.

Hon. He held, that a man might follow the Vices as well as the Virtues° of the Pilgrims; and that if he did both, he should be certainly saved.

Great-heart. How? If he had said, 'tis possible for the best to be guilty of the vices, as well as to partake of the vertues of Pilgrims, he could not much have been blamed; for indeed we are exempted from no Vice absolutely, but on condition that we Watch and Strive: But this I perceive is not the thing; but if I understand you right, your meaning is, that he was of that opinion, that it was allowable so to be?

Hon. Ai, ai, so I mean, and so he believed and practised.

Great-heart. But what grounds had he for his so saying?

Hon. Why, he said he had the Scripture for his warrant.

Great-heart. Prithee, Mr. *Honest*, present us with a few particulars.

Hon. So I will. He said: To have to do with other mens wives, had been practised by *David*, God's beloved, and therefore he could do it. He said: To have more women than one, was a thing that *Solomon* practised, and therefore he could do it. He said, that *Sarah* and the godly midwives of *Egypt* lied, and so did save *Rahab*, and therefore he could do it. He said, that the disciples went at the bidding of their Master, and took away the owner's *Ass*, and therefore he could do so too. He said, that *Jacob* got the inheritance of his father, in a way of° Guile and dissimulation, and therefore he could do so too.

---

got Persuaded; **Vices as well as the Virtues** The Ranter belief that the elect cannot sin; **in a way of** By means of. The Ranter has understood the Scriptures literally.

Great-heart. High base!° indeed. And are you sure he was of this opinion?

Hon. I have heard him plead for it, bring Scripture for it, bring arguments for it, *&c.*

Great-heart. An opinion that is not fit to be with any allowance° in the World.

Hon. You must understand me rightly: He did not say that *any* man might do this; but, that those that had the Virtues of those° that did such things, might also do the same.

Great-heart. But what more false than such a conclusion? For this is as much as to say, that because good men heretofore have sinned of Infirmity, therefore he had allowance to do it of a presumptuous mind: Or if because a child, by the blast of the wind, or for that it stumbled at a stone, fell down and so defiled° itself in mire, therefore he might wilfully lie down and wallow like a boar therein. Who could ha' thought that any one could so far ha' been blinded by the power of Lust? But what is written must be true: They *stumble at the Word, being disobedient, whereunto also they were appointed.*   1 Peter 2. 8.

His supposing that such may have the godly man's Virtues, who addict themselves to their Vices, is also a delusion as strong as the other. ('Tis just as if the *dog* should say, I have, or may have the *qualities* of the *child*, because I lick up its stinking excrements.) To eat up the Sin of God's People, is no   Hos. 4. 8. sign of one that is possessed with their Virtues. Nor can I believe, that one that is of this opinion, can at present have Faith or Love in him. But I know you have made strong objections against him, prithee what can he say for himself?

Hon. Why, he says, to do this by way of Opinion, seems abundance° more honest than to do it, and yet hold contrary to it in opinion.

Great-heart. A very wicked answer; for though to let loose

High base Extremely degenerate; **to be with any allowance** "To be given any credence," but perhaps also "to be allowed." Bunyan did not favor complete religious toleration; **those that had the Virtues of those** The saints who had the virtues of the biblical examples as well as their vices; **defiled** Dirtied; **abundance** Abundantly.

the bridle to lusts, while our opinions are against such things, is bad; yet, to sin, and plead a Toleration° so to do, is worse; the one stumbles beholders accidentally, the other pleads° them into the snare.

Hon. There are many of this man's mind, that have not this man's mouth, and *that* makes going on Pilgrimage of so little esteem as it is.

Great-heart. You have said the truth, and it is to be lamented: But he that feareth the King of Paradise, shall come out of° them all.

Christ. There are strange opinions in the world. I know one that said, 'twas time enough to repent when they came to die.

Great-heart. Such are not over wise: That man would ha' been loth,° might he have had a week to run twenty mile in his life, to have deferred that Journey to the last hour of that week.

Hon. You say right, and yet the generality of them that count themselves Pilgrims, do indeed do thus. I am, as you see, an old man, and have been a traveller in this Road many a day; and I have taken notice of many things.

I have seen some that have set out as if they would drive all the world afore them, who yet have in few days died as they in the Wilderness, and so never gat sight of the Promised Land.

I have seen some that have promised nothing at first setting out to be Pilgrims, and that one would ha' thought could not have lived a day, that have yet proved very good Pilgrims.

I have seen some that have run hastily forward, that again have, after a little time, run as fast just back again.

I have seen some that have spoke very well of a Pilgrim's Life at first, that after a while have spoken as much against it.

I have heard some, when they first set out for Paradise, say positively, there is such a place, who when they have been almost there, have come back again, and said there is none.

Toleration Permission; **pleads** Persuades; **come out of** Both "be delivered from" and "stand out from"; **loth** Unwilling.

I have heard some vaunt° what they would do in case they should be opposed that have even at a false alarm fled Faith, the Pilgrim's Way, and all.

Now as they were thus in their Way, there came one running to meet them, and said, Gentlemen, and you of the weaker sort,° if you love life, shift for° yourselves, for the Robbers are before you.

Great-heart. Then said Mr. *Great-heart*, they be the three that set upon *Little Faith* heretofore. Well, said he, we are ready for them; so they went on their Way: Now they looked at every turning when they should ha' met with the villains: But whether they heard of Mr. *Great-heart*, or whether they had some other game, they came not up to the Pilgrims.

Christ. Christiana then wished for an Inn for herself and her children, because they were weary. Then said Mr. *Honest*, There is one a little before us, where a very honourable disciple, one *Gaius*,° dwells. So they all concluded to turn in thither, and the rather, because the old gentleman gave him so good a report. So when they came to the door, they went in, not knocking, for folks use not to knock at the door of an Inn. Then they called for the Master of the House, and he came to them: So they asked if they might lie there that night?

Gaius. Yes, Gentlemen, if you be true men,° for my house is for none but Pilgrims. Then was *Christiana, Mercy*, and the boys, the more glad, for that the Innkeeper was a lover of Pilgrims. So they called for rooms, and he shewed them one for *Christiana* and her children, and *Mercy*, and another for Mr. *Great-heart* and the old gentleman.

Great-heart. Then said Mr. *Great-heart*, good *Gaius*, What hast thou for supper? for these Pilgrims have come far to-day, and are weary.

Gaius. It is late, said *Gaius*, so we cannot conveniently go

Fresh News of trouble.

Part I. *p.* 143. *Great-heart's Resolution.*

Christiana *wisheth for an Inn.*

Rom. xvi. 23. Gaius. *They enter into his House.*

Gaius *entertains them, and how.*

---

vaunt Boast; **the weaker sort** Women and children; **shift for** Look after; **Gaius** Described by Paul as "mine host, and of the whole church" (Romans 16:23; KJV); **if you be true men** Few of the pilgrims are literally men, in the sense of adult males.

out to seek food; but such as we have you shall be welcome to, if that will content.

Great-heart. We will be content with what thou hast in the house, forasmuch as I have proved° thee; thou art never destitute of that which is convenient.

Gaius *his Cook.*

Then he went down and spake to the cook, whose name was, *Taste-that-which-is-Good*, to get ready Supper for so many Pilgrims. This done, he comes up again, saying, Come, my good friends, you are welcome to me, and I am glad that I have a house to entertain you; and while supper is making ready, if you please, let us entertain one another with some good Discourse: So they all said, content.

Talk between Gaius *and his Guests.*

Gaius. Then said *Gaius*, Whose wife is this aged matron?[38] and whose daughter is this young damsel?

Great-heart. The woman is the wife of one *Christian*, a Pilgrim of former times; and these are his four children. The maid is one of her acquaintance; one that she hath persuaded to come with her on Pilgrimage. The boys take all after their father, and covet to tread in his steps: Yea, if they do but see any place where the old Pilgrim hath lain, or any print of his foot, it ministereth joy to their hearts, and they covet to lie or tread in the same.

Mark this.

Gaius. Then said *Gaius*, Is this *Christian's* wife, and are these *Christian's* children? I knew your husband's father, yea, also his father's Father. Many have been good of this stock, their ancestors dwelt first at *Antioch*.° *Christian's* progenitors (I suppose you have heard your husband talk of them) were very worthy men. They have, above any that I know, shewed themselves men of great virtue and courage, for the Lord of the Pilgrims, his ways, and them that loved him. I have heard of many of your husband's relations that have stood all trials for the sake of the Truth. *Stephen*,° that was one of the first of the Family from whence your husband sprang, was knocked o' th' head with stones. *James*, another of this generation, was slain with the edge of the sword. To say nothing of *Paul* and

Acts 11. 26. *Of* Christian's *Ancestors.*

Acts 7. 59, 60.

chap. 12. 8.

---

proved Tested; **Antioch** "The disciples were called Christians first in Antioch" (Acts 11:26; KJV); **Stephen** The first Christian martyr.

Peter,[39] men anciently of the family from whence your husband came: There was *Ignatius*, who was cast to the Lions: *Romanus*, whose flesh was cut by pieces from his bones; and *Polycarp*, that played the man in the fire.[40] There was he° that was hanged up in a basket in the Sun, for the wasps to eat; and he° who they put into a sack, and cast him into the Sea to be drowned. 'Twould be impossible, utterly to count up all of that family that have suffered injuries and death, for the love of a Pilgrim's life. Nor can I but be glad, to see that thy husband has left behind him four such boys as these. I hope they will bear up their Father's name, and tread in their Father's steps, and come to their Father's end.

Great-heart. Indeed, Sir, they are likely° lads; they seem to choose heartily their father's ways.

Gaius. That is it that I said, wherefore *Christian's* family is like still to spread abroad upon the face of the ground, and yet to be numerous upon the face of the earth: Wherefore, let *Christiana* look out some damsels for her sons, to whom they may be betrothed, *&c.* that the name of their father, and the house of his progenitors may never be forgotten in the world. *Advice to Christiana about her Boys.*

Hon. 'Tis pity this family should fall and be extinct.

Gaius. Fall it cannot, but be diminished it may; but let *Christiana* take my advice, and that's the way to uphold it.

And *Christiana*, said this Inn-keeper, I am glad to see thee and thy friend *Mercy* together here, a lovely couple. And may I advise, take *Mercy* into a nearer relation to thee: If she will, let her be given to *Matthew* thy eldest son; 'tis the way to preserve you a posterity in the earth. So this match was concluded, and in process of time they were married: But more of that hereafter.

Gaius also proceeded, and said, I will now speak on the behalf of Women, to take away their reproach.° For as Death *Gen. 3.*

---

he Marcus, fourth-century bishop of Arethusa, whose grisly martyrdom is described by Foxe; **he** Various martyrs were killed by drowning; **likely** Promising; **their reproach** Gaius rehearses the favorite arguments of seventeenth-century feminist works, such as Aemelia Lanyer's "Salve Deus Rex Judeorum" (1611; Hail, God, King of the Jews).

Gal. 4.

and the Curse came into the world by a woman, so also did Life and Health: *God sent forth his Son, made of a woman.* Yea, to shew how much those that came after, did abhor the act of their Mother, this sex in the old Testament coveted children, if happily this or that woman might be the Mother of the Saviour of the World. I will say again, that when the Saviour was come, women rejoyced in him, before either man or angel. I read not, that ever any man did give unto Christ so much as one groat, but the women followed him, and ministered to him of their substance. 'Twas a woman that washed his feet with tears, and a woman that anointed his body to the burial. They were women that wept when he was going to the Cross; and women that followed him from the cross, and that sat by his sepulchre when he was buried: They were women that were first with him at his Resurrection-morn; and women that brought tidings first to his disciples, that he was risen from the dead: Women therefore are highly favoured, and shew by these things, that they are sharers with us in the Grace of Life.

Why women of old so much desired children.

Luke 2.
chap. 8. 2, 3.

chap. 7. 37, 50.
John 11. 2.
chap. 12. 3.
Luke 23. 27.
Mat. 27. 55,
56, 61.

Luke 24. 22,
23.

Supper ready.

Now the cook sent up to signify that Supper was almost ready, and sent one to lay the cloth, the trenchers, and to set the salt and bread in order.

Then said *Matthew*, The sight of this cloth, and of this fore-runner of a supper, begetteth in me a greater appetite to my food than I had before.

What to be gathered from laying of the Board with the Cloth and Trenchers.

Gaius. So let all ministring doctrines *to* thee in this life, beget *in* thee a greater desire to sit at the Supper of the great King in his Kingdom; for all preaching, books and ordinances here, are but as the laying of the trenchers, and as setting of salt upon the board, when compared with the Feast that our Lord will make for us when we come to his House.

Levit. 7. 32, 33,
34. ch. 10.
14, 15.
Psalm 25. 1.
Heb. 13. 15.
Deut. 32. 14.
Judg. 9. 13.
John 15. 1.

So Supper came up, and first a *heave-shoulder*, and a *wave-breast* were set on the table before them;[41] to shew that they must begin their meal with Prayer and Praise to God. The *heave-shoulder David* lifted his Heart up to God with, and with the *wave-breast, where his Heart lay*, with that he used to lean upon his harp, when he played. These two dishes were very fresh and good, and they all eat heartily-well thereof.

The next they brought up, was a bottle of wine, red as blood.° So *Gaius* said to them, Drink freely, this is the juice of the true Vine,° that makes glad the heart of God and man. So they drank and were merry. Deut. 32. 14. Judg. 9. 13. John 15. 1.

The next was a dish of milk well crumbed: But *Gaius* said, *Let the boys have that, that they may grow thereby.* 1 Pet. 2. 1, 2. A Dish of Milk.

Then they brought up in course a dish of *butter* and *honey.* Then said *Gaius,* Eat freely of *this,* for this is good to chear up, and strengthen your judgments and understandings; this was our Lord's dish when he was a child: *Butter and honey shall he eat, that he may know to refuse the Evil, and choose the Good.* Of Honey and Butter. Isa. 7. 15.

Then they brought them up a dish of apples, and they were very good tasted fruit. Then said *Matthew,* may we eat apples, since they were such, by and with which, the Serpent beguiled our first Mother? A Dish of Apples.

Then said *Gaius,*

> *Apples were they* with *which we were beguiled,*
> *Yet* Sin, *not Apples,*° *hath our Souls defiled;*
> *Apples forbid, if eat, corrupt the blood:*
> *To eat such, when commanded, does us good;*
> *Drink of his Flagons then, thou Church, his Dove,*
> *And eat his Apples, who are sick of Love.*

Then said Matthew, *I made the Scruple,*° *because I a while since was sick with eating of fruit.*

Gaius. Forbidden fruit will make you sick, but not what our Lord has tolerated.

While they were thus talking, they were presented with another dish, and 'twas a dish of *Nuts.* Then said some at the table, *Nuts* spoil tender teeth, 'specially the teeth of the children: Which when *Gaius* heard, he said: Song 6. 61. A Dish of Nuts.

---

red as blood The communion wine that represents the blood of Christ; **the true Vine** John 15:1: "I am the true vine, and my Father is the husbandman" (KJV); **Sin, not apples** Matthew is instructed that the symbolic reading supercedes the literal; **Scruple** Caveat.

> *Hard* Texts *are* Nuts,° *(I will not call them* Cheaters)
> *Whose* Shells *do keep their* Kernels *from the* Eaters.
> *Ope then the shells, and you shall have the Meat,*
> *They here are brought, for you to crack and eat.*

Then were they very merry, and sat at the table a long time, talking of many things. Then said the old gentleman, My good landlord, while ye are here cracking your *Nuts*, if you please, do you open° this Riddle.

A Riddle put forth by Old Honest.

> *A man there was, tho' some did count him mad,*
> *The more he cast away, the more he had.*

Then they all gave good heed, wondering what good *Gaius* would say; so he sat still a while, and then thus replyed:

Gaius opens it.

> *He that bestows his Goods upon the Poor,*
> *Shall have as much again, and ten times more.*

Joseph wonders.

Then said *Joseph*, I dare say, Sir, I did not think you could ha' found it out.

Oh! said *Gaius*, I have been trained up in this way a great while: Nothing teaches like experience; I have learned of my Lord to be kind, and have found by experience, that I have gained thereby. *There is that scattereth, yet increaseth; and there is that with-holdeth more than is meet, but it tendeth to Poverty: There is that maketh himself Rich, yet hath nothing; there is that maketh himself poor, yet hath great Riches.*

Prov. 11. 24. chap. 13. 7.

Then *Samuel* whispered to *Christiana* his mother, and said, Mother, this is a very good man's house, let us stay here a good while, and let my brother *Matthew* be married here to *Mercy*, before we go any further.

The which *Gaius* the host over-hearing, said, *With a very good will, my child.*

Hard Texts are Nuts Gaius repeats Bunyan's case against those who criticized his allegorical method; **open** Solve.

So they stayed there more than a month, and *Mercy* was given to *Matthew* to wife.

Matthew *and* Mercy *are married.*

While they stayed here, *Mercy*, as her custom was, would be making coats and garments to give to the poor, by which she brought a very good report° upon the Pilgrims.

But to return again to our Story: After supper, the lads desired a bed, for that they were weary with travelling: Then *Gaius* called to shew them their chamber; but said *Mercy*, I will have them to bed. So she had them to bed, and they slept well, but the rest sat up all night: For *Gaius* and they were such suitable° company, that they could not tell how to part. Then after much talk of their Lord, themselves, and their Journey, old Mr. *Honest*, he that put forth the riddle to *Gaius*, began to nod. Then said *Great-heart*, What, Sir, you begin to be drowsy; come, rub up,° now here is a *Riddle* for you. Then said Mr. *Honest*, Let's hear it.

The Boys go to bed, the rest sit up.

Old Honest *nods.*

Then said Mr. *Great-heart*,

He that will kill, must first be overcome:
Who live abroad would, first must die at home.

A Riddle.

Ha! said Mr. *Honest*, it is a hard one, hard to expound, and harder to practise. But, come, landlord, said he, I will, if you please, leave my part to you, do you expound it, and I will hear what you say.

No, said *Gaius*, 'twas put to you, and it is expected you should answer it.

Then said the old Gentleman,

He first by Grace must conquer'd be,
That Sin would mortify:
And who, that lives, would convince me,
Unto himself must die.

The Riddle opened.

It is right, said *Gaius*, good Doctrine and Experience teaches this. For first, untill Grace displays itself, and over-

---

report Reputation; **suitable** Sympathetic; **rub up** Wake up.

comes the soul with its glory, it is altogether without heart° to oppose Sin; besides, if Sin is Satan's cords, by which the soul lies bound, how should it make resistance, before it is loosed from that Infirmity?

Secondly, Nor will any, that knows either reason or Grace, believe that such a man can be a living monument of Grace, that is a slave to his own Corruptions.

A Question worth the minding. And now it comes in my mind, I will tell you a story worth the hearing. There were two men that went on Pilgrimage, the one began when he was young, the other when he was old: The young man had strong corruptions° to grapple with, the old man's were decayed with the decays of nature:° The young man trod his steps as even as did the old one, and was every way as light as he: Who now, or which of them had their Graces shining clearest, since both seemed to be alike?

A Comparison. *Hon.* The young man's, doubtless. For that which heads it° against the greatest opposition, gives best demonstration that it is strongest; specially when it also holdeth pace with that that meets not with half so much; as to be sure old age does not.

A Mistake. Besides, I have observed, that old men have blessed themselves with this mistake; namely, taking the decays of nature for a gracious conquest over corruptions, and so have been apt to beguile themselves. Indeed old men that are gracious, are best able to give Advice to them that are young, because they have seen most of the emptiness of things: But yet, for an old and a young to set out both together, the young one has the advantage of the fairest discovery of a work of Grace within him, though the old man's corruptions are naturally the weakest.

Thus they sat talking till break of day. Now when the family was up, *Christiana* bid her son *James* that he should read a *Another question.* chapter; so he read 53d of *Isaiah:* When he had done, Mr. *Honest* asked why it was said, *that the Saviour is said to come*

---

without heart Both "pointless" and "insincere"; **corruptions** Fleshly temptations; **decays of nature** The declining sexual desire of old age; **heads it** Makes headway.

out of a dry ground, and also that he had no Form nor Comeliness in him.[42]

Great-heart. Then said Mr. *Great-heart;* To the first I answer; Because the Church of the *Jews,* of which Christ came, had then lost almost all the sap, and Spirit of religion.[43] To the second I say, the words are spoken in the person of the Unbelievers, who because they want that Eye that can see into our Prince's heart, therefore they judge of him by the meanness of his outside.

Just like those, that know not that precious stones are covered over with a homely crust; who when they have found one, because they know not what they have found, cast it again away, as men do a common stone.

Well, said *Gaius,* now you are here, and since, as I know, Mr. *Great-heart* is good at his Weapons, if you please, after we have refreshed ourselves, we will walk into the fields, to see if we can do any good. About a mile from hence, there is one *Slay-good,* a giant, that doth much annoy the King's Highway in these parts: And I know whereabout his haunt is, he is master of a number of thieves; 'Twould be well if we could clear these parts of him.°

So they consented and went, Mr. *Great-heart* with his *Sword, Helmet,* and *Shield;* and the rest with Spears and Staves.

When they came to the place where he was, they found him with one *Feeble-mind* in his hands, whom his servants had brought unto him, having taken him in the Way; now the *Giant* was rifling him,° with a purpose, after that, to pick his bones; for he was of the nature of *Flesh-eaters.*°

Well, so soon as he saw Mr. *Great-heart* and his friends at the mouth of his Cave, with their Weapons, he demanded what they wanted.

Great-heart. We want thee; for we are come to revenge the Quarrel of the many that thou hast slain of the Pilgrims,

Giant Slaygood *assaulted and slain.*

He is found with one Feeble-mind *in his hand.*

'Twould be well . . . of him For the first time, the pilgrims take the offensive, actively seeking out their opponents; **rifling him** Going through his pockets; **Flesh-eaters** Cannibals.

when thou hast dragged them out of the King's High-way;
wherefore come out of thy Cave. So he armed himself and
came out, and to a battle they went, and fought for above an
hour, and then stood still to take wind.

Slay. Then said the Giant, Why are you here on my
ground?

Great-heart. To revenge the blood of Pilgrims, as I also told
thee before; so they went to it again, and the giant made Mr.
Great-heart give back; but he came up again, and in the greatness of his mind he let fly with such stoutness at the giant's
head and sides, that he made him let his weapon fall out of
his hand; so he smote him, and slew him, and cut off his

Feeble-mind
rescued from
the Giant.

Head, and brought it away to the *Inn.* He also took *Feeble-
mind* the Pilgrim, and brought him with him to his lodgings.
When they were come home, they shewed his head to the
Family, and set it up as they had done others before, for a terror to those that shall attempt to do as he, hereafter.

Then they asked Mr. *Feeble-mind,* how he fell into his
hands?

How Feeble-
mind *came to*
be a Pilgrim.

Feeble-mind. Then said the poor man, I am a sickly man,
as you see, and because *Death* did usually once a day *knock at
my door,* I thought I should never be well at home: So I betook myself to a Pilgrim's life; and have travelled hither from
the town of *Uncertain,* where I and my father were born. I am
a man of no strength at all of body, nor yet of mind, but
would, if I could, though I can but *crawl,* spend my life in the
Pilgrim's Way. When I came at the Gate that is at the head of
the Way, the Lord of that place did entertain me freely; neither objected he against my weakly looks, nor against my *feeble mind;*° but gave me such things that were necessary for my
Journey, and bid me hope to the end. When I came to the
House of the *Interpreter,* I received much kindness there; and
because the Hill of *Difficulty* was judged too hard for me, I
was carried up that by one of his Servants. Indeed I have
found much relief from Pilgrims, though none was willing to
go so softly as I am forced to do: Yet still as they came on, they

---

my feeble mind An attribute of this figure, not his essence;

bid me be of good cheer, and said, that it was the will of their
Lord, that comfort should be given to the *feeble-minded*, and 1 Thes. 5. 4.
so went on their *own* pace. When I was come to *Assault-Lane*,
then this Giant met with me, and bid me prepare for an *Encounter:* But alas! feeble one that I was, I had more need of a
Cordial:° So he came up and took me: I conceited° he should
not kill me; also when he had got me into his Den,° since I
went not with him *willingly*, I believed I should come out
alive again. For I have heard, that not any Pilgrim that is *Mark this.*
taken captive by violent hands, if he keeps heart-whole towards his Master, is, by the Laws of Providence, to die by the
hand of the Enemy. *Robbed* I look'd to° be and robbed to be
sure I am; but I am as you see escaped with life, for the which
I thank my King as Author, and you as the means. Other
brunts I also look for, but this I have resolved on, to wit, to
run when I can, to *go*° when I cannot run, and to *creep*° when
I cannot go. As to the main, I thank him that loves me, I am
fixed;° my Way is before me, my mind is beyond the River *Mark this.*
that has no bridge, tho' I am, as you see, but of a *feeble mind*.

Hon. Then said old Mr. *Honest*, Have not you some time
ago, been acquainted with one Mr. *Fearing* a Pilgrim.

Feeble. Acquainted with him, Yes; he came from the town
of *Stupidity*, which lieth four degrees *Northward* of the City Mr. Fearing
of *Destruction*, and as many off, of where I was born; yet we Mr. Feeble-
were well acquainted, for indeed he was mine uncle, my fa- mind's *Uncle.*
ther's brother; he and I have been much of a temper,° he was
a little shorter than I, but yet we were much of a complexion.

Hon. I perceive you know him, and I am apt to believe also, Feeble-mind
that you were related one to another; for you have his whitely° *has some of*
look, a cast like his with your eye, and your speech is much alike. Mr. Fearing's
features.

Feeble. Most have said so, that have known us both; and
besides, what I have read in him,° I have for the most part
found in myself.

Cordial Medicine; conceited Understood; Den Bunyan's word for "prison";
look'd to Expected to; go Walk; creep Crawl; fixed Both "mended" and "set
in my purpose"; of a temper Alike; whitely Pale; what I have read in him
Feeble-Mind has been reading *The Pilgrim's Progress*.

Gaius
comforts him.

Gaius. Come, Sir, said good *Gaius*, be of good cheer, you are welcome to me, and to my house, and what thou hast a mind to, call for freely; and what thou would'st have my servants do for thee, they will do it with a ready mind.

Notice to be
taken of
Providence.

Then said Mr. *Feeble-mind*, This is an unexpected favour, and as the Sun shining out of a very dark cloud: Did Giant *Slay-good* intend me this Favour when he stopped me, and resolved to let me go no further? Did he intend, that after he had rifled my pocket, I should go to *Gaius* mine host! Yet so it is.°

Tidings how
one Not-right
was slain by a
thunder-bolt,
and Mr.
Feeble-
mind's
comment
upon it.

Now, just as Mr. *Feeble-mind* and *Gaius* were thus in talk, there comes one running, and called at the door, and told, that about a mile and a half off, there was one Mr. *Not-right* a Pilgrim struck dead upon the place where he was, with a *Thunder-bolt.*

Feeble. Alas! said Mr. *Feeble-mind*, is he slain? He overtook me some days before I came so far as hither, and would be my company-keeper: He also was with me when *Slay-good* the Giant took me, but he was nimble of his heels, and escaped: But it seems, he escaped to Die, and I was took to Live.

What, one would think, doth seek to slay outright,
Oft-times delivers from the saddest plight.
That very Providence, *whose Face is Death,*
Doth oft-times to the lowly, Life bequeath:
I was taken, he did escape and flee;
Hands crost, give Death to him, and Life to me.

Now about this time, *Matthew* and *Mercy* were married; also *Gaius* gave his daughter *Phebe*° to *James*, *Matthew's* brother, to wife; after which time, they yet staid above ten days at *Gaius's* house; spending their time, and the Seasons, like as Pilgrims use to do.

When they were to depart, *Gaius* made them a feast, and

Yet so it is Even the wicked fulfill God's providence; **Phebe** Greek for "shining."

they did eat and drink, and were merry. Now the hour was *The Pilgrims prepare to go forward.*
come that they must be gone; wherefore Mr. *Great-heart*
called for a reckoning.° But *Gaius* told him, that at his house
it was not the custom for Pilgrims to pay for their entertain- Luke 10. 33, 34, 35.
ment. He boarded them by the year, but looked for his pay
from the good *Samaritan*,° who had promised him, at his re- *How they greet one another at parting.*
turn, whatsoever charge he was at with them, faithfully to
repay him. Then said Mr. *Great-heart* to him,

Great-heart. Beloved, thou dost faithfully, whatsoever thou 3 John 5. 6.
dost, to the Brethren and to Strangers,° which have borne
witness of thy Charity before the Church, whom if thou (yet)
bring forward on their Journey, after a Godly sort,° thou shalt
do well.

Then *Gaius* took his leave of them all, and of his children, *Gaius's last kindness to Feeble-mind.*
and particularly of Mr. *Feeble-mind*. He also gave him some-
thing to drink by the Way.

Now Mr. *Feeble-mind*, when they were going out of the
door, made as if he intended to linger. The which when Mr.
Great-heart espied, he said, Come, Mr. *Feeble-mind*, pray do
you go along with us, I will be your conductor, and you shall
fare as the rest.

Feeble. Alas! I want a suitable companion; you are all lusty *Feeble-mind for going behind.*
and strong, but I, as you see, am weak; I choose therefore
rather to come behind, lest by reason of my many Infirmities,
I should be both a burden to myself and to you. I am, as I
said, a man of a weak and a feeble mind, and shall be offended and made weak at that which others can bear. I shall
like no Laughing: I shall like no gay Attire: I shall like no unprofitable Questions. Nay, I am so weak a man, as to be of- *His Excuse for it.*
fended with that which others have a liberty to do. I do not
know all the truth: I am a very ignorant *Christian man:*
Sometimes, if I hear some rejoice in the Lord, it troubles me,
because I cannot do so too. It is with me, as it is with a weak
man among the strong, or as with a sick man among the Job 12. 5.

---

reckoning Bill; the good Samaritan In Luke 10, Jesus tells the parable of a
Samaritan who helps a stranger; to the Brethren and to Strangers An echo
of 3 John 1:5, where the words are also addressed to Gaius; sort Manner.

healthy, or as a lamp despised, (he that is ready to slip with his feet, is as a lamp despised in the thought of him that is at ease:) so that I know not what to do.

Great-heart's
commission.
1 Thes. 5. 15.
Rom. 14.
1 Cor. 8.
chap 9. 22.

A Christian
spirit.

Great-heart. But brother, said Mr. *Great-heart*, I have it in Commission to comfort the *feeble-minded*, and to support the weak. You must needs go along with us; we will wait for you, we will lend you our help; we will deny ourselves of some things both *Opinionative* and *Practical*,° for your sake: We will not enter into doubtful disputations before you; we will be made all things to you, rather than you shall be left behind.

Psalm 38. 17.
Promises.

Now all this while they were at *Gaius's* door; and behold, as they were thus in the heat of their discourse, Mr. *Ready-to-halt* came by, with his *Crutches* in his hand, and he also was going on Pilgrimage.

Feeble. Then said Mr. *Feeble-mind* to him, Man! How camest thou hither? I was but just now complaining that I had not a suitable companion, but thou art according to my wish. Welcome, welcome, good Mr. *Ready-to-halt*, I hope thee and I may be some help.

Feeble-mind
glad to see
Ready-to-halt
come by.

Ready-to-halt. I shall be glad of thy company, said the other; and good Mr. *Feeble-mind*, rather than we will part, since we are thus happily met, I will lend thee one of my crutches.

Feeble. Nay, said he, though I thank thee for thy good-will, I am not inclined to halt° afore I am lame. Howbeit, I think, when occasion is, it may help me against a dog.

Ready-to-halt. If either myself, or my crutches can do thee a pleasure, we are both at thy command, good Mr. *Feeble-mind*.

Thus therefore they went on; Mr. *Great-heart* and Mr. *Honest* went before, *Christiana* and her children went next, and Mr. *Feeble-mind* and Mr. *Ready-to-halt* came behind with his crutches. Then said Mr. *Honest*,

New talk.

Hon. Pray, Sir, now we are upon the Road, tell us some profitable things of some that have gone on Pilgrimage before us.

Great-heart. With a good will: I suppose you have heard

---

both Opinionative and Practical The pilgrims will not drive Feeble-mind away with opinionated discourse or excessively strict behavior; halt Limp.

how *Christian* of old did meet with *Apollyon* in the Valley of *Part* I. *pp.* 66, 73, 82–88.
Humiliation, and also what hard work he had to go through
the Valley of the *Shadow of Death*. Also I think you cannot but
have heard how *Faithful* was put to it with Madam *Wanton*,
with *Adam* the First, with one *Discontent* and *Shame;* four as
deceitful villains, as a man can meet with upon the Road.

Hon. Yes, I have heard of all this; but indeed good *Faithful*
was hardest put to it with *Shame;* he was an unwearied one.

Great-heart. Ay, for as the Pilgrim well said, he of all men
had the wrong name.

Hon. But pray, Sir, where was it that *Christian* and *Faithful*
met *Talkative?* That same was also a notable one.

Great-heart. He was a confident Fool, yet many follow his
ways.

Hon. He had like to ha'° beguiled *Faithful*.

Great-heart. Ay, but *Christian* put him into a way quickly
to find him out. Thus they went on till they came at the place
where *Evangelist* met with *Christian* and *Faithful*, and proph- *Part* I. *p.* 101.
esied to them what should befall them at *Vanity-Fair*.

Great-heart. Then said their guide, Hereabouts did *Christian* and *Faithful* meet with *Evangelist*, who prophesied to
them of what troubles they should meet with at *Vanity-Fair*.

Hon. Say you so! I dare say it was a hard chapter that then
he did read unto them.

Great-heart. 'Twas so, but he gave them encouragement *Part* I. *p.* 107.
withal. But what do we talk of them, they were a couple of
lion-like men; they had set their faces like flints. Don't you remember how undaunted they were when they stood before
the Judge?

Hon. Well, *Faithful* bravely suffered.

Great-heart. So he did, and as brave things came on't; for
Hopeful and some others, as the story relates it, were converted by his death.

Hon. Well, but pray go on; for you are well acquainted with
things.

---

had like to ha' Both "would have liked to have" and "was likely to."

Part I. *p.* 115.

Great-heart. Above all that *Christian* met with after he had passed through *Vanity-Fair*, one *By-Ends* was the arch° one.

Hon. By-Ends, what was he?

Great-heart. A very arch° fellow, a down-right Hypocrite; one that would be religious which way ever the world went; but so cunning, that he would be sure neither to lose nor suffer for it.

He had his *mode* of religion for every fresh occasion, and his wife was as good at it as he. He would turn and change from opinion to opinion; yea, and plead for[44] so doing too. But so far as I could learn, he came to an ill end with his *By-Ends;*° nor did I ever hear that any of his children were ever of any esteem with any that truly feared God.

They come within sight of Vanity-Fair. [Ps. 21. 16.? 1ST EDIT.]

Now by this time they were come within sight of the town of *Vanity*, where *Vanity-Fair* is kept. So when they saw that they were so near the town, they consulted with one another how they should pass through the town, and some said one thing, and some another. At last Mr. *Great-heart* said, I have, as you may understand, often been a Conductor of Pilgrims through this town; now I am acquainted with one Mr. *Mnason°* a *Cyprusian* by nation, an old disciple, at whose house we may lodge. If you think good, said he, we will turn in there?

They enter into one Mr. Mnason's to lodge.

Content, said Old *Honest;* content, said *Christiana;* content, said Mr. *Feeble-mind;* and so they said all. Now, you must think, it was even-tide° by that° they got to the outside of the town; but Mr. *Great-heart* knew the way to the old man's house. So thither they came; and he called at the door, and the old man within knew his tongue so soon as ever he heard it; so he opened, and they all came in. Then said *Mnason*, their host, How far have ye come to-day? So they said, from the house of *Gaius* our friend. I promise you, said he, you have gone a good stitch,° you may well be a weary; sit down. So they sat down.

---

arch Worst; **very arch** Utterly despicable; **with his By-Ends** The allegorical qualities are, once again, distinguished from the character himself; **Mr. Mnason** Acts 21:16 refers to "one Mnason of Cyprus, an old disciple with whom we should lodge" (KJV); **even-tide** Evening; **by that** By that time; **stitch** Distance.

Great-heart. Then said their Guide, Come, what cheer, Sirs, I dare say you are welcome to my friend.

Mnason. I also, said Mr. *Mnason*, do bid you welcome; and whatever you want, do but say, and we will do what we can to get it for you.

They are glad of entertainment.

Honest. Our great want, a while since, was Harbour° and good Company, and now I hope we have both.

Mnason. For harbour, you see what it is; but for good company, that will appear in the trial.

Great-heart. Well, said Mr. *Great-heart*, will you have the Pilgrims up into their lodging?

Mnason. I will, said Mr. *Mnason*. So he had them to their respective places; and also shewed them a very fair dining-room, where they might be, and sup together until time was come to go to rest.

Now when they were set in their places, and were a little cheary after their Journey, Mr. *Honest* asked his landlord, if there were any store of good people in the town?

Mnason. We have a few, for indeed they are but a few when compared with them on the other side.°

Honest. But how shall we do to see some of them? For the sight of good men to them that are going on Pilgrimage, is like to the appearing of the Moon and Stars to them that are sailing upon the Seas.

They desire to see some of the good people in the Town.

Mnason. Then Mr. *Mnason* stamped with his foot, and his daughter *Grace* came up: So he said unto her, *Grace*, go you, tell my friends, Mr. *Contrite*, Mr. *Holy-man*, Mr. *Love-saint*, Mr. *Dare-not-lie*, and Mr. *Penitent*, that I have a friend or two at my house that have a mind this evening to see them.

Some sent for.

So *Grace* went to call them, and they came; and after salutation made, they sat down together at the table.

Then said Mr. *Mnason*, their landlord, My neighbours, I have, as you see, a company of *Strangers* come to my house; they are *Pilgrims:* They come from afar, and are going to Mount *Sion*. But who, quoth he, do you think this is? point-

---

Harbour A resting place; **the other side** The rigid social polarization in
ity reminds us that England had just been through a civil war.

ing with his finger to *Christiana:* It is *Christiana*, the wife of *Christian*, that famous Pilgrim, who with *Faithful* his brother, were so shamefully handled in our town.° At that they stood amazed, saying, We little thought to see *Christiana*, when *Grace* came to call us, wherefore this is a very comfortable° surprize. Then they asked her of her welfare, and if these young men were her husband's sons. And when she had told them they were; they said, the King whom you love and serve, make you as your father, and bring you where he is in peace.

Some talk betwixt Mr. Honest and Mr. Contrite.

Hon. Then Mr. *Honest* (when they were all sat down) asked Mr. *Contrite* and the rest, in what posture° their town was at present.

The fruit of Watchfulness.

Contrite. You may be sure we are full of hurry in Fair-time. 'Tis hard keeping our hearts and spirits in any good order, when we are in a cumbered° condition. He that lives in such a place as this is, and that has to do with such as we have, has need of an *Item*° to caution him to take heed every moment of the day.

Honest. But how are your neighbours now for quietness?

Persecution not so hot at Vanity-Fair *as formerly.*

Contrite. They are much more moderate now than formerly.[45] You know how *Christian* and *Faithful* were used at our town: But of late, I say, they have been far more moderate. I think the blood of *Faithful* lieth with load upon them° till now; for since they burned him, they have been ashamed to burn any more; in those days we were afraid to walk the streets, but now we can shew our heads. *Then* the name of a professor was odious; *now*, specially in some parts of our town, (for you know our town is large) Religion is counted honourable.

Then said Mr. *Contrite* to them, Pray how fareth it with you in your Pilgrimage? How stands the country affected towards you?

---

in our town Mnason and his friends were conspicuous by their absence from Vanity in part one; **comfortable** Pleasant; **posture** Political and religious stance; **cumbered** Burdened. Compare Bunyan's *Christ A Complete Savior* (1692): "Worldly cumber is a devilish thing" (*Works*, vol. 1, p. 206); **Item** Written reminder; **lieth with load upon them** Makes them feel guilty.

Hon. It happens to us, as it happeneth to wayfaring men; sometimes our Way is clean, sometimes foul; sometimes up hill, sometimes down hill; we are seldom at a certainty:° The wind is not always on our backs, nor is every one a Friend that we meet with in the Way. We have met with some notable rubs° already; and what are yet behind° we know not; but for the most part we find it true, that has been talked of of old: *A good man must suffer trouble.*

Contrite. You talk of rubs, what rubs have you met withal?

Hon. Nay, ask Mr. *Great-heart*, our Guide, for he can give the best account of that.

Great-heart. We have been beset three or four times already: First, *Christiana* and her children were beset with two ruffians, that they feared would take away their lives. We were beset with giant *Bloody-man*, giant *Maul*, and giant *Slay-good:* Indeed we did rather beset the last, than were beset of him; and thus it was: After we had been some time at the house of *Gaius, mine host, and of the whole Church,* we were minded upon a time to take our weapons with us, and so go see if we could light upon any of those that were Enemies to *Pilgrims;* (for we heard that there was a notable one thereabouts.) Now *Gaius* knew his *haunt* better than I, because he dwelt thereabout; so we looked and looked, till at last we discerned the mouth of his Cave; then were we glad, and plucked up our spirits. So we approached up to his den, and lo, when we came there, he had dragged, by mere° force, into his net, this poor man, Mr. *Feeble-mind*, and was about to bring him to his end. But when he saw us, supposing, as we thought, he had had another prey; he left the poor man in his hole, and came out. So we fell to it full sore,° and he lustily laid about him; but, in conclusion, he was brought down to the ground, and his head cut off, and set up by the Way-side, for a Terror to such as should after practise such Ungodliness. That° I tell

---

We are seldom at a certainty Refers to the fluctuations in Charles II's policy toward dissenters; **rubs** Blows; **behind** Ahead, in terms of time, but behind in the sense of "hidden"; **mere** Sheer; **full sore** Very fiercely; **That** To prove that.

you the truth, here is the man himself to affirm it, who was as a lamb taken out of the mouth of the lion.

Feeble-mind. Then said Mr. *Feeble-mind,* I found this true, to my cost and comfort; to my cost, when he threaten'd to pick my bones every moment; and to my comfort, when I saw Mr. *Great-heart* and his friends, with their weapons, approach so near for my deliverance.

Holy-man. Then said Mr. *Holy-man,* there are two things that they have need to be possessed with that go on Pilgrimage, *Courage,* and an *Unspotted° Life.* If they have not courage, they can never hold on their Way; and if their lives be loose, they will make the very name of a *Pilgrim* stink.

Love-saint. Then said Mr. *Love-saint;* I hope this caution is not needful amongst you. But truly there are many that go upon the road, that rather declare themselves Strangers to Pilgrimage, than *Strangers and Pilgrims in the Earth.*

Dare-not-lie. Then said Mr. *Dare-not-lie,* It is true, they neither have the Pilgrim's *weed,°* nor the Pilgrim's *Courage;* they go not uprightly, but all *awry* with their feet; one shoe goeth *inward,* another *outward,* and their hosen out° behind; here a rag, and there a rent,° to the disparagement of their Lord.

Penitent. These things, said Mr. *Penitent,* they ought to be troubled for; nor are the Pilgrims like to have that Grace upon them and their *Pilgrims Progress,°* as they desire, untill the Way is clear'd of such spots and blemishes.

Thus they sat talking and spending the time, untill supper was set upon the table. Unto which they went, and refreshed their weary bodies; so they went to rest. Now they staid in the Fair a great while,[46] at the house of Mr. *Mnason,* who, in process of time, gave his daughter *Grace* unto *Samuel, Christian's* son, to wife, and his daughter *Martha* to *Joseph.*

The time, as I said, that they lay here, was long, (for it was not now as in former times.) Wherefore the Pilgrims grew ac-

---

Unspotted Immaculate; **weed** Clothing; **hosen out** Stockings torn; **rent** Tear; **their Pilgrims Progress** Self-referential; these false pilgrims will lack the grace needed to interpret *The Pilgrim's Progress* correctly.

quainted with many of the good People of the town, and did them what service they could. *Mercy*, as she was wont, laboured much for the Poor, (wherefore their bellies and backs blessed her,) and she was there an ornament to her profession. And, to say the truth for *Grace, Phebe*, and *Martha*, they were all of a very good nature, and did much good in their places. They were also all of them very fruitful, so that *Christian's* name, as was said before, was like to live in the world.

While they lay here, there came a *Monster*° out of the *A Monster.* woods, and slew many of the people of the town. It would also carry away their children, and teach them to suck its whelps.° Now no man in the town durst so much as face this *Monster*; but all men fled when they heard of the noise of his coming.

The *Monster* was like unto no one beast upon the earth: Its *Rev. 17. 3.* body was like a Dragon, and it had seven heads and ten *His Shape.* horns. *It made great havock of children, and yet it was governed* *His Nature.* *by a woman.*° This *Monster* propounded conditions to men; and such men as loved their Lives more than their Souls, accepted of those conditions. So they came under.°

Now this Mr. *Great-heart*, together with these that came to visit the Pilgrims at Mr. *Mnason's* house, enter'd into a covenant to go and engage° this beast, if perhaps they might deliver the people of this town from the paw and mouths of this so devouring a Serpent.

Then did Mr. *Great-heart*, Mr. *Contrite*, Mr. *Holy-man*, Mr. *Dare-not-lie*, and Mr. *Penitent*, with their weapons, go forth to meet him. Now the *Monster* at first was very rampant, and *How he is* looked upon these enemies with great disdain; but they so be- *engaged.* labour'd him, being sturdy men at arms, that they made him make a retreat: So they came home to Mr. *Mnason's* house again.

The *Monster*, you must know, had his certain Seasons to come out in, and to make his attempts upon the children of

---

a **Monster** The Antichrist; **to suck its whelps** Nurture (suckle) its offspring; a **woman** The Whore of Babylon; **came under** Fell under the sway of Antichrist; **engage** Fight.

the people of the town: Also these seasons did these valiant Worthies watch him in, and did continually assault him; insomuch, that in process of time he became not only wounded, but lame; also he had not made the havock of the townsmen's children, as formerly he has done. And it is verily believed by some, that this beast will certainly die of his wounds.°

This therefore made Mr. *Great-heart* and his fellows of great Fame in this town; so that many of the people that wanted their taste of things,° yet had a reverend esteem and respect for them. Upon this account therefore it was, that these Pilgrims got not much hurt here. True, there were some of the baser sort, that could see no more than a mole, nor understand more than a beast; these had no reverence for these men, nor took they notice of their valour and adventures.

Well, the time grew on that the Pilgrims must go on their Way, wherefore they prepared for their Journey. They sent for their friends, they conferred with them, they had some time set apart therein to commit each other to the Protection of their Prince. There were again, that brought them of such things as they had, that were fit for the weak and the strong, for the women and the men, and so laded them with such things as were necessary.

Acts 28. 10.

Then they set forwards on their Way, and their friends accompanying them so far as was convenient, they again committed each other to the protection of their King, and departed.

They therefore that were of the Pilgrims company, went on, and Mr. *Great-heart* went before them; now the women and children being weakly, they were forced to go as they could bear; by this means Mr. *Ready-to-halt* and Mr. *Feeble-mind* had more to sympathize with their condition.°

---

die of his wounds The final defeat of Antichrist presages the Apocalypse, to which Bunyan looks forward as his text nears its conclusion; **wanted their taste of things** Lacked their interpretation of religion; **sympathize with their condition** It is not specifically feminine weakness, but human weakness in general, that Bunyan depicts here; Ready-to-Halt and Feeble-mind are in the same condition as the rest.

When they were gone from the townsmen, and when their friends had bid them farewel, they quickly came to the place where *Faithful* was put to death: Therefore they made a stand, and thanked him that had enabled him to bear his Cross so well; and the rather, because they now found that they had a benefit by such a manly Suffering as his was.

They went on therefore after this, a good way further, talking of *Christian* and *Faithful*, and how *Hopeful* joined himself to *Christian*, after that *Faithful* was dead.

Now, they were come up with the hill *Lucre*, where the *Silver-Mine* was, which took *Demas* off from his Pilgrimage, and into which, as some think, *By-ends* fell and perished; wherefore they considered that. But when they were come to the old Monument that stood over-against the hill *Lucre*, to wit, to the Pillar of Salt, that stood also within view of *Sodom*, and its stinking lake; they marvelled, as did *Christian* before, that men of that knowledge and ripeness of wit as they were, should be so blinded as to turn aside here. Only they considered again, that nature is not affected with the harms that others have met with, specially if that thing, upon which they look, has an attracting virtue° upon the foolish eye.

Part I. *p.* 123.

I saw now that they went on till they came at the River that was on this side of the Delectable Mountains.

Part I. *page* 127.

To the River where the fine Trees grow on both sides; and whose leaves, if taken inwardly,° are good against surfeits, where the meadows are green all the year long, and where they might lie down safely.

Psalm 23.

By this River side, in the meadow, there were cotes and folds for sheep, a house built for the nourishing and bringing up of those lambs, the babes of those women that go on Pilgrimage. Also there was here One that was entrusted with them, who could have compassion, and that could gather these lambs with his arm, and carry them in his bosom, and that could gently lead those that were with young.[47] Now to the care of *this Man, Christiana* admonished her four Daugh-

Heb. 5. 2.
Isa. 40. 11.

---

virtue Power; **inwardly** Spiritually, metaphorically.

Jer. 23. 4.
Ex. 34. 11, 12,
   13, 14, 15,
   16.

ters to commit their little ones, that by these waters they might be housed, harboured, succoured, and nourished, and that none of them might *be lacking in time to come.* This man, if any of them go astray, or be lost, he will bring them again; he will also bind up that which was broken, and will strengthen them that are sick. Here they will never want meat and drink and cloathing; here they will be kept from thieves and robbers; for this man will die before one of those com-

John 10. 16.

mitted to his Trust shall be lost. Besides, here they shall be sure to have good *nurture* and *admonition,* and shall be taught to walk in right Paths, and that you know is a Favour of no small account. Also here, as you see, are delicate *waters,* pleasant *meadows,* dainty *flowers,* variety of *trees,* and such as bear wholsome *fruit;* fruit not like that that *Matthew* eat of, that fell over the wall, out of *Beelzebub's* garden; but fruit that procureth Health where there is none, and that continueth and increaseth where it is.

So they were content to commit their little ones to him; and that which was also an encouragement to them so to do, was, for that all this was to be at the charge of the King, and so was an Hospital to young children and *orphans.*

*They being
come to* By-
Path *stile,
have a mind
to have a
pluck with
Giant*
Despair. Part
I. *p.* 127–137.

Now they went on; and when they were come to *By-Path* meadow, to the stile over which *Christian* went with his fellow *Hopeful,* when they were taken by Giant *Despair,* and put into *Doubting Castle;* they sat down, and consulted what was best to be done; to wit, now they were so strong, and had got such a man as Mr. *Great-heart* for their conductor, whether they had not best to make an attempt upon the Giant, demolish his Castle,[48] and if there were any Pilgrims in it, to set them at liberty, before they went any further. So one said one thing, and another said the contrary. One questioned, if it was lawful to go upon *unconsecrated* ground; another said they might, provided their end was good; but Mr. *Great-heart* said, though that assertion offered last, cannot be universally true, yet I have a commandment to resist Sin, to overcome Evil, to fight the good fight of Faith: And I pray, with whom should I fight this good fight, if not with Giant *Despair?* I will therefore attempt the taking away of his life, and the demol-

ishing of *Doubting Castle*. Then, said he, who will go with me?
Then said old *Honest*, I will; and so will we too, said *Christian's* four sons, *Matthew, Samuel, James*, and *Joseph*, for they   1 John 2. 13,
were young men and strong.   14.

So they left the women in the Road, and with them Mr.
Feeble-mind and Mr. *Ready-to-halt*, with his crutches, to be
their guard, until they came back; for in that place the Giant
Despair dwelt so near, they keeping in the Road, *a little child*   Isa. 11. 6.
might lead them.

So Mr. *Great-heart*, old *Honest*, and the four young men,
went to go up to *Doubting-Castle*, to look for Giant *Despair*.
When they came at the Castle-Gate, they knocked for entrance with an unusual noise. At that the old Giant comes to
the gate, and *Diffidence* his wife follows: Then said he, Who
and what is he, that is so hardy, as after this manner to molest
the Giant *Despair*? Mr. *Great-heart* replyed, It is I, *Great-
heart*, one of the King of the Cœlestial Country's conductors
of Pilgrims to their place: And I demand of thee, that thou
open thy gates for my entrance; prepare thyself also to fight, for
I am come to take away thy head, and to demolish *Doubting-
Castle*.

Now Giant *Despair*, because he was a Giant, thought no   Despair *has*
man could overcome him; and again, thought he, since   *overcome*
heretofore I have made a conquest of Angels,° shall *Great-*   *Angels.*
heart make me afraid? So he harnessed° himself, and went
out: He had a cap of steel upon his head, a breast-plate of fire
girded to him, and he came out in iron shoes, with a great
club in his hand. Then these six men made up to him, and
beset him behind and before: Also when *Diffidence* the Gi-
antess came up to help him, old Mr. *Honest* cut her down at
one blow. Then they fought for their lives, and Giant *Despair*
was brought down to the ground, *but was very loth to die:* He   Despair *is*
struggled hard, and had, as they say, as many lives as a cat; but   *loth to die.*
Great-heart was his death, for he left him not till he had sev-
ered his head from his shoulders.

I have made . . . Angels Satan and his followers, the fallen angels, are in despair; **harnessed** Equipped.

Then they fell to demolishing *Doubting-Castle*, and that you know might with ease be done, since Giant *Despair* was dead. They were seven days in destroying of that, and in it of Pilgrims they found one Mr. *Despondency*, almost starved to death, and one *Much-afraid* his daughter; these two they saved alive. But it would ha' made you ha' wondered, to have seen the dead bodies that lay here and there in the castle-yard, and how full of dead men's bones the dungeon was.

When Mr. *Great-heart* and his companions had performed this exploit, they took Mr. *Despondency*, and his daughter *Much-afraid* into their protection, for they were honest people, though they were prisoners in *Doubting-Castle* to that tyrant Giant *Despair*. They therefore, I say, took with them the head of the Giant, (for his body they had buried under a heap of stones) and down to the road, and to their companions they came, and shewed them what they had done. Now when *Feeble-mind* and *Ready-to-halt* saw that it was the head of Giant *Despair* indeed, they were very jocund° and merry. Now *Christiana*, if need was, could play upon the *viol*,° and her daughter *Mercy* upon the *lute:*° So since they were so merry disposed, she played them a lesson,° and *Ready-to-halt*

would dance. So he took *Despondency's* daughter *Much-afraid* by the hand, and to dancing they went in the road. True, he could not dance without one crutch in his hand; but I promise you, he footed it well; also the girl was to be commended, for she answered the musick handsomely.

As for Mr. *Despondency*, the musick was not much to him, he was for feeding rather than dancing, for that he was almost starved. So *Christiana* gave him some of her bottle of Spirits, for present relief, and then prepared him something to eat, and in little time the old gentleman came to himself, and began to be finely revived.

Now I saw in my dream, when all these things were finished, Mr. *Great-heart* took the head of Giant *Despair*, and set

---

jocund Jolly; **viol** Viola; **lute** Stringed instrument, emblematic of poetry; **lesson** Piece.

it upon a pole by the High-way-side, right over against the Pillar that *Christian* erected for a *caution* to Pilgrims that came after, to take heed of entring into his grounds.

Then he writ under it upon a marble-stone, these verses following:

A Monument of Deliverance.

> *This is the* Head *of him, whose* Name *only*
> *In former times did Pilgrims terrify.*
> *His Castle's down, and* Diffidence *his wife*
> *Brave Master* Great-heart *has bereft of life.*
> Despondency, *his daughter* Much-afraid,
> Great-heart, *for them also the Man has play'd.*
> *Who hereof doubts, if he'll but cast his eye,*
> *Up hither, may his scruples satisfy.*
> *This head also, when doubting cripples dance,*
> *Doth shew from Fears they have Deliverance.*

When these men had thus bravely shewed themselves against *Doubting Castle*, and had slain Giant *Despair*, they went forward, and went on till they came to the *Delectable* mountains, where *Christian* and *Hopeful* refreshed themselves with the varieties of the place. They also acquainted themselves with the Shepherds there, who welcomed them, as they had done *Christian* before, unto the *Delectable* mountains.

Now the Shepherds seeing so great a train follow Mr. *Great-heart*, (for with him they were well acquainted;) they said unto him, Good sir, you have got a goodly company here; pray where did you find all these? Then Mr. *Great-heart* replyed,

> *First, here's* Christiana *and her train,*
> *Her Sons, and her Sons wives, who, like the wain,*°
> *Keep by the Pole, and do by Compass steer,*
> *From Sin to Grace, else they had not been here:*

The Guide's Speech to the Shepherds.

---

wain The group of stars also known as "the big dipper"; it was also sometimes called "King Charles's Wain." A wain was a heavy wagon used on farms.

Though *Doubting-Castle* be demolished,
And the Giant *Despair* hath lost his head,
Sin can rebuild the Castle, make't remain,
And make *Despair* the Giant live again.

Next here's old Honest *come on Pilgrimage,*
Ready-to-halt *too, who I dare engage,°*
True hearted is, and so is Feeble-mind,
Who willing was, not to be left behind.
Despondency, *good man, is coming after,*
And so also is Much-afraid *his daughter,*
May we have entertainment here, or must
We further go? Let's know whereon to trust?

Then said the Shepherds; This is a comfortable Company; you are welcome to us, for we have for the *feeble,* as for the *strong;* our Prince has an eye to what is done to the least of these. Therefore Infirmity must not be a block to our entertainment. So they had them to the Palace door, and then said unto them, Come in Mr. *Feeble-mind,* come in Mr. *Ready-to-halt,* come in Mr. *Despondency,* and Mrs. *Much-afraid,* his daughter. These, Mr. *Great-heart,* said the Shepherds to the Guide, we call in by name, for that they are most subject to draw back;° but as for you, and the rest that are *strong,* we leave you to your wonted liberty.[49] Then said Mr. *Great-heart,* This day I see that Grace doth shine in your faces, and that you are my Lord's Shepherds indeed; for that you have not *pushed* these diseased neither with side nor shoulder, but have rather strewed their way into the Palace with flowers, as you should.

So the feeble and weak went in, and Mr. *Great-heart* and the rest did follow. When they were also set down, the Shepherds said to those of the weakest sort, What is it that you would have? For, said they, all things must be managed here to the supporting of the weak, as well as the warning of the unruly.

So they made them a feast of things easy of digestion, and that were pleasant to the palate, and nourishing: The which when they had received, they went to their rest, each one respectively unto his proper place. When morning was come,

Their entertainment.

Mat. 25. 40.

A description of false Shepherds. Ezek. 34. 21.

---

engage Affirm; **subject to draw back** Both "prone to draw back" and "subjected to drawbacks"; the pilgrims are both subjects and objects.

because the mountains were high, and the day clear; and because it was the custom of the Shepherds to shew to the Pilgrims, before their departure, some rarities; therefore, after they were ready, and had refreshed themselves, the Shepherds took them out into the fields, and shewed them first what they had shewed to *Christian* before.

Then they had them to some new places. The first was *Mount-Marvel*, where they looked, and behold a man at a distance, *that tumbled the hills about with words.*[50] Then they asked the Shepherds what that should mean? So they told them, that that man was the son of one Mr. *Great-grace,*° of whom you read in the First Part of the records of the *Pilgrim's Progress.* And he is set there to teach Pilgrims how to believe down, or to tumble out of their ways, what difficulties they should meet with; by Faith. Then said Mr. *Great-heart,* I know him, he is a man above many.

Then they had them to another place, called *Mount Innocent;* and there they saw a man cloathed all in white; and two men, *Prejudice* and *Ill-will,* continually casting dirt upon him. Now behold the dirt, whatsoever they cast at him, would in little time fall off again, and his garment would look as clear as if no dirt had been cast thereat.

Then said the Pilgrims, What means this? The Shepherds answered; this man is named *Godly-man,* and the garment is to shew the innocency of his life. Now those that throw dirt at him, are such as hate his *well-doing;* but, as you see, the dirt will not stick upon his cloaths, so it shall be with him that liveth truly innocently in the world. Whoever they be that would make such men dirty, they labour all in vain; for God, by that a little time is spent, will cause that their *Innocence* shall break forth as the light, and their *righteousness* as the noon-day.

Then they took them, and had them to *Mount Charity,* where they shewed them a man that had a bundle of cloth lying before him, out of which he cut coats and garments for

Mount-Marvel.

Part I. p. 135.

Mark 11. 23, 24.

Mount Innocent.

Mount Charity.

Mr. **Great-grace** Faith is produced by grace.

the poor that stood about him; yet his bundle, or roll of cloth, was never the less.

Then said they, What should this be? This is, said the Shepherds, to shew you, that he that has a heart to give of his labour to the poor, shall never want where-withal. He that watereth, shall be watered himself. And the cake that the widow gave to the prophet, did not cause that she had ever the less in her barrel.°

They had them also to a place, where they saw one *Fool*, and one *Want-wit*, washing of an *Ethiopian*,[51] with intention to make him white; but the more they washed him, the blacker he was. They then asked the Shepherds, what that should mean? So they told them, saying, thus shall it be with the vile person; all means used to get such an one a good name, shall in conclusion tend but to make him more abominable. Thus it was with the *Pharisees*,[52] and so shall it be with all *Hypocrites*. *The Work of one* Fool, *and one* Want-wit.

Then said *Mercy*, the wife of *Matthew*, to *Christiana* her mother, I would, if it might be, see the hole in the Hill; or that commonly called the *By-way* to Hell. So her mother brake her mind to the Shepherds. Then they went to the door; it was in the side of an hill, and they opened it, and bid *Mercy* hearken awhile. So she hearkened, and heard one saying, *Cursed be my father for holding of my feet back from the way of Peace and Life;* and another said, *O that I had been torn in pieces, before I had, to save my life, lost my soul;* and another said, *If I were to live again, how would I deny myself rather than come to this place.* Then there was, as if the very Earth had groaned and quaked under the feet of this young woman for fear; so she looked white, and came trembling away, saying, Blessed be he and she, that is delivered from this place. *Part* I. *p.* 139. *Mercy has a mind to see the hole in the Hill.*

Now when the Shepherds had shewed them all these things, then they had them back to the palace, and entertained them with what the house would afford: But *Mercy* being a young and breeding° woman, longed for something *Mercy longeth, and for what.*

---

her barrel In 1 Kings 17 a widow gives cake to the prophet Elijah, and her barrel is miraculously replenished; **breeding** Pregnant.

that she saw there, but was ashamed to ask. Her mother-in-law then asked her what she ailed, for she looked as one not well. Then said *Mercy, There is a Looking-Glass*[53] *hangs up in the dining-room*, off of which I cannot take my mind; if therefore I have it not, I think I shall miscarry. Then said her mother, I will mention thy wants to the Shepherds, and they will not deny it thee. But she said, I am ashamed that these men should know that I longed. Nay, my daughter, said she, it is no shame, but a vertue, to long for such a thing as that; so *Mercy* said, Then mother, if you please, ask the Shepherds, if they are willing to sell it.

It was the Word of God. James 1. 23.

Now the Glass was one of a thousand. It would present a man, one way with his own feature exactly; and turn it but another way, and it would shew one the very face and similitude° of the Prince of Pilgrims himself. Yea, I have talked with them that can tell, and they have said, that they have seen the very Crown of Thorns upon his head, by looking in that Glass; they have therein also seen the holes in his hands, in his

1 Cor. 13. 12.
2 Cor. 3. 18.

feet, and his side. Yea, such an excellency is there in that Glass, that it will shew him to one, where they have a mind to see him; whether living or dead, whether in Earth or Heaven; whether in a state of Humiliation, or in his Exaltation; whether coming to Suffer, or coming to Reign.

Christiana therefore went to the Shepherds apart, (Now the names of the Shepherds are *Knowledge, Experience, Watchful*, and *Sincere*) and said unto them, there is one of my daughters a breeding woman; that, I think doth long for something that she hath seen in this house, and she thinks she shall miscarry, if she should by you be denied.

Part I. *p.* 138.

She doth not lose her longing.

Experience. Call her, call her, she shall assuredly have what we can help her to. So they called her, and said to her, *Mercy*, what is that thing thou wouldst have? Then she blushed and said, The great Glass that hangs up in the dining-room: So *Sincere* ran and fetched it, and with a joyful consent it was given her. Then she bowed her head, and gave

---

the very face and similitude Both the actual face and signs of the face.

thanks, and said, By this, I know that I have obtained favour in your eyes.

They also gave to the other young women such things as they desired, and to their husbands great commendations, for that they joined with Mr. *Great-heart*, to the slaying of Giant *Despair*, and the demolishing of *Doubting-Castle*.

About *Christiana's* neck the Shepherds put a bracelet, and so they did about the necks of her four daughters; also they put ear-rings in their ears, and jewels on their foreheads. *How the Shepherds adorn the Pilgrims.*

When they were minded to go hence, they let them go in peace, but gave not to them those certain Cautions which before were given to *Christian* and his companion. The reason was, for that these had *Great-heart* to be their Guide, who was one that was well acquainted with things, and so could give them their cautions more seasonably;° to wit, even then when the danger was nigh the approaching.° *Part I. p. 141.*

What cautions *Christian* and his companion had received of the Shepherds, they had also lost by that the time was come that they had need to put them in practice. Wherefore, here was the advantage that this company had over the other. *Part I. p. 151.*

From hence they went on singing, and they said,

> Behold, how fitly *are the Stages set!*
> For their *Relief that Pilgrims are become,*
> And how they us *receive without* one *let,*
> That make the other *Life the* mark *and Home.*
> What Novelties they have, to us they give,
> That we, tho' Pilgrims, joyful lives may live.°
> They do upon us too, such Things bestow,
> That skew we Pilgrims are, where-e'er we go.

When they were gone from the Shepherds, they quickly came to the place where *Christian* met with one *Turn-away*, that dwelt in the town of *Apostacy*. Wherefore of him Mr. *Part I. p. 143.*

---

seasonably At the right time; **nigh the approaching** About to approach; **that we . . . may live** In marked contrast to the life of struggle endured by the pilgrim in part one.

Great-heart, their Guide, did now put them in mind, saying, This is the place where *Christian* met with one *Turn-away*, who carried with him the character of his rebellion at his back.° And this I have to say concerning this man, he would hearken to no counsel, but once afalling, persuasion could not stop him.

How one Turn-away managed his apostacy. Heb. 10. 26, 27, 28, 29.

When he came to the place where the Cross and Sepulchre was, he did meet with one that did bid him *look there*, but he gnashed with his teeth, and stamped, and said, he was resolved to go back to his own town. Before he came to the Gate, he met with *Evangelist*, who offered to lay hands on him, to turn him into the way again. But this *Turn-away resisted him*, and having done much *despite* unto him, he got away over the Wall, and so escaped his hand.

Then they went on, and just at the place where *Little-faith* formerly was robbed, there stood a man with his sword drawn, and his face all bloody. Then said Mr. *Great-heart*, What art thou? The man made answer, saying, I am one whose name is *Valiant-for-truth*.[54] I am a Pilgrim, and am going to the Cœlestial City. Now, as I was in my Way, there were three men did beset me, and propounded unto me these three things: 1. Whether I would become one of them? 2. Or go back from whence I came? 3. Or die upon the Place? To the first I answered, I had been a true° man a long season, and therefore it could not be expected that I now should cast in my lot with thieves. Then they demanded what I would say to the second. So I told them that the place from whence I came, had I not found incommodity° there, I had not forsaken it at all; but finding it altogether unsuitable to me, and very unprofitable for me, I forsook it for this Way. Then they asked me what I said to the third. And I told them, my Life cost more dear far than that I should lightly give it away. Besides, you have nothing to do thus to put° things to my choice; wherefore at your peril be it, if you meddle. Then these three,

One Valiant-for-truth *beset with Thieves.*

Prov. 1. 10, 11, 13, 14.

---

who carried . . . at his back See page 143. Turn-away is a rare pilgrim who carries a sign announcing his allegorical meaning, as in a book of emblems; **true** Both "honest" and "real"; **incommodity** Inconvenience, unpleasantness; **you have nothing to do thus to put** You have no business putting.

to wit, *Wild-head, Inconsiderate*, and *Pragmatick*,° drew upon me, and I also drew° upon them.

So we fell to it, one against three, for the space of above three hours. They have left upon me, as you see, some of the marks of their valour, and have also carried away with them some of mine. They are but just now gone: I suppose they might, as the saying is, hear your horse dash,° and so they betook them to flight.

How he behaved himself, and put them to flight.

Great-heart. But here was great odds, three against one.

Valiant. 'Tis true; but *little* and *more* are nothing to him that has the Truth on his side: *Though an Host should encamp against me*, said one,° *my heart shall not fear: Though War should rise against me, in this will I be confident*, &c. Besides, said he, I have read in some records, that one man has fought an army: And how many did *Sampson* slay with the jaw-bone of an ass?°

Great-heart wonders at his valour.

Ps. 27. 3.

Great-heart. Then said the Guide, Why did you not cry out, that some might ha' came in for your succour?°

Valiant. So I did to my King, who I knew could hear, and afford invisible Help, and that was sufficient for me.°

Great-heart. Then said *Great-heart* to Mr. *Valiant-for-truth*, Thou hast worthily behaved thyself; let me see thy Sword; so he shewed it him.

When he had taken it in his hand, and looked thereon a while, he said, Ha! It is a right *Jerusalem* blade.°

Is. 2. 3.

Valiant. It is so. Let a man have one of *these blades*, with a hand to wield it, and skill to use it, and he may venture upon an Angel with it. He need not fear its holding, if he can but tell how to lay on. Its edges will never blunt. It will cut *flesh*, and *bones*, and *soul*, and *spirit* and all.

Ephes. 6. 12,
13, 14, 15,
16, 17.
Heb. 4. 12.

Pragmatick Dictatorial busybody; **drew** That is, drew their swords; **hear your horse dash** Hear you approach; **one** David, reputed author of the Psalms, invoked here for his defiance of physical odds in slaying Goliath; **And how many . . . an ass** One thousand (Judges 15:15–16); **succour** Aid; **invisible Help . . . sufficient for me** A material character named "Help" is no longer necessary; **Jerusalem blade** Ephesians 6:17: "The sword of the Spirit, which is the word of God."

Great-heart. But you fought a great while, I wonder you was not weary.

2 Sam. 23. 10.
The Word.

The Faith.
Blood.

Valiant. I fought till my Sword did cleave to my hand,° when they were joined together, as if a sword grew out of my arm; and when the blood ran through my fingers, then I fought with most courage.

Great-heart. Thou hast done well, thou hast resisted unto blood, striving against Sin; thou shalt abide by us, come in, and go out with us, for we are thy companions.

Then they took him and washed his wounds, and gave him of what they had to refresh him; and so they went together. Now as they went on, because Mr. *Great-heart* was delighted in him (for he loved one greatly, that he found to be a man of his hands)° and because there was with his company them that were feeble and weak: Therefore he questioned with him about many things; as first, what Country-man he was?

Valiant. I am of *Dark-Land* for there I was born, and there my father and mother are still.

Great-heart. Dark-Land, said the Guide, doth not that lie upon the same coast with the City of *Destruction?*

How Mr.
Valiant came
to go on
Pilgrimage.

Valiant. Yes, it doth. Now that which caused me to come on Pilgrimage, was this; we had one Mr. *Tell-true*° came into our parts, and he told it about what *Christian* had done, that went from the City of *Destruction:* Namely, how he had forsaken his wife and children, and had betaken himself to a Pilgrim's life. It was also confidently reported, how he had killed a *Serpent*,° that did come out to resist him in his Journey; and how he got through to whither he intended.° It was also told, what welcome he had at all his Lord's lodgings, specially when he came to the Gates of the Cœlestial City: For there, said the man, he was received with sound of Trumpet, by a

---

till my Sword did cleave to my hand Till the Word of God entered into my mind; **a man of his hands** A fighting man; **Mr. Tell-true** Note how this preacher lacks any ecclesiastical title; **a Serpent** Possibly Apollyon but, since Christian does not in fact kill him, probably an emblem of evil in general; **he got through to whither he intended** Both "he reached his intended destination" and "he conveyed his intended meaning."

company of shining ones. He told it also, how all the bells in the city did ring for joy at his reception, and what golden garments he was cloathed with; with many other things that now I shall forbear to relate. In a word, that man° so told the story of *Christian* and his Travels, that my heart fell into a burning haste, to be gone after him; nor could father or mother stay° me; so I got from them, and am come thus far on my Way.

Great-heart. You came in at the Gate, did you not?

Valiant. Yes, yes; for the same man° also told us, that all would be nothing, if we did not begin to enter this Way at the Gate.

He begins right.

Great-heart. Look you, said the Guide to *Christiana*, the Pilgrimage of your husband, and what he has gotten thereby, is spread abroad far and near.

Christian's name famous.

Valiant. Why, is this *Christian's* wife?

Great-heart. Yes, that it is; and these are also her four sons.

Valiant. What! and going on Pilgrimage too?

Great-heart. Yes verily, they are following after.

Valiant. It glads° me at heart! good man! How joyful will he be, when he shall see them that would not go with him, yet to enter after him, in at the Gates into the City?

He is much rejoiced to see Christian's wife.

Great-heart. Without doubt it will be a comfort to him; for next to the joy of seeing himself there, it will be a joy to meet there his wife and his children.

Valiant. But now you are upon that, pray let me hear your opinion about it. Some make a Question, whether we shall know one another when we are there?°

Great-heart. Do they think they shall know themselves then? or that they shall rejoice to see themselves in that Bliss, and if they think they shall know and do these, why not know others, and rejoice in their welfare also?

Again, since relations are our second self, though that state°

---

that man Mr. Tell-true seems to represent the author of *The Pilgrim's Progress*; stay Delay; the same man Now Tell-true blends into Evangelist, as well as Bunyan; glads Gladdens; Some make . . . we are there? The question of whether the saved would recognize each other in heaven was a favorite topic of controversy; that state The condition of fleshly, "blood relations."

will be dissolved there, yet why may it not be rationally concluded, that we shall be more glad to see them there, than to see they are wanting?

Valiant. Well, I perceive whereabouts you are as to this. Have you any more things to ask me about my beginning to come on Pilgrimage?

Great-heart. Yes; Was your father and mother willing that you should become a Pilgrim?

Valiant. Oh no. They used all means imaginable to persuade me to stay at home.

Great-heart. Why what could they say against it?

The great stumbling-blocks that by his friends were laid in his way.

Valiant. They said, it was an idle life;[55] and if I myself were not inclined to sloth and laziness, I would never countenance a Pilgrim's condition.

Great-heart. And what did they say else?

Valiant. Why, they told me that it was a dangerous Way, yea, the most dangerous Way in the world, said they, is that which the Pilgrims go.

Great-heart. Did they shew wherein this Way is so dangerous?

Valiant. Yes; and that in many particulars.

Great-heart. Name some of them.

The first stumbling block.

Valiant. They told me of the *Slough of Despond,* where *Christian* was well-nigh smothered. They told me, that there were archers standing ready in *Beelzebub-Castle,* to shoot them that should knock at the *Wicket* gate for entrance. They told me also of the Wood, and dark Mountains, of the Hill *Difficulty;* of the Lions, and also of the three Giants, *Bloody-man, Maul,* and *Slay-good:* They said moreover, that there was a foul *Fiend* haunted the Valley of *Humiliation;* and that *Christian* was by them almost bereft of life. Besides, said they, you must go over the *Valley of the Shadow of Death,* where the *Hobgoblins* are, where the Light is Darkness, where the Way is full of snares, pits, traps, and gins. They told me also of Giant *Despair,* of *Doubting-Castle,* and of the *ruin* that the Pilgrims met with there. Further, they said, I must go over the Enchanted ground, which was dangerous: And that, after all this, I should find a River, over which I should find no bridge;

and that that River did lie betwixt me and the Cœlestial Country.

Great-heart. And was this all?

Valiant. No; they also told me, that this Way was full of *deceivers*, and of persons that laid await there to turn good men out of the path.   *The second.*

Great-heart. But how did they make that out?

Valiant. They told me, that Mr. *Worldly-wise-man* did lie there in wait to deceive.   *The third.*

They also said, that there was *Formality* and *Hypocrisy* continually on the road. They said also, that *By-ends*, *Talkative*, or *Demas*, would go near to gather me up: that the *Flatterer* would catch me in his net; or that, with green-headed° *Ignorance*, I would presume to go on to the Gate, from whence he always was sent back to the hole that was in the side of the Hill, and made to go the by-way to Hell.

Great-heart. I promise you, this was enough to discourage; but did they make an end here?

Valiant. No, stay.° They told me also of many that had tried that Way of old, and that had gone a great way therein, to see if they could find something of the Glory there, that so many had so much talked of from time to time; and how they came back again, and befooled themselves for setting a foot out of doors in that path, to the satisfaction of all the Country. And they named several that did so, as *Obstinate* and *Pliable*, *Mistrust* and *Timorous*, *Turn-away* and old *Atheist*,° with several more; who, they said, had some of them gone far to see if they could find, but not one of them found so much advantage by going, as amounted *to the weight of a feather.*°   *The fourth.*

Great-heart. Said they any thing more to discourage you?

Valiant. Yes, they told me of one Mr. *Fearing*, who was a Pilgrim; and how he found this Way so *solitary*, that he never had a comfortable hour therein: Also that Mr. *Despondency* had like to° have been starved therein: Yea, and also which I

---

green-headed Naive; **stay** Wait; **old Atheist** Atheism long predates Christianity; **the weight of a feather** Note the quantitative terms of evaluation; **had like to** Was likely to.

had almost forgot *Christian* himself, about whom there has been such a noise, after all his ventures for a Cœlestial Crown, was certainly drowned in the black *River*, and never went a foot further; however, it was smothered up.°

Great-heart. And did none of these things discourage you?

Valiant. No, they seemed but as so many Nothings to me.

Great-heart. How came that about?

How he got over these stumbling-blocks.
Valiant. Why, I still believed what Mr. *Tell-true* had said, and that carried me beyond them all.

Great-heart. Then this was your Victory, even your Faith.

Valiant. It was so, I believed, and therefore came out, got into the Way, fought all that set themselves against me, and by believing, am come to this place:

> *Who would true Valour see,*
> *Let him come hither;*
> *One here will constant be,*
> *Come wind, come weather:*
>
> *There's no Discouragement*
> *Shall make him once relent,*
> *His first avow'd intent*
> To be a Pilgrim.
>
> *Whoso beset him round*
> *With dismal stories,*
> *Do but themselves confound,*
> *His Strength the more is.*
>
> *No Lion can him fright;*
> *He'll with a Giant fight,*
> *But he will have a right*
> To be a Pilgrim.

---

smothered up That is, the townsfolk believe that the news of Christian's demise was covered up.

> *Hobgoblin, nor foul Fiend*
> *Can daunt his spirit;*
> *He knows,* he at the End
> Shall Life inherit.

> *Then Fancies fly away,*
> *He'll fear not what men say,*
> *He'll labour Night and Day*
> To be a Pilgrim.

By this time they were got to the *enchanted Ground*, where the air naturally tended to make one *drowsy*: And that place was all grown over with briars and thorns, excepting here and there, where was an *enchanted Arbour*, upon which if a man sits, or in which if a man sleeps, 'tis a question, say some, whether ever they shall rise or wake again in this world. Over this Forest therefore they went, both one and another, and Mr. *Great-heart* went before, for that he was the Guide, and Mr. *Valiant-for-truth*, he came behind, being there a Guard, for fear, lest peradventure° some *Fiend*, or *Dragon*, or *Giant*, or *Thief*, should fall upon their rear, and so do mischief. They went on here, each man with his Sword drawn in his hand, for they knew it was a dangerous place. Also they cheered up one another, as well as they could; *Feeble-mind,* Mr. *Great-heart* commanded should come up after him, and Mr. *Despondency* was under the eye of Mr. *Valiant*.

Part I. *p.* 154.

Now they had not gone far, but a great Mist and Darkness fell upon them all; so that they could scarce, for a great while, see the one the other: Wherefore they were forced, for some time, to feel for one another, by words;° for they walked not by Sight.

But any one must think, that here was but sorry going for the best of them all; but how much worse for the women and children, who both of *feet* and *heart* were but tender. Yet so it

---

peradventure By chance; **feel . . . by words** Once again, words become phys-ical forces.

was, that through the encouraging words of he that led in the front, and of him that brought them up behind, they made a pretty good shift to wag° along.

The Way also was here very wearisome, through dirt and slabbiness.° Nor was there on all this Ground, so much as one *Inn*, or *Victualling-house*,° therein to refresh the feebler sort. Here therefore was *grunting*, and *puffing*, and *sighing:* While one tumbleth over a bush, another sticks fast in the dirt; and the children, some of them, lost their shoes in the mire: While one cries out, I am down; and another, Ho, where are you? And a third, The bushes have got such fast hold on me, I think I cannot get away from them.

An Arbour on the Enchanted Ground.

Then they came at an *Arbour*, warm, and promising much refreshing to the Pilgrims: For it was finely wrought above-head, beautified with *greens*,° furnished with *benches* and *settles*.° It also had in it a soft couch, whereon the weary might lean. This, you must think, all things considered, was tempting; for the Pilgrims already began to be foiled with the badness of the Way; but there was not one of them that made so much as a motion to stop there. Yea, for ought I could perceive, they continually gave so good heed to the advice of their Guide, and he did so faithfully tell them of *dangers*, and of the *nature* of dangers when they were at them, that usually when they were nearest to them, they did most pluck up their Spirits, and hearten one another to deny the Flesh. This *Ar-bour* was call'd, *The Slothful's friend*, on purpose to allure, if it might be, some of the Pilgrims there, to take up their Rest, when weary.

The name of the Arbour.

I saw then in my dream, that they went on in this their *solitary* ground, till they came to a place at which a man is apt to lose his Way. Now, though when it was light, their Guide could well enough tell how to miss those ways that led wrong, yet in the dark he was put to a stand:° But he had in his pocket a *map*° of all ways leading to or from the Cœlestial City;

The Way is difficult to find.

---

shift to wag Effort to trot; slabbiness Muddiness; Victualling-house Pub selling food; greens Greenery; settles Seats; put to a stand Forced to pause; a map The Bible.

wherefore he struck a light, (for he never goes also without his tinder-box) and takes a view of his Book or map, which bids him be careful in that place, to turn to the Right-hand-way. And had he not here been careful to look in his map, they had all in probability been smothered in the mud; for just a little before them, and that at the end of the cleanest Way too, was a Pit, none knows how deep, full of nothing but mud; there made on purpose to destroy the Pilgrims in. *The Guide has a Map of all ways leading to or from the City.*

Then thought I with myself,° who, that goeth on *Pilgrimage*, but would have one of these maps about him, that he may look when he is at a *stand*, which is the Way he must take. *God's Book.*

They went on then in this *enchanted Ground*, till they came to where there was another *Arbour*, and it was built by the High-way-side. And in that *Arbour* there lay two men, whose names were *Heedless* and *Too-bold*. These two went thus far on Pilgrimage; but here, being wearied with their Journey, they sat down to rest themselves, and so fell fast asleep. When the Pilgrims saw them, they stood still, and shook their heads; for they knew that the Sleepers° were in a pitiful case.° Then they consulted what to do, whether to go on, and leave them in their sleep, or step to them, and try to awake them. So they concluded to go to them, and wake them; that is, if they could; but with this caution, namely to take heed that themselves did not sit down nor embrace the offered benefit of that *Arbour*. *An arbour, and two asleep therein.*

So they went in, and spake to the men, and called each by his name, (for the Guide it seems did know them) but there was no voice, nor answer. Then the Guide did shake them, and do what he could to disturb them. Then said one of them, *I will pay you when I take my Money.* At which the Guide shook his head. *I will fight so long as I can hold my Sword in my hand,*° said the other. At that, one of the children laughed. *The Pilgrims try to wake them.*

---

thought I with myself The narrator's thoughts are distinguished from his self; **Sleepers** Note that according to the dream motif, the narrator is himself recounting experiences he had while asleep; **case** Condition; **I will fight . . . my Sword in my hand** The sleepers are dreaming of money and violence, as opposed to the edifying dream enjoyed by the narrator.

Then said *Christiana*, What is the meaning of this? The Guide said, *They talk in their sleep;* if you strike them, beat them, or whatever else you do to them, they will answer you after this fashion; or as one of them said in old time, when the waves of the Sea did beat upon him, and he slept as one upon

the mast of a ship; *When I awake, I will seek it again.* You know, when men talk in their sleep, they say any thing, but their words are not governed either by Faith or Reason. There is an incoherency in their words now, as there was before betwixt their going on Pilgrimage, and sitting down here. This then is the mischief on't, when *heedless* ones go on Pilgrimage, 'tis twenty to one but they are served thus. For this *Enchanted Ground* is one of the last refuges that the Enemy to Pilgrims has; wherefore it is, as you see, placed almost at the end of the Way,° and so it standeth against us with the more advantage. For when, thinks the Enemy, will these Fools be so desirous to sit down, as when they are weary? and when so like to be weary, as when almost at their Journey's end? Therefore it is, I say, that the *Enchanted Ground* is placed so nigh to the Land *Beulah*, and so near the end of their race. Wherefore, let Pilgrims look to themselves, lest it happen to them, as it has done to these, that, as you see, are fallen asleep, and none can wake them.

Then the Pilgrims desired with trembling to go forward, only they prayed their Guide to strike a light, that they might go the rest of their Way by the help of the light of a Lantern. So he strook a light, and they went by the help of that through the rest of this Way, though the darkness was very great.

But the children began to be sorely weary, and they cried out unto him that loveth Pilgrims, to make their Way more comfortable. So by that they had gone a little further, a wind arose, that drove away the fog, so the air became more clear.

Yet they were not off (by much) of the *Enchanted Ground*, only now they could see one another better, and the Way wherein they should walk.

---

almost at the end of the Way The temptation to sleep is greatest near the end of life; the sleepers may be suffering from senile dementia.

Now, when they were almost at the end of this ground, they perceived that a little before them was a *solemn* noise, of one that was much concerned. So they went on, and looked before them, and behold they saw, as they thought, a man upon his knees, with hands and eyes lift up, and speaking, as they thought, earnestly to one that was above; they drew nigh, but could not tell what he said; so they went softly till he had done. When he had done, he got up, and began to run towards the Cœlestial City. Then Mr. *Great-heart* called after him, saying, soho,° friend, let us have your company, if you go, as I suppose you do, to the Cœlestial City. So the man stopped, and they came up to him. But so soon as Mr. *Honest* saw him, he said I know this man. Then said Mr. *Valiant-for-Truth*, Prithee,° who is it? 'Tis one, said he, that comes from whereabouts I dwelt, his name is *Standfast;* he is certainly a right good Pilgrim.

Standfast upon his knees in the Enchanted Ground.

The story of Standfast.

So they came up one to another, and presently *Standfast* said to old *Honest*, Ho, Father *Honest*, are you there? Ay, said he, that I am, as sure as you are there. Right glad I am, said Mr. *Standfast*, that I have found you on this Road. And as glad am I, said the other, that I espied you upon your knees. Then Mr. *Standfast* blushed, and said; But why, did you see me? Yes, that I did, quoth the other, and with my heart was glad at the sight. Why, what did you think, said *Standfast?* Think, said old *Honest*, what should I think? I thought we had an honest man upon the road, and therefore should have his company by and by. If you thought not amiss, how happy am I? But if I be not as I should, I alone must bear it. That is true, said the other; but your fear doth further confirm me, that things are right betwixt the Prince of Pilgrims and your soul: For he saith, *Blessed is the man that feareth always.*

Talk betwixt him and Mr. Honest.

Valiant. Well, but brother, I pray thee tell us what was it that was the cause of thy being upon thy knees even now? Was it for that some special Mercy laid obligations upon thee, or how?

They found him at Prayer.

---

soho Originally a hunting cry, here a greeting; **Prithee** Please.

What it was
that fetch'd
him upon his
knees.

Standfast. Why, we are, as you see, upon the *Enchanted Ground;* and as I was coming along, I was musing with myself of what a dangerous Road the Road in this place was, and how many that had come even thus far on Pilgrimage, had here been stopt, and been destroyed. I thought also of the manner of the death, with which this place destroyeth men. Those that die here, die of no violent distemper;° the death which such die, is not grievous to them. For he that goeth away in a *Sleep* begins that Journey with desire and pleasure. Yea, such acquiesce in the Will of that disease.

Hon. Then Mr. *Honest* interrupting of him, said, Did you see the two men asleep in the arbour?

Standfast. Ay, ay, I saw *Heedless* and *Too-bold* there; and for

Prov. 10. 7.

ought I know, there they will lie till they rot. But let me go on with my tale: As I was thus musing, as I said, there was one in very pleasant attire, but old, that presented herself unto me, and offered me three things, to wit, her body, her purse, and her bed. Now the truth is, I was both weary and sleepy: I am also as poor as a howlet,° and that perhaps the witch knew.[56] Well, I repulsed her once and twice, but she put by° my repulses, and smiled. Then I began to be angry, but she mattered° that nothing at all. Then she made offers again, and said, if I would be ruled by her, she would make me great and happy. For, said she, I am the mistress of the World, and men

Madam
Bubble: Or
this vain
World.

are made happy by me. Then I asked her name, and she told me it was Madam *Bubble.*[57] This set me further from her; but she still followed me with enticements. Then I betook me, as you see, to my knees, and with hands lift up, and cries, I prayed to him that had said he would help. So just as you came up, the gentlewoman° went her way. Then I continued to give thanks for this my great deliverance; for I verily believe she intended no good, but rather sought to make stop of me° in my Journey.

Hon. Without doubt her designs were bad. But stay, now

---

distemper Disease; howlet Owlet, a proverbial figure for poverty; **put by** Disregarded; **mattered** Cared about; **gentlewoman** Madame Bubble is of a high social class; **make stop of me** Make me stop.

you talk of her, methinks I either have seen her, or have read some story of her.

Standfast. Perhaps you have done both.

Hon. Madam *Bubble!* is she not a tall, comely dame, something of a swarthy complexion?

Standfast. Right, you hit it, she is just such an one.

Hon. Doth she not speak very smoothly, and give you a smile at the end of a sentence?

Standfast. You fall right upon it again, for these are her very actions.

Hon. Doth she not wear a great purse by her side, and is not her hand often in it, fingering her money,° as if that was her heart's delight?

Standfast. 'Tis just so; had she stood by all this while, you could not more amply have set her forth before me, nor have better described her features.

Hon. Then he that drew her picture was a good limner,° and he that wrote of her said true.

Great-heart. This woman is a *Witch*, and it is by virtue of her sorceries,° that this ground is *enchanted:* Whoever doth lay their head down in her lap, had as good lay it down upon that block over which the axe doth hang; and whoever lays their eyes upon her beauty, are counted the Enemies of God. This is she that maintaineth in their splendor, all those that are the enemies of Pilgrims. Yea, this is she that has bought off° many a man from a Pilgrim's life. She is a great gossipper; she is always, both she and her daughters, at one Pilgrim's heels or other, now commending, and then preferring the excellencies of this life. She is a bold and impudent slut; she will talk with any man. She always laugheth poor Pilgrims to scorn, but highly commends the rich.° If there be one cunning to get Money in a place, she will speak well of him from house to house; she loveth banqueting and feasting mainly

The World.

Jam. 4. 4.
1 John 2. 15.

---

fingering her money Money is an efficacious sign, comparable to those used in witchcraft; **limner** Sketcher; **sorceries** Spells; **bought off** Bribed; **the rich** That is, "rich people," not "rich pilgrims": Bunyan assumes that pilgrims are by definition poor.

well; she is always at one full table or another. She has given it out in some places, that she is a Goddess, and therefore some do Worship her.° She has her times, and open places of cheating; and she will say, and avow it, that none can shew a Good° comparable to hers. She promiseth to dwell with children's children,° if they will but love and make much of her. She will cast out of her purse gold, like dust, in some places, and to some persons. She loves to be sought after, spoken well of, and to lie in the bosoms of men. She is never weary of commending her commodities,° and she loves them most that think best of her. She will promise to some crowns and kingdoms, if they will but take her advice; yet many has she brought to the halter, and ten thousand times more to Hell.

Standfast. Oh! said *Standfast*, what a Mercy is it that I did resist her; for whither might she hav' drawn me?

Great-heart. Whither! nay, none but God knows whither. But in general, to be sure she would hav' drawn thee *into many foolish and hurtful Lusts, which drown men in Destruction and Perdition.*

1 Tim. 6. 9.

'Twas she that set *Absalom* against his Father, and *Jeroboam* against his Master.[58] 'Twas she that persuaded *Judas* to sell his Lord; and that prevailed with *Demas* to forsake the Godly Pilgrim's life; none can tell of the mischief that she doth. She makes variance° betwixt rulers and subjects, betwixt parents and children, 'twixt neighbour and neighbour, 'twixt a man and his wife, 'twixt a man and himself, 'twixt flesh and the heart.

Wherefore, good Master *Standfast*, be as your name is, and when you have done all, *stand.*

At this discourse, there was among the Pilgrims, a mixture of joy and trembling, but at length they brake out and sang:

---

some do **Worship her** Idolatry, like money and magic, involves putting one's faith in an efficacious sign; **Good** Both "benefit" and "commodity"; **with children's children** Who will inherit their grandparents' money; **commending her commodities** Commodification is the last significant temptation we hear of in *The Pilgrim's Progress*, just as it is the final temptation described in *Grace Abounding*; **variance** Differences; the socially corrosive effect of money was one reason behind the English civil war.

What danger is the Pilgrim in?
How many are his Foes?
How many ways there are to Sin,
No living mortal knows.
Some in the ditch shy are, yet can
Lie tumbling on the mire.
Some, though they shun the frying-pan,
Do leap into the fire.

After this, I beheld until they were come unto the land of *Beulah*, where the Sun shineth night and day. Here, because they were weary, they betook themselves a while to rest. And because this country was common for Pilgrims, and because the orchards and vineyards that were here, belonged to the King of the Cœlestial Country, therefore they were licensed to make bold with any of his things. But a little while soon refreshed them here; for the bells did so ring, and the trumpets continually sound so melodiously, that they could not sleep, and yet they received as much refreshing, as if they had slept their sleep never so soundly. Here also all the noise of them that walked the streets, was, *More Pilgrims are come to town.* And another would answer, saying, And so many, went over the Water, and were let in at the Golden Gates to day. They would cry again, There is now a Legion of shining ones just come to town; by which, we know, that there are more Pilgrims upon the road; for here they come to wait for them, and to comfort them after all their sorrow. Then the Pilgrims got up, and walked to and fro: But how were their ears now filled with heavenly noises and their eyes delighted with Cœlestial Visions? In this land they *heard* nothing, *saw* nothing, *felt* nothing, *smelt* nothing, *tasted* nothing, that was offensive to their stomach or mind; only when they tasted the water of the River, over which they were to go, they thought that tasted a little *bitterish* to the palate, but it proved sweeter when 'twas down.

In this place there was a Record kept of the names of them that had been Pilgrims of old, and a history of all the famous Acts that they had done. It was here also much discoursed,

Part I. p. 172.

Death bitter to the Flesh, but sweet to the Soul.

Death hath its ebbings and flowings like the Tide.

how the River to some had had its *flowings*, and what *ebbings* it has had while others have gone over. It has been in a manner *dry* for some, while it has overflowed its banks for others.

In this place, the Children of the town would go into the King's Gardens, and gather nosegays° for the Pilgrims, and bring them to them with much affection. Here also grew *camphire*, with *spikenard*, and *saffron*, *calamus*, and *cinnamon*, with all its trees of *frankincense*, *myrrh*, and *aloes*, with all *chief* spices.° With these the Pilgrims' chambers were perfumed while they staid here; and with these were their bodies anointed, to prepare them to go over the River, when the time appointed was come.

A messenger of Death sent to Christiana.

Now while they lay here, and waited for the good hour, there was a noise in the town, that there was a post come from the Cœlestial City, with matter of great importance to one *Christiana*, the wife of *Christian* the Pilgrim. So enquiry was made for her, and the house was found out where she was, so the post presented her with a letter: The contents whereof

His message.

were, *Hail good woman! I bring thee tidings, that the Master calleth for thee, and expecteth that thou shouldest stand in his Presence, in clothes of Immortality, within this ten days.*

When he had read this letter to her, he gave her therewith a true token[59] that he was a true messenger, and was come to bid her make haste to be gone. The token was, *an Arrow with*

How welcome is Death to them that are willing to die.

a point sharpened with Love, let easily into her heart, which by degrees wrought so effectually with her, that at the time appointed she must be gone.

When *Christiana* saw that her time was come, and that she was the first of this company that was to go over, she called

Her speech to her Guide.

for Mr. *Great-heart* her Guide, and told him how matters were. So he told her, he was heartily glad of the news, and could have been glad, had the post come for him. Then she

---

nosegays Garlands carried by bridesmaids; camphire . . . spices As Keeble notes, these are "Biblical spices, all mentioned in the Song of Solomon, whose love poetry was held to express Christ's love for his church" (Keeble, ed., *The Pilgrim's Progress*, p. 284).

bid that he should give advice how all things should be prepared for her Journey.

So he told her, saying, thus and thus it must be, and we that survive, will accompany you to the River-side.

Then she called for her children, and gave them *her Blessing*, and told them, that she yet read with comfort, the Mark that was set in their foreheads, and was glad to see them with her there, and that they had kept their garments so white. Lastly, she bequeathed to the Poor that little she had, and commanded her sons and her daughters to be ready against° the messenger should come for them. *To her Children.*

When she had spoken these words to her Guide, and to her children, she called for Mr. *Valiant-for-Truth*, and said unto him, Sir, you have in all places shewed yourself true-hearted, be *faithful unto Death*, and my King will give a *Crown of Life*. I would also intreat you to have an eye to my children; and if at any time you see them faint, speak comfortably to them. For my daughters, my Sons' wives, they have been faithful, and a fulfilling of the Promise upon them will be their end. But she gave Mr. *Standfast* a ring. *To Mr. Valiant.* *To Mr. Standfast.*

Then she called for old Mr. *Honest*, and said of him, *Behold an Israelite indeed, in whom is no Guile*. Then said he, I wish you a fair day, when you set out for Mount *Sion*, and shall be glad to see that you go over the River dry-shod.° But she answered, come *wet*, come *dry*, I long to be gone; for however the weather is in my Journey, I shall have time enough when I come there, to sit down and rest me, and dry me. *To Old Honest.*

Then came in that good man Mr. *Ready-to-halt*, to see her. So she said to him, thy travel hither has been with difficulty; but that will make thy Rest the sweeter. But watch and be ready; for at an hour when you think not, the messenger may come. *To Mr. Ready-to-halt.*

After him came in Mr. *Despondency*, and his daughter *Much-afraid;* to whom she said, you ought, with Thankfulness, for ever, to remember your deliverance from the hand of *To Despondency, and his Daughter.*

---

against For when; **dry-shod** With dry feet, but Honest means that he hopes she will have a painless death.

Giant *Despair*, and out of *Doubting-Castle*. The effect of that mercy, is that you are brought with safety hither. Be ye watchful, and cast away Fear; be sober, and hope to the end.

To Feeble-mind. Then she said to Mr. *Feeble-mind*, Thou wast delivered from the mouth of Giant *Slay-good*, that thou mightest live in the Light of the Living for ever, and see the King with comfort: Only I advise thee to repent thee of thy aptness to fear and doubt of his Goodness, before he sends for thee; lest thou shouldest, when he comes, be forced to stand before him for that fault, with blushing.

Her last day, and manner of departure. Now the day drew on, that *Christiana* must be gone. So the Road was full of people, to see her take her Journey. But behold all the banks beyond the River were full of horses and chariots, which were come down from above, to accompany her to the City Gate. So she came forth, and entred the *River*, with a *beckon* of farewell, to those that followed her to the River-side. The last word she was heard to say, here, was *I come, Lord, to be with thee, and bless thee.*

So her children and friends returned to their place, for that those that waited for *Christiana* had carried her out of their sight. So she went and called, and entred in at the Gate with all the ceremonies of Joy, that her husband *Christian* had done before her.

At her departure her children wept, but Mr. *Great-heart* and Mr. *Valiant* play'd upon the well-tuned cymbal and harp for Joy. So all departed to their respective places.

Mr. Ready-to-halt summoned. In process of time, there came a post to the town again, and his business was with Mr. *Ready-to-halt*. So he enquired him out, and said to him, I am come to thee in the name of him whom thou hast Loved and followed, tho' upon *Crutches:* And my message is to tell thee, that he expects thee at his table to sup with him in his Kingdom, the next day after *Easter;* wherefore prepare thyself for thy Journey.

Eccles. 12. 6. Then he also gave him a token that he was a true messenger, saying, *I have broken thy golden bowl, and loosed thy silver cord.*

After this, Mr. *Ready-to-halt* called for his fellow Pilgrims, and told them, saying, I am sent for, and God shall surely visit you also. So he desired Mr. *Valiant* to make his *Will*. And because he had nothing to bequeath to them that should survive him, but his *crutches*, and his *good wishes*, therefore thus he said: *These crutches I bequeath to my son, that shall tread in my steps, with an hundred warm wishes, that he may prove better than I have done.* *Promises His Will.*

Then he thanked Mr. *Great-heart* for his conduct and kindness, and so addressed himself to his Journey. When he came at the brink of the River, he said, Now I shall have no more need of these *crutches*, since yonder are Chariots and Horses for me to ride on: The last words he was heard to say, was, *Welcome Life.* So he went his Way. *His last Words.*

After this, Mr. *Feeble-mind* had tidings brought him, that the post sounded his horn at his chamber-door. Then he came in, and told him, saying, I am come to tell thee that thy Master has need of thee; and that in very little time thou must behold his Face in Brightness: And take this as a token of the truth of my message: *Those that look out at the windows, shall be darkned.* *Feeble-mind summoned.*

Then Mr. *Feeble-mind* called for his friends, and told them what errand had been brought unto him, and what token he had received of the truth of the message. Then he said, Since I have nothing to bequeath to any, to what purpose should I make a will? As for my *feeble Mind*, that I will leave behind me,° for that I have no need of that in the place whither I go; nor is it worth bestowing upon the poorest Pilgrims: Wherefore, when I am gone, I desire, that you, Mr. *Valiant*, would bury it in a dunghill. This done, and the day being come in which he was to depart, he entered the River as the rest: His last words were, *Hold out, Faith and Patience.* So he went over to the other side. *He makes no will.* *His last Words.*

When days had many of them passed away, Mr. *Despondency* was sent for; for a post was come, and brought this

---

that I will leave behind me Feeble-mind abandons his alienated, allegorical earthly identity as he enters the celestial city.

Mr.
Despondency'
s summons.

message to him: *Trembling man, these are to summon thee to be ready with thy King by the next Lord's Day, to shout for Joy, for thy deliverance from all thy doubtings.*

And, said the messenger, that my message is true, take this for a proof. So he gave him the *grasshopper*[60] to be a *burden* unto him. Now Mr. *Despondency's* daughter, whose name was *Much-afraid*, said, when she heard what was done, that she would go with her father. Then Mr. *Despondency* said to his friends; myself and my daughter, you know what we have been, and how troublesomely we have behaved ourselves in every company. My will, and my daughter's is, that our *Desponds* and slavish fears be by no man ever received, from the day of our departure, for ever: For I know, that after my death, they will offer themselves to others. For, to be plain with you, they are *ghosts,*° the which we entertained when we first began to be Pilgrims, and could never shake them off after: And they will walk about, and seek entertainment of the Pilgrims; but for our sakes, shut ye the doors upon them.

When the time was come for them to depart, they went to the brink of the River. The last words of Mr. *Despondency*, were, *Farewel night, Welcome day.* His daughter went through the River singing, but none could understand what she said.

Then it came to pass a while after, that there was a post in the town, that enquired for Mr. *Honest.* So he came to his house, where he was, and delivered to his hands these lines: *Thou art commanded to be ready against this day seven-night, to present thyself before thy Lord, at his Father's house.* And for a token that my message is true, *All thy daughters of Musick shall be brought low.* Then Mr. *Honest* called for his friends, and said unto them, I die, but shall make no will. As for my Honesty, it shall go with me; let him that comes after, be told of this. When the day that he was to be gone was come, he addressed himself to go over the River. Now the River at that time over-flow'd the banks in some places; but Mr. *Honest* in

Eccles. 12. 5.
His Daughter goes too.
His Will.
His last Words.
Mr. Honest summoned.
Eccles. 12. 4.
He makes no Will.

---

ghosts Images, idols.

his life-time had spoken to one *Good-Conscience* to meet him there, the which he also did, and lent him his hand, and so helped him over. The last words of Mr. *Honest* were, *Grace Reigns:* So he left the World.

Good-Conscience helps Mr. Honest over the River.

After this; it was noised abroad, that Mr. *Valiant-for-Truth* was taken with a summons by the same post as the other; and had this for a token that the summons was true, *That his pitcher was broken at the fountain.* When he understood it, he called for his friends, and told them of it. Then, said he, I am going to my Father's, and tho' with great difficulty I am got hither, yet now I do not repent me of all the trouble I have been at to arrive where I am. *My Sword* I give to him that shall succeed me in my Pilgrimage, and my *Courage* and *Skill* to him that can get it. My *marks* and *scars* I carry with me, to be a witness for me, that I have fought His battles, who now will be my Rewarder. When the day that he must go hence was come, many accompany'd him to the River-side, into which as he went, he said, *Death, where is thy Sting?* And as he went down deeper, he said, *Grave, where is thy Victory?°* So he passed over, and all the Trumpets sounded for him on the other side.

Mr. Valiant summoned.

Eccles. 12. 6.

His Will.

His last words.

Then there came forth a summons for Mr. *Standfast;* (this Mr. *Standfast* was he that the rest of the Pilgrims found upon his knees in the *Enchanted ground;*) for the post brought it him open in his hands. The contents whereof were, *That he must prepare for a change of life, for his Master was not willing that he should be so far from him any longer.* At this Mr. *Standfast* was put into a muse: Nay, saith the Messenger, you need not doubt of the truth of my message; for here is a token of the truth thereof: *Thy wheel is broken at the cistern.* Then he called to him Mr. *Great-heart,* who was their Guide, and said unto him, Sir, although it was not my hap to be much in your good company in the days of my Pilgrimage, yet, since the

Mr. Standfast is summoned.

Eccl. 12. 6.

He calls for Mr. Great-heart.

Death . . . Victory 1 Corinthians 15:55: "O death, where is thy string? O grave, where is thy victory?" (KJV)

His speech to him.

time I knew you, you have been profitable to me. When I came from home, I left behind me a wife, and five small children; let me intreat you, at your return, (for I know that you will go and return to your Master's house, in hopes that you may yet be a conductor to more of the Holy Pilgrims) that you send to my family, and let them be acquainted with all that hath, and shall happen unto me. Tell them moreover of my happy arrival to this place, and of the present late° blessed condition

His errand to his family.

that I am in. Tell them also of *Christian* and *Christiana* his wife, and how *she* and her children came after her husband. Tell them also, of what a happy end she made, and whither she is gone. I have little or nothing to send to my family, except it be Prayers and Tears for them; of which it will suffice if you acquaint them, if peradventure they may prevail.

When Mr. *Standfast* had thus set things in order, and the time being come for him to haste him away, he also went down to the River. Now there was a great calm at that time in the River; wherefore Mr. *Standfast*, when he was about halfway in, stood a while, and talked to his companions that had waited upon him thither: And he said,

His last Words.
Jos. 3. 17.

This River has been a terror to many, yea, the thoughts of it also have often frighted me; but now methinks I stand easy, my foot is fixed upon that upon which the feet of the Priests that bare the Ark of the Covenant stood, while *Israel* went over this *Jordan*. The waters indeed are to the palate bitter, and to the stomach cold; yet the thoughts of what I am going to, and of the conduct that waits for me on the other side, doth lie as a glowing coal at my heart.

I see myself now at the end of my Journey; my *toilsome* days are ended. I am going now to see *that* Head that was crowned with thorns, and *that* Face that was spit upon for me.

I have formerly lived by hear-say and Faith; but now I go where I shall live by Sight, and shall be with him in whose company I delight myself.

---

late Both "recent" and "final."

I have loved to hear my Lord spoken of; and where-ever I have seen the print of his shoe in the earth, there I have coveted to set my foot too.

His Name has been to me as a *civet-box;*° yea, sweeter than all perfumes. His Voice to me has been most sweet; and his Countenance I have more desired than they that have most desired the light of the Sun. His Word I did use to gather for my food, and for antidotes against my faintings. He has held me, and I have kept me from mine iniquities; yea, my steps hath he strengthened in his Way.

Now, while he was thus in discourse, his countenance changed, his *strong man*° bowed under him; and after he had said, *Take me, for I come unto Thee,* he ceased to be seen of them.

But Glorious it was to see, how the open Region was filled with Horses and Chariots, with Trumpeters and Pipers, with Singers and Players on stringed instruments, to welcome the PILGRIMS as they went up, and followed one another in at the Beautiful Gate of the City.

As for *Christian's* children, the four boys that *Christiana* brought with her, with their wives and children, I did not stay where I was till they were gone over. Also since I came away, I heard one say, that they were yet alive, and so would be for the increase of the Church° in that place where they were, for a time.

Shall it be my lot to go that way again, I may give those that desire it, an account of what I here am silent about; mean time, I bid my Reader *Adieu.*

THE END.

---

civet-box Package containing fragrances; **strong man** Physical strength; **the increase of the church** Bunyan guarantees the physical survival of the saints through Christiana's descendants.

Endnotes

Unless otherwise specified, references to Keeble, Owens, and Sharrock are to their editions of The Pilgrim's Progress. *In the endnotes and footnotes, all references to text from the Bible are to the King James Version.*

Part One

1. (p. 5) I writing of the Way: Sharrock argues that "the book referred to is probably *The Heavenly Footman*" (*John Bunyan*, p. 387; see "For Further Reading"), and Owens agrees that "the work referred to here is almost certainly Bunyan's *The Heavenly Footman*" (Owens, ed., *The Pilgrim's Progress*, p. 291). Certainly this line is reminiscent of the opening of that work, which was published posthumously in 1692: "If thou wouldst so run as to obtain the kingdom of heaven, then be sure that thou get into the way that leadeth thither. For it is a vain thing to think that ever thou shalt have the prize, though thou runneth never so fast, unless thou art in the way that leads to it" (*The Works of John Bunyan*, edited by George Offor, vol. 3, p. 383). But Bunyan might also refer to *Grace Abounding to the Chief of Sinners*, which depicts many of Christian's allegorical encounters in psychological terms. Joan Webber comments that this work "goes very far toward making allegories of [Bunyan] and his congregation" (*The Eloquent "I,"* p. 22), and Offor believes that Bunyan means "most probably his own spiritual experience" (*Works*, vol. 3, p. 7).

2. (p. 5) Race of Saints: This is the first of many Pauline images, from the Bible, 1 Corinthians 9:24: "Know ye not that they which run in a race run all, but one receiveth the prize? So run, that ye may obtain." As Bunyan's use of the term "saints" implies, this verse was often cited in support of Calvinist predestination.

3. (p. 5) Fell suddenly into an Allegory: Stanley Fish observes that, for Bunyan, "the source of danger and of potential error is to be located in the world as it usually appears" (*Self-consuming Artifacts*, p. 237). Luxon perceptively expands: "Virtually the entire plot of Bunyan's allegory is generated by a string of occasions in which the pilgrim characters temporarily forget the allegorical status of their experiences in this world. Mistaking

341

this-worldly experience for reality, they fall, as it were, back into the allegory and take it for the real thing" (*Literal Figures*, p. 160).

4. (p. 5) *to divert my self in doing this, / From worser thoughts*: Greaves claims that in early 1668 Bunyan was worried by changes in Charles II's policy toward dissenters: "The 'worser thoughts' that prompted Bunyan to write *The Pilgrim's Progress* probably were triggered by reports that the King had yielded to parliamentary calls for a repressive policy, leading Bunyan to conclude that he might never be freed" (*Glimpses of Glory*, p. 217).

5. (p. 7) *Dark Clouds bring Waters*: Bunyan's words are "dark" in the sense of "obscure," but they will produce rain and so bring to fruition the ideas that grow in the fertile soil of the reader's mind. Bunyan may also be thinking of baptismal water.

6. (p. 7) *If that a Pearl may in a Toad's head dwell*: Valuable "toadstones" were believed to grow in the heads of toads. See Shakespeare's *As You Like It* (act 2, scene 1): "Sweet are the uses of adversity, / Which, like the toad, ugly and venomous, / Wears yet a precious jewel in his head."

7. (p. 8) *That this your Book will stand when soundly try'd*: Here, as at many other points in the book, Bunyan parodies legalistic reasoning by introducing a trial motif. His entire theology is based on the superseding of the law of the Old Testament by the grace of the New.

8. (p. 8) *Metaphors make us blind*: The danger is that Bunyan's use of iconic imagery may produce idols in the mind, obscuring our access to truth and thus making us "blind" in the sense of "ignorant of religion."

9. (p. 8) *Types, Shadows and Metaphors*: A "type" is an object, person, or event, described literally in the Old Testament, but also "spiritualized" as an image prefiguring its "antitype" in the New. Samson, for example, was a "type" of which Christ was the "antitype." "Shadows" means "images." Roger Pooley cites Samuel Parker's *A Discourse of Ecclesiastical Politie* (1670): "And herein lies the most material difference between the sober Christians of the Church of England, and our modern sectaries, that we express the Precepts and Duties of the Gospel in plain and intelligent terms, whilst they trifle them away by childish Metaphors and Allegories, and will not talk of Religion but in barbarous and uncouth similitudes" (Keeble, ed., *John Bunyan: Conventicle and Parnassus*, p. 94).

10. (p. 9) *And find There darker lines. . . . there are worse lines too*: The complainer's "real" life is, properly examined, just as full of obscure, hidden meaning as Bunyan's allegory. Already Bunyan is suggesting that the alienated, iconic world he depicts is more "real" than the world of experience.

11. (p. 9) *Sound words I know, Timothy is to use*: In 1 Timothy 1:4, Paul advises

his correspondent: "Neither give heed to fables and endless genealogies, which minister questions, rather than godly edifying which is in faith."

12. (p. 10) abuse: That is, use an illegitimate image or figure. George Puttenham's *English Poesie* (1589) uses "abuse" to translate the Greek *catachresis*, which is when "for lacke of naturall and proper terme or worde we take another, neither naturall nor proper and do untruly applie it to the thing which we would seeme to expresse" (quoted in Hawkes, *Idols of the Marketplace*, p. 79). It was often used to refer to idolatry, as in one of John Donne's sermons: "If the true use of pictures be preached unto them, there is no danger of an abuse" (p. 81).

13. (p. 10) I find that men . . . will write / Dialogue-wise: The dialogue, typically between teacher and pupil, was a favorite genre of religious texts. Arthur Dent's *The Plaine Man's Pathway* (1601), a prominent influence on Bunyan, is in dialogue form, for example, and Bunyan uses dialogue himself in *The Life and Death of Mr. Badman* (1680). Here Bunyan points out that this unimpeachably religious form also uses fictional characters.

14. (p. 10) let Truth be free / To make her salleys upon Thee, and Me: Compare Milton's *Areopagitica* (1644): "So Truth be in the field, we do injuriously by licensing and prohibiting, to misdoubt her strength. Let her and Falsehood grapple; who ever knew Truth put to the worse, in a free and open encounter?" (*Complete English Poems, Of Education, Areopagitica*, p. 746).

15. (p. 11) This Book is writ in such a Dialect: Since it represents a fallen, alienated world, allegory will appeal to fallen, alienated men. Compare Bunyan's "Prison Meditations" (1665): "Hark yet again, you carnal men, / And hear what I shall say / In your own dialect, and then / I'll you no longer stay" (*Works*, vol. 1, p. 66).

16. (p. 13) a Book: The Book is the Bible. The words of Holy Scripture often become physical forces in Bunyan's writing. Hill notes: "In *Grace Abounding* texts are hurled at Bunyan's head like thunderbolts of God" (*The World Turned Upside Down*, p. 95). In that book, Bunyan mentions: "I have sometimes seen more in a line of the Bible than I could well tell how to stand under" (*Grace Abounding to the Chief of Sinners and A Relation of the Imprisonment of Mr. John Bunyan*, 1987, p. 83).

17. (p. 14) but they began to be hardened: In Exodus 7:3 God "hardens" Pharaoh's heart to prevent him from seeing the meaning behind the visible "signs" God sends, and this prevents Pharaoh from freeing the Israelites from slavery. The connection between literalism and cruelty features largely in Shakespeare's *The Merchant of Venice*, where Shylock cruelly insists on the letter of the law, and in *A Relation of the Imprisonment of Mr.*

John Bunyan, where the obsessive literalism of Justice Chester reflects his hardness of heart in his dialogue with Bunyan's wife: " 'But it is recorded, woman, it is recorded,' said Justice Chester; as if it must be of necessity true, because it was recorded. With which words he often endeavoured to stop her mouth, having no other argument to convince her, but 'it is recorded, it is recorded' " (*Works*, vol. 1, p. 60). See also Bunyan's *On the Fear of God*: "Take heed of hardening thy heart at any time, against convictions or judgments. I bid you before to beware of a hard heart; now I bid you beware of hardening your soft heart" (*Works*, vol. 3, p. 487).

18. (p. 14) *a Man named* Evangelist: This character has a small but vital role in part one; part two gives much greater emphasis to the need for spiritual guidance. In Bunyan's life, this part was played by John Gifford, pastor of the Bedford church that Bunyan joined after his conversion.

19. (p. 15) *Wicket Gate*: A wicket gate is a small gate, usually part of a larger door. The passage to heaven is represented as a "strait gate" in Luke 13:24. Some critics believe the gate represents Christ, but in his pamphlet *The Strait Gate* (1676) Bunyan argues that this is not so: "The master of the house is not the door" (*The Works of John Bunyan*, edited by George Offor, vol. 1, p. 366).

20. (p. 15) *his Wife and Children*: In *Grace Abounding* Bunyan recalls his surprise "when I found professors much distressed and cast down when they met with outward losses, as of husband, wife, child, etc. Lord, thought I, what a do is here about such little things as these!" (p. 24). However, he also remembers that parting from his family to go into prison was "as the pulling the flesh from the bones" (p. 80). Davies comments, regarding Christian's desertion of his family: "Only if we read this action gracefully, understanding Christian's desertion of his family within the compass of an allegorical ode that takes advantage of literal-metaphorical hesitations in making the unseen visible, can we accept such apparently unchristian behavior unproblematically" (*Graceful Reading*, p. 277).

21. (p. 17) *wiser in their own eyes than seven men that can render a Reason*: Works of Restoration philosophy such as John Locke's *Essay Concerning Human Understanding* (1689) use "reason" as an antidote to the religious faith of "enthusiasts" like Bunyan: "If the boundaries be not set between faith and reason, no enthusiasm or extravagancy in religion can be contradicted" (1867 edition, p. 589).

22. (p. 18) *I can better conceive of them with my Mind, than speak of them with my Tongue*: Compare Milton's *Paradise Lost* (1667), where the archangel Raphael also uses iconic imagery to express the unspeakable: "what sur-

mounts the reach / Of human sense I shall delineate so, / By likening spiritual to corporeal forms, / As may express them best" (book 5, lines 571–574).

23. (p. 20) *The name of the Slough was* Despond: The name means "depression." Offor cites Bunyan's *The Jerusalem Sinner Saved* (1688): "Satan casts the professor into the mire. . . . He bedaubeth us with his own foam, and then tempts us to believe that the bedaubing comes from ourselves" (*Works*, vol. 3, p. 92).

24. (p. 20) *a man came to him, whose name was* Help: Regarding this episode, Carolynn Van Dyke observes: "Bunyan's point is precisely that Christian escapes from a disabling experience into an allegorical understanding of it in terms of Christian doctrine" (*The Fiction of Truth*, p. 171).

25. (p. 22) *The gentleman's name that met him, was Mr.* Worldly Wiseman: This character is often identified specifically as Edward Fowler (see Introduction). Greaves objects: "But unlike Fowler Worldly Wiseman is not a minister. Instead he must represent those gentry who readily conformed at the Restoration, finding in Latitudinarianism an antidote to the sharply defined religious principles that had contributed to the upheavals of the 1640's and 1650's" (p. 258). According to Sharrock, "This figure may be specially intended to satirize the Latitudinarian party in the Church of England" (*John Bunyan*, p. 388). Keeble finds a more general "type of the complacent believer who rests securely in his high opinion of his own moral behavior without ever having experienced the desperate need for grace represented in the Slough of Despond" (Keeble, ed., *The Pilgrim's Progress*, p. 266). Offor cites the gloss from W. Mason's edition (1778), which connects Wiseman's legalism with antinomian libertinism: "Self-righteousness is as contrary to the faith of Christ as indulging the lusts of the flesh" (*Works*, vol. 3, p. 94).

26. (p. 25) *Yes, very well:* Since it stands for the fleshly law, Mount Sinai is clearly visible to Christian's senses. Compare his response here to page 15, where Evangelist asks if he sees the "Shining Light," which represents the Word of God, and he replies, "I think I do."

27. (p. 25) Christian *was afraid to venture further, lest the Hill should fall on his head:* In *Grace Abounding*, Bunyan recalls how, tormented by guilt over his worldly pleasure in bell-ringing, he was forced to flee the church "for fear it should fall upon my head" (p. 14).

28. (p. 29) Strive to enter in at the Strait Gate: "Strait" means "narrow." Christian is learning the allegorical nature of the "strait gate"; it represents the small number of the predestined elect. As Bunyan explains in *The Strait*

Gate (1676): "The straitness of this gate is not to be understood carnally, but mystically. You are not to understand it, as if the entrance into heaven was some little pinching wicket; no, the straitness of the gate is quite another thing" (*Works*, vol. 1, p. 366).

29. (p. 35) *the house of the* Interpreter: The Holy Spirit is manifested in the faculty of interpretation. Offor cites a note from T. Scott's edition (1797): "With great propriety Bunyan places the house of the Interpreter *beyond* the strait gate; for the knowledge of Divine things, that precedes conversion to God by faith in Christ, is very scanty, compared with the diligent Christian's subsequent attainments" (*Works*, vol. 3, p. 98). Keeble observes: "The instruction of the new convert by the inner light of the Holy Spirit . . . takes the form of a series of emblems, some of which had appeared in such earlier collections as Francis Quarles's *Emblems* (1635)" (p. 268). Greaves, on the other hand, suggests that the Interpreter is "modeled on Bunyan's pastoral experience" (p. 232).

30. (p. 38) *The name of the eldest was* Passion, *of the other* Patience: Offor cites George Cheever's *Lectures on the Pilgrim's Progress and on the Life and Times of John Bunyan* (1846): "Passion stands for the men of this world, Patience of that which is to come" (*Works*, vol. 3, p. 99).

31. (p. 39) *Then I perceive it is not best to covet things:* Paul twice equates "covetousness" with idolatry: in Colossians 3:5 and in Ephesians 5:5. In *Christian Behaviour* (1663), Bunyan explains: "It engageth the very heart of man in it, to mind earthly things. . . . Thus it changeth the object on which the heart should be set, and setteth it on that which it should not" (*Works*, vol. 2, p. 567). In the same text, like many of his contemporaries, he identifies "covetousness" with what we would call the "market" (see Introduction).

32. (p. 41) *a man in an Iron Cage:* Keeble identifies this figure as "John Child, who conformed to the Church of England in 1660, was visited after his lapse by Baptists who may have included Bunyan, and who in 1684 committed suicide" (p. 268). It may also allude to Francis Spira, an Italian Protestant who returned to Catholicism and was punished with agonizing remorse and despair. In *Grace Abounding* Bunyan says of Spira: "Every groan of that man . . . his tears, his prayers, his gnashing of teeth, his wringing of hands, his twining and twisting, languishing and pining away under the mighty hand of God that was on him, was as knives and daggers in my soul" (p. 41).

33. (p. 42) *I am now a man of* Despair, *and am shut up in it, as in this Iron Cage:* Note that the man is aware that the cage is only a symbol for his despair. Because he is unable to distinguish symbols from reality, however, it has

the same effect as a literal prison. The man's situation is in every respect the reverse of Bunyan's.

34. (p. 42) *But now every one of those things also bite me, and gnaw me, like a burning Worm:* A conventional image for conscience, as in Mark 9:46, where Jesus refers to Hell as a place for the punishment of sinners "where their worm dieth not, and their fire is not quenched."

35. (p. 43) *and some sought to hide themselves under the mountains:* Recall Christian's fear that Mount Sinai would fall on his head, when he was still under the law. Legalists will be buried under mountains on Judgment Day.

36. (p. 44) *gird up his loins:* This common biblical phrase means, literally, "tie his clothes about his middle" and, figuratively, "prepare himself for action." In biblical societies, where people dressed in flowing robes, the first would be a prerequisite for the second.

37. (p. 45) *the third also set a Mark on his forehead, and gave him a Roll:* Assurances of elect status and so of salvation. But Davies finds that the roll "seems intimately bound up not with election but with faith in the scriptural promises of deliverance" (*Graceful Reading*, p. 44). In other words, it signifies the Lutheran principle of justification by faith alone rather than the Calvinist doctrine of predestination.

38. (p. 46) *The name of the one was* Formalist, *and the name of the other* Hypocrisy: U. Milo Kaufmann identifies three distinct species of hypocrite in seventeenth-century religious discourse: the "privie" hypocrite, who deceives only himself; the "grosse" hypocrite, who deceives only others; and the "formal" hypocrite, who deceives both himself and others (Keeble, ed., *John Bunyan: Conventicle and Parnassus*, p. 174). See Thomas Traherne's "Right Apprehension": "His gold and he / Do well agree, / For he's a formal hypocrite / Like that unfruitful though on th'outside bright" (lines 77–80).

39. (p. 47) *a thousand years:* According to Keeble, this is "the length of time Roman Catholicism had, in Puritan eyes, obscured the doctrine of justification by faith through its insistence on the merit of works and had substituted for inner Christian commitment a formal religion of external observance and ceremony such as the established Church of England continued to promote by its determination to enforce conformity to its liturgy" (p. 269).

40. (p. 47) *we are also in the Way:* Fish observes that Formalist and Hypocrisy misinterpret the "way" as a literal, physical place, thus "betraying an inability to think symbolically" (p. 228).

41. (p. 47) *I walk by the Rule of my Master, you walk by the rude working of your*

your fancies: This is an assertion of the guiding value of scripture, rather than the "inner light" followed by the Quakers, or the "divine spark" of reason to which Latitudinarians often appealed.

42. (p. 51) *a couple of Lions:* Offor identifies the lions as "civil despotism and ecclesiastical tyranny" (*Works*, vol. 3, p. 106). Sharrock opines that "the lions represent persecution, civil and ecclesiastical, of Nonconformists under the Clarendon Code" (Sharrock, ed., *The Pilgrim's Progress*, p. 391). Greaves observes that "the lions evoke the Foxian accounts of martyrs torn apart by wild beasts" (p. 245).

43. (p. 54) *there was a very stately palace before him, the name of which was* Beautiful: The palace Beautiful represents the congregation or church. John R. Knott points out: "The three major places in which [Christian] receives instruction—the Interpreter's House, the Palace Beautiful, and the Delectable Mountains—mark stages in his understanding of Scripture and his ability to relate his experience to it" (in Keeble, ed., *John Bunyan: Conventicle and Parnassus*, p. 166).

44. (p. 57) *she ran to the door and called out* Prudence, Piety, *and* Charity: Sharrock notes: "The fact that the principle keepers of the House Beautiful are women reminds us of the important role played by women in the Bedford congregation" (p. 391).

45. (p. 61) *I have a Wife and four small Children:* So did Bunyan when he first entered prison in 1660. But *Offor* notes that this conversation was added to the second edition of 1678, and concludes that "if he referred to his own family, it was to his second wife" (*Works*, vol. 3, p. 108).

46. (p. 61) *Then* Christian *wept:* Compare Bunyan's reflections on the consequences of his impending imprisonment for his family in *Grace Abounding:* "I . . . have often brought to mind the many hardships, miseries, and wants that my poor family was like to meet with, should I be taken from them, especially my poor blind child, who lay nearer my heart than all I had besides; O the thought of the hardship I thought my blind one might go under, would break my heart to pieces" (p. 80).

47. (p. 65) *the Sword also with which their Lord will kill the Man of Sin:* The Man of Sin is the Antichrist. Protestants identified Antichrist with the Pope, but for Bunyan he is a more generalized source of illusion, as he explains in *Of Antichrist and His Ruin* (1692): "Antichrist is the adversary of Christ; an adversary *really*, a friend *pretendedly*: So then, Antichrist is one that is *against* Christ; one that is *for* Christ, and one that is *contrary* to him: And this is that mystery of iniquity"(*Works*, vol. 2, p. 45).

48. (p. 65) *we will . . . show you the Delectable Mountains:* Offor cites the note

from Scott's edition: "The Delectable Mountains, as seen at a distance, represent those distinct views of the privileges and consolations, attainable in this life, with which believers are sometimes favoured" (*Works*, vol. 3, p. 110).

49. (p. 65) Emanuel's Land: "Emmanuel" is Hebrew for "God is with us." Owens suggests: "It is perhaps significant that Emmanuel was a favorite name for Christ among the millenarian group known as Fifth Monarchists" (p. 298).

50. (p. 66) *So they went on together, reiterating their former discourses:* As Greaves explains: "Bunyan's periodic recapitulation of previous action . . . serves a catechetical function, and during the course of the allegory Christian develops from catechumen to catechizer" (*Glimpses of Glory*, p. 222).

51. (p. 66) *His name is* Apollyon: The name is Greek for "destroyer"; see Revelation 9:11. Owens notes: "As well as symbolizing the power of the devil, Apollyon also represents the oppressive power of the state" (p. 298). In *Grace Abounding*, Bunyan recalls: "Sometimes I have thought I should see the devil, nay, thought I have felt him, behind me, pull my clothes" (p. 29).

52. (pp. 74–75) *That Ditch is it, into which the blind have led the blind. . . . a very dangerous Quag:* Offor cites Mason: "The ditch on the right hand is error in principle, into which the blind, as to spiritual truth, fall. The ditch on the left hand means outward sin and wickedness" (*Works*, vol. 3, p. 114). Sharrock notes: "It has been suggested that the ditch represents reliance on works, while the 'quag' is that antinomianism that considers that the gift of grace absolves from the moral law" (p. 392). Christian's stumbling between the two echoes Bunyan's vacillation between legalism and license (see Introduction).

53. (p. 79) *grown so crazy and stiff in his joints:* In Sharrock's opinion, "This reference to the weakness of Papal power could hardly have been written after the Declaration of Indulgence in 1672 had occasioned renewed Protestant fear of Catholic influence" (p. 393). But Bunyan may have been thinking in the longer term: See *Of Antichrist and His Ruin* (1692), where he refers to the Papacy: "Do but look back and compare Antichrist four or five hundred years ago, with Antichrist as he is now, and you shall see what work the Lord Jesus has begun to make with him" (*Works*, vol. 2, p. 48).

54. (p. 80) *Then did* Christian *vain-gloriously smile:* Fish comments: "If the last is first, the first is Faithful, who is never more ahead of Faithful than when he is overrun by him. . . . If the unfolding of the scene disallows Christian's claims to be first, it also disallows the mimetic claims of the spatial image in which he and the reader momentarily believe" (pp. 226–227).

55. (p. 81) *he is a turncoat!:* Cowardly soldiers or servants would turn their

coats inside out so that their allegiance could not be discerned. In the 1660s the term referred to dissenters who had conformed after the Restoration, such as Bunyan's Latitudinarian opponent Edward Fowler (see Introduction).

56. (p. 84) *saw one coming after me:* This is Moses, representing the law. Davies notes, with regard to Faithful's conversion, "What is emphasized is not a Calvinist predestination but a basic need to recognize the impossibility of fulfilling the law" (p. 231). Bunyan is more of a Lutheran than a Calvinist.

57. (p. 85) *For that the Valley was altogether without* Honour: Bernard de Mandeville makes this argument with apparent seriousness in *An Enquiry into the Origin of Honour* (1732): "Honour is diametrically opposite to Christianity" (1971 ed., p. 89).

58. (p. 86) *all Natural Science:* Sharrock points out: "Shame appeals to intellectual snobbery in a highly topical manner: the new physical science was very popular (e.g. at court) in the Restoration period" (p. 393), and Owens calls this "a topical remark, since the Royal Society had received its charter in 1662" (p. 300). The Baconian empiricism espoused by such institutions rapidly undercut the intellectual foundations of Christianity; here, Bunyan identifies natural science as the ideology of the ruling class.

59. (p. 88) *a man whose name was* Talkative: Luxon notes of this episode: "Christian and Faithful first bring Talkative into being as a personified projection of their own error, then they proceed to exteriorize and condemn him as a false pilgrim, an other" (p. 176). Hill observes that "Bunyan thought Ranters talked too much" (*The World Turned Upside Down*, p. 201). Bunyan says the same of the Quakers, whom he associated with the Ranters, in *Some Gospel Truths Opened* (1656): "Who are the men who at this day are so deluded by the quakers, and other pernicious doctrines; but those who thought it enough to be talkers of the gospel, and grace of God, without seeking and giving all diligence to make it sure unto themselves?" (*Works*, vol. 2, p. 133).

60. (p. 91) *so will he talk when he is on the* ale-bench: This indicates that Talkative may be a Ranter rather than a Quaker. In *A Vindication of Some Gospel Truths Opened* (1657), Bunyan accused the Ranters of making their doctrines "threadbare at an alehouse" (*Works*, vol. 2, p. 183).

61. (p. 95) *You lie at the Catch:* "Lie in wait to catch out in conversation" (Sharrock, p. 394). Offor cites Bunyan's *Jerusalem Sinner Saved* (1688): "This is doing things with a high hand against the Lord our God, and a taking Him, as it were, *at the catch!*" (*Works*, vol. 3, p. 124; emphasis in original).

62. (p. 98) *you had ought else but Notion:* Bunyan discusses "notionists" in *Some*

Gospel Truths Opened (1656), in connection with other groups he considered antinomian, like the Ranters and Quakers. He describes them as covert legalists, warning against those "who slip into high notions, and rest there; taking that for true faith which is not. I shall desire thee seriously to consider this one character of a NOTIONIST. Such an one, whether he perceives it or not, is puffed up in his fleshly mind" (*Works*, vol. 2, p. 133).

63. (p. 101) *you must through many Tribulations enter into the Kingdom of Heaven:* Evangelist continues his prophecy of persecution. According to Offor, this speech "peculiarly relates to the miseries endured by Nonconformist ministers in the reign of Charles II" (*Works*, vol. 3, p. 126).

64. (p. 101) *Vanity-Fair:* Hill observes: "There has been some dispute as to whether Vanity Fair represents the Church of Rome or the money power. I do not see why we have to choose: Bunyan could perfectly well have intended both" (*A Tinker and a Poor Man*, p. 225). I take the town of Vanity to represent the world, and the Fair to stand for the market.

65. (p. 102) *houses, lands . . . precious stones, and what not:* Note that Bunyan omits the essential differences between the commodities; they are all made equivalent for the purposes of exchange. Greaves shows the influence of Max Weber's thesis that Protestantism created an ideological climate favorable to capitalism when he comments that in Vanity Fair, "Bunyan ignored an obvious place to incorporate a defense of nonconformity on the grounds that it was conducive to economic development" (p. 225). But in fact, as R. H. Tawney has argued in *Religion and the Rise of Capitalism*, Weber underestimates the opposition to capitalism among radical Protestants, and Bunyan is a good example.

66. (p. 104) *bedlams:* Madmen. Compare the account of Bunyan's old enemy, the Quaker George Fox, of his visit to Lichfield: "As soon as I was got within the town the word of the Lord came to me again, to cry, 'Woe unto the bloody city of Lichfield!' So I went up and down the streets, crying with a loud voice, 'Woe to the bloody city of Lichfield!' It being market-day, I went into the market-place, and to and fro in several parts of it, and made stands, crying as before, 'Woe to the bloody city of Lichfield!' And no one laid hands on me, but as I went crying through the streets, there seemed to me to be a channel of blood running down the streets, and the market-place appeared like a pool of blood" (Carey, *Eyewitness to History*, pp. 185–186).

67. (p. 105) *Turn away mine eyes from beholding Vanity:* Offor cites Ivimey's edition of 1824: "Holy Hunt of Hitchin, as he was called, a friend of Bunyan's, passing the market-place where mountebanks were performing, one cried after him, 'Look there, Mr. Hunt!' Turning his head another way,

he replied, 'Turn away mine eyes from beholding vanity'" (*Works*, vol. 3, p. 128).

68. (p. 106) *partakers of their misfortunes:* Offor cites the *Narrative of Proceedings against Nonconformists* (1670): "In 1670, the town porters of Bedford being commanded to assist in a brutal attack upon the Nonconformists, ran away, saying, 'They would be hanged, drawn, and quartered, before they would assist in that work'; for which cause the justices committed two of them . . . to the jail" (*Works*, vol. 3, p. 129).

69. (p. 107) *they had made Commotions and Divisions in the Town, and had won a Party:* Dissenters remained a potent political force in England for more than two centuries, especially within the Whig Party, later the Liberals, and eventually in the British Labor Party, which is traditionally said to owe "more to Methodism than to Marx."

70. (p. 108) *there came in three witnesses, to wit,* Envy, Superstition, and *Pickthank:* Sharrock (p. 394) glosses this as "flatterer" and cites Shakespeare's *The First Part of Henry IV* (act 3, scene 2): "smiling pickthanks and base newsmongers." More generally, it means one who tries to extort gratitude, or thanks, from another.

71. (p. 112) *whoever would not fall down and worship his Golden Image:* Nebuchadnezzer, who imprisoned the Israelites in Babylon, was a conventional figure for the alienation caused by idolizing worldly wealth and power. In *Grace Abounding,* Bunyan mentions: "I should often also think on Nebuchanezzar, of whom it is said, *He had given him all the kingdoms of the earth* (Dan. 5:18, 19). Yet, thought I, if this great man had all his portion in this world, one hour in hell fire would make him forget all. Which consideration was a great help to me" (p. 21). A franker statement of Nietzschean *ressentiment* (ill feeling) would be hard to find.

72. (p. 114) *Christian for that time escaped them:* The implausible ease of Christian's escape reminds us to avoid the temptation of reading naturalistically. Bunyan felt he had "escaped" from prison with similar ease, albeit in a purely metaphorical sense.

73. (p. 116) *That is not my name, but indeed it is a nick-name that is given me by some that cannot abide me:* By-Ends makes the now familiar mistake of the bad characters; he fails to understand that he is an allegorical figure so that his name constitutes his essence. But some readers repeat his error. Samuel Taylor Coleridge, for instance, claimed that in *The Pilgrim's Progress* "we go on with his characters as real persons, who had been nicknamed by their neighbors" (*Biographia Literaria,* in *Collected Works,* edited

by Kathleen Coburn, Princeton, NJ: Princeton University Press, 1969–; vol. 7, 1987, p. 103).

74. (p. 117) *in the county of* Coveting, *in the north:* Sharrock finds here "the old joke about Scottish close-fistedness" (p. 395), but the "north" is associated with witchcraft and evil in European folklore, and the "king of the north" is an enemy of Israel in Daniel 11.

75. (p. 118) *cozenage:* The word means "fraud." Compare Bunyan's indictment of market economics in *The Life and Death of Mr. Badman* (1680): "If it be lawful for me to sell my commodity . . . as dear as I can, then there can be no sin in my trading, how unreasonably soever I manage my calling, whether by lying, swearing, cursing, cheating, for all this is but to sell my commodity as dear as I can" (p. 113).

76. (p. 118) *Let us be wise* as Serpents: Echoing Jesus' injunction to the disciples in Matthew 10:16—"Behold, I send you forth as sheep in the midst of wolves: be ye therefore wise as serpents, and harmless as doves"—but the phrase acquires a sinister connotation in the mouth of Hold-the-World.

77. (p. 119) *a good man* shall lay up Gold as Dust: Hold-the-World displays his literalism; the phrase from Job 22:24 ("Then shalt thou lay up gold as dust, and the gold of Ophir as the stones of the brooks") is of course meant figuratively. Greaves notes: "In the figure of Hold-the-World Bunyan satirized those . . . who sought an accord between the capitalist spirit and religion" (p. 255).

78. (p. 120) *his desire after that benefice makes him . . . a better man:* Moneylove's argument parallels that of the political economists. They argued that the pursuit of economic self-interest provided a motive to self-improvement that would benefit society as a whole. Their descendants make a similar case today.

79. (p. 123) *Silver-Mine:* This is both figural and literal; the precious metals from American mines had monetarized the European economy, producing such avaricious characters as By-Ends.

80. (p. 124) *son of* Abraham: But By-Ends does not specify whether he descends from Isaac (the son of the free woman, hence the gospel) or Ishmael (the son of the bondwoman, hence the law).

81. (p. 128) *here is the easiest going:* Offor cites Mason: "The transition into the by-path is easy, for it lies close to the right way; only you must get over a stile, that is, you must quit Christ's imputed righteousness, and trust in your own inherent righteousness; and then you are in By-path meadow directly" (*Works*, vol. 3, p. 138).

82. (p. 131) *walking up and down in his fields:* Owens find that this image "sug-

gests the power of the landowning gentry" (p. xxxvi), and James Turner points out: "The units of topographical space (heights and depths, lands, fields, hills, houses, and roads) are inseparable in Bunyan's imagination from the social means of their control, from lordships, tenure and sale, trespass actions and enclosure claims" (in Newey, ed., *The Pilgrim's Progress: Critical and Historical Views*, p. 97). Certainly Despair's ownership of the land is heavily stressed, but Bunyan also alludes to Satan's description of himself "going to and fro in the earth, and . . . walking up and down in it" (Job 1:7). And theologically, Bunyan is instructing us that self-righteousness leads to despair. As with Vanity Fair, there is no need to choose between these interpretations; Bunyan considered class oppression to be an earthly manifestation of Satan's power.

83. (p. 131) *a very dark Dungeon:* In Vanity Fair the pilgrims were publicly exhibited in a cage; here the misery of their imprisonment comes from their being kept hidden away.

84. (p. 132) *bitter Lamentations:* Greaves mentions: "Several critics have recognized that Bunyan's treatment of despair in the allegory goes beyond the typical puritan understanding and reflects mental illness" (p. 233).

85. (p. 132) *fits:* Despair is erratic. If we anachronistically apply our medical terminology to Bunyan it would seem, from this account and from the details he gives of his depression in *Grace Abounding*, that he was "bi-polar" or "manic depressive."

86. (p. 135) Promise: In *Grace Abounding*, Bunyan recalls that he was rescued from the depths of despair by the "promise" contained in John 6:37 ("And him that cometh to me I will in no wise cast out"): "I should in these days, often in my greatest agonies, even flounce towards the promise, as the horses do towards sound ground that yet stick in the mire" (p. 63). According to John R. Knott, "The suddenness with which Bunyan remembers . . . suggests the miraculous intervention of grace" (Keeble, ed., *John Bunyan: Conventicle and Parnassus*, p. 168). As in Vanity Fair, the ease with which Christian escapes also suggests the illusory nature of physical prisons.

87. (p. 135) *a pillar:* Offor cites Bunyan's *Of the House of the Forest of Lebanon* (1692): "The church in the wilderness . . . is full of pillars—apostles, prophets, and martyrs of Jesus. There are hung up also the shields that the old warriors used, and on the walls are painted the brave achievements they have done" (*Works*, vol. 3, p. 110).

88. (p. 137) *Safe for those for whom it is to be safe:* Stuart Sim finds a statement of predestination here: "There is an entire theological position encapsu-

lated in that line, one unmistakably based on the Calvinist doctrines of election and justification by faith, that is central to Bunyan's narrative practice" (in Laurence et al., eds., *John Bunyan and His England, 1628–88*, p. 149).

89. (p. 138) Hymeneus *and* Philetus: In 2 Timothy 2:17–18, Paul criticizes these figures for "saying that the resurrection is past already." The dead bodies show that this is a self-fulfilling prophecy.

90. (p. 140) *such as sell their Birth-right with* Esau: Esau sold his rights as Isaac's first-born to his brother Jacob for a "mess of pottage" in Genesis 25:30–34. The most fearful and persistent temptation faced by Bunyan in *Grace Abounding* is the desire to "sell" Christ (see Introduction). He eventually acquiesces, causing himself to be tortured by "the aforementioned scripture, concerning Esau's selling of his birthright," although he eventually concludes that his closest biblical counterpart is Judas.

91. (p. 140) *that Lie and dissemble, with* Ananias *and* Sapphira *his wife:* This is another instance of "selling" Christ for money. In Acts 5, this couple violates the early Christians' practice of communism: "But a certain man named Ananias, with Sapphira his wife, sold a possession, / And kept back part of the price, his wife also being privy to it, and brought a certain part, and laid it at the apostles' feet. / But Peter said, Ananias, why hath Satan filled thine heart to lie to the Holy Ghost, and to keep back part of the price of the land?"

92. (p. 141) *So I awoke from my Dream:* Keeble notes that this is "usually taken to signify Bunyan's release from prison and hence to imply the remainder of part one was written when he was at liberty" (p. 275). This is also Sharrock's conclusion, but he notes that "some critics have thought the break between the two dreams artistically justifiable on the grounds that Christian has decisively overcome his despair" (p. 396). Others, such as Greaves, suggest that Bunyan refers to a temporary release in 1669–1670, and that part one was completed following his re-incarceration.

93. (p. 141) *As other good people do:* As Vincent Newey comments, "The reader cannot but see something of himself in Ignorance" (Keeble, ed., *John Bunyan: Conventicle and Parnassus*, p. 213).

94. (p. 142) *be content to follow the Religion of your country, and I will follow the Religion of mine:* Hill points out that "Bunyan contributed nothing to the theory of toleration" (*A Tinker and a Poor Man*, p. 340). In *Grace Abounding* he ascribes to "the tempter" the thought "that the Turks had as good scriptures to prove their Mahomet the Saviour, as we have to prove our Jesus is. . . . Every one doth think his own religion rightest, both Jews, and

Moors, and Pagans; and how if all our faith, and Christ, and Scriptures, should be but a think-so too?" (p. 27).

95. (p. 143) *for he was loth to lose his Money:* Luxon notes: "Had he not been 'loth to lose his Money,' that is to say, were he unconcerned about the things of this world, the thieves would be no threat; they would not even exist" (p. 193).

96. (p. 144) *his Jewels . . . his spending-money:* Offor cites Mason: "By his jewels, we may understand those radical graces of the Spirit—faith, hope, and love. By his spending-money, the sealing and earnest of the Spirit in his heart" (*Works*, vol. 3, p. 147). Later, he cites Bunyan's *Grace Abounding*: "Now I could look from myself to [Christ], and should reckon that all those graces of God that now were green in me, were yet but like those cracked groats and four pence-halfpennies, that rich men carry in their purses, when their GOLD is in their trunks at home. Oh! I saw that my gold was in my trunk at home, in Christ my Lord and Saviour" (*Works*, vol. 3, p. 148). Keeble believes that "the stolen money represents his assurance of election" (p. 275). Given Bunyan's association of money with the law, however, it seems more likely that Little-faith's "money" represents his "works" and that his "jewels" stand for his faith. Money is a mere sign representing an arbitrary and irrational, merely human form of value, whereas jewels are naturally valuable because of their inherent qualities.

97. (p. 146) *themselves outright to boot:* To be carnal was to alienate, or "sell," one's self. In Romans 7:14, Paul declares, "I am carnal, sold under sin." A slave is legally an object, and carnality was a form of slavery, as Paul's allegory of the bondwoman indicates (see Introduction).

98. (p. 148) *some do say of him:* The qualification indicates that Bunyan favored Paul for this role. Like Luther, he agreed with Paul's insistence, over Peter's opposition, that Christians need not follow the Judaic law.

99. (p. 150) *Leviathan:* This sea monster is mentioned at several points in the Bible. It symbolizes Satan in Isaiah 27:1: "In that day the Lord with his sore and great and strong sword shall punish leviathan the piercing serpent, even leviathan that crooked serpent; and he shall slay the dragon that is in the sea." Political theorist Thomas Hobbes used it as a symbol of state power in his *Leviathan* (1642).

100. (p. 150) *since the Lion and the Bear have not as yet devoured me, I hope God will also deliver us from the next uncircumcised* Philistine: David says this of Goliath in 1 Samuel 17:36: "Thy servant slew both the lion and the bear: and this uncircumcised Philistine shall be as one of them, seeing he hath defied the armies of the living God."

101. (p. 150) *a man black of Flesh, but covered with a very light Robe:* Here Bunyan describes the Lutheran "white devil" of self-righteousness, though
Sharrock finds a more composite figure: "It looks as if the idea of false pastors with winning words has been combined with the notion of the devil
as a flatterer, and popular superstition believed that the devil appeared as
a black man" (p. 396).

102. (p. 155) *the Good of my Soul:* Kaufmann accurately calls the following account of Hopeful's conversion "*Grace Abounding* in miniature" (*The Pilgrim's Progress and Traditions in Puritan Meditation*, p. 228).

103. (p. 157) *Debt:* The metaphor of sin as debt was very common; Christ redeemed our debt, while Satan would exact interest on it. This figure was al-
luded to constantly during debates over the ethical status of usury.

104. (p. 161) He is Mediator between God and us: See Galatians 3:19–20:
"Wherefore then serveth the law? It was added because of transgressions,
till the seed should come to whom the promise was made; and it was ordained of angels in the hand of a mediator. Now a mediator is not a mediator of one, but God is one."

105. (p. 161) *This was a Revelation of Christ to your soul indeed; But tell me particularly what effect this had upon your spirit?:* Offor cites Scott: "Christ did
not appear to Hopeful's senses, but to his understanding; and the words
spoken are no other than texts of Scripture taken in their genuine meaning" (*Works*, vol. 3, p. 156).

106. (p. 165) *Thus Faith maketh not Christ a justifier of thy person, but of thy actions:* The Quakers actually espouse the idea of work's righteousness,
though they are ignorant of this. Compare Bunyan's *The Strait Gate* (1676):
"The poor ignorant world miss of heaven . . . because they lean upon their
own good meanings, and thinkings, and doings" (*Works*, vol. 1, p. 384).

107. (p. 166) *This conceit would loosen the reins of our Lust:* Keeble observes: "Ignorance cogently points to antinomianism, the complete separation of the
moral life from the scheme of salvation, as the apparent consequence of
Calvinism's stress on the imputation of Christ's righteousness to the pre-
determined elect" (p. 276). In *Grace Abounding*, Bunyan recalls that in his
youth he "let loose the reins to my lust" (p. 8).

108. (p. 172) *Beulah:* The word "Beulah" means, literally, "married," used in Isaiah 62:4 to describe the union of God with His people: "Neither shall thy
land any more be termed Desolate: but thou shalt be called Hephzibah,
and thy land Beulah: for the Lord delighteth in thee, and thy land shall be
married." According to Greaves, this land "represents psychological well-
being and spiritual contentment" (p. 240).

109. (p. 174) *there met them two Men:* Offor (*Works*, vol. 3, p. 162) notes the specifically human nature of these beings. He suggests that these may be "glorified inhabitants of the Celestial City," and observes that John is addressed from heaven by a "fellowservant" (Revelation 22:9).

110. (p. 180) *then the Pilgrims gave in unto them each man his Certificate:* The certificate is usually held to refer to their election, though Davies disagrees: "The 'Certificate' Christian and Hopeful tender at the Celestial Gate is not of their election . . . but of their faith in the efficacy of salvation by grace alone" (p. 238). Of course, the elect would enjoy such a faith in any case, but the distinction is not unimportant; it is the difference between Calvinist and Lutheran theology.

111. (p. 181) *he fumbled in his bosom for one, and found none:* Either he was not one of the predestined elect, or he did not grasp the doctrine of justification by faith alone. Luxon believes that Ignorance "is damned precisely because he never believed sufficiently in the invisible things. . . . Like the Jew of Protestant typology he lived and breathed in the unreal world of temporal things, always mistaking them for the invisible reality of the promises. He is the personification of the true pilgrims' fleshly existence" (p. 181).

Part Two

1. (p. 187) *Christiana:* While the fact of her gender is certainly significant, Christiana's primary role is to symbolize the church (see Introduction). Kaufmann argues: "While in the first part Bunyan is concerned to disturb the comfortable, ensuring a close examination of the reader's own calling, in the second part his concern is plainly to comfort the disturbed" (in Keeble, ed., *John Bunyan: Conventicle and Parnassus*, p. 178).

2. (p. 187) *his Wife and Children are:* The first part of *The Pilgrim's Progress* had been a huge popular success, appearing in three editions during its first year. See Bunyan's *Christian Behaviour* (1663): "One of God's ends in instituting marriage is that, under such a figure, Christ and His church should be set forth" (*Works*, vol. 3, p. 558).

3. (p. 190) *above their Gold:* See *Grace Abounding:* "Thus I continued for a time all on a flame to be converted to Jesus Christ, and did also see at that day such glory in a converted state, that I could not be contented without a share therein. Gold! Could it have been gotten for gold, what could I have given for it! Had I a whole world, it had all gone ten thousand times over, for this, that my soul might have been in a converted state" (p. 22).

4. (p. 190) *stripling:* Youth. See *The Heavenly Footman* (1692): "You that are old professors, take you heed that the young striplings of Jesus, that began to strip but the other day, do not outrun you" (*Works*, vol. 3, p. 393).

5. (p. 192) Besides, what my first Pilgrim left conceal'd . . . Sweet *Christiana* opens with her Key: According to Offor: "After the author had heard the criticisms of friends and foes upon the First Part, he adopts this second narrative to be a key explaining many things which appeared dark in Christian's journey" (*Works*, vol. 3, p. 170).

6. (p. 198) *unbecoming behaviour towards her husband:* Davies observes: "The burden Christiana bears at the beginning of *Part II* teeters dangerously upon the brink of not being guilt over sin at all: it seems to be a more specifically gendered anxiety over being an unworthy spouse" (p. 337).

7. (pp. 198–199) *rent the caul of her heart:* See Hosea 13:8: "I . . . will rend the caul of their heart." Owens notes: "A caul is any membrane enclosing organs of the body, in particular the heart, and the fetus before birth" (p. 310). In the Bible, the term is most frequently used in relation to the liver.

8. (p. 200) *Secret:* Offor cites Scott "The intimations of Secret represent the teachings of the Holy Spirit, by which the sinner understands the real meaning of the Sacred Scriptures as to the way of salvation" (*Works*, vol. 3, p. 174). According to Keeble, "The character represents divine knowledge of, and concern about, men's innermost longings and anxieties, and underlines the essentially private nature of the saints' experience of grace as they are let into the secret of God's mercy" (p. 278). More generally, it reminds us of the imperative to search out the hidden meanings behind appearances.

9. (p. 206) *Madam* Wanton's: Here it is made more clear than in part one that she is the "madam" of a brothel. This figure stands for the sin of "concupiscence"—that is, fleshly lust pursued as an end in itself, rather than as a means to the end of spiritual love—which was closely connected with covetousness in the puritan imagination. "Wanton" means "wayward," especially in the sexual sense; a modern cognate would be "horny." Compare John Milton's hymn "On the Morning of Christ's Nativity" (1629), where the term is applied to "Nature:" "It was no season then for her / To wanton with the sun, her lusty paramour" (lines 35–36).

10. (p. 206) *for all the gold in the* Spanish *Mines:* The flood of gold from America had monetarized the European economy during the past two centuries, destroying traditional values and enhancing the alienation of human beings from God's creation.

11. (p. 207) *all things in common:* Mercy's servitude to Christiana does not in-

volve any diminution of her status; like the early Christians, Bunyan's pilgrims practice communism.

12. (p. 207) *her own Salvation:* "Her own" can refer to either Mercy or Christiana; Mercy achieves her salvation through empathy with Christiana's. Keeble comments: "[Mercy's] affection for Christiana is given precedency. Friendship between women can no less serve as a means of grace than the love for a husband which draws Christiana" (in Laurence et al., eds., pp. 135–136).

13. (p. 208) *worse than formerly:* According to Sharrock, "There is implied satire here on the strict Baptists of London, with whom Bunyan had conducted a controversy in 1672–3. It is suggested that their strict conditions for church membership would have driven believers away" (p. 401). But the deterioration of the slough may also reflect a more general degeneration in society.

14. (p. 209) *Mr.* Sagacity: Keeble calls Mr. Sagacity a "false start. Bunyan soon realizes he is redundant, and Mr. Sagacity leaves him 'to Dream out my Dream by myself.' This gets rid of Mr. Sagacity, but it is . . . inconsistent: since Bunyan's dream hitherto has not been of Christiana and her family but of Mr. Sagacity telling him about them, Mr. Sagacity *is* his dream" (p. 278). For Davies, however, the narrational shift from Mr. Sagacity to the dreamer is more artful and indicates the importance of the wicket gate, through which Christiana is about to pass. It might also suggest the dreamer's growing comprehension of the story's significance, so that he no longer needs a guide. Perhaps we are to understand that human wisdom is unnecessary once the pilgrims have begun to view the world in allegorical terms.

15. (p. 211) *I am come for* that *unto which I was never invited, as my friend* Christiana *was:* Keeble comments: "Bunyan's point is that, although Mercy fears she has not, like Christiana, received a call, her coming itself witnesses to a vocation whether or no she be conscious of spiritual regeneration" (p. 279). Sharrock observes: "Mercy has not received a definite call like Christiana; she goes on pilgrimage out of friendship to the latter: she is to be saved not by her deeds, but by displaying a truly Christian sensibility. Her character illustrates how much more subtle Bunyan's understanding of grace had become since he wrote the first part, which is confined to the dramatic either/or aspect of religious conversion" (p. 400).

16. (p. 217) *being ye knew that ye were but weak women:* Sharrock notes in another context that Bunyan means to commend women in part two, not to criticize them: "Women played an important role in the Bedford church; in the first list of members they were in a considerable majority, and in

1683 there was a demand for separate prayer-meetings for women, which was rejected: Bunyan may have felt that recognition of the female contribution was required to offset this rebuff" (p. 405).

17. (p. 221) *no way but downwards:* Compare John Milton's depiction of Mammon (money) in *Paradise Lost* (1667): "Even in heaven his looks and thoughts / Were always downward bent; admiring more / The riches of heaven's pavement, trodden gold, / Than aught divine or holy else enjoyed / In vision beatific" (book 1, lines 679–683).

18. (p. 222) *a very great Spider:* See Proverbs 30:28: "The spider taketh hold with her hands, and is in kings' palaces." In the *A Book for Boys and Girls; or, Temporal Things Spritualized* (1686; later titled *Divine Emblems; or, Temporal Things Spiritualized*), which has verses attached to its pictures, Bunyan guides the reader through the same process of interpretation that Mercy and Christiana are about to follow. The spider tells the sinner: "Since I an ugly ven'mous creature be, / There is some semblance 'twixt vile man and me" (*Works*, vol. 3, p. 753). Davies explains: "The emblem, the women's preliminary misunderstanding of it, and the subsequent revelation of its "true" meaning enact in miniature the overall conversion movement from ignorance, fear, and sinful self-reproach to faith and a forgiving acceptance that Bunyan's theology consistently promotes" (p. 331).

19. (p. 228) *thou are a* Ruth: The biblical book of Ruth describes how she, a Moabite, left her native land to live with her Israelite husband, out of regard for her mother-in-law, Naomi, as Mercy has gone on pilgrimage out of love for Christiana.

20. (p. 229) *Bath:* This is a reference to baptism by total immersion. Sharrock notes: "There is no treatment of baptism in the first part and Bunyan may have been under pressure from fellow Baptists; his own Bedford church was Open Communion and practiced adult baptism not as a necessary condition but as an optional sign of church membership" (p. 402).

21. (p. 230) Great-heart: Greaves explains that Great-heart "is Bunyan the minister, and by extension every committed dissenting pastor. Great-heart is not a role model for believers, or even male ones, but for ministers of gathered churches, and his function in the allegory is to underscore the importance of looking to such men for spiritual leadership" (p. 501).

22. (p. 237) *let them hang:* John R. Knott observes: "Mercy's uncharitable sentiments seem surprising, even unintentionally ironic, to a modern reader, but they reflect an uncompromising attitude toward unregenerate sinners and temptations to sin that runs through *The Pilgrim's Progress*" (in Gay et al., eds., *Awakening Words*, p. 52). But the apparent cruelty of Mercy's state-

ments evaporates if we read the executed figures as allegorical depictions of qualities within her own mind, rather than taking them literally, as referring to independent characters.

23. (p. 237) *be a Sign:* This emphasizes Mercy's burgeoning comprehension of the allegorical nature of the world. As Bunyan predicted in the part two's preparatory verse, this volume instructs the reader about how to read part one.

24. (p. 239) *James:* The boys are not given allegorical titles, but realistic, biblical names. This is the beginning of the process whereby various characters shed the constraints of their allegorical definitions as they approach the holy city.

25. (p. 241) *Lions:* Sharrock notes: "The lions which were asleep when Faithful passed are now awake: this reflects the renewed period of persecution in 1681–4" (p. 403). Whereas in part one the two lions stood for the civil and ecclesiastical powers, here they represent the latter only.

26. (p. 241) *Now the name of that man was* Grim, *(or* Bloody-Man*):* According to Keeble, "the civil authority responsible for the persecution of nonconformists with renewed vigor during the 'Tory Revenge' of the early 1680s following the defeat of the Whigs in the Exclusion Crisis."

27. (p. 242) *downright:* Here the word means "forceful." John Knott observes of Great-heart's various combats: "The violence and bloodiness of the victories . . . suggest a delight in prospect of vengeance for the oppression of the true church" (Gay et al., eds., p. 58).

28. (p. 242) *Now the Lions were chained, and so of themselves could do nothing:* The Anglican Church is powerless against dissenters unless backed by the power of the state. Note that, if Grim represents the state, Great-heart's slaughter of him comes close to advocating political revolution.

29. (p. 243) *such poor women:* Opinions differ about the pilgrims' need for a guide in part two. Aileen Ross claims: "Once Christiana's authority has been handed over to the male characters, notably Mr. Great-heart, and the women made thoroughly aware of their weak status, any adventure becomes a male prerogative" (in Gay et al., eds., p. 162). However, Melissa D. Aaron finds that Bunyan "postulates an alternative Puritan society in the second part. . . . He creates an extended family structure where 'the last shall be first.' Humility becomes the critical value, and the model for humility is female" (Gay et al., eds., p. 169).

30. (p. 251) *cried her down at the Cross:* As Owens notes: "This refers to the practice in the seventeenth century by which a man could take his wife to the local market cross (sometimes leading her by a symbolic halter) and

sell her to the highest bidder" (p. 314). The practice continued well into the nineteenth century; it is described in Thomas Hardy's *The Mayor of Casterbridge* (1886).

31. (p. 253) *pills:* Compare Bunyan's *Seasonable Counsel* (1684): "Alas! we have need of those bitter pills, at which we so wince and shuck: and it will be well if at last we be purged as we should thereby" (*Works*, vol. 2, p. 693).

32. (p. 256) *Learn to remember* Peter's *Sin:* That is, when he denied knowing Jesus three times before cock-crow. Bunyan is fond of this example, and generally ambivalent about Saint Peter, who opposed Saint Paul and who reputedly became the first pope.

33. (p. 265) *such a shape:* Compare John Milton describing Death in *Paradise Lost* (1667): "The other shape, / If shape it might be called that shape had none" (book 2, lines 666–667). The line number is clearly significant, for in the biblical book of Revelation, 666 is the "number of the beast [Antichrist]."

34. (p. 266) *something 'most like a Lion:* Both "almost like a lion" and "resembling a lion more closely than anything else." See 1 Peter 5:8: "Be sober, be vigilant; because your adversary the devil, as a roaring lion, walketh about, seeking whom he may devour."

35. (p. 268) Maul *a giant:* According to Sharrock: "The Roman Catholic Church. The reference to his spoiling the pilgrims with sophistry suggests the activity of the Jesuits, that to 'my master's kingdom' raises the question of the foreign allegiance of Catholics, a common charge in the age of the Popish Plot" (p. 404). Greaves concurs: "The linkage between Giants Pope and Maul effectively associates the repressive policies of the Tory-Anglicans with Catholicism" (p. 512). But Owens disagrees: "The charge of sophistry was certainly leveled at the Jesuits, but there is little else to suggest that Bunyan had a specific reference in mind. It seems just as likely that Maul (a maul being a heavy hammer) represents a more general enemy of pilgrims. In *The Jerusalem Sinner Saved* (1688), the temptation to doubt one's salvation is described as Satan's 'Maul, his Club, his Master-piece'" (p. 316).

36. (p. 277) *pipe:* Sing happily. William Blake, who loved Bunyan and illustrated *The Pilgrim's Progress*, may have had this line in mind in his "Introduction" to the *Songs of Innocence* (1789): "'Pipe a song about a lamb!' / So I piped with merry chear. / 'Piper, pipe that song again.' / So I piped: he wept to hear" (lines 5–8).

37. (p. 280) *but he would always be like himself,* self-willed: Honest stresses the propriety of the name. Compare Bunyan's *The Life and Death of Mr. Bad-*

man (1680), in which the title character is theoretically capable of acting honestly, but "had he done so, he had not done like himself, like Mr. *Bad-man*" (p. 89, emphasis in original).

38. (p. 284) *Whose wife is this aged matron?:* Christiana has not been so de-scribed before; we gather that she has aged during the journey, as we later find that her sons have grown to manhood. This is another example of the increased naturalism in part two.

39. (pp. 284–285) Paul *and* Peter: In Paul's epistle to the Galatians, and in Luther's *Commentary on Galatians*, the quarrel between Peter and Paul embodies the conflict between works and faith. Paul was Bunyan's biblical model, but here he reconciles the two apostles in their shared martyrdom.

40. (p. 285) *There was* Ignatius, *who was cast to the Lions:* Romanus, *whose flesh was cut by pieces from his bones; and* Polycarp, *that played the man in the fire:* The deaths of the early Christians Ignatius, Romanus, and Polycarp were familiar to Bunyan from Foxe's *Acts and Monuments* (1563). Keeble notes that they are "the only non-biblical historical figures mentioned in *PP*" (p. 282).

41. (p. 286) *first a* heave-shoulder, *and a* wave-breast *were set on the table be-fore them:* Leviticus 10:14: "And the wave breast and heave shoulder shall ye eat in a clean place; thou, and thy sons, and thy daughters with thee." Bunyan does not refer to the literal ceremonial of the Jewish law, but to their spiritual antitypes. The heave-shoulder and the wave-breast are parts of the sacrificial animal.

42. (pp. 290–291) that the Saviour is said to come out of a dry ground, and also that he had no Form nor Comeliness in him: Isaiah 53 contains a series of prophecies concerning the advent of Christ, as in 53:2: "For he shall grow up before him as a tender plant, and as a root out of a dry ground: he hath no form nor comeliness; and when we shall see him, there is no beauty that we should desire him."

43. (p. 291) *Because the Church of the* Jews . . . *had then lost almost all the sap, and Spirit of religion:* Compare George Herbert's "The Jews" (1633): "Poore nation, whose sweet sap, and juice / Our cyens have purloin'd, and left you dry" (lines 1–2).

44. (p. 298) *plead for:* Here the phrase means "rationalize." The Latitudinari-ans argued that their lack of principle was itself a principle. Compare Bun-yan's description of Edward Fowler as "a glorious latitudinarian, that can, as to religion, turn and twist like an eel on the angle; or rather like the weather-cock that stands on the steeple" (*Works*, vol. 2, p. 281).

45. (p. 300) *They are much more moderate now than formerly:* Sharrock notes:

"Presumably since the Declaration of Indulgence to Nonconformists in 1672; this statement does not allow for the recurrence of persecution in the last years of Charles II's reign and may therefore have been written before that period" (p. 406).

46. (p. 302) *a great while:* Their behavior is in striking contrast to Christian's in part one. As Melissa D. Aaron claims, "These new pilgrims, consisting of women, children, and feeble men, are able to live in Vanity Fair for years without being tainted by it in any way. They have in effect set up a new society" (in Gay et al., eds., p. 177).

47. (p. 305) *Also there was here One . . . and that could gently lead those that were with young:* Isaiah 40:11: "He shall feed his flock like a shepherd: he shall gather the lambs with his arm, and carry them in his bosom, and shall gently lead those that are with young."

48. (p. 306) *demolish his Castle:* Keeble comments: "The allegory appears unsound at this point. . . . It is difficult to understand how [Great-heart] could ensure other believers should not be subject to the temptation to despair" (p. 283). But perhaps the fact that the pilgrims are able to demolish Doubting Castle suggests the imminence of Apocalypse, and even hints at social revolution.

49. (p. 311) *These . . . we call in by name . . . but as for you, and the rest that are strong, we leave you to your wonted liberty:* At this stage, the weaker characters must still be identified by their allegorical names, to remind them of their alienated status and prevent them from retreating. The stronger pilgrims, however, are now ready to enjoy "liberty" from their allegorical confinements.

50. (p. 312) *The first was Mount-Marvel, where they looked, and behold a man at a distance,* that tumbled the hills about with words: Mark 11:23: "For verily I say unto you, That whosoever shall say unto this mountain, Be thou removed, and be thou cast into the sea; and shall not doubt in his heart, but shall believe that those things which he saith shall come to pass; he shall have whatsoever he saith." The mountain is an emblem of faith, and as Keeble notes, the tumbling man is "a literal presentation of the test from Mark cited in the margin" (p. 283). As so often in Bunyan, a biblical text becomes a physical force.

51. (p. 313) *one* Fool, *and one* Want-wit, *washing of an* Ethiopian: The impossibility of washing an Ethiopian white was proverbial. The specific reference here is to Moses' Ethiopian wife. In *A Book for Boys and Girls* (1686), Bunyan explains: "Moses was a type of Moses' law, / His wife likewise of one that never saw / Another way unto eternal life" (*Works*, vol. 3, p. 757).

52. (p. 313) *Thus it was with the* Pharisees: Compare Bunyan's *The Pharisee and the Publican* (1685): "The Pharisee goes on boldly, fears nothing, but trusteth in himself that his state is good; he hath his mouth full of many fine things, whereby he strokes himself over the head, and calls himself one of God's white boys" (*Works*, vol. 3, p. 215).

53. (p. 314) *Looking-Glass:* Mercy is referring to the Word of God. Compare *A Book for Boys and Girls* (1686): "Unto this glass we may compare the Word, / For that to man advantage doth afford / (Has he a mind to know himself and state), / To see what will be his eternal fate" (*Works*, vol. 3, p. 759).

54. (p. 316) *I am one whose name is* Valiant-for-truth: He represents the church militant, the practical, political power of the godly. He is the last significant pilgrim to enter the narrative, because the earthly rule of the saints presages the Day of Judgment. For the same reason, George Herbert makes "The Church Militant" the final poem in *The Temple* (1633).

55. (p. 320) *They said, it was an idle life:* This seems to argue against Max Weber's thesis that "the Protestant ethic" was considered conducive to industry in the accumulation of worldly goods. Valiant-for-truth's parents assume he is choosing a life of idleness and poverty.

56. (p. 328) *and that perhaps the witch knew:* Witchcraft was very common in seventeenth-century England, and Bunyan himself was accused of this crime. It involved the magical manipulation of signs to practical effects, and it was widely believed to be carried out in alliance with the devil. Here, the workings of the market economy are equated with the efficacious rituals of witchcraft.

57. (p. 328) *Madame* Bubble: This woman is a conventional figure for the world, suggesting ephemerality. In *Some Gospel Truths Opened* (1656), Bunyan cites Luke 12:20 and Proverbs 7:7 as referring to "the world, held forth by the similitude of a woman with the attire of a harlot" (*Works*, vol. 2, p. 165).

58. (p. 330) *'Twas she that set* Absalom *against his Father, and* Jeroboam *against his Master:* In the Old Testament, Absalom rebelled against his father, King David, and Jeroboam turned away from God to idolatry, for reasons of worldly ambition. In the New Testament, Judas betrayed Jesus, and Demas abandoned Paul, out of similar motives. The former are types of the latter, who are in turn types of Madame Bubble, who is herself an emblem of the market.

59. (p. 332) *he gave her therewith a true token:* In addition to their summonses, each pilgrim receives a "token" of its authenticity. Except for Christiana's,

these are texts from the biblical book of Ecclesiastes, the main message of which is the "vanity" of earthly life.

60. (p. 336) *So he gave him the* grasshopper: Ecclesiastes 12:5: "Also when they shall be afraid of that which is high, and fears shall be in the way, and the almond tree shall flourish, and the grasshopper shall be a burden, and desire shall fail: because man goeth to his long home, and the mourners go about the streets."

Inspired by The Pilgrim's Progress

Literature

For centuries second only to the Bible in popularity, *The Pilgrim's Progress from This World to That Which Is to Come* (1678) is one of the most influential books in the English language. In its own day, Bunyan's allegory inspired numerous imitations and adaptations. Six years after its release, Bunyan published his own sequel, *The Pilgrim's Progress: The Second Part* (1684), which relates the attempt of Christian's wife and sons to reunite with him. In this second volume Bunyan eases the ardent psychological and spiritual investigation of *The Pilgrim's Progress* in favor of increased realism and comedy. As in this edition, both parts of *The Pilgrim's Progress* are commonly combined to represent Bunyan's full work.

Two years before the second installment of Bunyan's tale appeared, a spurious sequel made its way into public view: Thomas Sherman's *The Second Part of the Pilgrim's Progress* (1682). The first verse adaptation of *The Pilgrim's Progress* appeared soon afterward, at the hand of "S. M.," under the title *The Heavenly Passenger* (1687). Another versification, by Ager Scholae, appeared ten years later, the second of many that would appear over the centuries. Not all the imitations were loving tributes. In the eighteenth century, English poet and dramatist John Gay, primarily known for *The Beggar's Opera* (1728) penned *The What D'Ye Call It: A Tragi-Comi-Pastoral Farce* (1715)—a title reflecting Shakespeare's *Hamlet*, specifically Polonius's description of the actor's wide-ranging set of skills: "The best actors in the world, either for tragedy, comedy, history, pastoral, pastoral-comical, historical-pastoral, tragical-historical, tragical-comical-historical-pastoral . . ." (act 2, scene 2). *The What D'Ye Call It* includes an irreverent parody of Bunyan's allegory in which a condemned man comically blubbers over the title page of the eighth edition of *The Pilgrim's Progress*. The following is from the opening scene in the second act of Gay's farce:

[A condemned man is offered a prayer book and, urged to make use of it, he cries out:]

> I will! I will!
> Lend me thy handkercher. '*The pilgrim's pro—*' [reads and weeps]
> (I cannot see for tears) '*pro-progress*': Oh!
> '*The Pilgrim's Progress, eight edi-ti-on:*
> *Lon-don print-ed–for–Ni-cho-las Bod-ding-ton:*
> *With new ad-di-tions never made before*':
> —Oh! 'tis so moving, I can read no more.
> [drops the book]

Almost fifty years later, John Mitchell published yet another imitation of Bunyan's work called *The Female Pilgrim: or, the Travels of Hephzibah, under the Similitude of a Dream* (1762).

Early novelists were influenced by Bunyan's allegory. In the first pages of Laurence Sterne's *The Life and Opinions of Tristram Shandy, Gentleman* (1759–1767), the narrator, in the process of predicting his own widespread fame, succinctly summarizes the popularity of Bunyan's work. He writes: "As my life and opinions are likely to make some noise in the world, and, if I conjecture right, will take in all ranks, professions, and denominations of men whatever,—be no less read than the *Pilgrim's Progress* itself—and in the end, prove the very thing which Montaigne dreaded his Essays should turn out, that is, a book for a parlour-window—I find it necessary to consult every one a little in his turn."

One of England's most eminent eighteenth-century poets, William Cowper, who, among other things, translated Homer's *Iliad* into English blank verse, deeply admired Bunyan's allegory. As a young student at private school, Cowper suffered at the hands of bullies, a daily torment to which he gave vent in his poem *Tirocinium, or, a Review of Schools* (1784). A vehement satire, *Tirocinium* also includes an appreciation of *The Pilgrim's Progress*:

> O thou, whom, borne on Fancy's eager wing,
> Back to the season of life's happy spring,
> I pleased remember, and, while Memory yet
> Holds fast her office here, can ne'er forget;
> Ingenious dreamer, in whose well-told tale

> Sweet fiction and sweet truth alike prevail;
> Whose humorous vein, strong sense, and simple style
> May teach the gayest, make the gravest smile;
> Witty, and well employ'd, and, like thy Lord,
> Speaking in parables his slighted Word;
> I name thee not, lest so despised a name
> Should move a sneer at thy deserved fame;
> Yet e'en in transitory life's late day,
> That mingles all my brown with sober gray,
> Revere the man whose Pilgrim marks the road,
> And guides the Progress of the soul to God.

In 1830 Robert Southey's comprehensive biography of Bunyan generated major interest in the writer and his works. One of the period's most popular writers, Charles Dickens, was greatly affected by having read Bunyan in his youth. He subtitled his novel *Oliver Twist* (1838) "The Parish Boy's Progress." Attempting to demonstrate the notion that poverty leads to crime, the novel depicts the orphan Oliver's travails in the London underworld, where he encounters a gallery of characters who serve as allegories for various vices. Nell, the main character of Dickens's *The Old Curiosity Shop* (1841), takes a journey toward the afterlife that is specifically modeled on that of Christian.

For the title of his renowned satire of society and manners, Dickens's rival William Makepeace Thackeray borrowed the name "Vanity Fair" from *The Pilgrim's Progress*. Serialized monthly between January 1847 and July 1848, Thackeray's *Vanity Fair: A Novel without a Hero* chronicles the witty and upwardly mobile Becky Sharp and her friend, the unworldly Amelia Sedley. Bunyan's "Vanity Fair" is an ancient, year-round carnival on the outskirts of the town of Vanity Fair that attempts to lure men away from Heaven. In Thackeray's work, Vanity Fair is society itself, along with all its attending frivolities, venal feuds, and a notable lack of heroism of any kind—in the end, one colossal distraction.

Among Americans, writer Nathaniel Hawthorne was deeply influenced by Bunyan. His short story "The Celestial Railroad" (1843) is a satirical allegory criticizing those who call themselves as Christians but ignore the duty and hard work required by biblical Christianity. Accompanied by Mr. Smooth-it-away, the narrator of the story takes the same path as Christian from the City of Destruction to the Celestial City. The narrator discovers, though, that he need not travel by foot: He can take the Celestial Railroad instead. At the end of the story, Mr. Smooth-it-away and the so-called Celestial City are revealed to be evil in disguise—the narrator's just dessert for circumventing the route of Bunyan's Christian. Indeed, *The Pilgrim's Progress* pervades Hawthorne's entire oeuvre. The characters in his best-known work, *The Scarlet Letter* (1850), have strong allegorical traits, drawn in a technique suggestive of Bunyan. Hawthorne's *The Blithedale Romance* (1852), based on the author's experience with the failed utopian community Brook Farm, evokes Bunyan directly. The narrator calls the founder of the fictional Blithedale "an exemplification of the most awful truth in Bunyan's book of such, from the very gate of heaven there is a by-way to the pit!"

Louisa May Alcott's *Little Women* (1868) makes abundant use of *The Pilgrim's Progress* in terms of structure and content. The preface, which adapts the apology that introduces the second part of *The Pilgrim's Progress*, bids: "Go then, my little Book, and show to all / That entertain and bid thee welcome shall, / What thou dost keep close shut up in thy breast." The first chapter, "Playing Pilgrims," has the mother of the four March girls ask, "Do you remember how you used to play Pilgrim's Progress when you were little things? Nothing delighted you more than to have me tie my piece bags on your backs for burdens, give you hats and sticks and rolls of paper, and let you travel through the house from the cellar, which was the City of Destruction, up, up, to the housetop, where you had all the lovely things you could collect to make a Celestial City." Several chapters in *Little Women* reflect person and place names in Bunyan's allegory—"Beth Finds the Palace Beautiful," "Amy's Valley of Humiliation," "Jo Meets Apollyon," "Meg Goes to Vanity Fair," and "The Valley of the Shadow." Following a modest early career in writing, Alcott hoped to obtain as large an audience as possible for *Little Women*, which she wrote at the commission of her publisher. It is no coincidence, then, that she chose *The Pilgrim's Progress* as the model for her work: Alcott's own lifetime coincided with the period of Bunyan's greatest popularity in America. Like *The Pilgrim's Progress* and many other works associated with it, *Little Women* was enormously popular upon its initial publication and continues to be read widely.

Alcott's philosophical opposite, the humorist Mark Twain, peppers several of his works with references to *The Pilgrim's Progress*. Most notably, Twain's travelogue *The Innocents Abroad; or, the New Pilgrim's Progress* (1869) likens the author's steamship journey through Europe, Egypt, and Palestine to Christian's search for Heaven. The publication of *The Innocents Abroad*, which employs history, statistics, irascible argument, and inimitable wit to lambaste tourists too dependent upon their guidebooks, heralded Twain's most productive, mature, and popular period. In Twain's masterpiece *Adventures of Huckleberry Finn* (1884), the eponymous character describes the contents of a library, remembering, "There was some books too, piled up perfectly exact, on each corner of the table. One was a big family Bible, full of pictures. One was 'Pilgrim's Progress,' about a man that left his family it didn't say why. I read considerable in it now and then. The statements was interesting, but tough."

Stage adaptations of *The Pilgrim's Progress* appeared in 1894 and 1920; the 1920 version, *The Play of Pilgrim's Progress*, based on the first part of Bunyan's allegory, was written by C. R. Haines. Playwright George Bernard Shaw reviewed the 1894 play by G. G. Collingham. He opens the review, entitled "Better than Shakespeare," by remarking, "When I saw a stage version of 'The Pilgrim's Progress' announced for production, I shook my head, knowing that Bunyan is far too great a dramatist for our theater." Commenting remarkably little on the actual play, Shaw does not miss the opportunity to take a jab at one of his favorite targets, William Shakespeare. He writes, "All that you miss in Shakespeare you find in Bunyan, to whom the true heroic came obviously and naturally. The world was to him a more terrible place than it was to Shakespeare."

The Pilgrim's Progress remained relevant to many twentieth-century readers. E. M. Forster's short story "The Celestial Omnibus" (1911) is a spirited and fantastic defense of literature. A young English boy, pure of heart, notices a sign near his home that points into an alley and reads, "To Heaven." His parents tell him the sign was a prank played by a derelict named Shelley, an allusion to atheist Romantic poet Percy Bysshe Shelley. The boy enters the alley and catches the Celestial Omnibus, which takes him to a magical world inhabited by the characters in Dickens and Homer, where, as Keats writes, he "visit[s] dolphin deep in coral seas." Astounded, the boy invites an older neighbor to visit with him; the neighbor, who pretends to love literature, is a philistine at heart. The city rejects the man, and he falls through the clouds to his death.

During World War I, *The Pilgrim's Progress* was important to many Britons who desperately needed hope in the face of disaster. Rudyard Kipling's poem "The Holy War" (1917) praises Bunyan for the spiritual guidance he gives those affected by the terrible events of combat. The last stanza reads:

> A pedlar from a hovel,
> The lowest of the low,
> The Father of the Novel,
> Salvation's first Defoe,
> Eight blinded generations
> Ere Armageddon came,
> He showed us how to meet it,
> And Bunyan was his name!

Between the two world wars, modernist authors viewed Bunyan with a more critical eye. James Joyce, in the "Oxen of the Sun" chapter of *Ulysses* (1922), parodies the moral-allegorical style of Bunyan, as well as that of Defoe, Gibbon, and Charles Lamb, among others. In *The Enormous Room* (1922), poet E. E. Cummings makes significant use of Bunyan's work in both structure and technique, yet he reevaluates the earlier author's wholesale faith in a higher authority. *The Enormous Room*, based on Cummings's wrongful imprisonment in a French detention center during World War I, conveys a deep-seated mistrust of government, bureaucracy, and the establishment.

Visual Art

William Hogarth adapted the idea of *The Pilgrim's Progress* in two series of engravings that made him one of the best-known artists in eighteenth-century England. The first series, *The Harlot's Progress* (1731–1732), which shows the rise and fall of a young country-girl-*cum*-prostitute named Moll Hackabout, was inspired by Bunyan's work as well as others, including Daniel Defoe's tale of disgrace and redemption, *Moll Flanders* (1722). As Kipling's poem "The Holy War" indicates, Bunyan was often cited as a precursor to Defoe in terms of storytelling.

The first engraving shows Moll's arrival in the city and her acquaintance with the seemingly kind Mother Elizabeth Needham, the madam of a brothel. Moll retains an admirable amount of control over her life in the second engraving, despite the fact that she has already become a prostitute. The picture shows Moll living in the apartment of a rich older man; the drama consists of her successful attempt to usher her handsome young lover out of the apartment before the older gentleman returns. Moll's downfall begins in the third panel. Her new apartment is unkempt and inexpensively furnished, and Moll shows signs of venereal disease. The fourth painting finds her in prison, the fifth on her deathbed, and the sixth in a coffin, her toddler son dressed in mourning on the floor beside it. Hogarth followed this popular series with *A Rake's Progress* (1735), a less sympathetic portrayal of a young man who squanders two fortunes: his father's and his wife's.

Music

During World War I, British composer Sir Edward Elgar began a symphonic drama based on *The Pilgrim's Progress* that he never completed. American composer and critic Edgar Stillman Kelley, known for his symphonies *Gulliver* (1913–1937), based on Swift's *Gulliver's Travels*, and *New England* (1913), adapted Bunyan's work in his oratorio *The Pilgrim's Progress* (1918).

British composer Ralph Vaughan Williams wrote an opera of *The Pilgrim's Progress*, which he finished in 1951. Williams's works include *A London Symphony* (1914; revised 1934), *A Pastoral Symphony* (1921), and the Sixth Symphony (1947). His music combines the pastoral with a striking sense of the visual, and *The Pilgrim's Progress*—an amalgam of many works he had released throughout the years—provides a deeply religious, contemplative listening experience. Williams's wife, Ursula Vaughan Williams, derived the poetic libretto from Bunyan's original. *The Pilgrim's Progress*, which took Williams forty years to write, became his chief work, the one that established him as a paramount composer of his generation, but one that could never be widely popular due to its explicit morality.

Muckraking

At the turn of the twentieth century, industrialization was transforming urban America at an astounding rate; meanwhile, the nation's social conscience began to crystallize. The determinations of that conscience were delivered to the public by a remarkable group of journalists, among them Lincoln Steffens, Ida Tarbell, Brand Whitlock, Jacob Riis, David Graham Phillips, Ray Stannard Baker, Samuel Hopkins Adams, and Upton Sinclair. Their carefully documented findings exposed the monopoly and corruption lurking in the big business trusts and shed light on the atrocious working conditions at the heart of the system. The scandal produced by such provocative writing spurred imitators to publish sensationalistic articles deliberately calibrated to arouse public outcry. In response U.S. President Theodore Roosevelt publicly condemned irresponsible journalism. Quoting from Bunyan's *The Pilgrim's Progress*, Roosevelt likened the journalist to the Man with the Muck Rake—"the man who could look no way but downward, with the muck rake in his hand; who was offered a celestial crown for his muck rake, but who would neither look up nor regard the crown he was offered, but continued to rake to himself the filth of the floor." The term "muckraking" soon came into use to describe writers who attempt to expose corruption. Sinclair's *The Jungle* (1906) became the paradigm of the muckraking genre, as it led directly to social change: The Food and Drug Act went into effect just months after the novel's private publication. Later muckrakers include figures as diverse as Rachel Carson, Jane Jacobs, Angela Davis, Gloria Steinem, Eric Schlosser, and Michael Moore.

Comments & Questions

In this section, we aim to provide the reader with an array of perspectives on the text, as well as questions that challenge those perspectives. The commentary has been culled from sources as diverse as reviews contemporaneous with the work, letters written by the author, literary criticism of later generations, and appreciations written throughout the work's history. Following the commentary, a series of questions seeks to filter John Bunyan's The Pilgrim's Progress *through a variety of points of view and bring about a richer understanding of this enduring work.*

Comments

JONATHAN SWIFT

Some gentlemen, abounding in their university erudition, are apt to fill their sermons with philosophical terms, and notions of the metaphysical or abstracted kind; which generally have one advantage, to be equally understood by the wise, the vulgar, and the preacher himself. I have been better entertained, and more informed by a few pages in the *Pilgrim's Progress*, than by a long discourse upon the will and the intellect, and simple or complex ideas. Others again are fond of dilating on matter and motion, talk of the fortuitous concourse of atoms, of theories, and phenomena; directly to reconcile their former tenets with every new system of administration.

—from *A Letter to a Young Clergyman,*
Lately Entered into Holy Orders (1720)

BENJAMIN FRANKLIN

In crossing the bay, we met with a squall that tore our rotten sails to pieces, prevented our getting into the Kill, and drove us upon Long Island. In our way, a drunken Dutchman, who was a passenger too, fell overboard; when he was sinking, I reached through the water to his shock pate, and drew him up, so that we got him in again. His ducking sobered him a little, and he went to sleep, taking first out of his pocket a book, which he desir'd I would dry for him. It proved to be my old favorite author, Bunyan's *Pilgrim's Progress*, in Dutch,

377

finely printed on good paper, with copper cuts, a dress better than I had ever seen it wear in its own language. I have since found that it has been translated into most of the languages of Europe, and suppose it has been more generally read than any other book, except perhaps the Bible. Honest John was the first that I know of who mix'd narration and dialogue; a method of writing very engaging to the reader, who in the most interesting parts finds himself, as it were, brought into the company and present at the discourse. De Foe in his *Crusoe*, his *Moll Flanders, Religious Courtship, Family Instructor*, and other pieces, has imitated it with success; and Richardson has done the same, in his *Pamela*, etc.

—from his *Autobiography* (1771)

SAMUEL JOHNSON

Pilgrim's Progress has great merit, both for invention, imagination, and the conduct of the story; and it has had the best evidence of its merit, the general and continued approbation of mankind. Few books, I believe, have had a more extensive sale. It is remarkable, that it begins very much like the poem of Dante; yet there was no translation of Dante when Bunyan wrote. There is reason to think that he had read Spenser.

—from James Boswell's *The Life of Samuel Johnson* (1791)

SIR WALTER SCOTT

The distinctions between the first and second part of *The Pilgrim's Progress* are such as circumstances render appropriate; and as John Bunyan's strong mother wit enabled him to seize upon correctly. Christian, for example, a man, and a bold one, is represented as enduring his fatigues, trials, and combats, by his own stout courage, under the blessing of heaven: but to express that species of inspired heroism by which women are supported in the path of duty, notwithstanding the natural feebleness and timidity of their nature, Christiana and Mercy obtain from the interpreter their guide, called Great-heart, by whose strength and valour their lack of both is supplied, and the dangers and distresses of the way repelled and overcome. . . .

In whatever shape presented, John Bunyan's parable must be dear to many, as to us, from the recollection that in youth they were endued with permission to peruse it at times when all studies of a nature merely entertaining were prohibited. We remember with interest the passages where, in our childhood, we stumbled betwixt the literal story and metaphorical explanation; and can even recall to mind a more simple and early period, when Grim and Slaygood, and even he

Whose castle's Doubting, and whose name's Despair,

were to us as literal Anakim as those destroyed by Giant-killing Jack. Those who can recollect the early development of their own ideas on such subjects, will many of them at the same time remember the reading of this work as the first task which gave exercise to the mind, before taste, grown too fastidious for enjoyment, taught them to be more disgusted with a single error than delighted with a hundred beauties.

—from the *Quarterly Review* (1830)

THOMAS BABINGTON MACAULAY

The characteristic peculiarity of the *Pilgrim's Progress* is that it is the only work of its kind which possesses a strong human interest. Other allegories only amuse the fancy. The allegory of Bunyan has been read by many thousands with tears.

—from the *Edinburgh Review* (1830)

SAMUEL TAYLOR COLERIDGE

I know of no book, the Bible excepted, as above all comparison, which I, according to my judgment and experience, could so safely recommend as teaching and enforcing the whole saving truth according to the mind that was in Christ Jesus, as the *Pilgrim's Progress*. It is, in my conviction, incomparably the best *Summa Theologiae Evangelicae* ever produced by a writer not miraculously inspired.

—from *The Literary Remains of
Samuel Taylor Coleridge*, vol. 3 (1838)

HENRY DAVID THOREAU

I think that *Pilgrim's Progress* is the best sermon which has been preached from [The New Testament]; almost all other sermons that I have heard, or heard of, have been but poor imitations of this.

—from *A Week on the Concord and Merrimack Rivers* (1849)

ROBERT LOUIS STEVENSON

Pilgrim's Progress [is] a book that breathes of every beautiful and valuable emotion.

—from the *British Weekly* (May 13, 1867)

GEORGE ELIOT

I am reading old Bunyan again after the long lapse of years, and am profoundly struck with the true genius manifested in the simple, vigorous, rhythmic style.

—from *George Eliot's Life as Related in Her Letters and Journals* (1885)

ANDREW LANG

People have wondered why he fancied himself such a sinner? He confesses to having been a liar and a blasphemer. If I may guess, I fancy that this was merely the literary genius of Bunyan seeking for expression. His lies, I would go bail, were tremendous romances, wild fictions told for fun, never lies of cowardice or for gain. As to his blasphemies, he had an extraordinary power of language, and that was how he gave it play. "Fancy swearing" was his only literary safety-valve, in those early days, when he played cat on Elstow Green. . . .

Bunyan is everybody's author. The very Catholics have their own edition of the Pilgrim: they have cut out Giant Pope, but have been too good-natured to insert Giant Protestant in his place. Unheralded, unannounced, though not uncriticised (they accused the Tinker of being a plagiarist, of course), Bunyan outshone the Court wits, the learned, the poets of the Restoration, and even the great theologians.

—from *Essays in Little* (1891)

RICHARD GARNETT

John Bunyan, the one man who has attained to write a successful prose allegory on a large scale, and to infuse true emotion into an exercise of ingenuity, and who probably owed less to study and training than any other of the great authors of the modern world, was born at Elstow, a village in the neighbourhood of Bedford, in November, 1628. He is usually described as a 'tinker,' but, as he was not an itinerant, 'brazier' would be a more correct appellation. . . .

It is unnecessary to dwell at any great length upon the characteristics of so famous and universally known a book as *Pilgrim's Progress*. Though professedly a vision, and treating of spiritual things, it ranks with *Robinson Crusoe* and *Gulliver's Travels* as one of the great realistic books of the English language. All three are examples of the possibility of rendering scenes wholly imaginary, and in fact impossible, truer to the apprehension than experience itself by the narrator's own air of absolute conviction, and by unswerving fidelity to truth of detail. In Bunyan's case the triumph is the more remarkable, as his personages are not even imaginary men and women, but mere embodiments of moral or theological qualities. Yet Faithful and Hopeful are as real as Crusoe and Friday. Before he began to write he must have realized what he wished to describe with a vividness only conceivable by regarding it as an outward expression of his own spiritual experience. He had himself been Christian and Faithful and the captive in Doubting Castle; he had gazed on Vanity Fair, and passed through the Valley of the Shadow of Death.

—from *The Age of Dryden* (1895)

GEORGE BERNARD SHAW

Two and a half centuries ago our greatest English dramatizer of life, John Bunyan, ended one of his stories with the remark that there is a way to hell even from the gates of heaven, and so led us to the equally true proposition that there is a way to heaven even from the gates of hell.

—from his preface to *Three Plays for Puritains* (1900)

WILLIAM JAMES

Bunyan became a minister of the gospel, and in spite of his neurotic constitution, and of the twelve years he lay in prison for his nonconformity, his life was turned to active use. He was a peacemaker and doer of good, and the immortal Allegory which he wrote has brought the very spirit of religious patience home to English hearts.

But neither Bunyan or Tolstoy could become what we have called healthy-minded. They had drunk too deeply of the cup of bitterness ever to forget its taste, and their redemption is into a universe two stories deep. Each of them realized a good which broke the effective edge of his sadness; yet the sadness was preserved as a minor ingredient in the heart of the faith by which it was overcome. . . .

The "hue of resolution" is there, but the full flood of ecstatic liberation seems never to have poured over poor John Bunyan's soul.

—from *The Varieties of Religious Experience* (1902)

SAMUEL BUTLER

The Pilgrim's Progress consists mainly of a series of infamous libels upon life and things; it is a blasphemy against certain fundamental ideas of right and wrong which our consciences most instinctively approve. . . .

What a pity it is that Christian never met Mr. Common-Sense with his daughter, Good-Humour, and her affianced husband, Mr. Hate-Cant; but if he ever saw them in the distance he steered clear of them, probably as feeling that they would be more dangerous than Giant Despair, Vanity Fair and Apollyon all together—for they would have stuck to him if he had let them get in with him. . . .

Bunyan, we may be sure, took all that he preached in its most literal interpretation; he could never have made his book so interesting had he not done so. The interest of it depends almost entirely on the unquestionable good faith of the writer and the strength of the impulse that compelled him to speak that which was within him. He was not writing a book which he might sell, he was speaking what was borne in upon him from heaven. The message he uttered was, to my thinking, both low and false, but it was truth of truths to Bunyan. . . .

Anything worse than *The Pilgrim's Progress* in the matter of defiance of literary canons can hardly be conceived. The allegory halts continually; it professes to be spiritual, but nothing can be more carnal than the golden splendour of the eternal city; the view of life and the world generally is flat blasphemy against the order of things with which we are surrounded. Yet, like the *Odyssey*, which flatly defies sense and criticism (no, it doesn't; still, it defies them a good deal), no one can doubt that it must rank among the very greatest books that have ever been written. How Odyssean it is in its sincerity and downrightness, as well as in the marvellous beauty of its language, its freedom from all taint of the schools and, not least, in complete victory of genuine internal zeal over a scheme initially so faulty as to appear hopeless.

—from *The Note-Books of Samuel Butler* (1912)

GEORGE SAINTSBURY

As for Bunyan, here as everywhere, he stands quite by himself. I think he had read a good deal more than some persons of worship fancy; but there is little doubt that the common idea as to the Bible furnishing him with his only formal models is correct enough. And by special genius he had managed to combine Biblical music with the style of the most ordinary, yet never in the least vulgar, vernacular after a fashion which seems to me almost more marvellous than Browne's weaving of the Biblical magic into his own splendour, or Taylor's decking texts with his prettiest trills and flourishes.

—from *A History of English Prose Rhythm* (1912)

ALDOUS HUXLEY

Most vices . . . demand considerable self-sacrifices. There is no greater mistake than to suppose that a vicious life is a life of uninterrupted pleasure. It is a life almost as wearisome and painful—if strenuously led—as Christian's in *The Pilgrim's Progress.*

—from *Along the Road: Notes and Essays of a Tourist* (1925)

MAX WEBER

The old mediæval (even ancient) idea of God's book-keeping is carried by Bunyan to the characteristically tasteless extreme of comparing the relation of a sinner to his God with that of customer and shopkeeper. One who has once got into debt may well, by the product of his virtuous acts, succeed in paying off the accumulated interest but never the principal.

—from *The Protestant Ethic and the Spirit of Capitalism,*
as translated by Talcott Parsons (1930)

C. S. LEWIS

There are books which, while didactic in intention, are read with delight by people who do not want their teaching and may not believe that they have anything to teach—works like Lucretius' *De Rerum Natura* or Burton's *Anatomy.* This is the class to which *The Pilgrim's Progress* belongs.

—from *Selected Literary Essays* (1969)

Questions

1. Can one obtain from *The Pilgrim's Progress* the satisfaction one usually expects from the reading of narrative fiction? Is this early example of the genre too far removed from our contemporary novels? Is its allegorical message too much in the way for you to enjoy the underlying story?

2. Do you think it is healthy or good sense to argue that the world we apprehend through our senses and experience is unreal—a mere appearance, an epiphenomenon—and that to see it as real is a sin? Taking this idea further, is it sensible to say that true reality is spiritual?

3. Commentators often note that in spite of its allegorical dimension, *The Pilgrim's Progress* is often realistic, with characters just like our neighbors but with labels attached. Find a passage in which this realism is particularly vivid. Also, find a passage in which attempts at realism fail.

4. As an argument for John Bunyan's religious views, is *The Pilgrim's Progress* convincing?

For Further Reading

Editions of The Pilgrim's Progress

Keeble, N. H., ed. *The Pilgrim's Progress*, by John Bunyan. Oxford: Oxford University Press, 1984.

Owens, W. R., ed. *The Pilgrim's Progress*, by John Bunyan. Oxford and New York: Oxford University Press, 2003.

Sharrock, Roger, ed. *The Pilgrim's Progress*, by John Bunyan. Baltimore, MD: Penguin, 1965.

Other Primary Texts

Bunyan, John. *Grace Abounding to the Chief of Sinners and A Relation of the Imprisonment of Mr. John Bunyan.* 1666. Edited by W. R. Owens. Harmondsworth: Penguin, 1987.

———. *The Works of John Bunyan.* 3 vols. Edited by George Offor. London: Blackie and Son, 1856.

———. *The Life and Death of Mr. Badman.* 1680. Edited by James F. Forrest and Roger Sharrock. Oxford: Clarendon Press, 1988.

Carey, John, ed. *Eyewitness to History.* New York: Avon Books, 1987.

Locke, John. *An Essay Concerning Human Understanding.* 1689. London: William Tegg, 1867.

Luther, Martin. *Commentary on the Epistle to the Galatians.* 1535. In *Selections from His Writings*, edited by John Dillenberger. New York: Anchor Books, 1962.

Mandeville, Bernard de. *An Enquiry into the Origin of Honour and the Usefulness of Christianity in War.* 1732. London: Frank Cass, 1971.

Milton, John. *Paradise Lost.* 1667. Edited by David Hawkes. New York: Barnes and Noble, 2004.

———. *Complete English Poems, Of Education, Areopagitica.* Edited by Gordon Campbell. London: J. M. Dent, 1993.

Thompson, E. P. *The Making of the English Working-class.* Harmondsworth: Penguin, 1968.

Criticism and Biography

Batson, E. Beatrice. *John Bunyan: Allegory and Imagination.* London: Croom Helm, 1984.

Beal, Rebecca. *"Grace Abounding to the Chief of Sinners:* Bunyan's Pauline Epistle." *Studies in English Literature* 21 (1981), pp. 147–160.

Benjamin, Walter. *The Origin of German Tragic Drama.* Translated by John Osbourne. London: NLB, 1977.

Davies, Michael. *Graceful Reading: Theology and Narrative in the Works of John Bunyan.* Oxford and New York: Oxford University Press, 2002.

Fish, Stanley E. *Self-consuming Artifacts: The Experience of Seventeenth-century Literature.* Berkeley and London: University of California Press, 1972.

Gay, David, James G. Randall, and Arlette Zinck, eds. *Awakening Words: John Bunyan and the Language of Community.* Newark: University of Delaware Press, 2000.

Goldman, Peter. "Living Words: Iconoclasm and Beyond in Bunyan." *New Literary History* 33 (2002), pp. 461–489.

Gordon, Scott Paul. *The Power of the Passive Self in English Literature, 1640–1770.* Cambridge and New York: Cambridge University Press, 2002.

Greaves, Richard L. *Glimpses of Glory: John Bunyan and English Dissent.* Stanford, CA: Stanford University Press, 2002.

Haskin, Dayton. "The Burden of Interpretation in *The Pilgrim's Progress." Studies in Philology* 79 (1982), pp. 256–278.

Hawkes, David. *Idols of the Marketplace: Idolatry and Commodity Fetishism in English Literature, 1580–1680.* New York: Palgrave, 2001.

Hill, Christopher. *The World Turned Upside Down: Radical Ideas during the English Revolution.* New York: Viking Press, 1972.

———. *A Tinker and a Poor Man: John Bunyan and His Church, 1628–1688.* New York: W. W. Norton, 1990.

———. *The English Bible and the Seventeenth-century Revolution.* New York: Penguin, 1993.

Kaufmann, U. Milo. *The Pilgrim's Progress and Traditions in Puritan Meditation.* New Haven, CT: Yale University Press, 1966.

Keeble, N. H., ed. *John Bunyan: Conventicle and Parnassus: Tercentenary Essays.* Oxford: Clarendon Press, 1988.

————, ed. *John Bunyan: Reading Dissenting Writing.* Oxford and New York: Peter Lang, 2002.

Laurence, Anne, W. R. Owens, and Stuart Sim, eds. *John Bunyan and His England, 1628–88.* London: Hambledon Press, 1990.

Lukács, Georg. *The Theory of the Novel.* 1920. Translated by Anna Bostock. Cambridge, MA: MIT Press, 1971.

Luxon, Thomas H. *Literal Figures: Puritan Allegory and the Reformation Crisis in Representation.* Chicago: University of Chicago Press, 1995.

Mullett, Michael A. *John Bunyan in Context.* Keele, UK: Keele University Press, 1996.

Newey, Vincent, ed. *The Pilgrim's Progress: Critical and Historical Views.* Totowa, NJ: Barnes and Noble, 1980.

Sharrock, Roger. *John Bunyan.* New York: Hutchinson's Universal Library, 1954.

Shell, Marc. *Money, Language and Thought: Literary and Philosophic Economies from the Medieval to the Modern Era.* Baltimore, MD: Johns Hopkins University Press, 1993.

Sim, Stuart. *Negotiations with Paradox: Narrative Practice and Narrative Form in Bunyan and Defoe.* Savage, MD: Barnes and Noble, 1990.

Spargo, Tamsin. *The Writing of John Bunyan.* Aldershot: Ashgate, 1997.

Van Dyke, Carolynn. *The Fiction of Truth: Structures of Meaning in Narrative and Dramatic Allegory.* Ithaca, NY: Cornell University Press, 1985.

Webber, Joan. *The Eloquent "I": Style and Self in Seventeenth-century Prose.* Madison: University of Wisconsin Press, 1968.

Notes

Notes

Look for the following titles, available now and forthcoming from
BARNES & NOBLE CLASSICS.

Visit your local bookstore for these fine titles.
Or to order online go to: WWW.BN.COM/CLASSICS

Title	Author	ISBN	Price
Adventures of Huckleberry Finn	Mark Twain	1-59308-000-X	$4.95
The Adventures of Tom Sawyer	Mark Twain	1-59308-068-9	$4.95
Aesop's Fables		1-59308-062-X	$5.95
The Age of Innocence	Edith Wharton	1-59308-143-X	$5.95
Alice's Adventures in Wonderland and Through the Looking-Glass	Lewis Carroll	1-59308-015-8	$5.95
Anna Karenina	Leo Tolstoy	1-59308-027-1	$8.95
The Art of War	Sun Tzu	1-59308-017-4	$7.95
The Awakening and Selected Short Fiction	Kate Chopin	1-59308-001-8	$4.95
The Brothers Karamazov	Fyodor Dostoevsky	1-59308-045-X	$9.95
The Call of the Wild and White Fang	Jack London	1-59308-200-2	$5.95
Candide	Voltaire	1-59308-028-X	$4.95
A Christmas Carol, The Chimes and The Cricket on the Hearth	Charles Dickens	1-59308-033-6	$5.95
The Collected Poems of Emily Dickinson		1-59308-050-6	$5.95
The Complete Sherlock Holmes, Vol. I	Sir Arthur Conan Doyle	1-59308-034-4	$7.95
The Complete Sherlock Holmes, Vol. II	Sir Arthur Conan Doyle	1-59308-040-9	$7.95
The Count of Monte Cristo	Alexandre Dumas	1-59308-151-0	$7.95
Cyrano de Bergerac	Edmond Rostand	1-59308-075-1	$3.95
Daisy Miller and Washington Square	Henry James	1-59308-105-7	$4.95
Daniel Deronda	George Eliot	1-59308-290-8	$8.95
David Copperfield	Charles Dickens	1-59308-063-8	$7.95
The Death of Ivan Ilych and Other Stories	Leo Tolstoy	1-59308-069-7	$7.95
Don Quixote	Miguel de Cervantes	1-59308-046-8	$9.95
Dracula	Bram Stoker	1-59308-114-6	$6.95
Emma	Jane Austen	1-59308-089-1	$4.95
Essays and Poems by Ralph Waldo Emerson		1-59308-076-X	$6.95
The Essential Tales and Poems of Edgar Allan Poe		1-59308-064-6	$7.95
Ethan Frome and Selected Stories	Edith Wharton	1-59308-090-5	$5.95
Frankenstein	Mary Shelley	1-59308-115-4	$4.95
Great American Short Stories: from Hawthorne to Hemingway		1-59308-086-7	$7.95
Great Expectations	Charles Dickens	1-59308-006-9	$4.95
Grimm's Fairy Tales	Jacob and Wilhelm Grimm	1-59308-056-5	$7.95
Gulliver's Travels	Jonathan Swift	1-59308-132-4	$5.95
Hard Times	Charles Dickens	1-59308-156-1	$5.95
Heart of Darkness and Selected Short Fiction	Joseph Conrad	1-59308-021-2	$4.95
The Histories	Herodotus	1-59308-102-2	$6.95
The House of Mirth	Edith Wharton	1-59308-153-7	$6.95

(continued)

(continued)

The Prince and the Pauper	Mark Twain	1-59308-218-5	$4.95
Pygmalion and Three Other Plays	George Bernard Shaw	1-59308-078-6	$7.95
The Red Badge of Courage and Selected Short Fiction	Stephen Crane	1-59308-119-7	$4.95
Republic	Plato	1-59308-097-2	$6.95
Robinson Crusoe	Daniel Defoe	1-59308-360-2	$5.95
The Scarlet Letter	Nathaniel Hawthorne	1-59308-207-X	$4.95
Selected Stories of O. Henry		1-59308-042-5	$5.95
Sense and Sensibility	Jane Austen	1-59308-125-1	$5.95
Six Plays by Henrik Ibsen		1-59308-061-1	$8.95
Sons and Lovers	D. H. Lawrence	1-59308-013-1	$7.95
The Souls of Black Folk	W. E. B. Du Bois	1-59308-014-X	$5.95
The Strange Case of Dr. Jekyll and Mr. Hyde and Other Stories	Robert Louis Stevenson	1-59308-131-6	$4.95
A Tale of Two Cities	Charles Dickens	1-59308-138-3	$5.95
Tao Te Ching	Lao Tzu	1-59308-256-8	$5.95
The Three Musketeers	Alexandre Dumas	1-59308-148-0	$8.95
The Time Machine and The Invisible Man	H. G. Wells	1-59308-032-8	$4.95
Tom Jones	Henry Fielding	1-59308-070-0	$8.95
Treasure Island	Robert Louis Stevenson	1-59308-247-9	$4.95
The Turn of the Screw, The Aspern Papers and Two Stories	Henry James	1-59308-043-3	$5.95
Twenty Thousand Leagues Under the Sea	Jules Verne	1-59308-302-5	$5.95
Uncle Tom's Cabin	Harriet Beecher Stowe	1-59308-121-9	$7.95
Vanity Fair	William Makepeace Thackeray	1-59308-071-9	$7.95
The Varieties of Religious Experience	William James	1-59308-072-7	$7.95
Villette	Charlotte Brontë	1-59308-316-5	$7.95
The Voyage Out	Virginia Woolf	1-59308-229-0	$6.95
Walden and Civil Disobedience	Henry David Thoreau	1-59308-208-8	$5.95
The War of the Worlds	H. G. Wells	1-59308-085-9	$3.95
Ward No. 6 and Other Stories	Anton Chekhov	1-59308-003-4	$7.95
The Waste Land and Other Poems	T. S. Eliot	1-59308-279-7	$4.95
The Wings of the Dove	Henry James	1-59308-296-7	$7.95
Wives and Daughters	Elizabeth Gaskell	1-59308-257-6	$7.95
Wuthering Heights	Emily Brontë	1-59308-044-1	$4.95

ℬ
BARNES & NOBLE CLASSICS

If you are an educator and would like to receive an
Examination or Desk Copy of a Barnes & Noble Classic edition,
please refer to Academic Resources on our website at
WWW.BN.COM/CLASSICS
or contact us at
B&NCLASSICS@BN.COM.

All prices are subject to change.